With love to my inspirational favourite Sister-in-law Sheila xx

The Staggering Seventies

by

R.T. Cain

R T Cain '08

authorHOUSE

AuthorHouse™ UK Ltd.
500 Avebury Boulevard
Central Milton Keynes, MK9 2BE
www.authorhouse.co.uk
Phone: 08001974150

© 2008 R.T. Cain. All rights reserved.

No part of this book may be reproduced, stored in a retrieval system, or transmitted by any means without the written permission of the author.

First published by AuthorHouse 3/14/2008

ISBN: 978-1-4343-7255-0 (sc)

Printed in the United States of America
Bloomington, Indiana

This book is printed on acid-free paper.

Table of Contents

Foreword	vii
"We must not allow ourselves to become dinosaurs…Eh? … Eh?"	1
"I demand an explanation."	17
"You can depend upon my wholehearted support."	25
"Sorry Gill….What's the cockeyed problem?"	39
"Why would anyone be interested in a bunch of old rags?"	53
"Please Reginald…..Please open it"	67
"Jezebel"	73
"Face? What face?"	79
"Did you ever see one of those Zombies for yourself Alf?"	87
"Sergeant…Her Ladyship wishes to speak to you in private."	109
"Bloody Norah!"	117
"I am delighted to see you looking so well."	123
"Yes it's a small world isn't it?"	129
"None are quite as beautiful as you."	141
"You're entitled to a little practice"	147
"Gentlemen…..Call me Blackie."	159
"You nasty old Bastard"	177
"Paddy is Larry's horse Serg."	185
"I'm Goff…..Has he mentioned me?"	195
"Oh no…..The mind boggles."	205
"What did you charge him with Bert?"	217
"Alright then….I got the name wrong."	229
"What a marvellous man he was and no mistake."	241
"My face went bright red."	253
"Alfred please pull another pint of bitter for our honoured guest."	261
"Right…..Now it is my turn."	271
"Thanks Ricky….I am honoured."	283
"I think we might have entered into the 'Staggering Seventies'"	289
The End (Or is it?)	295

Foreword

This book follows on from the many stories first related in, 'The Swaying 60's'. That revealing account of the real 1960's subsequently led to the publication of the first sequel, a continuation of those original stories, entitled, 'Still Swaying'. 'The Staggering 70's' is the third book in this ongoing series of novels all of which humorously demonstrate the fascinating reality of two remarkable decades experienced in the life and times of ordinary people who may well have lived in a small fictional Town called Lapley Vale, in a corner of South East Lancashire, during this memorable era of the 1960's carrying over into the 1970's. All the stories are intended to reflect the Author's efforts to realistically chronicle life as it might, quite reasonably, have been experienced by a small, yet significant, typical, cross section of ordinary British citizens living throughout this exceptionally exciting period of our most illustrious modern British history.

The stories you are about to read are now relating to a further move forward in the period of time being concentrated upon. The remarkable 1960's will come to a close with the thrilling prospects of a brand new decade, the 1970's, relentlessly approaching.

Modern British history, well supported by popular opinion, encouraged by myth and legend, has already accepted a reference to 'The Swinging 60's' as entirely appropriate as well as perfectly acceptable when being used as an indicative description of that particular decade but as anyone who has already read *'The Swaying Sixties'"* followed by *"Still Swaying"* will be keen to educate you by putting forward a strong argument that this Title was not entirely accurate when applied to many areas outside of London and the other main Metropolitan Districts.

Those fortunate Readers who are already familiar with Lapley Vale and quite a wide cross section of the local inhabitants will readily add fuel to the generalisation history has established. In addition to the two books previously mentioned another book has been published involving this fictitious Town of Lapley Vale. The Town is also featured, quite prominently, in, the fiction based upon fact, recollections of a young Police Officer who was serving with the Lancashire Constabulary during that relevant time. As a direct result of the rather hastily arranged marriage to the love of his life the main character was taken off the elite duties he carried out as a member of the famous 'Z' Car Crime Patrols to take up a married vacancy at the Lapley Vale Police Section. This associated story is, again humorously, related in the novel entitled *"Boydie"*.

A wide selection of the prominent Characters introduced to the readers in *"The Swaying Sixties"* and *"Still Swaying"* have survived from the Author's previously related encounters with some of the residents of Lapley Vale. Many of them will reappear once again in these latest recorded adventures. They will revive as well as regenerate their justifiable popularity, together with their fond familiarity, with the Readers as they enjoy reading the fourth of these individual novels. Readers will now be able to chart the effects that numerous inevitable changes have brought to all of those involved throughout this on-going saga. These radical alterations to the normal 'Status Quo' were having a profound affect upon the everyday life of the majority of people living in this typical small Mill Town during the relevant periods of time.

Many of the Personalities continue to slowly, but surely, respond and unconsciously adapt, to the massive social changes obviously taking place all around them. These clearly identifiable differences happening in most walks of life were definitely having a considerable impact on the everyday lives of most of the ordinary people. Some, forlornly, desperately, struggled to cling onto their long established traditions particularly in regard to their previously caring social attitudes openly displayed, without reservation, towards the others within their close community.

The storyline has been taken up after approximately six months have elapsed since the Readers left Lapley Vale at the conclusion of *"Still Swaying"*. In real time the Townsfolk of Lapley Vale were currently able to enjoy the particularly warm and sunny summer weather in the memorable year of 1969.

The continuously featured four mothers-to-be were all at differing stages in their own individual family development. Jenny McCabe and Linda Chumley were about to have their second babies. Newlywed Kay Best was about to experience her first encounter with childbirth. Susan Summers, the veteran of the group of friends, was now expecting her fifth child. All four were now well advanced in their confinements. Fortunately all were, so far, progressing smoothly in their happy conditions, devoid of any significant worries or troublesome problems.

Permit me to remind you of a couple of salient facts which will assist your comprehension and appreciation of the current situation. Jenny's lifelong friend Kay was married to Sam Best, who happened to be Eric McCabe's lifelong best friend as well as Jenny's Husband. As a direct consequence of their marriage, which took place on Christmas Eve, there now existed the quite staggering probability that all four of these women actually conceived at, more or less, the same time, on the same night, give or take an hour or so on either side. They were currently bonding even closer together through their developing friendship enhanced by their regular visits to the Anti-Natal Clinic at the Lapley Vale Cottage Hospital. Secretly they all hoped they could deliver their babies on, or around, the same day. Although this unlikely occurrence could be considered as a real possibility not many would have been prepared to place any kind of sizable wager that this would prove to be the actual outcome.

The Crown Green Bowlers at the Lapley Vale Bowling and Social Club continued to enjoy their expected local dominance over all of their rivals in the South East Lancashire Crown Green Bowling League. Their chosen sport had still not lost any of the well established attraction and popularity it had justifiably earned over many years. It continued to receive unbridled support amongst many regular, ultra keen, local participants. Woody Green and Eddie Brown were rapidly establishing themselves as top players in the All England County Crown Green Bowling League echelons after they had both received the great personal honour of being selected for and subsequently representing their beloved County as members of the official Lancashire Squad.

The ever popular, modestly aristocratic, Lady Lapley together with her faithful Staff at Lapley Vale Manor were diligently exploring many of the possibilities that were likely to be created after the opening of the new Safari Park and Visitor Centre inside the vast Lapley Manor Estate took place. This stunning and, hopefully, historic consideration had been forced upon Her Ladyship because of her steadily rising overheads which, together with exorbitant tax liabilities and many other personal fiscal dues, were being lawfully demanded from her. The planned introductions of these drastic domestic changes were hopefully going to pleasantly affect as well as seriously change her whole lifestyle in the future. Everyone concerned had been obliged to reluctantly take on these radical advancements because they had been sensibly considered as being essential in order to preserve, not only Her Ladyship's future financial status and standing, but also the livelihood and general welfare conditions of her numerous loyal, some almost completely dependant, cherished Staff.

The ready availability of comprehensive local and national news coverage was now being provided to the ordinary man in the street. An incredible mass of up to date information was now being welcomed by a wide, extremely keen, interested audience. Not only were the media providing news coverage there were also remarkable changes happening to the popular trends in all genres of music, fashion and dress. These innovations were in addition to all the many new and exciting forms of communication and fresh avenues of basic entertainment made available to them in abundance via their radio and television receivers. People were now more likely to be in touch with these modern trends and changing attitudes because of the obvious advancements especially through the rapid popularity of the medium of television. These unmistakable developments were clearly having a marked effect on the vast majority of the population of Lapley Vale. The immediate consequences of many of the social changes were being felt much more acutely by the members of the older generation who, quietly and possibly vainly, continued to quietly demonstrate their resistance to many of the advances reflected by the new 'Free for all attitudes' regrettably now being exhibited by the much less community minded persons who were clearly becoming more prevalent amongst there numbers in this emerging modern Society.

As the dawning of the new decade drew closer many ordinary people wondered, some even dreaded, just how much their lives were about to be changed for ever. Most of them courageously continued with their struggle, desperately trying to adapt to the effects of the enormous impact caused by many of the events which had already taken place during the 1960's decade. They were now inevitably being obliged to face up to all of the challenges facing them in the future, bravely, doing their level best to managing to reluctantly *'Stagger'* on into the unpredictable, 1970's.

"We must not allow ourselves to become dinosaurs…Eh? … Eh?"

The Clubroom at the Lapley Vale Bowling and Social Club was quite crowded. The sole female presence amid the assembled throng of males was Denise the popular, much experienced and greatly appreciated, barmaid. She was busy assisting Alf Morgan, the long standing Club Steward, behind the bar as they did their best to cope with the many pressing demands for their services from their thirsty Club Members. Despite the noticeable increase in the popularity of new lighter, trendier beers, called *Lagers*', most of the Club Members continued to enjoy and appreciate well established drinks, mostly pints of Best Bitter Beer, expertly supplied through the pumps by Alf and Denise. As a clear indication of the advancing times Alf has now stocked up with bottled lager beers due to the presence of a genuine demand mainly from young Ladies visiting the Club as guests.

The Club's Dart Team were all present and correct. They were playing a home fixture against opponents from 'The Flying Horse' one of the popular local Public Houses. Great interest was clearly being generated in the playing of this engaging contest. As a result of way events over the current season had unfolded this particular match had become a real top of the table Brewery League Championship decider. Many of the Members, who were not normally closely associated with the game of darts, were paying keen attention to the thrilling, ongoing, proceedings.

The Captain of the home side was Eric McCabe, son of Sergeant Bert McCabe, the local Chief of Police, and his wife Alice. Better known to all of his friends and relatives as 'Ricky' he was also the beloved husband of Jenny and the devoted father of their little baby daughter Amy.

Bert McCabe, a larger than life character who tended to dispense his own interpretation of law and order enforcement in the Town, was a regular drinker at the Club. He was presently enjoying a pint of best bitter whilst having a quiet, friendly, chat with some of his closest friends. Bert was seated at the bar with three of his associates, who could also be described as his long serving and much experienced drinking partners. Affectionately referred to by many as the *'Beer Brothers"*.

To Bert's right, seated on his personal, well established and easily recognised, stool, was Woody Green. Woody was the Head Green keeper and the fairly recently appointed Husband of Mavis. The couple originally met through her, since considered inspirational, appointment by Alf as the extremely efficient and capable Club Cleaner with additional catering, particularly cooking, duties thrown in whenever the demand arose.

To his left was Norman Smith. Norman was a familiar and prominent Club Member whose presence was a regular sight at the bar where he sat on his specially adapted bar stool. The stool had metal steps attached to the long wooden legs because Norman was very small in stature. Without attempting to be unkind, Norman could be correctly described as a genuine 'Dwarf'. Woody was responsible for making the small additions to Norman's stool which enabled him to discreetly and quite comfortably scale up the side of his bar stool thus avoiding the possible embarrassment of him being unable to reach the top of the seat without receiving assistance. However, what ever Norman might have lacked in height he had more than been able to make up for through his sharp, bright, intelligent, engaging, personality together with his proven and much admired abundance of personal courage, expressed and also implied whenever necessary. Norman's adapted stool had also been utilised on occasions as a useful platform for him to stand upon whilst throwing darts. He was an exceptionally skilled player as many challengers had found to their surprise and cost.

Eddie Brown, the third of Bert's companions, was seated on the stool next to Norman. Eddie, originally born in the West Indies, moved to England when he was still a young man. He spent all of his working life employed as an operative in a metal pressing Factory Mill situated close to his home in the Town. Now retired, he was well accepted as a popular and familiar local character. He was happily married to his childhood sweetheart. Together they raised their family in Lapley Vale. Eddie was the Grandfather of Kay who, as mentioned in the introduction to this story, was married to Eric McCabe's best friend Sam Best on the most memorable Christmas Eve just past. All of those who attended the ceremony and the subsequent celebrations would be happy to agree that this marriage had been responsible for providing a delightfully unforgettable Christmas for all concerned.

Sam was a regular member of the Club Dart Team. He was currently playing his match against Alan Marshall, one of the Flying Horse's best players. Eric was keenly watching as he actively supported his best friend whilst he was in action. He was standing in the company of their latest close friend Damien, nicknamed 'Specky', Harris. Damien, Sam and Eric all went through their schoolboy days together. Their other close childhood friend, Peter Franks, was now serving abroad as a Regular Soldier in Her Majesty's Armed Forces.

Specky did not play darts very well, probably due, in no small part, to his rather defective eyesight, although it had to be said that he was never much good at any kind of sport or games when they were together at school. Damien was noted as an academic achiever rather than as any sort of athlete or sportsman. Still, since he recently became so much closer to Eric and Sam he now regularly attended all the matches both at home and away, acting as an official scorer for the both the Club's Bowling and Darts Teams when required. It was a fact that all these close friends could quite easily be considered as formidable contenders for possible future selection as representatives in any England beer drinking teams. All were born and bred into a well established society where many lifestyles inevitably revolved around the accepted enjoyment derived from drinking alcoholic beverages of various kinds in the amply provided local Licensed Premises.

Damien and his fiancée Bernadette Dougan had been able to prove themselves invaluable to Eric, Jenny, Sam and Kay at a time when the McCabe's took a brave and bold step towards ensuring their future comfort and security by taking out long term mortgages to pay for Eric and Jenny's extended shop premises. This option was also applied when Sam and Kay bought their self contained flat conveniently situated above the McCabe's shop. Many young couples had been assessing the potential value of property ownership against the poor investments made by routinely paying rents which tended to line the pockets of others. The McCabe's were the first to be convinced of the soundness of their investment. The Best's, equally encouraged by Specky and Bernie, followed suit by committing themselves in the same fashion with regard to the ownership of their flat. Sam's expertise as an experienced and time served builder had been utilised to great effect when he and his old friend, mentor and retired colleague, Isaac Wells converted the flat, situated over the top of the shop within the same building, into a comfortable and desirable dwelling place. These vital and life changing moves had been carried out just prior to Sam and Kay's marriage. Without the knowledge and guidance they all received from Damien and Bernie the chances were that neither couple would have embarked upon such radical modern financial challenges. Although their monthly commitments were demanding at the present time they were all quietly confident that they had made the correct moves in the interests of their long term prosperity and happiness.

Bernie was soon to qualify as a fully fledged Solicitor and this proud personal achievement would trigger off the mechanism which would then activate their keenly awaited and much desired nuptial celebrations. Already in the early stages of planning, the devoted couple were keen to firm up all their provisional plans and the necessary arrangements were steadily being drawn together for their forthcoming matrimonial union.

In keeping with their sound professional standing they were utilising the most consummate care and keen attention to every detail.

Eric McCabe was already well established as the devoted husband of Jenny and the proud Father of their daughter Amy. He enjoyed the cherished honour of being officially appointed and recognised as the understudy to Woody Green who was the long standing, much herald and locally envied, Green keeper at the Bowling and Social Club. Their excellent Crown Bowling Green had been awarded the prestigious 'Highly recommended' plaque by the Lancashire County Crown Bowling Association the previous year. A well deserved, yet surprising, honour much appreciated by all connected with the Club and the also with their chosen game.

Eric also managed to work full time for Dickie Mitchell, the owner of the local Garden Centre and Nursery. He had been under Dickie's tutelage, learning to become a fully fledged Gardener, since leaving school at 15, with no real educational qualifications. He expected to be taking over from Dickie very soon as a full Partner and Co-owner of the Nursery because Dickie made no secret of his advanced preparations to take his well earned retirement.

Eric and Jenny had already established 'Bloomers', their Flower and Greengrocery Shop on the High Street, where Kay Best was employed by them as their Manageress. Eric was responsible for the supply of flowers, plants and all the other organic goods offered for sale to the public in the shop.

Sam and Kay had been delighted with their occupation of the newly extended and lovingly refurbished flat over the top of the McCabe's business premises. Kay had easy access to her place of employment downstairs. As you can well imagine Eric was fully occupied with the many aspects of his daily duties in connected with his various commitments. He had never been afraid of taking on any kind of honest toil. As a time served builder Sam was always in great demand, not just through his regular employment as an employee of Freddie Moore's Building Company, but he also had a long list of 'Pound note' jobs awaiting his convenience and availability. Friends and the friends of those friends were all anxious to save a little money on the cost of their normally minor, sometimes not so small, building and maintenance requirements. The recent growing trends in home ownership had boosted the opportunities for skilled tradesmen in the Building Industry to make considerable amounts of extra money. Freddie was well aware of the 'illegal', possibly unethical, activities of Sam and Isaac but, in truth, he actively encouraged them to take the smaller jobs away from his Firm. From humble beginnings both of the young couples were prospering and slowly reaping the rewards they duly merited through their hard work and a shared determination towards their future comfort and security.

As you have already been informed, both Jenny and Kay were pregnant. Miraculously, they suspect that they and their friends, Susan Summers and Linda Chumley all managed to conceive on the same night, identified as being last Christmas Eve. Their present conditions made them even more determined to build the best possible futures for themselves and their fledgling families. They and their husbands were fully committed and everyone was looking forward to their happy events, inevitably, due in September in the familiar surroundings of the Labour Ward at the Lapley Vale Cottage Hospital.

As usual Victor Callow, the Club Treasurer/Secretary, and the Club Chairman Ralph Jones were seated across the bar from where Woody and his friends were seated. Victor liked to be present whenever the Club were entertaining any groups of Visitors, especially on the now frequent occasions when darts and snooker matches were taking place.

As a former Bank Clerk, Victor was usually trusted to act as a trusted arbitrator whenever scores or any other numerical calculations became the subject of argument or dispute. Lately he was truly delighted to share this responsibility with Specky, who was currently employed as a Planning Officer with the Council at the Town Hall.

Joe Summers, husband of Susan, undoubtedly held the less than welcome, but genuinely justified, reputation for being the most disliked and avoided person inside the Clubroom. This was definitely the case until he took up crown green bowling under the unlikely tutelage of

Eddie Brown. As a result of some slightly suspicious circumstances, which were never fully investigated, Joe and Eric were urgently called upon to substitute for Billy 'Cockeye' Dawes and Charlie Walsh during the final of the Lancashire County Friendship Cup Competition held at the Trafalgar Hotel in Blackpool the previous summer. Joe ended up making himself the hero of the day when his final firing wood (A bowl sent across the crown of the green at such a speed it is intended to dislodge other bowls lying close to the jack) won the coveted and much cherished Cup for their beloved Club by one single point.

Because of his volatile nature, usually witnessed when he was under the influence of strong drink, Joe was still detested by a large number of ordinary self respecting people who lived in the Town. His wife Susan, on the other hand, the Mother of his four delightful children and expecting a fifth child, was highly respected as a friend by the other Ladies. She had comfortably bonded with Jenny, Kay and Linda Chumley to become a cherished and much respected companion and confidant to all of the other women. Susan was understandably the subject of much sympathy as Joe's long suffering Wife but many people diluted their commiseration for her predicament when they considered the fact that she did chose to marry him in the first place. Susan had to put up with what many Locals thought was a self inflicted wound. Some possibly looked upon the situation as an own goal in every sense of the word.

Joe was playing darts for the Flying Horse Team tonight because he had been thrown out of the home team last year following a dispute with Leo Banks. Although Leo subsequently resigned as Team Captain he remained a prized member of the home team. Eric and his team mates were understandably on edge because, as bad fortune would have it on the night, Joe had been drawn to play his game in the match against Leo.

The two men reluctantly shook hands before Joe took his first throw, aiming for any double scoring segment around the edges of the dart board. The game was soon under Leo's control. He was a much better player than Joe and very soon he stepped up to the oche requiring only

40 points to win the game. This remaining total meant that he needed to hit the double 20 with his dart in order to end the game successfully and, as it also happened, win the entire match for the home side. He was well ahead of Joe in the game because Joe found that he still required a large score to progress towards any finishing double because he had experienced a certain amount of difficulty starting after he failed to hit the required first double several times. Joe was unable to launch his initial attack into motion when he failed to land in any double with his first six attempts. In these official Brewery League dart matches the rules of engagement, which were rigorously enforced, required each player to start with a double before attempting to reduce their score from 501 points. After hitting any double on the board this score has to be gradually reduced by the total scored in each round of three dart throws until the player's total is sufficiently low to enable him to finish on a double i.e. if he had whittled his total down to 40 he would need to hit the double 20 segment on the board in order end up with zero points and therefore win. If he landed in the single segment, scoring only 20, he would then need to switch his attack to the double 10 and so on.

Leo confidently threw the first of his three darts. It missed, landing on the outside of the wire over the top of the double twenty segment on the board therefore failing to score anything at all. Joe laughed out aloud and he was encouraged to do so by his revolting friend and long time drinking companion Fred Bates. Fred had already lost his game to Sam without even managing to hit a double to get started. This was referred to as a 'Whitewash' by dart players and was not looked upon with any joy by any person on the receiving end, a bit like being knocked out in a boxing match or allowing a batsman to score a six off your bowling on the cricket field.

Charlie Walsh representing the home side and John Coates from the visiting team had been duly appointed as the Referees for all of the games. They immediately issued an official caution to Joe and also warned the other Members of his team about the punishments they would dish out for any further instances of unsporting conduct. This obvious breach of etiquette was considered to be highly undesirable as well as strictly forbidden under the rules.

Leo was completely unmoved by Joe's disgraceful un-gentlemanly conduct. He winked in the direction of Eric and Sam before he settled his stance to take careful aim. His second dart landed squarely in the single twenty segment of the board which left Leo still requiring another twenty points, achieved by hitting the double ten, in order to win and finish the game. Joe and Fred roared and then swiftly stifled their uncalled for laughter. They had to be given a firm and final warning by Johnny Coates.

Without even moving his position at the oche Leo threw his final dart. This one landed squarely in the centre of the double ten segment. Leo threw up his hands in delight as the home team Members and their supporters roared as an expression of their appreciation and approval. Joe's face contorted with instant rage. He glared at Leo before he literally spit his words out.

"You jammy…JAMMY…. Bastard……I suppose you think you're clever don't you? I wonder how bloody smart you'd feel with my fist rammed in you big gob…Eh?"

Joe lurched towards Leo with obvious malicious intent. He was physically restrained by his own team mates, including Fred Bates.

Whilst this confrontation was still simmering Bert McCabe had been closely watching proceedings from his position seated by the bar. Even before Joe launched his vicious attack Bert had already commenced his, famous, pre-violence ritual.

For those not familiar with Bert's tried and tested habit, he inevitably removed his spectacles and his false teeth whenever he suspected that physical contact of a violent nature was about to be required from him. Quickly wrapping his dentures in his pocket handkerchief he handed them to Norman for safe custody before he dashed across to the dart playing area.

Still struggling with his team mates Joe managed to spot the approach of Bert out of the corner of his eye. He instantly panicked because he was well aware of what Bert was capable of doing to him.

With enormous personal strength he wriggled clear of the restraint he was being held under to make a wild dash for the door, screaming in panic as he did so. Bert veered across the room to catch him as he reached the door leading onto the car park at the front of the Clubhouse. Joe's actual exit via the open door onto the car park was then aided by a well aimed kick from Bert's right boot. Joe screamed even louder as he lost his footing outside. The door closed behind the two men. Then even more pathetic screaming was clearly audible to all of those remaining inside the Clubroom.

Silence soon descended once again. An angry looking Bert returned into the Clubroom through the door. He pointed his finger directly at Fred Bates, who had turned white and was quaking with undiluted fear. Obviously still quite upset Bert spat out his words,

"Right! ... You! ... Bates! ... Get out there and look after your stupid Mate….Tell him I'll be seeing him tomorrow morning in my Office when he sobers up.……..Message understood? ... Eh? ... Eh?"

Frantically nodding his head Fred cautiously squeezed past Bert to join Joe outside. The disturbance had caused a deadly hush to fall over the whole Clubroom. Ralph leapt off his stool attempting to restore order and take control.

"O.K.……Fine.……That's it for tonight Gents….Sorry about that…. I'm sure you all know Joe as well as we do….What a Pillock….Still carry on please…..Come along now….All this delicious beer must not be wasted."

Ralph's final remark caused a sudden surge towards the bar where Alf and Denise were already pulling pints as fast as they possibly could.

Bert recovered his teeth and spectacles from the completely unmoved and unruffled Norman. He quickly returned his teeth to their rightful positions inside his mouth. He delicately exercised two trial bites to ensure they were correctly seated before he placed his spectacles on his nose. He was now ready to confidently address his friends.

"What a total waste of space that soft Bastard continues to prove he really is…Eh? ... Eh? ... I despair at times….That man is like that character in the book…You know? ... What's it called? ... Come on you know…Doctor Jekyll and Mr Hyde? … Eh? … Eh? … Mind you…He doesn't need any fancy chemical potions to set him off….Just let him have a few pints of best bitter and then stand back…If there was ever a cast iron case for enforced temperance or perhaps euthanasia I humbly suggest that you see a prime candidate before you in the shape and image of Joseph Kitchener Summers….Eh? … …Eh? … EH? … If he was engaged in an intelligence contest up against a wooden rocking horse the soft get would lose all hands down…Eh? … Eh? … When he's under the influence of the demon drink his brain ceases to function properly…Eh? … Eh? … What about his poor Missus? Susan…She must cringe every time anyone realises that he is her wedded husband…Eh? … Eh? … Not to mention also the Father of their four beautiful little children…Eh? … Eh? … She such a lovely woman and those kids are a credit to her.…Let's all hope for their sakes they continue to take after their Mother.…Eh? … Eh? … And I include the young lads in that as well…Eh? … Eh?"

Eric, Sam and Specky had now made their way from the alcove, where the dart board was situated, in order to join the group at the bar. Arriving whilst Bert was in full flow, Eric confidently took over the theme of the current conversation from his father.

"And those kids think the bloody world of him.…How the hell Susan managed to get lumbered with him is a mystery to my Jenny… And Kay and all the other people who know her.…Thanks for sorting him out again Dad.…Good job you were here that could have been quite nasty.…Leo would really love to smack Joe…Very much indeed."

Sam nodded his agreement.

"Yes and he's not on his own in wishing to get the opportunity to smack Joe neither…The problem is the famous Joe definitely is a different bloke when he's sober…Honestly…I mean it…It's just like Bert says.…He's really has got a dual personality.…What's it called? … There's a proper medical name for it isn't there?"

Specky, the brightest spark of the whole bunch by far, was happy to help out.

"Schizophrenia….That's what it's called…It's actually a medical or rather mental condition…But as Sam says it is a recognised serious medical condition…Happens when a person seems to have two separate individual personalities….I don't think they've actually found any cure for it yet….But who knows…I might be wrong….Genuine suffers can be quite dangerous if they have it bad enough."

Bert chipped in again, smiling broadly.

"I know exactly what you mean Damien my boy….I think we've all heard that famous adage….'You're never alone with schizophrenia'…. Eh? … Eh? … "

They all enjoyed a relieving laugh. Woody then joined in the levity by adding his comments.

"Spot on Bert there's another one going the rounds at the moment… .'Help to Preserve Local Wild Life….Please pickle a squirrel today'…. Bloody hell fire…Someone should pickle Joe…or at the very least Stuff him! … I'd like to be amongst the first to volunteer to carry out the necessary taxidermy myself."

The evening was now drawing to a gentle close as the clock moved on past the bewitching hour of midnight. Denise had already left to go home. Alf was subtly indicating that he was also ready for his bed. Well, if you could call walking around with his hot water bottle tucked under his arm an example of being subtle. He was always anxious not to upset any remaining "Bitter Enders" so he smiled in a friendly, suggestive and inviting fashion as he addressed Bert, Woody, Ralph and Victor, who were now the sole survivors of a long and enjoyable evening.

"Well Gentlemen…..I have to be up early in the morning….I have to pay a visit to the Brewery….They have introduced a new draft Lager Beer and they want me to sample it with a view to running some of it through our pumps in here….It has to be said that this Lager seems to be on sale and available at most Pubs and Clubs nowadays it's becoming very fashionable I believe…So…I don't want anyone to think we don't keep up with modern trends in here…Anyways bearing in mind that I need to have a clear head for my visit I wish to ask if there is a demand for anymore for anymore please Gents…Before I switch the pumps off for the night?"

Bert and Woody immediately pushed their empty glasses forward as Ralph and Victor eagerly endeavoured to drain theirs. Ralph raised his right hand as the back of his left hand was being utilised to wipe the excess liquid from around the vicinity of his mouth and lips.

"Well said Alfred my man….I will pay for these nightcaps and please refill your own glass as well….I know you will always put the best possible interests of this Club first in all matters concerning alcohol…. Five pints please Alf before we bid you a fond farewell."

Woody grimaced, spitting his words out,

"Lager….Lager Beer….That's a bloody girl's drink that is….I won't be requiring any of it Alfie… Oh no! … Not on your bloody Nellie…. Not whilst you still continue to keep stocks of common or garden cooking bitter available for sale to us all…Traditional Best Bitter is what I call a proper man's drink….Tasty….Dependable….Popular and I think reasonably priced…Delicious and suitable for consumption at numerous multifarious occasions…Including the successful and far from unpleasant treatment of warts and pimples when applied externally…. What? … What?"

There were grunts of amused agreement as Alf refilled their glasses. Bert looked quite pensive for a moment or two before he chose to speak.

"We mustn't be selfish Woody…Eh? … Eh?…We're the genuine lifeblood of this Club and will hopefully remain so for many many years to come but….But…Make no mistake about the validity of what I am about to relate to you now Gentlemen….Listen in Gents….Eh? … Eh? … Well…. As you are probably quite aware I visit all of the Licensed Premises in this area as a normal routine part of my arduous duties as the undisputed Supreme Commander of the Forces for Law and Order within the boundaries of Lapley Vale and some adjacent not to mention surrounding Urban Districts….Eh? … Eh? … I am convinced beyond a shadow of a doubt that there is a noticeable increase in the popularity of this pale and insipid looking fluid sold as an alternative to real beer….

The truth of the matter is that the stuff is mostly being supped by some of the youngsters….You know? … The much less experienced elements within our Society…It is absobloodylutely true I'm afraid… I have to say by some young Lads as well as the Lasses….You might expect Girls to want a light refreshing drink but a large number of the young Chaps are now supping this stuff in increasing quantities….Eh? … Eh? … We obviously need to encourage the younger people to patronise us in due consideration of our future prosperity and in the overall interests of this Club Eh? … Eh? … ….We must not allow ourselves to become dinosaurs….Eh? … Eh?"

Victor looked as if he wished to add his comments but gave up because of the apparent effort required for him to do so. This was due to the fact that his safe limit of personal alcoholic intake had been slightly exceeded even before he tackled his frothy nightcap. Ralph nodded his agreement and tacit approval for Bert's pertinent observations before he deemed to address his friends.

"Well said Bert…. Giving this stuff a chance is the only sensible thing to do…It's no skin off our noses is it? If there's little or no demand for it we don't have to order anymore of it do we? … Let's wait…Let's wait and see what the Brewery has got to offer…Eh? … Good luck to you in your discussions with the powers that be at the Brewery tomorrow Alf……Whatever you decide will be fine by us…Eh? … Just go with the flow Alf….As Bert has already mentioned we don't want to be left behind when it comes to us being able to supply and distribute any of the many and varied sorts of alcoholic liquor available to us all in these enlightened modern times…Anyways….Who was it who once said and I quote…..Ahem! … Listen in now Chaps…'There's no such thing as bad Beer' …Who was that…Eh? … Have we anyone present who might be familiar with that wise statement?"

Bert growled with obvious passion,

"Aye…That's true BUT some beer is definitely better than others."

Woody nodded, smiling, as he remarked,

"I have no idea who said it but as Bert has eloquently pointed out for us some beer is much better than others….And….Our Best Bitter takes some beating.....It's been good enough for me for the past fifty years or so." Grinning agreeably as he took Woody's point, Bert added,

"You'd require major plumbing work carried out on your digestive tract Woody....I've tasted this Lager...Eh? ... Eh? ... It was when one of the Landlords under my supervision and guidance forced a pint of it on to me....Believe me Gents....There is more chance of Woody becoming the next Pope than there is of him changing his favourite tipple....Eh? ... Eh? ... Tell the Brewery Bosses that Alf...And I think I can speak with confidence when I say that will be the case for the vast majority of dedicated drinkers in this Town...Eh? ... Eh?"

Alf was pleased to get the chance to respond as they now had full glasses in front of them.

"Thanks for that much appreciated vote of confidence Gents...I didn't mention....Sorry Gents...I failed to give you the full facts as they say...The Brewery are going to give us a free barrel to try out and after that the first order we give them will be available to us at half price....An introductory offer no less...So bearing those added facts in mind...Perhaps some of you might change your attitudes...What do you say to that Woody?"

Woody glared at Alf with undisguised disgust most apparent,

"Speaking for myself personally Alfie...I can honestly say...Without the slightest fear of contradiction...That I wouldn't sup the bloody stuff if you were giving it away free with every packet of crisps bought over the bar....Fifty years of dedicated common or garden bitter beer drinking speaks volumes for my preferences...I admit to liking the occasional bottle of Guinness for a refreshing change or if I feel the need for a tonic but I will always choose my beloved best bitter and I wouldn't change my habits for a gold watch or even a large cash bonus...I think I must speak for the vast majority of our Members when I state that anything other than draught bitter is a second class drink... But....I suppose we have to consider others...If I ever see any of our real beer drinkers being converted to drinking Lager I will willingly show me arse to all present wishing to bear witness to it...In here at ten o'clock on any suitable Saturday evening of your choice."

Victor, eager to demonstrate his support for Woody's stance and to also endorse his sincerely felt comments just about managed to slur a response.

"Thank Christ that is never likely to happen…Not even worth an outside bet….I'm with Woody one hundred and fifty per cent…Mind you…The thought of you showing your arse in public is enough to put anyone off their beer for life."

He chuckled to himself because he considered his statement to be pertinent as well as amusing. This action almost caused him to fall from his stool. Amazingly, in all the circumstances, Ralph was still alert enough to adeptly grab hold of his friend to prevent him from causing himself a nasty injury. They all roared with undiluted laughter before they happily tackled their waiting nightcaps.

Alf could not help smugly smiling as he considered that he had uttered the final word on the issue,

"Well I think I can take that as a definite maybe after due consideration I wonder how the mention of free offers and generous terms might have coloured some strongly held views….Still….If any of you Gentlemen want to test Lager for yourselves I promise to supply you with your first pints on the house."

The groans emitted in perfect unison gave a clear indication to Alf that 'The Bitter Enders' would not be taking him up on his offer.

"I demand an explanation."

Jack 'Peggy' Hackett, was standing in the front garden of his small, quite humble, yet neat and very well presented, red brick, terraced house on Church Street situated quite close to the Town Centre of Lapley Vale. He appeared to be preoccupied as he constantly peered up and down the street. Obvious anxiety was clearly apparent through his strange general behaviour and overall demeanour. He seemed to be unusually alert, possibly on the look out for someone or something. Whatever the reason might have been he was definitely very edgy and noticeably much more agitated than even a odd man like Peggy would be in normal circumstances.

Larry the Lamb, local Irish Tinker and popular Jobbing Gardener, come Odd Job Man, suddenly came into Peggy's view. He was walking along Church Street from the direction of the Town Centre towards Peggy's house. Larry was carrying some of his basic gardening utensils in his small, hand propelled, home constructed, cart. (Cart is quite an exaggeration really because this contraption he was utilising simply comprised of a large wooden box fastened onto the chassis and wheels of an old pram with a number of nuts and bolts. This unfortunate exposure gave a true indication of the pathetic extent of his powers of invention were unfortunately exhibited by the rather odd prominence of a basic pair of plastic covered handles on a push bar which remained, as they had always been, attached to the pram chassis thus providing his only means of basic propulsion.)

It certainly appeared that Larry was in unusually high spirits as he rapidly approached the frontage of Peggy's house. He was emitting a mixture of whistling and singing, neither of which was in tune. This outward sign of cheerfulness was not at all pleasant on the ears of anyone who might just have been unfortunate enough to be within earshot of him.

For those of you who are not familiar with these two Characters please allow me to briefly describe them for you. Jack Hackett acquired his long standing nickname 'Peggy' indirectly as a consequence of the injuries he sustained whilst serving as a Private Soldier during the Second World War. He was unfortunate enough to lose his leg whilst engaged in action with the British Army in France in 1944. Until quite recently Peggy had invariably worn an old fashioned 'Pirate type' wooden peg leg complete with thick rubber feral attached to the end of it. Experience and familiarity with this essential aid to his locomotion had gradually enabled him to become adept at most aspects of getting around. As a result of Woody Green's clandestine good fortune on Littlewood's Pools, which was still a secret to everyone with a couple of trusted exceptions, Peggy had been one of a number of the fortunate beneficiaries of Woody's anonymous generosity. Many mysterious gifts and cash donations emanated from the 'Kenneth Gordon Trust'. The unlikely truth of the origins of the Trust still remained unknown to all except certain Bank Officials, Bert McCabe and of course Mavis to that present day. Peggy was supplied and fitted with a superb artificial prosthetic limb at no cost to him. This Trust had been opened by Woody in order to enable him to distribute his treats to many of his friends and, in particular, to provide desperately needed injections of capital into his beloved Lapley Vale Bowling and Social Club's banking facilities without anyone being aware of the actual source of his unsolicited generosity. Woody's Christian names, Kenneth Gordon, used to identify the Trust, were completely unknown to even his closest friends, with the one notable exception of Bert McCabe who was able to solve the mystery using some of his typical guile and natural detecting abilities. The Kenneth Gordon Fund became the surprise provider of various gifts which were responsible for many of his friend's wildest dreams really coming true. In Peggy's case Woody did have a vested interest because of his position as the Head Green Keeper of their highly respected, renowned, and much admired Crown Bowling Green. Peggy, one of the stars of the bowling team, was known to play havoc with the carefully manicured and cosseted grass covering the surface of the sacred green with his wooden peg. He not only mildly peppered the grass but had occasionally sunk to a considerable depth beneath the surface, especially during bouts of inclement weather. To most people's astonishment Peggy took to his brand new artificial limb like a duck takes to water. Since the day he had been supplied and fitted with the state of the art prosthetic limb he had consistently preferred to wear it and the peg leg had almost become redundant, to become a thing of the past. Despite his new image Peggy still retained and also relished his affectionate nickname with all his close friends, fellow bowlers and other persons who were associated with him on a personal basis.

Now Larry the Lamb, who had just arrived in speaking distance, was another well known local character. Loosely described as a cross between an Irish Tinker and a Gypsy, unfortunately referred to regularly as the 'Stinker' by many local children, he shared his time between Lapley Vale and the nearby Town of Stretton. Larry commuted back and forth between the two Towns in his mobile home. This was a very old fashioned Gypsy caravan made entirely of carved, highly decorated, vividly painted, solid oak wood. This unique place of abode had been inherited from his late Father on whom Larry had modelled his whole existence and humble life style. When mobility was ever required by Larry, almost inevitably to travel between the two Towns, the caravan was efficiently towed by Larry's faithful horse, a fine and healthy cob, named Paddy.

Real name Lawrence Walter O'Brien, Larry the Lamb had the misfortune of being known to all and sundry in Lapley Vale by this nickname because of an alleged incident with a sheep when he was still in his youth. Nothing was ever proven and Larry had always vigorously denied any impropriety but never-the-less he retained, indeed he had been forced to accept, his familiar nickname. Strangely enough he was known as 'Wandering Wally' by all the people who were acquainted with him in Stretton. Larry was more contented with this nickname probably because he did not wish the gentle folk of Stretton to ask too many questions about his less comforting Lapley Vale handle.

Although it was fair to relate that Larry did tend to share his time between the two locations accommodated through the generous Christian hospitality shown to him by the Reverend Reginald Blackburn, better known as 'Whistling Reggie', the Vicar of 'All Soul's' Parish Church, Lapley Vale and the Reverend Emmanuel Snoddy, the Vicar of St Peter's Parish Church, Stretton,. both had facilitated him with adequate facilities for parking his caravan on safe land which was also able to provide Paddy with suitable pasture for him to graze upon, he actually spent much more of his time in vicinity of Lapley Vale. He could be correctly classified as being only a temporary dweller in Stretton albeit with moderate frequency.

Soon the probable cause of Peggy's odd and unusual behaviour became apparent when Jedd Clampett, the local Town Tramp, suddenly emerged from the narrow alleyway, which was commonly referred to as a *'Ginnel'* by the locals, at the side of Peggy's home. This ginnel and other similar enclosed passageways were strategically placed at regular intervals along the long rows of terraced houses in order to provide easy pedestrian access to the gardens and sheds conveniently situated at the rear of each neat block of houses. Jedd was carrying a pair of garden shears in one hand. He was also toting a large sack, which appeared to be stuffed with weeds, leaf and foliage cuttings as well as miscellaneous garden rubbish, in his other hand.

Jedd Clampett had been the resident Tramp in the Town since the late 1940's or early 1950's. Suddenly appearing from nowhere he soon made himself accepted and known to those amongst the Populous who were prepared to tolerate his presence and also supported him from time to time. He had been quite content to live, for many years, in relative squalor inside a large, hollow, disused concrete sewerage pipe at the side of the local Municipal Tip. Although he was unsightly, and frequently very smelly, Jedd enjoyed the reputation of being perfectly harmless when left alone and not provoked in any way. He could be a bit of a nuisance sometimes when he had consumed alcohol but he was tolerated by the vast majority of the people in the Town. He was considered to be neither Master nor Servant to any person. He worked for anyone who would employ him to carry out all kinds of odd menial domestic jobs. He was usually paid in kind, usually food or clothing, because he could become a potential nuisance if he was paid in cash due of his weakness for strong drink. He, just like Larry, would definitely have a severe drinking problem if he could afford it.

Jedd was Larry's natural rival in the Town because both derived their day to day living from a similar source. They both cherished and protected their own established circle of regular customers. Surprisingly enough the two men had never ever clashed over all the years, although they never attempted to hide or disguise their obvious disapproval and clear dislike as well as distrust for each other. For many years they had both gone to great lengths in their efforts to avoid any sort of personal contact. So far as anyone was aware they had never actually clashed with each other in any violent or distasteful way. Jedd had only fairly recently gained the nickname of 'Jedd Clampett' because of a popular American television series being shown on British TV's entitled *"The Beverley Hillbillies"*. Although his true name was thought to be Clampett his first name was certainly not Jedd although he accepted and responded to it without any sign of resentment.

There had been a quite recent, regrettable, incident which involved a large roll of linoleum, being carried over Larry's shoulder, and Peggy, who had, at the relevant time, been standing on the pavement, outside the Town's Post Office. This innocent looking roll was subsequently responsible for causing Larry the Lamb to accidentally, quite inadvertently, knock Peggy into the path of an oncoming vehicle when Larry happened to turn sharply to his left in order to respond to someone who chanced to address him. Peggy, who had been standing at the edge of the pavement chatting with Billy 'Cockeye' Dawes, was suddenly hit at the back of his head with the roll engaging such force that he was unable to stop his involuntary propulsion into the carriageway. The Curate at the Parish Church of All Souls, the Reverend Jeremy Smith-Eccles, despite his reputation for being accident prone and also as being a useless driver, almost completely avoided a collision occurring whilst he had been unfortunate enough to be driving his small green Mini car along the street at that very moment in time. The only actual contact occurred between the front nearside tyre of his vehicle and Peggy's new artificial limb. The prosthetic limb was squashed and quite badly damaged. Miraculously Peggy, although severely shocked, was physically unhurt. Larry was so relieved with this unlikely outcome and so filled with guilt that, without demand or invitation, he had volunteered to carry out all Peggy's gardening requisites, on a regular basis ever since that accident happened, free of any kind of charge. Incidentally, that particular incident provided Larry with yet another unwanted nickname. He was soon being called 'The Wild Linoleum Boy', in some highly amused quarters and this continued to be the case for quite some time afterwards. However, as events had turned out, Larry had failed to appear to perform his voluntary gardening duties at Peggy's home for some time over the preceding few weeks, probably as a result of his temporary absence from the Town during one of his regular, yet usually not pre-planned, visits to the Vicar of Stretton, Emmanuel Snoddy. It also had to be taken into consideration that he had quite a number of regular paying customers who resided in that nearby Town.

Peggy, without the suggestion of malice aforethought, had innocently engaged the readily available services of Jedd after he had happened to come across him wandering along their street looking, even more than usually, neglected and hungry. Peggy, incorrectly as it then appeared, thought that Larry must have considered that he had completed his period of penance and, because his gardens were in need of some immediate attention, he had taken the opportunity to engage Jedd to take care of all his horticultural needs in exchange for the welcome provision of a home made steak and kidney pudding dinner expertly prepared by Peggy's wife Lena, who was widely respected and acknowledged locally as a cook of great skill which had resulted in her enjoyment of well deserved favourable repute.

Although Peggy had a well earned a reputation for being somewhat, bordering upon extremely, argumentative at times he had never actually gone out of his way to unnecessarily upset anyone without just cause or reason. Clearly he had been aware of the possibility of the clash of interests when he engaged Jedd's services and his furtive behaviour could correctly be attributed to the fact that he was hoping that fate did not cause Larry to make a chance appearance in their vicinity until well after Jedd had finished his tasks and was well clear of the immediate area.

Jedd had completed his tasks in the gardens and having already enjoyed the delicious meal he was now preparing to take his leave. When Larry eventually caught sight of him at Peggy's home he immediately put two and two together which instantly caused him to become very angry, aggressive, and quite threatening.

"What the bloody hell is that scruffy old Bugger doing in your garden Peggy? ... Eh? ... Come on? ... I demand an explanation…..I do your gardening now….I'm your Head Gardener….He's got no right whatsoever to be stealing any of my regular customers from me."

Peggy had been justifiably embarrassed, not to mention flustered. He did not know what to do or say for the best. Jedd merely glared at Larry before turning his back on him to walk away down the road. Despite the obvious provocation he elected to completely ignore the obviously unwelcome presence of Larry. This casual course of action had resulted in aggravating Larry even more. He abandoned his cart in the middle of the road to rush after Jedd, now definitely consumed with undiluted malicious intent implied rather than aforethought. Just as he was about to grab Jedd from the rear the Tramp chanced to notice him. With astonishing dexterity and formidable ability, not to mention, surprising agility Jedd swiftly took hold of Larry to throw him bodily over his shoulder. Larry, emitting a loud and piercing scream, had landed flat on his back on the surface of the road. Without further ado

Jedd continued on his way without passing comment of any kind or indeed in the total absence of any form of detectable reaction at all.

Peggy dashed, subject to his age and disability, to see if Larry had been injured in anyway. Larry, lying motionless, was dazed but only his feelings had been hurt. He had been sufficiently surprised and stunned to completely lose any further desire to attack or to consider pursuing Jedd. Peggy, who had been joined by Lena alerted by the sound of the commotion going on outside her home, cautiously helped Larry back onto his feet. They carefully sat him down on their front garden wall. Mrs Hackett soon brought him out a mug of hot tea and a large slice of her home made fruit cake. The incident closed with Peggy ardently assuring Larry that he still remained his first choice Head Gardener and he went on to promise him that he would never ever ask Jedd to do any work for him in future without first consulting him. These comments seemed to comfort and reassure the pathetic looking man as he slurped his tea held in one hand whilst tightly grasping his slice of cake in the other.

Yet another fascinating and exciting incident had broken the so called peace and tranquillity of the quiet life normally expected in an ordinary working class Town. High powered Producers of motion pictures could not possibly visualise the level of intrigue and adventure hidden beneath the thin veneer of normality in everyday life regularly experienced within the aura of the "Swaying 60's".

"You can depend upon my wholehearted support."

Sergeant Bert McCabe was patiently waiting in the kitchen situated at the rear of the building at Lapley Vale Police Station. He was seated at the large wooden table which tended to dominate most of the total interior space available in the room. He was quietly drinking tea from his, personalised, large mug clearly identifiable because it had three very distinct broad stripes prominently painted on the side of it. He looked relatively calm and pensive as he quietly prepared himself for an 11am meeting with the Divisional Rural Inspector, his old friend and immediate superior, Bill Kinley, who was on his way to join him from the quite close by Whiston Sub-Divisional Headquarters of the Lancashire Constabulary.

Kitty, the reliable, revered, long serving, Station Cleaner, had completed all of her daily tasks. She was now preparing to vacate the premises when she suddenly became aware that Inspector Kinley had entered the Station from High Street through the open front door. She immediately turned all of her attention towards making the welcome visitor a fresh mug of tea.

The Inspector passed a few cheery words with the Duty Officer, Constable Eddie Littlejohn, affectionately known in the Town as the *'Gentle Giant.'*. Eddie was busily scribbling down incoming messages from Divisional Headquarters, which he was currently in the process of receiving via the large old fashioned telephone which was positioned alongside the purpose built switchboard, conveniently situated in the corner of the main office under the bright daylight available through the Police Station's large front bay windows. The Inspector swiftly made his way through to the kitchen area.

"Good morning Bert.....How are they hanging this morning my old and trusted friend?...Ahem....Not to mention my revered colleague and brother-in-arms....I'm pleased to note that I didn't miss out on the statutory tea testing ceremony......Thank you kindly Kitty....How are you my Dear? ... I trust I find you in rude health and high spirits this fine day...I have to confess it is always a pleasure to see you at any time of the day Dear....You are like a ministering angel to the battle weary warriors of the law enforcement ever fully engaged at the sharp end in the fight against crime and disorder in Lapley Vale and surrounding areas."

Kitty smiled coyly as she placed the third heaped spoonful of sugar into Bills' mug of tea. Slightly flustered and at all times most respectful she spluttered,

"Oh...Fine thank you Inspector....Thanks for asking....I've made you a nice brew Sir....Just the three sugars isn't it? ... Yes that's right isn't it? ... I thought it was."

Smiling broadly Bert intervened.

"Good Morning to you Sir...May I also remark what a pleasure it is to behold my 'Fearless Leader' at the said sharp end of proceedings in this constant battle we wage in order to ensure peace and tranquillity prevails for our appreciative...Not to mention....Ahem...Also adoring...General Public....Eh? ... Eh? ... In answer to your question Sir they hang appropriately thank you....As you have already observed our Kitty is...As ever....An angel in disguise Eh? Eh? And might I add how appropriate it is that you happen to know that statement to be true for a fact....Eh....Eh? ... Thank you Dear Kitty....You get off home now...That pile of dirty washing won't do itself will it? ... Eh? ...Eh?"

Kitty blushed, as she quickly gathered her bits and pieces together, before she disappeared through the open doorway and out of their sight. Bill and Bert settled down to enjoy their tea, whilst they continued to amuse each other with their normal exchange of the familiar, well practised, enjoyable pleasantries. Bill coughed politely before he cautiously made a point of glancing in the direction of the Office towards the front of the building where Eddie was taking the messages from Divisional Headquarters.

"Will Eddie be making himself scarce soon Bert?....I want to have a private and very personal word with you this morning....On one of those occasions when...Only those persons who qualify as being amongst the needing to know are present....If you catch my drift Bert....I find it necessary to be cloaked in secrecy accompanied by any other kind of unadulterated bullshit you may care to mention...Need I say anymore?"

Bill touched the end of his nose with his finger as he winked to Bert in a sly and sneaky way.

Despite the fact that he was slightly puzzled by his Inspector's comments, Bert immediately sprung to his feet. Without comment he marched through to the Front Office where he could see that Eddie was then in the process of fastening up the silver buttons on his tunic, having just completed his business on the telephone. Bert grinned at him in a friendly way,

"Nothing that needs my urgent attention I trust Eddie....Eh? ... Eh?"

Smiling broadly, all across his round friendly features, Eddie responded,

"Oh no....Nothing as serious as that Serg....I was about to partake of a nice brew unless you have some other plans involving vital tasks to be urgently and instantly undertaken by me."

Bert was shaking his head as he spoke calmly to his subordinate,

"Excellent...Good....No...That's fine Eddie....But....I wonder if you would be kind enough to make a noise like an egg for me and then beat it...Eh?... Eh? ... Why don't you make one of your rare excursions out into the open air for a short while? Eh? ... Eh? ... Take your well earned tea break with one of our many grateful and admiring shopkeepers in the Precinct please...The Boss and I have matters of great importance…Not to mention issues covered in gold plated secrecy to….Er…Well….To discuss in camera so to speak… Eh? … Eh?"

Nodding and smiling Eddie obliged without the slightest sign of any kind of dissent or any indication of the presence of latent curiosity. He placed his helmet on the top of his head before he boldly strode forth towards the open front door.

"Yes….Message received and understood Serg…I need to have a little word with Dick Rigby at the Butcher's Shop….I think he wants my expert opinion on his new….Deeper filled….Meat pies….It's a Bastard of a job but someone has to do it….If that particular venture happens to be thwarted in any way I am also required to test the new recipe scones at the 'Currant Bun' Baker's Shop in the Precinct…The pressures brought to bear from this job are one hell of a heavy burden at times….Still….See you later Serg….Shall I shut the front door behind me Serg? … Keep the public at bay so to speak whilst the summit talks are conducted to their natural conclusion?"

Bert was about respond in the negative when the Inspector called through from the kitchen.

"Yes…..Close it as you leave please Eddie….Drop the catch on it as well…It is our ardent wish to be undisturbed for the next half hour or so."

Eddie, as usual responded cheerfully.

"Whatsoever you say Sir….Tatty bye for now….Oh by the way….I've switched the trusty switchboard over onto automatic pilot so you shouldn't be interrupted Gentlemen….See you in an hour or so."

Although it was clear, even to a casual observer, that Bert currently appeared to be in excellent spirits and most receptive to Bill's idiosyncrasies he was, nevertheless, slowly but surely, becoming more curious about the whole situation as it was painfully unfolding. Bill Kinley suddenly seemed to be uncharacteristically anxious and somewhat on edge. Bert wondered what was in store for him as he made his way back into the kitchen.

"There we are then….All ship shape and Bristol fashion as the sailors always say…Aye….Aye Sir….Not to mention we are now one hundred per cent secure….Eh? … Eh? … Now then I want to tell you about some interesting developments now occurring inside the hallowed grounds of Lapley Vale Manor….But….As you requested to speak to me first….Please…Carry on…Fire ahead…Eh? … Eh? … How's the tea? … Up to the usual high standard you have come to expect from the premier portion of your vast Empire I trust? … Eh? … Eh?"

Bill appeared to be unusually, not to mention quite strangely for him, ill at ease as he stared into Bert's, now turning decidedly anxious, features.

"Bert…..You know how together you and I have always made a habit of applying….Each and every year…For your invaluable service to be extended beyond your contracted thirty years of distinguished commitment to the Chief Constable of this great Lancashire Constabulary…Usually authorised and annually rubber stamped thus permitting you to carry on regardless with your selfless and dedicated service to the Public? … The report we have submitted each and every year since you actually exceeded the upper age limit when all Sergeant and Constables are obliged to submit themselves to compulsory retirement as laid down by Statute…If I may be bold enough to remind you Bert that age limit is in fact at the age of fifty five?"

Bert nodded without making any comment.

"Well….I'm afraid I have bad news for you my old friend….There's no easy way to tell you this…Brace yourself Bert….What I am about to relate to you comes straight from the Chief Constable's Office at Preston…You will be required to retire on your full pension before you reach your sixtieth birthday…Later this year….10th of October I believe….Sorry Bert….When you've got to go you've just got to go…."

Clearly stunned, Bert stared into Bill's empathetic and tortured features. For once in his lifetime Sergeant Bert McCabe was suddenly lost for words. This particular scenario was as rare as a month of Sundays or the discovery of a deposit of rocking horse droppings lying on the High Street, as an indication, if indeed one was needed, of the seriousness of the statement of intent outlined by the Inspector on behalf of the Chief Constable.

Both men were speechless for a few moments, which actually seemed much longer to both of them. It fell upon Bill to break the uncomfortable silence.

"Nothing personal against you Bert....Even the Chief Constable is obliged to comply with all of these Home Office Regulations.... And...I'm afraid to say that the news I have just given to you is not the end of all of the bad news neither."

Bert gulped noisily as he visibly steeled and braced himself.

"My sixtieth birthday falls on the day before yours.....So....Fate has decreed that we both hanging our boots up together....My Missus...Well she won't hear of me asking for any extension even if I had the remotest chance of getting one....She has been making plans for our retirement for a number of years now....It's one hell of a grievous situation Bert.... But....We find ourselves in the same boat I'm afraid."

Bert, rapidly recovering his composure, responded almost instantly,

"Up the creek without a bloody paddle if you ask me Bill....How the hell can the Chief Constable contemplate the loss of both of us in one savage....Foul and devastating sweep...Eh? ... Eh? ... Talk about leaving the Force on the bones of its arse...Eh? ... Eh? ... Bloody hell fire Bill....You've actually managed to put me off my dinner delivering news like that....And that's just my bloody luck because we have both been cordially invited to partake of our luncheon with Her Ladyship at Lapley Manor so that we can engage in an informal meeting with her in the company of her esteemed Estate Manager Major Sebastian Kinsley-Porter....Definitely an appointment not to be missed under any normal circumstances....Eh? ... Eh? ... Her Ladyship will have ordered the Cook to chill a few bottles of best bitter and also to prepare some of the finest cheese and onion butties ever tasted by man or beast with no crusts on them....Eh? ... Eh?"

Silence fell over the room once again as both men desperately struggled to come to terms with what could only be described as a cruel and devastating *'Coup de grace'*. Shaking his head sadly Bill muttered something about being shafted by the fickle finger of fate, or something on those lines.

Again Bill was the first to speak.

"On the plus side Bert….We can arrange to hold a joint 'Leaving Do' and split the cost of the ale and butties between us when the dreaded time arrives."

Bert, looking horrified, shrugged his broad shoulders as he replied,

"Oh…That's on the plus side is it? … Eh? … Eh? … I wasn't planning on breaking my life long well established habit of not paying for anything like that out of my own pocket in the first place…Bloody hell fire Bill."

With an overdone flourish, Inspector Kinley produced the official letter signed by the Chief Constable, detailing Bert's fate, from the inside pocket of his unfastened top coat. He purposefully shoved it across the table to his still visibly shocked colleague. Bert scanned the text. He sighed, deeply, displaying a clear indication that he was reluctantly having to force himself to accept the inevitable on this occasion. He was very gradually beginning to come to terms with his prospective future fate. In true McCabe tradition he soon began to swing back towards the positive side.

"Still we've got a few months left to sort things out for ourselves and our futures yet Bill.…Eh? … Eh? … Cross our bridges when we come to them.…Eh? … Eh? … Don't allow uncalled for panic to creep in and cloud any of our personal decisions.…That's always been my motto in life…Eh? … Eh?"

There was definite evidence that Bert's normal spark of unbridled enthusiasm was returning but Bill had readily appreciated the devastating extent of the shattering shock his visit and the imparting of such unwelcome tidings had inflicted upon his old friend and colleague of many long years standing.

Bill glanced at his wrist watch as he swiftly rose to his feet. He was re-buttoning his uniform great coat as he spoke.

"I'm very sorry Bert but I'll have to postpone the pleasure of taking luncheon with Her Ladyship on this occasion…..I have to see the Chief Superintendent at Rochdale at 1pm sharp today….I think he wants to gauge our initial reaction to this devastating news from Headquarters for himself….He is buying my dinner for me in his posh Officer's Mess situated right next to the Other Ranks and Peasants Canteen….That's one for the diary Bert….Christ….He's almost as tight with his money as you and I are….Eh? … What? … And that's watertight isn't it? Eh? … Like the proverbial duck's arse under water."

They both relaxed as they enjoyed a little chuckle. It was then Bert who took up the conversation.

"Well I will naturally offer your humble apologies to Lady Lapley and I'll do my level best under extreme pressure to polish off your share of the beer and butties….No….No….Don't thank me….Please…Please don't hug me impulsively through sheer unadulterated hero worship…. Not to mention the genuine appreciation and heartfelt admiration you are now feeling for my willing self sacrifice …Eh? … Eh? … Anyways…. I've no idea what she wants…..I must confess that things have been rather quiet at the Manor recently….Local rumour has it that Her Ladyship is having more that a bit of hassle from those traitors to common decency who call themselves Her Majesties Inspectors of Taxes…..Eh? … Eh? … Please give the Chief Superintendent my compliments William…. Tell him he has my full authority to inform the Chief Constable that Sergeant Bert McCabe unequivocally states that he….The Chief Pussy Cat of this whole extensive bloody shooting match in the County of Lancashire…Eh….Eh? Can kiss the Sergeant's arse on both cheeks…. What a bloody carry on Bill….And I thought this was going to be another ordinary…Yet never-the-less….Peaceful tranquil and most enjoyable day….Eh? … Eh? … Little did I know…..Incidentally……Let's keep this news under our hats for the time being…Eh? … Eh? … We don't want any of our Colleagues to know about our impending fate until they absolutely have to….I want to make sure the public at large are sufficiently prepared for the obvious shock they will experience with the removal in one foul sweep of their beloved and esteemed leaders and protectors….Eh? … Eh? … We don't want anyone taking uncalled for liberties with advantageous knowledge of our impending loss of status do we? … Eh? … Eh?"

Inspector Kinley fastened the final silver button on his greatcoat before he headed in the direction of the front door. He stood to one side in order to allow Bert the space required to release the Yale lock as he concluded their conversation with obvious sincerity.

"My lips will be sealed you may rest assured on that Bert my old friend and valued Colleague…But don't leave them in the dark for too long we want to give them plenty of time to collect all the large cash donations for our leaving presents…Stands to reason that they'll be insisting upon buying something extra special for us…Eh? … It's a bugger Bert but….Well….It's a well known phrase or saying but… You know it to be true….All good things must come to end….'Illegitimo nil carborundum' has always been my favourite and cherished motto…."

Bert was able to instantly translate the words as Bill's lips moved, his retort was immediate.

"Yes I know that one…Never let the Bastards grind you down….. Eh? Eh? What might be most appropriately and aptly called appropriate in view of all of these current prevailing circumstances….Eh? Eh?"

As if Bert had not been subjected to enough unwanted news he was now about to receive yet another shock when Lady Lapley and the Major settled down with him for their planned discussion, in the Withdrawing Room at Lapley Vale Manor. This was after suitable refreshments had been taken and duly enjoyed by all present. As anticipated Bert comfortably managed to dispatch all the specially prepared cheese and onion sandwiches. Lady Lapley was aware, not to mention amused, that they remained his undisputed favourites. Bert had washed them down with four large bottles of chilled best bitter.

Lady Lapley seemed composed and confident, possibly a little excited, as she related her bombshell to the already apprehensive Bert.

"I hope you have enjoyed your repast Sergeant Bert… I am sorry Inspector Kinley could not join us here today but….As you may have heard on the grapevine…So to speak… I am presently being subjected to pressures on the financial front of the type never ever faced up to by any of my illustrious predecessors throughout our long and honourable history....I have to find ways of paying enormous tax bills to Her Majesties Inspector of Taxes....Duly owed by the Lapley Manor Estates for many years....I have been forced to make decisions which would have been unthinkable in the time of my late and beloved Father.... The Duke...After many considerations have been rigorously examined I wish to inform you Sergeant Bert....My dear friend...Lapley Vale Manor Estate will be opening up as a tourist attraction under the guise of what is now commonly known as a Safari Park in the near future."

Her Ladyship paused to gauge Bert's reaction. His expression did not give anything away. Calling upon all the vast reserves of her aristocratic background and breeding she managed to continue without exposing her true inner feelings of sadness and regret for the necessary action she was being forced to take in order to combat the cruel and impossible position in which she had found herself wallowing. She continued,

"The Major and I have already held meetings with an international company known as the Chadderton Brothers who have been responsible for the initial setting up followed by the development of many similar facilities in other parts of....Well...Not only our beloved Country but throughout the whole wide World....Their experience enables them to attend to all the red tape and licences and all those other necessary arrangements including the structural alterations necessary when wild animals are being kept in securely fenced and supervised expanses of open land....The Safari Park will take up the whole of the West side of the Estate....These vital preparations will take a few months to complete Sergeant Bert but the Lapley Vale Safari Park is scheduled to be ready for the expected opening to the public on the first day of September this very year...This target will be achieved....Without fail I am assured.... Obviously there is a need for you and possibly your Superiors to kept up to date with all the fast moving developments and the Major is looking forward to working closely with you personally so that we will all be singing from the same hymn sheet....So to speak."

There was a pregnant pause purposefully engineered to enable Bert to absorb the stunning information. Her Ladyship and the Major appeared to be noticeably anxious as they patiently awaited Bert's valued response.

Suddenly a smile flickered across Bert's gnarled, yet still quite handsome, features. He sat forward, speaking with undisguised enthusiasm.

"Well…If that's the decision you have made My Lady….You can depend upon my wholehearted support….Not to mention my full and undiluted total co-operation…Eh? … Eh? … One hundred and ten per cent…The only thing nagging at the back of my mind is how these radical changes will affect the many members of your loyal and trusted Staff….Those who have lived and worked on this Estate all of their lives as their Fathers and so on and so forth before them…Eh? … Eh?"

The Major was keen to respond positively.

"Not a thing to worry anyone with that particular score Sergeant…. Their jobs will be secure…There will also be exciting openings for a considerable number of local people….Not just for employment as Game Wardens and the like but in the offices of administration…The proposed and envisaged extensive catering facilities….Not to mention the imperative need for added security requirements….Each and every person currently on the Staff will be guaranteed their future employment and those who live in tied property will be protected for life….We expect to be recruiting extra Staff as early as the end of July or more likely the beginning of August at the very latest…"

On receiving this information Bert's expression suddenly changed. He managed to sound hopefully curious.

"I dare say you might require the services of an experienced local Police Officer on a full time basis when the time is right….Eh? … Eh? … I don't wish to jump the gun but I might be persuaded to resign from the Lancashire Constabulary to join you in such an exciting venture if the terms of employment could be laid down to suit all our individual needs….Eh? … Eh?"

Lady Lapley was absolutely delighted.

"Oh Sergeant Bert…It would be a great relief to myself and indeed to all my Staff if you could sacrifice your career to provide us with your wealth of experience in everyday dealings with the public at large.…We were only discussing this very prospect with Horace Pink my trusted Gamekeeper yesterday…He feels he would definitely need much guidance and expertise from someone.…Like yourself Sergeant Bert…Yet I was apprehensive when I rationally considered just how much of a loss you would be to the Lancashire Constabulary and what a wrench it would be for you to leave your post.…Oh Sergeant Bert you have made me very happy today.…I would welcome you with open arms…So would we all…What say you Major?"

The Major nodded his head with genuine enthusiasm. Unbridled delight was apparent from their demeanour.

"I am sure all the fine details can be worked out with the Legal Team but I can promise that you will not be remunerated on any less of a salary than you presently derive and enjoy through the Police Service.…Do you need further time to consider your future position Sergeant Bert? … Shall we meet again next week perhaps?"

Bert found that he could not stop himself from smiling broadly as he responded.

"My Lady…My dear…Dear Lady Lapley.…Please take my word for it.…I am all yours for the taking .…Eh? … Eh?.…Name the date.… Allow me enough time to give the Chief Constable at least a month's notice please.…It's only fair because he will probably need to promote two or possibly three top Constables to fill my boots.…Eh? … Eh? … As you rightly commented it will be a great tug for the Force and myself but I am prepared to make the sacrifice to assist you in this fabulous project…Eh? … Eh?"

They all laughed as Lady Lapley tugged on her bell rope to summon Smithers, the arrogant snob of a Butler into the room.

Smithers, a naturally pompous man, his nose permanently stuck up in the air, knocked on the door, before he swiftly entered the room.

"You rang My Lady?"

"Yes Smithers indeed I did….Be kind enough to ask Cook to provide us with some cake and then pour a whisky for Sergeant Bert…The Major and I will join him as well….We have good reason to celebrate."

Without the slightest visible change in his features Smithers responded.

"Very good My Lady".

Appearing to be almost bowing from the ankles he departed, his prominent nose still stuck up in the air. Bert gazed upon him with disbelief.

Once he was well clear of the Manor grounds Bert stopped his car in a lay by. He climbed out and after checking that he was not being overlooked of observed, he threw his cap into the air and cheered loudly as he performed an impromptu gig. As he continued with his journey back to Lapley Vale Police Station Bert, not normally a religious person, muttered a brief but nevertheless heartfelt prayer of thanks.

"Sorry Gill….What's the cockeyed problem?"

Not one of the numerous persons who just happened to find themselves in the vicinity of High Street, Lapley Vale at 11.30am on, what might be fairly be described as a nothing out of the ordinary, Tuesday morning would have been able to appreciate, for even one fleeting moment, the astonishing significance and rarity of an event openly taking place before their very eyes. If they had chanced to take particular notice, Billy Dawes was about to enter the Betting Office which was owned and managed by the local friendly Bookmaker 'Degsy' Franks. The truth of the matter was the vast majority of people could not be expected to pay the slightest heed to this less than momentous event when an elderly man just happens to walk into a Betting Office. However, this unremarkable incident could possibly have had a quite staggering impact upon those local persons who were familiar with Billy. Clearly a forthright explanation was required for the information of all concerned.

Firstly: Billy had not ever seen the inside of a Betting Office nor had he involved himself in gambling in any shape or form throughout his whole life prior to this particular visit. These perfectly legal establishments, now becoming regular features in many Town Centres, had recently proved to be amongst the most popular of the new additions to the ever increasing variety of highly commercial service outlets being found not only on High Streets but also in many other similar shopping facilities. These extra businesses were becoming increasingly available to the general public in numerous Town Centres throughout the whole of the Country. In the old days the only facilities available to potential gamblers were the familiar, rather shady, clandestine, men known to all as *'Bookies Runners'*. These fugitives from law enforcement skilfully received and placed bets from the then illegal gamblers, or *'Punters'*, using many various, on occasions quite devious and clever, means of doing so. They existed within a world where many ordinary working class men, who wished to indulge themselves with the opportunity to place a bet or wager, frequently, depended upon them to utilise all of their skills in outwitting the Police to conduct the practice of illegal gambling on their behalf. Purposely uninviting by design, as laid down by the law, these Betting Offices establishments, although increasing in numbers, were still a comparatively recent innovation. The high level of demand for their services had swiftly established them as familiar sights alongside all the other traditional shops in many typical shopping centres. Their now overt presence and obvious popularity was recognised as one of the increasing noticeable instances or examples of positive indications that some long standing social restraints, originally introduced with the intention of providing some protection to people from their own personal undesirable, possibly fraught with danger, weaknesses, were now quite liberally being tolerated as well as sanctioned by the Government of the day.

Secondly: There was the astonishing fact that Billy was not actually there to place any kind of wager on his own behalf. He was about to place a bet with Degsy for his fellow Committee Member Bernie Price. It was well known by anyone remotely acquainted with these two men that they did not like each other. This was understating their long standing animosity towards each other to say the very least. They could be fairly described as incompatible to the enth degree. Whenever their paths chanced to cross Bernie inevitably attempted to grasp any opportunity offered to belittle, ridicule, or find many other ways of tormenting or upsetting Billy. Billy, as a result of his charitable nature, naivety, together with a total absence of a sharp responsive mind, tended to make him a rather soft, vulnerable, target. Although, it must be said, the much less abrasive and likeable, it was Billy who usually ended up being comforted and often supported by most of their many shared friends and acquaintances. They, generally, appeared to have little or no time for the brash as well as frequently rude and confrontational Bernie.

Billy had responded to a request, received indirectly via Bernie's wife Agnes, to rally to the immediate assistance of his sworn adversary in order to render urgently needed personal aid to him. Agnes explained to Billy that Bernie had been temporarily confined to his bed with what normal people would classify as a severe cold, described by him as being in the early stages of something approaching double pneumonia. Being temporarily incapacitated he had realised that he would be unable to make one of his regular and frequent visits to Degsy's Betting Office. Despite their intense dislike for each other Billy was not the sort of person who would refuse to do a good turn for any of his fellow beings. The fact that Billy had suffered considerable emotional stress in Bernie's hands recently before he eventually ended up well on top in their ubiquitous personal disputes he had, immediately and without hesitation, responded to Bernie's unusual request without giving his own personal feelings a second thought.

Billy cautiously entered into the stuffy, dimly lit, smoke filled, atmosphere inside the obligatorily bland and less than inviting interior of the shop. The Regulations were very strict with regard to the provision of any sort of amenities permitted to be extended to the Punters inside any Licensed Shop. It was as if the Government did not really want Punters to linger inside the premises whilst gambling. Perhaps they felt that they should not be encouraged to enjoy themselves whilst they were engaged in the process of placing their bets. No toilet facilities for the Punters were permitted which at least kept the usual crowd of customers reasonably fit walking the fifty odd yards up the street to use the Public Conveniences situated alongside the Shopping Precinct. These necessary calls of nature could possibly hold the answer to the lingering mystery of why the ginnel alongside the Betting Office invariably smelt like a neglected urinal.

Peggy Hackett almost dropped his pencil in a spontaneous reaction to the shock of seeing his long standing old friend and admired bowling companion in such unfamiliar surroundings. He really wished to say something very witty but he was so surprised by Billy's appearance, even Peggy, found himself, for once in his life, quite speechless.

Probably because Billy had never ever placed any kind of bet before, either legally or illegally, he was much relieved and clearly delighted to see a familiar face looking out at him from behind the enclosed office counter. The Betting Office counter resembled that of the General Post Office but thankfully the notorious *'Terrible Twins*', Bella Briggs and Lily Forest, were nowhere to be seen. Gillian Best, one of fellow bowling team member Charlie Walsh's married daughters, had worked for Degsy Franks ever since the Office officially opened. She had been familiar with Billy and his family from her earliest days when she was an enchanting, delightful and respectful, little schoolgirl. Positively encouraged and gaining in confidence very slightly, Billy surged forward in the direction of Gillian's position from the public side of the cashier's window. She was also most surprised, perhaps better described as being shocked, to see him inside the shop. She was friendly and encouraging, greeting him with a broad, inviting, smile.

"Hello Mr Dawes…..This really is a rare treat….I don't think I've ever had the pleasure of seeing you in here ever before have I? Welcome…. What can I do for you?"

Rather self-consciously Billy pulled out a small sealed envelope from the inside pocket of his tweed sports jacket. He handed it over to Gillian with a nervous smile flickering across his ageing features.

"Sorry…Er….Yes Gill….Er….Hello….How nice to see you…..I'm not surprised you've never seen me inside here before….I've never placed a cockeyed bet in my life up to now Gill love…I'm only in here to put a bet on for Bernie Price because he finds himself cut down with the cockeyed flu or something just as cockeyed bad….His Missus came out of their house to hand this to me….Actually…I think she might well have been waiting for anyone who just happened to be walking past… Anyways….She handed me this envelope but I have to admit I haven't the faintest idea as to what the cockeyed procedure is in here at all…Please tell me what I have to do…Please Gill."

Gillian smiled sweetly as she deftly opened the envelope.

"Don't worry Mr Dawes….I'll make the slip out for you and give you the copy to hand back to Mrs Price….It's no trouble I know exactly what sort of bet Bernie usually puts on….Now let me see………"

She discarded the envelope to carefully read the contents of the note. She immediately gasped, clearly shocked. Her eyes opened wide as she stared at the note with a look of total horror and disbelief. She struggled to pull herself together before swiftly passing the note and the envelope back to Billy. He was naturally puzzled by Gillian's reaction, to say the very least. He rummaged around in his jacket and then his trouser pockets in an effort to locate the whereabouts of his spectacles. Placing them on his nose he leant back to carefully read the note. He still did not appear to understand why any sort of problem had arisen. Gillian nodded to him, in a helpful, understanding, fashion, as she anxiously instructed him,

"Read it carefully Mr Dawes….Please…Look at those names…. There….Look….The horse's names."

Billy's glare was fixed upon the note. He continued to appear totally perplexed.

"Sorry Gill….What's the cockeyed problem….His Missus told me that Bernie told her he wants a single bet on the one horse and a double on the other two….That's what she said to me anyways…Don't you know what that means Gill? … Because to be honest and speaking for myself personally I haven't got a cockeyed clue what she was going on about….Honestly."

Gillian was trying her level best to be discreet. She leant forward to whisper to him as loudly as she might dare bearing in mind all the prevailing circumstances.

"Read the names Mr Dawes….The horse's names….Read them carefully….I think Bernie might be having a bit of a joke at your expense…Please study those names."

Billy readjusted his national health issue glasses to ensure the full focus of his gaze was once again concentrated on the note. Then, very much to Gillian's chagrin, he started to read out aloud,

"Yes…O.K…. certainly…Here we go Gill the first one is….Hoof Hearted….Yes that's right….This handwriting isn't too cockeyed clever but it says Hoof Hearted…Well…That obviously must be it's cockeyed name….The others….The two put together for the cockeyed double are…Here we go now Gill love…Whale Oil……Beef Hooked… What's the cockeyed problem there Gill? I have no problem reading their names…..What's wrong? What is it?"

Gillian was cringing, desperately trying her best not to appear to be too embarrassed, as the dozen or so other Punters inside the shop immediately burst out laughing. Peggy was the first to take advantage of Billy's naivety.

"I bet you won't get any decent odds on the first one Billy….Not with your track record in the farting stakes…You must be the odds on to be the outstanding clear favourite….Eh? … You're asking a question Billy….Who farted? Hoof Hearted? Who Farted? Think about it Billy…. Got it yet?"

Billy's unexpected presence together with his subsequent strange conduct had now attracted everyone's undivided attention. Billy was still unable to completely comprehend what was causing the problem or the reason behind the obvious hilarity he was causing. Bearing in mind Peggy's comments he once again concentrated all of his attention upon the words written on the note. He slowly read them over to himself again. His lips moved slowly as he painfully studied the horse's names. Suddenly he shouted.

"It's….Who farted! … And the other two…Well I'll be fuc! Oo OOOh! … What kind of a cockeyed twisted prank would you call this?….Eh?….Sorry about that Gill….Wait till I get my hands on that so called cockeyed joker….This is the last time I volunteer to do any cockeyed favours for Bernie Price."

Blushing and looking absolutely shattered as well as, more than slightly, embarrassed and pathetic, Billy, rather rudely, snatched the offending envelope out of Gillian's hand before turning on his heels to stomp out of the shop with an air of deliberate urgency.

As the door slammed closed behind him and despite her best efforts in the willpower department, Gillian could not hold herself back from joining in with all the other laughing people standing around inside the shop. They laughed until tears ran down their cheeks and their sides started to ache. Lurking in the background at the rear of the shop, not usually known for possessing any trace of a sense of humour, even Degsy allowed himself to display a silly smirk which spreads across his gnarled features as he struggled to choke back a chuckle.

When he arrived outside Bernie's home, looking as if he was about to commit murder, Billy was slightly surprised and not a little perturbed to see Bernie, albeit wrapped in his thick winter overcoat, tweed cap and knotted scarf, standing, in full view, inside his open front door. Excitedly Bernie shouted over his right shoulder and Mrs Price almost instantly shoved her husband out of her way so that she could stand alongside him. Both were obviously highly amused and they appeared to be delighted to witness Billy's obvious distress. Billy stopped with a purpose at the closed gate located at the bottom of their short garden path. He was extremely agitated as he clearly experienced great difficulty controlling his temper. He forcefully addressed Bernie and Agnes.

"What a rotten cockeyed trick to play on a person who thought he was going out of his way to do another person a cockeyed favour.....You are nothing but a menace Bernie....A cockeyed menace....Don't ever ask me for anything ever again ever...."

Bernie and Agnes were now almost helpless laughing. Billy's distressed demeanour seemed to add to their amusement even more. Billy was then very close to completely losing his temper. He had to exercise maximum personal self control in order to force a necessary, undignified, retreat back along the street. He managed to shout his final remarks with pure venom present in his tone.

"You want locking up Bernie.....Both of you should be thrown in a cell...You're cockeyed menaces....Yes cockeyed menaces....Piss off inside the house Mister and take your cockeyed Dragon in there with you....You're as bad as each other if you ask me...You deserve each other....Cockeyed menaces....A pair of cockeyed menaces...."

Billy wanted to say more but realised that he was now in grave danger of making himself look and sound even more stupid, if that was at all possible, as a result of this particular situation.

Bernie and Agnes actually found Billy's final comments were almost too hilarious for them to cope with. Desperately clinging to each other they both gradually dropped down on their knees in obvious agony brought on through their uncontrolled bouts of laughing. Turning briefly, when he had walked about 20 yards away from them, Billy stopped to look back down the Street. He was obviously incensed and clearly in a state of acute frustration. He found himself unable to actually speak another word. With a genuinely threatening expression flashing across his face he slowly bent both of his knees ever so slightly in order to accentuate a sincerely intended two fingered gesture, using both hands in vicious unison accompanied by a fully blown raspberry. Bernie and Agnes were now rolling around on their garden path completely out of control. They were in imminent danger of actually wetting themselves.

***

Alf Morgan was gainfully employed stocking the shelves at the back of the bar in the Bowling and Social Club. He had recently opened the doors to four elderly men who regularly visited the Club at lunchtimes to quietly play slow games of dominoes whilst they sipped a couple of pints of best bitter. His attention was instantly drawn to the sudden appearance of Billy as he stormed in through the door, purposefully allowing it to slam closed behind him. He made straight towards Alf where he plonked himself on a stool alongside the bar. Alf then made the mistake of asking Billy if anything was wrong. Billy was absolutely shattered when Alf found he was unable to prevent himself from laughing out aloud as Billy related the sorry tale of his visit to Degsy Frank's shop. He just burst out laughing when Billy subsequently showed him the offending betting slip. Billy completely failed to see any humour whatsoever in the situation. He sat sulking with his back turned away from Alf as the Steward remained standing behind his bar quietly attempting to stop himself from chuckling.

The rear door entrance into the Clubroom then swung wide open. Woody Green and his apprentice Eric McCabe were taking their luncheon break. They were coming into the Clubroom from the vicinity of the bowling green, which was situated at the rear of the premises. As you may recall Eric had now become Billy's grandson-in-law since he had married his beloved Jenny. Woody headed straight for his personal stool as Alf slapped two frothing pints of best bitter on the bar in front of the two talented Gardeners. Eric pulled his face as he addressed them, pausing for a moment or two before he raised the glass to his lips.

"Bloody hell fire Woody….Alf……I've got a bloody long day in front of me yet….I wasn't going to bother with a lunchtime pint today."

Woody wryly lifted his tatty cap off his head for a second to allow him the space to gently scratch the top of his head before he responded.

"Oh Aye….I'd like to see anyone trying to take that away from you now you've smelt it Young'un…Eh?….What do you say Billy? … Christ Billy you look as if you've lost a quid and found a shilling….No true son of Bert McCabe….Or grandson of Billy Dawes would ever refuse the offer of a pint of delicious and refreshing beer….What do you say Billy? … Billy? … Christ what's up with you?"

The two men were soon becoming increasingly aware that Billy was genuinely upset about something. Billy declined to respond to Woody. Alf, more au fait with the circumstances, attempted to be helpful.

"You'll have to excuse Billy for a few minutes Boys….Yes….I'm afraid he's been the victim of that twisted Bastard Bernie Price's warped sense of humour again….Do you want me to tell them about it Billy?"

Billy gruffly nodded as he took a long drink from his pint glass. Woody and Eric were then very anxious to hear every word Alf was about to say.

Alf noticed that Billy still had the offending note stuck in his jacket pocket. He leant over to cautiously take possession of it. Billy was about to object but decided to let him have it.

"It would appear that Bernie and his Missus duped Billy into thinking Bernie was ill and unable to place his bet on a Degsy Frank's Betting Shop today…You know Degsy's place on High Street?"

Both men nodded, looking on in anticipation.

"Well Agnes gave Billy this envelope containing a written note.… Now Billy not being a betting man himself merely passed the envelope containing the note over the counter to Charlie Walsh's daughter Gillian.…You know Gill don't you? … His eldest girl…Married that Insurance Bloke."

They nodded again indicating, by their expressions, that they wanted Alf to get to the crux of the matter without further delay.

"Well…Agnes told Billy that Bernie wanted a single win bet on the first horse and a double on the other two.…Well I think you'll see that they were having Billy on when you read the horse's names as written down of this note."

Woody took the paper from Alf. His lips moved as he slowly read the names. He read them over again to make sure. He then sat back stifling a chuckle before he quickly passed the note over to Eric. Eric eagerly snatched the piece of paper from him. He also read with moving lips. He stared vacantly for a second or two and then after re-reading the contents again he suddenly identified the joke. He was unable to prevent a loud laugh emanating because of his own ultra sensitively active sense of humour. This immediately caused Woody to burst out laughing aloud which caused Billy to jump off his stool in a gesture of sheer disgust. He then stamped off in the direction of the door, actually leaving some beer in his glass. Eric ran after him. He managed to stop the old man before he reached the front door.

"Billy.….Billy.…Come back to the bar.…Finish your drink.…Here let me buy you another one.…Come on.…I'm sorry Billy.…I didn't mean to laugh at you but .…Bloody hell fire Billy.…Surely you twigged something was wrong when you read out those bloody names."

Billy reluctantly allowed Eric to steer him back to his stool. Eric nodded to Alf who immediately started to pull Billy another pint. Woody walked away from the bar desperately attempting to conceal his obviously high level of amusement. On seeing Billy returning to the bar he swiftly ducked into the secluded sanctuary of the nearby Gents toilets.

Billy was obviously upset but he was now sufficiently in control of his emotions to be capable of speaking.

"Hell fire Ricky…I didn't think you and Woody would be taking the cockeyed mickey out of me as well…I might have expected something a little better from my so called friends and cockeyed relatives…That Bernie Price is a cockeyed menace….A cockeyed menace not to mention his cockeyed Missus…She's just as bad as him."

Eric placed a comforting arm around Billy's shoulders. He was now just about managing to control his own level of amusement. He desperately wanted to comfort the obviously distressed old man. Woody returned from the toilet, his face indicated that he had been laughing until tears had run down his cheeks, but he was also back under control as he climbed onto his familiar stool. Eric glanced sympathetically at the other two men as he spoke.

"Billy…..No-one thinks you're a twit because a silly Bugger as despised as the likes of Bernie Price and his equally daft Missus are chose to take the piss out of you…And…Incidentally….Managed to achieved their aim by taking advantage of your good nature in a cowardly and cruel fashion….Wait till I see the Bastard…He thinks he's funny but he'll meet his match one day…And…Believe me……He who laughs last laughs laughing lasts….Or what ever."

The additional pint appeared to be providing the required soothing action for Billy. Still clearly upset he was slowly, yet surely, beginning to make a noticeable recovery. All four men then enjoyed a few moments of silent contemplation as the tension started to gradually clear from the prevailing ambience. Billy perked up sufficiently to order some beer.

"Thanks Ricky….Thanks Alf….And you Woody…..I must confess I was upset by that cockeyed clown's antics but far worse things happen at sea....Eh?...Eh Alf?...You'd be the best man to comment on that...Eh? ... Look....Set another round of drinks up please Alfred....Include yourself...I'm in the chair....I hope that Bernie's next cockeyed pint... Well...I hope it cockeyed chokes him....I mean that."

Silence reigned once again as the friends took possession of their freshly pulled pints. Eric had now forgotten about the heavy workload facing him for the rest of his working day. The ambience was clearly close to normal again as little Norman Smith entered the room. Billy nodded to Alf as he stepped up to the pump to pull a pint for Norman. Norman deftly scrambled up to the top of his specially adapted stool whilst exchanging the usually greetings with his friends. Before Norman could enter into any kind of conversation Woody grinned, turning to address Billy.

"I bet Degsy wouldn't have given any decent odds against you being responsible for any farting that might have taken place...Eh? ... Come on be honest...What do you say Billy?"

Eric and Alf glared at Woody with total disbelief, Norman had no idea what they were talking about, as Billy silently stared into Woody's grinning face. To everyone's relief Billy began to nod as a little smile swiftly turned into a full blooded laugh before he readily agreed.

"I suppose you're right there Woody....I always get the blame whenever any cockeyed farting is involved....Mind you....To be fair...I have to admit...It usually is me....Eh? What?"

In order to ensure the improved ambience was truly cemented Eric injected some personal well placed humour into the conversation.

"I bet these chaps don't know what Nan and the rest of family call you when you're at home do they Billy? ... Eh?"

Billy giggled, this time he was merely pretending to be embarrassed.

"Ask Nan if you don't believe me....Old Billy the Poo....Eh? ... That's what he's called by his nearest and dearest loved ones so I guarantee you're quite correct in your statement Woody....Mind you Woody.... I can vouch for the fact that there's a certain Head Green keeper not a million miles away from where we are standing at this moment in time…Eh? … Who can rip them off like a German sub machine gunner some mornings out there in that pavilion especially when he has had a heavy session on the bitter in here the previous evening or should I say night before….Eh? … What say you 'Old mighty arse'….Eh?"

Woody was trying his best to look offended but they all ended up enjoying a genuine laugh. The laughing was being generated through sheer relief as much as anything else. Norman innocently joined in the merriment although he quietly wished that someone would let him in on the joke.

"Why would anyone be interested in a bunch of old rags?"

Constable Eddie Littlejohn was affectionately known to many of the local people as "Eddie the Gentle Giant". A simple trusting type of person Eddie sometimes suspected that all of the heralded and well publicised modern advancements and the staggering technical advances, in various areas of general Policing methods, had somehow managed to pass by without the slightest involvement of the Lapley Vale Police Section. 'The Bert McCabe School of Policing', his very own unique method of 'Policing for small Towns and Villages within the County of Lancashire' was still alive and kicking. Perhaps the most annoying outcome of this was the strong and supportive level of continued public support his methods generally received and the considerable success it still enjoyed.

Eddie had arrived at his sad conclusion soon after he had given some serious consideration to the ready availability of all of the latest advances designed and adapted with a view to improving the overall efficiency now being seen in areas where the vast majority of Police Officers up and down his own County, never mind the rest of the Country, were taking full advantage of most of these new, useful and extremely helpful, resources. For one example swifter response times were being noticed as well as appreciated by the public. For a further sample of the improvements an extremely efficient, recently enhanced, radio communication system with wide ranging capabilities, was now being used throughout the entire Lancashire Constabulary Area. Eddie wondered why he had not been able to avail himself of any of them. The presence of many of these welcome advances had been quite apparent even to any casual untrained observers. The general public had witnessed that the majority of these day by day improvements, in all round services delivered to everyone by the Lancashire Constabulary as well as other modern Police Forces, were now unmistakably present. Somehow the Lapley Vale Police Section had sadly missed out on anything remotely resembling the introduction of any modern technological advancement. Eddie did find this state of affairs was providing him with much food for serious thought, especially as the new decade, introducing the 1970's, was relentlessly drawing ever closer. The truth of this entire issue was that Eddie and his colleagues did have a considerable amount of spare time on their hands even when the Police at Lapley Vale were most in usual demand.

This particular feeling of deprivation was being enhanced today as Eddie found himself patiently standing on the rear platform of the Huddersfield to Rochdale Express Omnibus. He was by way of responding to a reported, potentially serious, incident which may have occurred on the Rochdale Canal. This Canal actually formed the official boundary dividing the Lancashire Constabulary Police area with that belonging to the County Borough of Rochdale Police Force. The Borough prided itself upon providing an efficient, trusted and independent Police Force. Although considered to be fairly small in numbers, the whole Force consisted of a Chief Constable and about 200 Police Officers, it was well equipped, self sufficient, proud and clearly identifiable as the sole force for law and order in Rochdale. It was considered to be a competent outfit quite capable of dealing with most of the daily policing demands likely to be made upon their service by their General Public.

Eddie's Sergeant, the famous Bert McCabe, was enjoying a well earned rest day. Bert had already left home earlier in the day driving Mrs McCabe to the nearby much larger Town of Oldham in his Ford Prefect saloon car to carry out her weekly shop. This privately owned vehicle was the only vehicular form of transport actually available, albeit in a fairly limited way, to Lapley Vale Police Section. Bert received what he considered to be a paltry car allowance for any essential official use made of his car. Bert had been granted an interest free loan from the Lancashire County Treasurer to enable him to purchase the vehicle from new. He was permitted to claim a maximum mileage allowance for payment over and above his usual monthly salary. Any payments, in relation to the use of privately owned vehicles, which were the subject of any car allowance claim, were laid down within strictly enforced rules and limitations. When Bert was on leave or when he was off duty his Constables were obliged to either utilised their own bicycles which, incidentally, entitled them make a claim for a payment of seven pence per day when used on duty, or, in an emergency they could send for the Area Patrol Car. This apparently useful facility had to travel across to them from where it was based at the Whiston Sub Divisional Headquarters and was often engaged dealing with urgent matters in the rest of their Area when they were required. The remaining alternative courses of action left for Bert's small band of dedicated men was to walk or find any other legitimate means of transporting themselves around their area of responsibility.

Eddie now wished he had taken the time to repair the long standing puncture on the tyre on his bicycle when he had the chance to do so. This routine maintenance had been ignored until it was too late, when he actually needed to use the machine in earnest for his own convenience.

Eddie had received information relayed to him from Divisional Headquarters to the effect that an anonymous 999 telephone call had been made which indicated that there was a suspicious object floating in the Canal near to the Huddersfield Road Bridge which passed over from the Lancashire County side of the Boundary into the County Borough of Rochdale. This Bridge was possibly the furtherest possible distance away from Lapley Vale Police Station, situated as it was on High Street, consequently it was also a long, not to mention time consuming, walk on foot. The Public Transport Buses were handy because they never charged any fares from uniformed Police Officer travelling with them so they provided a reliable and efficient, if not very frequent, alternative means of available transport.

Displaying his ubiquitous broad, friendly, smile Eddie politely thanked the Bus Conductor as he alighted at the appropriate stop closest to the Canal Bridge. He stood on the Bridge to take a look along the extensive stretch of water below him. He was soon pleased to see a familiar face, even if it did happen to belong to Cyril Snead, known by many by his less than complimentary nickname of *"Snidey Snead"*, because of his reputation for being a nosey parker and gossip monger, as he was making his way toward him. Eddie greeted him with a friendly nod. Cyril soon made it clear that he was keen to inform Eddie about something of note and great importance.

"I was wondering who they would send all the way down here to the outer reaches of Bert McCabe's Empire to deal with this Eddie….. I thought the great man himself…Our Bert….Bless him…Might have graced us all with one of his rare personal appearances."

Eddie was amiably responsive,

"Hello Cyril….Nice to see you….Bert is taking a well earned day of rest today…Was it you who telephoned us using the 999 system Cyril?"

Cyril appeared to be slightly bemused. He slowly shook his head,

"Sorry Eddie I don't know what you're talking about….I haven't phoned anyone for a bloody long time…What I was going to tell you about…For your information…Is what I personally considered to be the strange antics of two Constables and a Sergeant from Rochdale Town Police which took place just a bit further down the Canal….Over yonder….On the far side of the Bridge….Just further down there…This was about half an hour ago….They seemed to be pushing something heavy along in the water…It looked like a bundle of old rags to me but I wasn't that close to see anything properly…Aye they were definitely pushing it along in the water with a couple of those long poles…You know?….Like the barge people use….They were buggering about there for about twenty minutes or perhaps even a little more pushing the rags away from some weeds they looked as if they were tangled up in near to the embankment…They eventually managed to steer it into the main current of the water.…They waited until it was well under way.…They seemed to be very pleased with themselves…Cheering and jumping for joy I would say…Anyways…They got the bundle floating along nicely…Look over there you can see the main run of the water is in middle of the Cut.…Starts over there near to where I told you I saw them messing about…It slowly floated along under this Bridge that we're standing on…Apparently much to their added delight for some reason beyond my understanding…Then the rags slowly carried on until they became snagged on some branches that were either floating in the water or were stuck up over the top of the water or something.…Anyways they were sticking up and the ragas got caught on them just down there not far from that Cotton Mill on the far side of the Cut.…It had definitely been making it's way towards the old Cotton Mill and might have floated past there if it hadn't finished up getting itself stuck.…There it is Eddie…You can just make it out if you look hard enough.…Some thirty or forty yards away down there."

Eddie strained his eyes peering along the straight course of the Canal. He immediately spotted the cluster of branches protruding out of the water.

"Come on Cyril.…Show me please…"

Cyril stepped back, pulling his face to demonstrate his instant displeasure at this suggestion.

"Bloody hell Eddie.…It was only a bunch of old rags.…I haven't got time to play around showing you bundles of bloody old rags…I'm on my way to Degsy's Betting Office and the bus is due any minute now.…I've picked out a couple of dead certs running at Haydock Park this afternoon and I want to make sure I get my money on them in good time before they run…Look.…You can't miss those rags bobbing about on the top of the water.…I'll have to press on.…Please don't read anything too much into this Eddie but I just though it was strange seeing three bloody big Coppers all playing in the water like little kids less than half an hour or so before you made one of your rare appearances around these necks of the woods….Roused my curiosity that's all…Why would anyone be interested in a bunch of old rags? … It beats me."

Not even Cyril's selfish attitude could upset the pleasant demeanour of the Gentle Giant. He nodded before he started to make his way down to the Tow Path alone. As he walked towards the place on the Canal where the branches were quite visible, Cyril cupped his hands around his mouth to yell out to him,

"It's a bloody pity all you Coppers don't find something a bit better to do with your time…Catching crooks or the like for instance…That's if anyone cares to ask me for my opinion….Eh? … What? … I've seen it all now….Like bloody little kids…..Playing in the Cut….Anyways…If anyone did happen to fall in there they'd probably die of leprosy or some other deadly disease before they actually drowned….That water's full of all kinds of shite….And I mean shite Mister….In fact you couldn't actually swim in it…You would only be able to go through the motions….Eh? … Get it Eddie? … Eh? … Go through the motions?"

Eddie continued to smile as he acknowledged Cyril's humorous remarks with a casual backhanded wave.

Reaching the actual spot on the side of the Canal where the branches were clearly visible, Eddie immediately noticed that there was more to the bundle of rags than even nosey parker Cyril had managed to observe. The rags belong to a human body which was floating face down in the water. Glancing all around Eddie was relieved when he noticed two Asian men walking along the cobbled road which ran adjacent to the Tow Path. They were obviously making their way towards the Mill to take up their shifts because this particular road did not lead to anywhere else.

Waving, Eddie shouted to them, frantically keen to attract their attention. The two men initially appeared to panic but then at Eddie's insistence they rather reluctantly joined him on the Tow Path. Still smiling in his usual friendly manner, Eddie politely addressed both of the men.

"Look sorry to delay you on your way into work Lads but I'm afraid I will need some assistance if you don't mind."

Eddie nodded in the direction of the body. Both men instantly and in view of all of the circumstances surprisingly calmly, appreciated the gravity of the situation and they responded willingly to the Constable's obvious call for urgent assistance to carry out his duties.

Without exchanging one word they actively assisted Eddie to carry out the gruesome task. After some difficulty and utilising considerable physical effort they did eventually manage to drag the heavy water soaked body out of the water. They needed to utilise all their combined strength in order to haul it up from the Canal onto the cobbled Tow Path. This awkward manoeuvre exhausted all three of the men. They all took a quick breather before Eddie carefully turned the body over to take a first look at the face. To his astonishment, despite some obvious distortion, he immediately recognised that the unfortunate body belonged to Jedd Clampett, the Lapley Vale resident tramp. Jedd's body was cold and very stiff as a result of the effects of exposure and the onset of *'Rigor Mortis'*. He was quite clearly dead.

Eddie spoke earnestly to the two men, who had ably assisted him,

"Listen Lads…You've been a great help…Thank you….As you can see this is a tragic situation and as such will need to be dealt with in a correct manner and also without any avoidable delay…Will one of you please stay here with the body whilst I quickly nip up to the Mill to use their telephone?….I'll need a Doctor and the local Undertaker to come here before I can shift this body…Plus someone will need to inform the Coroner through my Divisional Headquarters….Will one of you stay here whilst the other shows me where I can use a phone inside the Mill premises please?"

Still without a word being spoken to Eddie, the elder of the two men nodded to his companion. He then rather curtly spoke to him in some language well beyond Eddie's comprehension. The younger of the two men then headed off in the direction of the Mill frantically using hand gestures to indicate to Eddie that he should follow behind him.

About an hour and a half later Jed's body, now wrapped up and out of sight inside a black plastic, zipped up, bag was placed inside a coffin shell ready to be transported to the Public Mortuary at Rochdale Infirmary by Leonard Skillet, the local Undertaker. Leonard together with his son, David, were authorised to move bodies on behalf of H.M. Coroner. They had become skilled and efficient at carrying out their often unpleasant, yet essential, duties. Leonard, never ever addressed as Lenny, and David, never called Dave, always working together were commonly referred to as *'The Body Snatchers'* by all those familiar with the specialised services they competently happened to provide. Eddie was grateful for the prompt and efficient service they inevitably offered as he squeezed himself into the front of their hearse to accompany them and Jedd's body to the Public Mortuary at Rochdale Hospital.

Silly as it might seem to anyone not aware of the restrictions placed upon a Police Officer when he deals with sudden deaths the only person permitted to assume that a body is dead, or certifying that life is extinct as the Law demands, is a fully qualified Doctor. A Doctor must attend to pronounce that life is extinct even if the corpse is in several pieces or possibly in a state of advanced decomposition.

Reacting to Eddie's call from inside the Mill DHQ had contacted Doctor Berry at his Surgery. The Doctor had attended promptly to perform the necessary legal formalities. Local General Practitioner, Malcolm Berry, was the unofficial Police Surgeon for Lapley Vale and surrounding Districts. He never objected to his services being requested because he inevitably received a nice little cheque from H.M. Coroner's Office in payment for his availability and professionalism. Malcolm often disposed of this bonus money in the company of Bert McCabe at one of the local hostelries. They affectionately referred to it as *'Malcolm's Funny Money*'; this little monetary perk was never to be brought to the attention of H.M. Inspector of Taxes under any circumstances whatsoever.

***

The following morning Bert collected Eddie from the Mortuary after the Pathologist had completed his post mortem examination of Jedd's body. The obvious cause of death was found to be drowning and samples of his blood and other bodily fluids had been taken to be sent off for scientific analysis. These essential courses of action involving the magic of Forensic Science were always undertaken with a view to establishing the possible presence, or absence, of alcohol or any other noxious fluids in the body of the deceased at the time his death.

Back at Lapley Vale Police Station the two men enjoyed a nice cup of hot tea brewed and served by the every obliging Kitty the Cleaner. The two men sat facing each other across the large wooden table in the kitchen at the rear of the building. Eddie was able to concentrate his full attention on the investigation of Jedd's sudden death because his colleague Constable 'Sooty' Sutcliffe was now the official Duty Officer and as such had full responsibility for covering the day to day demands of Policing in the Town.

Eddie briefed his Sergeant with all the known and relevant facts available to them to date.

"Those sneaky lazy Bastards from the Borough Police…A Sergeant and two Constables bear in mind, definitely floated Jedd down the Canal from their area into ours Serg…I ask you…What a carry on?…. Christ there's hundreds of them all walking around down there with their fingers up their arses looking out for vicious motorists double parked or even worse…Dealing with real desperadoes who feloniously park their cars on those yellow lines…Still….When all's said and done Jedd's better off being dealt with by people who knew and cared for him….I'm glad to say that he didn't have much personal property on him Serg….Apart from several….And when I say several I mean numerous…Yes numerous…Layers of tatty clothing he was wearing and he had a soggy part eaten packet of rich tea biscuits in his army greatcoat pocket…There was his tobacco tin and papers…He also had an all but empty half bottle of cheap vodka in the other pocket….A few bob in coins and believe it or not Serg….A bloody comb….I couldn't find that tatty old trilby hat he always seemed to be wearing whenever I spotted him out and about….Probably still floating down the Cut well on it's way to Leeds by now."

The two men sat together in silent contemplation for a few moments. Bert was the first to speak.

"Well Eddie…..My Bonny Boy…You and I are going to have to take a bit of a look around inside that rat infested flea ridden concrete pipe down by the Municipal Tip….You know that place where Jedd lived… Eh? Eh? … The place he actually called his home….That's been the closest thing we will find to any permanent address you could possibly describe for an illusive old tripe hound like Jedd….He's hung about there all the many years I've ever known him….He had a television aerial sticking out of the top of it the last time I was down that way but I don't think he ever had a real television set….Kids messing I bet…. Eh? … Eh? … Be someone's idea of a bloody joke I suppose…..Eh? … Eh? … I don't fancy this particular job one little bit…We'll both need to call home to get our wellies and a bloody big thick pair of overalls each before we even think about venturing down that particular neck of the woods…Might just save us from getting ourselves all shit up to the eyeballs….Eh? … Eh? Or…Bloody hell fir Eddie…Even worse…. Infested!….Eh? Eh?"

A couple of hours later the two men were back sitting at the table in the kitchen drinking yet another mug of tea each. They were both visibly moved as well as adversely affected by their ordeal of searching through Jed's very humble place of dwelling. They had found very little of value but Bert did uncover a metal biscuit tin which Jedd had securely tied up with string as well as a piece of electric flex for added security. This box contained quite a number of important looking documents, all in a poor state of preservation to say the least. There was a letter written on official H.M. Government headed paper inside an envelope addressed to A.B. Clampett at an address which had become illegible due to the poor condition it was now in. Bert was always under the impression that Jedd's real Christian names were Trevor Ralph but he had never had occasion or reason to check on their authenticity. Another rather battered, almost unreadable, letter from H.M. War Office, was addressed to A.B. Clampett M.M. There was little actual information to be gleaned from these documents but Bert, recognising Military Medal, instantly decided to contact the War Office or hopefully the subsequent Government Department using the telephone number shown on the letter heads now in their possession. Bert retired to the privacy of his own Office to make the important telephone call without being disturbed.

Eddie walked into Bert's office just as he was replacing the telephone receiver. Bert appeared to be strangely intrigued and somehow suitably impressed as he concluded his rather lengthy telephone call to London. Astonishingly Bert had been able to speak to someone sensible within a matter of a few minutes after ringing the only contact number they had at their disposal.

Eddie could see that Bert was genuinely stunned. He had scribbled a few notes in his desk jotter whilst he had been talking on the phone. Eddie, appreciating Bert's untypical condition, was obviously concerned.

"Bloody hell fire Serg….Are you all right? I'm sorry to inform you but you look like the colour of boiled shite…What's up? Are you ill? Has the stench and filth of Jed's hovel eventually got through to you?"

Bert abruptly waved his hand indicating to Eddie that he was in need of a few moments to gather together all his thoughts. Eddie was now becoming even more anxiously intrigued as he waited to hear his Sergeant speak. Bert looked and sounded strangely emotional.

"Eddie….I've just spoken to an Army Major at the Ministry of Defence as a result of my ringing that number we found on Jedd's correspondence.…I'm not sure if there still is an actual War Office but he seemed to know what I was talking about and very soon gave me the sort of information we will require for the Coroner's Court.…I still find this hard to believe Eddie but unbeknown to any of us… And I'm absolutely sure of this.…We have been loosely acquainted with a 22 carat gold Second World War Hero …Yes I said a Hero here in Lapley vale within our midst for many years.…Eh? … Eh? … "

Eddie's eyes were now wide open indicating a mixture of disbelief and acute curiosity. Bert consciously steadied himself before he managed to continue. "Captain Arthur Benjamin Clampett…Eh? Eh? … Formerly of the Wartime Special Operations Service was awarded the Military Medal and several other bravery awards for outstanding personal conduct under fire in France and Italy during the last three years of the War.…There's no doubt about his identity Eddie.…On returning to his home he found his wife had moved in a Lover she had met and fallen for during Jedd's long enforced absences.…To make it even worse…His darling little Wife was also found to be up the duff.…Eh? … Eh? … Actually carrying this Boyfriend's child.…Gilt edged proof of someone guilty of some serious infidelity if proof had ever been needed…Eh? … Eh? … This was too much for him to bear and Jedd.…Or should I say Arthur.…Flipped.…He had a complete nervous breakdown.…As far as the Army are concerned the last they heard of him was when he was sent carefully strapped into a straight jacket on his way to a very hush hush Military Hospital somewhere in the County of Kent…That was in the Summer of 1946.…Eh? … Eh? … He suddenly disappeared from there before he had been officially discharged by the Medical Staff and he has never been heard of since that time.…The Army are sending a Liaison Officer up here to help us sort everything out.…He will be bringing all the available official Service Records with him.… Could well disclose if Jedd.…Sorry Arthur had any living relatives.… Or possibly if he ever got around to writing out or making his last Will and Testament .…Eh? … Eh? … Not a very likely possibility bearing in mind the subsequent circumstances of his miserable life I dare say…But who knows? … Eh? … Eh? … Someone could be worth a considerable amount of money because Jedd has never ever drawn any of his Army pay or touched his full Army Pension which had been arranged for him whilst he was detained at the Military Hospital…And now his next of kin or perhaps his nominated beneficiaries are entitled to claim it all together with a tidy sum in added compound interest.…Eh? … Eh? … Bloody hell fire…What do you think of that Eddie? What a turn up for the books.…Eh? … Eh? Right.…I'd better ring Inspector Kinley because he needs to be put in the picture without further delay....I just hope we are able to establish without any nasty difficulties that poor Old Jedd merely got himself pissed as we are all aware was always a distinct possibility and then unfortunately fell into the Canal by accident Eddie my Bonny Boy....Or else we could well be looking down the barrel at what 'The powers that be' class as a suspicious death....Eh? ... Eh? ... A possible homicide....A murder."

Poor naïve and inexperienced Eddie was now very close to collapsing into a full blown faint. His condition had been brought about by a combination of shock and sheer excitement. He was rendered speechless.

***

When Lenny Jopson, the Editor of the Lapley Vale Examiner, got wind of the exciting events he immediately triggered off a huge surge of National Media interest in the demise of Captain Arthur Benjamin Clampett M.M. Bert had enjoyed the unbridled hospitality of the *'Gentlemen of the Press'* that evening and into the night enjoying the luxurious, not to mention expensive, surroundings of the Vaughan Arms, Lapley Vale's finest watering hole by a long distance.

The following morning every National Newspaper in the Country carried the astonishing story of the War Hero turned Tramp. One or two of the publications had managed to get hold of an old photograph of the young Jedd in full uniform which had been taken from his Army records when he was still serving a serving Officer, as he did throughout the whole of the last World War. This picture of the handsome, dashing, young Officer bore little or no resemblance to the dirty, scruffy, old Tramp who had become such a familiar sight around the Town over many years. No person could really remember exactly when Jedd first appeared on the scene but it was a good few years after his initial arrival before they started to call him by his nickname, Jedd. This suddenly became his popular and accepted name as a result of a very popular and keenly viewed television programme entitled *'The Beverley Hillbillies'*. This light hearted American produced entertainment featured a scruffy character that had struck oil and became a multi millionaire. His screen name was Jedd Clampett and became almost as well known as Mickey Mouse. As an integral essence of the programmes plot this character Jedd was well known and famous for dressing and acting like a Tramp despite the fact that he had, quite by chance, become an Oil Magnate.

The chief, almost the only, topic of conversation throughout Lapley Vale and all surrounding Districts was firmly focussed for the next few days on the amazing revelations brought about by the sudden death of a most familiar, yet to most people insignificant, Member of their Society. The National Newspapers had certainly brought the little Town of Lapley Vale into some prominence.

Lenny Jopson entertained all of his closest friends at the Bowling and Social Club bar in the company of Bert McCabe after all the other visiting Newspaper Reporters had, mostly passed out, but had all eventually retired for the night in the comfort of their bedrooms at the Vaughan Arms. The small but jubilant group of not previously disclosed close and dear friends of the late Jedd remained there with Alf, Woody, Ralph and Victor until the wee early hours of the morning. This particular and stunning occurrence was unanimously considered to be one of the most remarkable revelations ever to come to the surface in their small Mill Town.

"Please Reginald…..Please open it"

The Vicar of All Souls, the Parish Church of Lapley Vale, the Reverend Reginald Blackburn together with his Curate, the Reverend Jeremy Smith-Eccles, had just enjoyed an excellent meal prepared for them by 'Whistling Reggie's' devoted wife Sybil.

For those of you who are not acquainted with the Vicar he earned his long established nickname, 'Whistling Reggie', due to the fact that he was unfortunate enough to have been cursed with very large, protruding front teeth. Whenever Reggie spoke he was inclined to make involuntary whistling noises especially when he is pronouncing any words commencing with the letter 'S' or other similar sounding letters. This noisy impediment was emphasised even more when he was in a state of excitement or agitation. Perhaps you might ponder what cruel fate had caused him to meet and marry his wife, bearing in mind her name is Sybil, but that was another story.

Sometimes naïve and accident prone, the young Curate Jeremy, probably in his mid thirties in age, remained a single man. He currently lodged at the Vicarage with the Vicar and Sybil. He had made a rather unfortunate start to his short career as a Clergyman. This was despite the obvious fact that he was completely committed and devoted to his calling. On the face of it, Jeremy definitely appeared to possess all the necessary dedication required to make a success of his chosen station in life. Alas he inevitably usually only managed to succeed in making a complete and total *'Pigs ear'* of most of his everyday undertakings.

Jeremy's roots were in a minor aristocratic family whose Country Seat was situated somewhere in the beautiful countryside of rural Surrey. Jeremy was less than impressive throughout his school life from his early Preparatory School days through to University. However he did eventually gain his appropriate degree in Divinity through his attendance at a rather obscure College of Theology, carefully chosen for him by his rather protective family. He was a caring, loving, decent man but, through no fault of his own, he was almost totally out of his depth living amongst the ordinary working class people of South East Lancashire. He had inevitably become a figure of ridicule amongst many of the Local Inhabitants including even some of the youngest who regularly attended his Sunday School Classes. One person in particular, Harry 'Bleeding' Longfellow, well known local driving instructor, who derived his nickname through his frequent use of the word 'Bleeding' in most of his conversations, told wondrous stories about his experiences during an extended period of time during which he was attempting to teach Jeremy how to master the expertise necessary to drive a motor car and pass his driving test. Even the local aristocrat, Lady Lapley, tended to treat him with, what might be described as, cautious forbearance since an incident at the Manor involving her front lawn, some rubber balls, and Her Ladyship's rather over-exuberant Labrador Dog, named Bruce. His propensity for clumsiness was first noted when he disappeared into an open grave whilst conducting a solemn funeral service, albeit in inclement weather conditions.

Jeremy suddenly astonished everyone by passing his driving test following a clandestine, intensive, residential driving course near his family home down South. He was rewarded for his feat with the present of a brand new British Racing Green Mini Car from his proud parents who were probably just as amazed as anyone else that Jeremy had actually managed to accomplish something tangible at last. There were some people who would probably still question Jeremy's overall ability as a competent driver, including Albert Snooks the Park Keeper at Lapley Vale Memorial Park. Albert had the misfortune to be almost mown down, whilst innocently standing upon a footpath deep inside the Park, by Jeremy driving his car through an area obviously intended for use by pedestrians only. On the other hand there were those who had reason to admire his swift reflexes and driving skills especially on one occasion when Larry the Lamb belted Peggy Hackett at the back of his head with the end of a roll of linoleum which involuntarily propelled him from the security of the pavement into the busy street at uncontrolled speed. This sudden action necessitated Jeremy having to brake hard whilst swerving in order to avoid and prevent a potentially serious road traffic accident. Incidentally, Larry was carrying the long roll of floor covering over his shoulder as he walked along the street when he turned to speak to someone who attracted his attention outside the Post Office. The rotation of the lino accidentally struck the unfortunate Peggy on the back of his head whilst he was causally passing the time of day with Billy Dawes as they stood together near to the edge of the footpath. This accounted for Larry's third nickname, 'The Wild Linoleum Boy'. As some of you may recall Larry shared his time travelling between Lapley Vale and the nearby Town of Stretton where, strangely enough, most of the locals who are familiar with him call him 'Wandering Walter'.

However, The Vicar, his wife Sybil and their Curate were quietly sipping their coffee after finishing their evening meal when Jeremy elected to update them of the days' happenings particularly with regard to the tragic and unexpected demise of Jedd Clampett.

"Yes Reginald….Sybil….I don't know if all of the facts are known to you but the unfortunate Mr Clampett ended up drowning in the Canal…It is strongly suspected that he had been enjoying an evening socialising which involved the consumption of excessive amounts of alcohol….It is sad to say that Mr Clampett was no stranger to extended excursions into drunkenness on the odd occasions….I digress….It subsequently became apparent to the Police that Mr Clampett was a War Hero decorated with one of the Country's highest honours by the late King George VI…."

Reginald was already aware of the brief details but this information was all new to Sybil. She was visibly shocked and genuinely saddened.

"Oh Dear....The poor man....What a terrible fate....I suspected that there was much more to that man than was apparent despite his ragged clothes and his lack of attention to his personal hygiene....He often enjoyed my cooking and was always grateful and most gracious to me....Never scrounged handouts or accepted charity....Always insisted upon working for his supper....I must confess that I actually admired the man....Even though I could not tolerate the stench he invariably emitted from his person on the many occasions our paths happened to cross."

Reginald added his observations.

"I have known Jedd for many years.... He was never known to be a burden upon anyone....Such a sinful waste of life....Dear oh dear the Lord works in mysterious ways his wonders to perform...What?"

Suddenly it was Sybil who appeared to be inspired.

"Reginald....Oh Reginald do you remember many years ago I told you that Mr Clampett entrusted me with the safe custody of a sealed envelope?...To keep for him?....You placed it inside your safe in the Study....I do hope it still remains there after all this time...Please Reginald....I am sorry to disturb you so soon after your repast but will you please check inside your safe for me?....Please Dear?"

Smiling broadly, Reginald returned from his Study to the Dining Room where Sybil and Jeremy were waiting agog with suspense.

"My goodness Sybil....I have to confess I was initially somewhat concerned but my fears were instantly put to rest I think this is the letter to which you are alluding My Dear."

He passed over the sealed missive to his wife. She carefully placed her spectacles on her nose to enable her to read the hand written inscription, *"To be opened by the Vicar only upon the occasion of my death."*

Sybil was clearly relieved and visibly excited.

"Please Reginald....Please open it."

Jeremy joined in

"Oh yes please do Reginald."

The contents of the letter, dated 1959 and signed by A.B.Clampett, asked for the Vicar to contact the Army Benevolent Society after his death had been confirmed. He intimated that he had left some form of documentation with them. There was a contact telephone number together with a coded reference included in the text of the short letter. It ended with expressions of his gratitude to the Vicar for all his and his wife's kindnesses and subsequently thanked them for any action they would necessarily have to take on his behalf.

All three were really excited by this fascinating turn of events. Reginald was the first to speak,

"I will take this letter to Sergeant Bert McCabe without delay.... I will call in at the Police Station to speak to him after Mrs Wardle's funeral service tomorrow morning....Unless you are able to call in earlier than that Jeremy."

Jeremy was delighted to be in a position to respond positively,

"Yes....Oh yes Reginald....I have no appointments of an urgent nature to concern me tomorrow morning and you can entrust this mission to me....I will take the letter directly to Sergeant Bert first thing after breakfast and our prayers tomorrow."

Sybil headed for the kitchen to make a fresh pot of coffee because their first cups had been allowed to go stone cold with all the abounding excitement. They were all genuinely intrigued by their surprising role in the on-going, highly topical, incident of popular note.

"Jezebel"

Shortly after his arrival at Lapley Vale Station at 8.30am the following day Sergeant Bert McCabe was quickly informed that a Solicitor from Herefordshire would be contacting him as a matter of urgency on the telephone by arrangement at 9am.

Bert duly accepted this expected telephone call. He found himself speaking to a very posh sounding Solicitor who, as it turned out, was representing Mrs Ursula Clampett the legal Wife and lawful heir to the estate of Arthur Benjamin Clampett as she was his sole surviving next of kin. He informed Bert that Mrs Clampett had instructed him to take the necessary steps required for him to apply on her behalf for probate in the anticipated absence of any legal last Will and Testament ever being made by her late husband. During the course of their conversation Bert managed to discover that Mrs Clampett had never actually been divorced from her Husband despite the fact that she had not laid eyes on him or had any contact whatsoever with him since the summer of 1946. Although she had lived with a former French Soldier for many years and had bore him three children, Ursula had never sought to annul their lawful marriage. Although she was known to be less than well placed in financial terms she was also known to be a long way from being declared a destitute. Her paramour had died leaving her a tidy sum which she had more or less spent buying her comfortable home near Hamel Hempstead where she resided whilst raising their illegitimate offspring.

Inspector Bill Kinley arrived as Bert was still noticeably simmering as a consequence of his recent contact with the Solicitor representing Ursula. They sat facing each other in the kitchen sipping mugs of tea made by the ever loyal and faithful Kitty. Bert could not disguise his utter disgust.

"What a carry on Bill….Eh? … Eh? … The bloody Woman has never cared a rat's arse for Jedd all these many passing years….She reads about his demise in the Daily Mail…Which incidentally….Has been kind enough to publish an estimate of his possible wealth bearing in mind the fact that it has been steadily building up and has remained unclaimed over those many years….Eh? … Eh? … And she has no hesitation whatsoever in swiftly jumping upon the bloody gravy train…. Eh? … Eh? … Or should that be the bloody bandwagon….Eh? … Eh?"

Bill blew on his tea before carefully taking a sip. He placed the mug on the table in front of him as he responded.

"Unfortunately Bert….I think she might be well within her rights….If she is still his lawful Wife she is his next of kin in the eyes of the Law….Better pass this information along to the Coroner's Office Bert….As you correctly remark….It stinks but what can we do?"

Shaking his head with unbridled disgust Bert agreed,

"Aye….You're right there Bill…I wonder if she'll even bother to turn up at his funeral….There will be an Inquest but the body has been cleared for burial because the cause of death is definitely drowning and he had enough alcohol in his bloodstream to have comfortably made at least twenty average normal people pissed….Eh? … Eh? … And that's just by the smelling of his breath alone….Eh? … Eh? … We now know for a fact…And we have taken written statements to this effect that he carried out some gardening work and picked up some monies owed to him before he spent the whole of his final fatal evening drinking in the 'Black Swan' Public House situated down by the Canal….There are no suspicious circumstances at all…He was so pissed he probably just stepped into the Cut thinking it was the main road which would take him to that festering stinking pit he called home….Sad but there you are….A lesson to us all perhaps…Poor Bastard….Still…Could have been worse....Eh? ... Eh? ... Might have be required to send for the Circus at Headquarters if there had been the slightest possibility that he was killed....We need that mob of pissyarsed Detectives crawling around all over our patch like we need an attack of septic piles....Eh? ... Eh?"

Both men laughed and relaxed, as they enjoyed their hot drinks. Constable Sooty Sutcliffe dashed into the kitchen looking distressed.

"Bloody hell fire...Excuse me Sir....Serg...There's been a little bump in the side street outside....No-one hurt but an Army Jeep and Jeremy whatshisname the Curate have definitely touched bumpers...They say they don't want to make a fuss....There's two people in the Station waiting to see you Serg...One is the aforementioned Jeremy and other is an Army Captain smartly dressed in full uniform....His driver is outside trying to straighten out the little dents on both of the vehicles.... Mostly on the Curate's mini car as it so happens."

Bert was on his feet. He rushed through to meet a shocked looking Jeremy now standing in the passageway between the Enquiry Office and his own private Office. Jeremy was flushed, obviously upset.

"Good morning Sergeant Bert I must apologise for the little incident outside I did not expect to find an Army vehicle parked in the little side street and unfortunately I must confess that my reflex braking left a little to be desired on this occasion....However...I can see you are extremely busy so I will pass this letter to you on behalf of the Vicar and swiftly take my leave....I will be taking a little lie down before facing the rest of the day....Good Morning to you all."

Jeremy was gone in a flash.

Bert was pleased to see that Sooty had already seated the Captain in his Office. Bert strode forward.

"That's right Captain....Please...Make yourself at home....Eh? Eh? ... We don't stand on any ceremony here...Not like in the Forces.... Eh? ... Eh? ... I assume you are the representative from that Office in Whitehall I contacted about the dear departed Jedd....Sorry...I do humbly beg your pardon....Arthur Benjamin Clampett.....Eh? ... Eh? ... How do you do.... Sergeant Bert McCabe at your service Sir....

Oh….Permit me to introduce you to my Commanding Officer this is Inspector William Kinley."

The Captain removed his cap and right glove to shake hands with Bill and then Bert.

"Good Morning Gentlemen….My name is David Fletcher I am temporarily attached to the Department dealing with all matters concerning Army Welfare….I have the late Captain Clampett's full Army records in my brief case….What an extraordinary man he was to be sure."

Whilst the Captain opened his briefcase Bill Kinley politely addressed him,

"Well thank you for attending so promptly Captain….We need to inform you that we have already heard from the late Captain's Widow through her Solicitor…May I also make it clear right away that the death is no longer being treated as suspicious although H.M. Coroner is enquiring into all aspects of the cause. There will have to be an Inquest because of his death being in the open but that will be arranged by the Coroner."

Captain Fletcher wryly shook his head.

"Didn't take her long to stake her claim….As you may have already surmised there is quite a large sum of money involved but our initial reaction is Mrs Clampett as his lawful Wife will be able to claim every penny of it in the absence of any Will….Pity."

Bert had now opened the letter that Jeremy had just handed to him. He interrupted to enquire quite urgently.

"Excuse me for asking Captain but are you aware of any documents being held by your Benevolent Society on behalf of Captain Clampett? … I'm not sure but….This letter I have just received from the Curate might shed some new light on this whole situation….Eh? … Eh?"

After reading the contents of Jedd's letter the Captain made a private telephone call before he returned to the ongoing conversation between Bill and Bert. Captain Fletcher was now smiling broadly.

"Well….I've just spoken to the appropriate person at the Army Benevolent Society and he has opened a sealed letter kept in their vaults after I supplied him with the secret code…The word….'Jezebel'.… Inscribed in this letter to the Vicar.…I am more than a bit delighted to inform you that Captain Clampett left a signed and witnessed last Will and Testament which he made in 1947 but appears to be nevertheless valid and legal.…He leaves all his worldly wealth to the Army Benevolent Fund with a stipulation that his wife Ursula should not in any circumstances touch one red cent of it.…I think we can safely say that Captain Clampett took the trouble to make sure his estate would be put to excellent purpose before he decided to bury himself in the twilight lifestyle he allowed himself to degenerate into.…Don't worry.…The Army will ensure his wishes are respected to the last letter and they will use each and every tool available to their legal team if called upon to do so.…Turned out nice again after all.…What say you Gentlemen?"

Bill, Bert and Sooty, who just happened to be eavesdropping, cheered in unison. Bert rubbed his hands together in a business like fashion before he responded to Captain Fletcher.

"Absobloodylutely.… Turned out nicely yes.…You can say that again Sir.… Absolutely fantastic…Eh? … Eh? … I'd love to see that Woman's face when she hears about these developments…Eh? … Eh? … Now then Captain Fletcher the delightful Kitty has prepared a fresh pot of tea for us so will you please accompany me to our Officer's Mess.… I actually mean the kitchen but I was showing off a bit…Eh? … Eh? … This welcome refreshment will provide us with the first opportunity to practice drinking a toast to Jedd as we knew and loved him with tea before we find somewhere suitable to partake of luncheon together after we have sorted out all the vital and various legally necessary paperwork…Eh? … Eh?"

The Captain grinned with sincere, genuine, pleasure.

"Sergeant the luncheon will be paid for by the Army.…I have access to a generous expense account which I am satisfied should be utilised in these exceptional circumstances…Eh? … What? … So let's not spare any expense."

Bert and Bill could hardly contain their delight as the happy throng move into the kitchen.

"Face? What face?"

The four pregnant Mothers really did look a picture of health as they patiently sat together on rather uncomfortable plastic and metal chairs which had been placed in neat rows inside the Waiting Room at the Ante-natal Clinic of the Maternity Wing in the Annex of Lapley Vale Cottage Hospital. As you may recall Jenny McCabe, Susan Summers, Linda Chumley and Kay Best all fell pregnant at, as close as dammit is to swearing, the same time. There was an undetermined element of certainty about this amazing situation because on the previous Christmas Eve there had been cause for extra celebration due to the marriage of Kay Brown to Sam Best which had taken place on that memorable day. For many obvious reasons they were all confident that they had conceived during that night or possibly early the following morning, that was then on Christmas day.

Jenny and Linda were both expecting their second babies, Susan was about to bring number five into the big wide World, Kay was the novice in this group, she was having her first baby. Although they appreciated the probable odds must be stacked against them they sincerely hoped that they would all deliver on the same day. Only time would tell if their wishes would come to fruition bearing in mind that any human behaviour is impossible to predict with any degree of accuracy.

As usual the Waiting Room was packed with women of all shapes, sizes, ages and stages of confinement. They majority of them seemed to be happily chattering away together as they patiently waited for their names to be called out by Sister Murphy, the rather abrupt, authoritarian, unpopular yet vastly experienced Midwife, who was in overall charge of the Clinic. Any innocent person passing this room with their eyes closed would be forgiven for thinking they had strayed into a battery hen farming complex if they were to go by the level of noise alone which was echoing around the large and very typical hospital waiting room.

Linda was happily addressing her close friends.

"Well Ladies the Town of Lapley Vale has been well and truly featured in all the headlines for the past few weeks or so….That poor old man Jedd…You know the scruffy old Tramp?....Did you see the lavish funeral ceremony shown in full colour on both the BBC and ITV Channels television news? ... I thought your Father-in-law looked particularly smart Jenny in his best uniform with all those shinny medals on display….I bet you were very proud of him."

Jenny smiled wryly as she responded.

"Trust Bert to be in front of all the cameras…He was even in shot when they showed the line of soldiers firing their guns in the air whilst they were standing over Jedd's grave…Mind you…To be fair he and Eddie Littlejohn put a hell of a lot of time and effort into the detailed investigation of the poor man's death….Dad managed to get a few late night drinking sessions out of it as well…Mind you he can always be depended upon to find some excuse to indulge in the popular local pastimes of swigging beer….I just hope for all our sakes we are now well and truly back to normal again….It was nice being in the spotlight for once but I think most of us in the Town of Lapley Vale prefer to rest in the shadows if offered any sort of choice."

Susan added her considered observations.

"I was bloody glad that the grasping bitch of a so called Wife of the poor Man didn't manage to get her greedy little hands on any of his money…. I bet she thought she could just swan in and boldly inherit all of his wealth despite treating the man in such a treacherous and uncaring fashion….She had a bloody nerve and no mistake."

Kay shook her head rather sadly.

"At the end of the day a brave Man with a broken heart died in tragic circumstances and I for one think a considerable number of those dozens of local people who fell over themselves to attend the funeral were hypocrites to say the least…Most of them wouldn't have given him the time of day when he was alive….My Sam thinks they were all swept along with the intense interest and unbridled enthusiasm shown by all those National Newspaper Reporters and that crowd of television people…Mind you every cloud has a silver lining as they say….The turn over of wreaths and flowers broke all records at the shop didn't they Jen? … As Jenny says let's hope we are back to normal at last….I don't know about anyone else but I'm starving…My stomach thinks my throat's been cut…I've got a hell of an appetite at the moment…I eat almost as much as my Sam and everyone knows that he can eat two more tatters than a pig….I'm ravenous…Honestly."

Linda attempted to console and offer some comfort to her young friend.

"It's all part and parcel of the ongoing process of pregnancy Kay love….Mind you… There is a definite need to err on the side of caution because you might well find out that it's very easy to put the weight on and not so easy to lose it again afterwards….I got a bit of a shock the first time I was carrying when I thought I could get all my old favourite clothes out of the back of the wardrobe after I eventually got rid of the lump…I tried to convince myself that all the garments had shrunk but I had to face the fact that I was carrying more weight than I had realised and believe me that soon curbed my desire for chocolate and other nice but naughty things to eat….So be warned Kay love."

Jenny and Susan tactfully indicated their considered agreement with Linda's considered comments and observations. Jenny decided to attempt to settle them down again,

"Right well that's a date then….As soon as we get the all clear from here it's straight around to Connie's Café our favourite oasis for refreshment to enjoy a nice pot of tea and some of her delicious sticky buns….All those in favour say….Aye."

The response was enthusiastic as well as unanimous. Then they all burst out giggling like small schoolgirls.

The whole ambience was suddenly changed when every person present inside the confines of the Clinic had their full attention drawn to the unavoidable, distinct, loud sound of raised voices and muffled screams clearly emanating from the corridor which connected their Annex to the other main parts of the Hospital complex.

Suddenly a frantic looking middle aged man, small in stature and balding, dashed into their Waiting Room. He was dressed in a Hospital issue thin cotton gown with 'X-Ray Department' printed on the front and back of the rather flimsy material. This desperate looking man stopped directly in front of Sister Murphy's reception desk. With a determined grunt he deliberately turned to face all of the Ladies seated upon the rows of plastic and metal chairs. With great theatrical emphasis placed upon his provocative stance he boldly shouted out, "Dah….. DAAAAH." as he ripped off the gown to expose his completely naked body to everyone present in the area in front of him inside the room. Without explaining in far too much indelicate detail it was fair to say that this man was clearly in a state of advanced sexual arousal and frantic excitement.

To his complete astonishment his outrageously deliberate act was met, first of all with sniggers which soon turned into roars of unbridled laughter from the majority of the Ladies present. Definitely not the sort of reaction he was anticipating at all.

A large, muscular, anxious looking, male Nurse accompanied by a uniformed Security Guard arrived, emerging from the corridor leading to the entrance into the Clinic; they paused in the doorway to carefully scan the scene laid out before them. They almost instantly focussed their attention on the naked man standing proud in front of the rows of pregnant ladies.

Before they were able to reach the now quite bewildered man, Sister Murphy boldly strode out from behind her desk to confront and challenge the man who had dared to disrupt her Clinic. Without issuing any sort of threat or warning she floored him with a deftly delivered right hook, which Henry Cooper, the famous Heavyweight Boxing Champion, would certainly have been very proud of. The man's body hit the cold polished floor sounding something like a large portion of prepared wet tripe hitting the top of a slab of marble after being dropped from a great height.

The male Nurse and the Guard immediately pounced on the lifeless body which was now lying motionless on the cold floor. They expertly and swiftly covered up the exposed naughty bits, utilising the discarded X-Ray Department gown as well as the security guard's peaked cap.

Inevitably Susan had to be the first to shout out a pertinent comment.

"Sorry Sonny….If you wanted to shock or impress any of these Ladies in here by showing them your….Sorry…..But…Your rather inferior looking wedding tackle I don't think you could have chosen an audience anywhere on earth which would be less likely to suit your purpose….We all know what a naked man looks like….Eh? … Don't we girls? … That's probably one of the many and varied reasons why most of us find ourselves sitting in this place this very day….Eh? … Well done Sister Murphy…What a punch….I think you've just rocketed up the popularity scale in most of all these assembled persons estimations… That poor chap….Let's face it….He must be a raving nut case…. Surely….Eh?"

Her remarks were greeted with even more laughter and general jollity. The offending man was making no effort whatsoever to struggle free as he was unceremoniously lifted up bodily off the floor to be removed from their presence without any further delay. This final action was accompanied by a perceivable chorus of combined female voices chanting *'Oh Bless him'* in a strangely empathetic manner.

As the Ladies began to recover from their amusing interlude Jenny suddenly appeared to be strangely inspired. She addressed Susan in an excited and enquiring fashion.

"Susan…Su….Listen Su…Did you see his face? It was him! The Flasher! We've met him before…Remember?"

Susan, never one to miss any chance to exercise her renowned acute sense of humour replied,

"His face? What face? I'm sorry Jenny love I never actually got around to noticing his face….Did you Linda? Kay?"

They all burst out laughing again which possibly indicated a slight element of guilt. Jenny was determined to make her point. She continued even more forcibly.

"Susan remember when we were confronted by that Flasher in the Memorial Park when we were pushing our babies in their prams along the leafy tree lined paths?….It was only last year?…Remember?…It was warm and sunny…During the summertime?….Not that long after our babies had been born?…Of course you do….Think on Su….Come along Susan….Surely you can recall that shocking incident…Eh? …Remember now?"

The penny dropped for Susan. All the other Patients appeared to be settling back into their well practised routine of waiting their turn to have their names called out before they could be seen by the Doctor. The volume and intensity of the chattering seemed to be much more excited and audible following the rude interruption. Susan appeared to be relieved as she now found herself in a position to respond positively to Jenny's earnest question.

"Aye Jenny love….I do believe you're right…..Correct me if I'm wrong….The former accountant who had managed to escape from a secure nursing home somewhere in the Royston area….The one who went completely loopy after he was jilted at the altar by his Fiancé….She ran off with a Lingerie Salesman from the other side of Oldham?…Yes Jen….I do actually think you're absolutely correct…Later on he almost threw a tantrum trying to smash the door down at the Police Station in his indecent haste to give himself up after he had confronted us ."

Jenny giggled,

"Perhaps he's got around to taking your advice after all this time Su….If you recall you threatened to give him a swift kick in his couple…Telling him he would be showing his tackle to the Nurses in here if he didn't make himself scarce…Eh? … What on earth is he doing here today?….The poor man should be locked up in a rubber room with boxing gloves fastened on his hands for his own protection as much as for ours or anybody else's…I wonder what's happened….He must be rated as the worse Flasher in the whole World….What a carry on."

They were soon informed by Sister Murphy, who was now sporting a cold compress across the knuckles of her right fist, was making a formal announcement after demanding that everyone paid her due heed and attention.

"Ladies!….Ladies!….May I on behalf of the Lapley Vale Cottage Hospital apologise to you all for that unseemly display in here a short time ago…The offending man was sent here for some barium meal X-rays because he has been suffering from some acute indigestion problems….He was supposed to be under the supervision of two attendants from the Mental Hospital near to Whiston where he is a long term permanent resident…They apparently found chatting to some of our less experienced and flighty young Nursing Staff to be more riveting than properly guarding their charge….May I assure you all that he is now safely on his way back to the Hospital where he certainly does belong under lock and key…Safely secured in a straight jacket and I have been given to understand that internal disciplinary proceedings have already commenced investigating the conduct of the two miscreants who were responsible for the entirely unnecessary and less than amusing fiasco…Thank you Ladies….I sincerely hope none of you have been upset or offended by this unfortunate incident…Right…..Come on settle down…PLEASE! … Next…..Mrs McCabe….Mrs Best…..Mrs Chumley…..Oh yes….If you'd be so kind please Mrs Summers…And Mrs Greening please follow me into the cubicles…Right away come along….Come on…Others are still waiting….CHOP! … CHOP!"

Again Susan managed to steal the spotlight. She smiled ever so sweetly at her old adversary, Sister Murphy, as she humorously added,

"Don't you worry Sister….I don't image any of the Ladies here present today would be likely to find themselves offended by a…Ahem! A little thing like that….Am I right girls?"

Again the room exploded into raucous laughter.

"Did you ever see one of those Zombies for yourself Alf?"

The victorious, jubilant, perhaps rather immodest, Members of the Lapley Vale Bowling Club Team together with their appointed Officials together with their band of avid Supporters, were enjoying the company of their freshly defeated opponents from the Flying Horse Public House. They were slowly starting the inevitable process of drinking up their refreshing pints of best bitter beer before having to reluctantly make their way out of the, still fairly crowded, Clubroom after the conclusion of a very one sided Bowls Match. The home team, even without their two star players, Woody and Eddie, had well and truly thrashed their enthusiastic, but alas hapless, embarrassingly inferior, Visitors in every game.

The reason for Woody and Eddie being absent was the Club's star players were playing in an 'International' friendly fixture where they were representing the Lancashire County Crown Bowling Association against a visiting team of Bowlers from over the borders in Scotland. This match was currently taking place on the magnificent and hallowed turf of the Trafalgar Hotel Bowling Green in Blackpool. Although the friendly visit by the Jocks was the last of the pre-season warm up matches being played by way of preparation for the National County Bowls League matches, the competition was very keen. No quarter was asked for and therefore none given. This contest also represented the final opportunity for the new, up and coming, players to impress the powers that be by exhibiting their skills for public examination in competitive mode. The new season in earnest would be commencing with an eagerly awaited battle against the old enemy, Yorkshire on the opening day. This match was scheduled to take place in two weeks time on a brilliantly sited and maintained green close to the promenade at the popular seaside resort of Scarborough.

In the comparatively short time since Woody and Eddie had been honoured by becoming members of the County Squad they had already managed to impress as they competently justified their rather surprising original selection.

Due to his long standing connections with the County hierarchy, in particular his former professional association with the Tony Shuttleworth, The Chairman, Sergeant Bert McCabe had been adopted in an unofficial role as the Manager of the two Lapley Vale players. Apart from his genuine, yet passive, interest in the noble art of bowls Bert was possibly even more attracted by the regular availability of free accommodation and the liberal provision large quantity of booze as well as a more than generous payment policy which was readily available, on application, to those who had volunteered to provide the means to facilitate all of the players' transport requirements. This combination of lucrative and desirable enticements had already ensured the presence of Bert whenever Woody and Eddie were called upon to bowl at this higher level. They had also managed to establish the necessary attendance of Norman Smith to accompany them, again with all expenses paid, as one of the duly appointed Official Scorers.

In the absence of the two undoubtedly outstanding players another two Junior Members were now emerging from amongst the remainder of the Lapley Vale Team as potential future stars. These rising stars were Eric McCabe and Joe Summers. Both relatively young men, definitely in comparison with their Team Mates, they were continuing to improve their all round skills with every match they were now regularly competing in. They were beginning to exceed even their own original high expectations, slowly but surely they were establishing themselves as preferred selections for the first eight bowlers proudly chosen to represent their beloved Club.

The present contest had been particularly memorable because each and every member of the home Team managed to win their individual games. Billy Dawes managed to beat his opponent 21 points to nil. This was commonly referred to as a *'Whitewash'* in crown bowling circles. It was a most rare occurrence particularly in the ranks of organised League Bowls Competitions.

Billy, the undisputed Hero of the hour, had had to be almost forcibly removed from the bar by Eric McCabe, who, as you might recall, was happily married to his beloved granddaughter Jenny. The reason for this cruel, draconian, behaviour by Eric was quite clear cut. Eric always enjoyed eating his tea at Nan Dawes's table every Saturday evening. Jenny and their little baby daughter Amy had spent the whole afternoon at the Dawes's house whilst Eric and Billy had been engaged with their sport. The famous Lancastrian delicacy; *'Meat and Tatter Pie"*, was always served at 6pm prompt, accompanied by mushy peas and as much pickled red cabbage as any group of normal persons could reasonably devour at one sitting. Nan was an excellent cook and Eric would never miss his regular Saturday treat at any price. With the benefit of hindsight perhaps it was fortuitous that Eric had been present because Billy had degenerated into talking in, what was commonly referred to locally, as the *'Language of broken biscuits'*. This condition had been brought on by numerous generous and admiring persons insisting upon buying him pints of his favourite bitter beer.

The place did seem strangely odd without the ubiquitous presence of Woody, Eddie, Bert and Little Norman. This trio would normally be seated on their usual perches next to the bar after any home match has taken place on their beloved Crown Bowling Green.

Bert McCabe had been able to cunningly re-arrange his schedule to enable him to be available to act as official Volunteer Driver taking them to Blackpool in his car on his re-arranged day off. This selfless act also enabled him to pocket a more than generous allowance for doing so from *'The Powers that be'*. They had made a promise to Alf that they would positively avoid getting involved in any drinking sessions after their match with the Scots was over. They had assured Alf that they would be back in Lapley Vale well before closing time, whenever that might happen to be. The Club had never paid too much attention to the permitted hours for drinking intoxicants as laid down by the Licensing Justices when the Club was originally granted and also at the time of every renewal of their Licence. They operated an open ended demand and supply approach to their provision of alcoholic beverages. Most of the members had no idea what the prescribed permitted hours actually were. Alf, who still resided in the flat, conveniently situated directly above the Clubroom, ceased serving alcohol and closed the bar when every one of those present indicated that they had consumed their fill. This could sometimes coincide with the commencement of the dawn chorus heralding the break of day.

Ralph Jones, the popular and respected Chairman, together with Victor Callow, the Treasurer/Secretary, basked in the well deserved glory after the Team's convincing victory on their home green. They were in the company of fellow team mates Bernie Price and Peggy Hackett. Peggy was confidently as well as comfortably wearing his, recently acquired, state of the art, artificial prosthetic leg. Neither Bernie nor Peggy had been able to produce their best form but both had nevertheless managed wins in the eventual and inevitable massacre which had assuredly taken place.

Victor, enjoying an enormous sense of well being, addressed his friends,

"An auspicious day without a doubt Gentlemen….I don't think there can be much doubt about the final outcome of the coveted League Championship once again this year….That magnificent silver trophy proudly displayed here behind the bar will only need to be removed for the annual engraving and necessary polishing….The place would look strangely odd without it….Could I also take this opportunity to inform you all?.....Thank you….The Members are rapidly getting accustomed to seeing the recently awarded plaque honouring our green over there on the pillar but we still need to go through the process of winning that trophy fairly and squarely every year but…As I have already stated I am cautiously confident of the inevitable outcome once again….Billy Cockeye played like a man possessed….That Chap he annihilated is not a novice you know…Goodness me no….One of their better players…. God knows what the overall score might have been if the now famous Woody and Eddie had turned out to play in our team as usual today…. Eh? ... What?"

Bernie begrudgingly had to demonstrate his agreement with the comments made including the compliment paid to his arch enemy Billy Dawes. Bernie had quite recently been subjected to a considerable amount of adverse publicity amongst the majority of the members when they were eventually made aware of his reprehensible behaviour after he had played a cruel trick on Billy. This was a sorry deception involving Degsy Franks the Bookmaker and Billy's well known willingness and aptitude for helping others in need. Bernie's twisted; unpleasant sense of humour had been commented upon and highlighted to his detriment in every quarter it had happened to reach. Bernie, being Bernie, could not prevent himself from saying something derogatory about Billy's magnificent achievement,

"And his performance today was not aided by his musical arse in any shape or form….I never heard him fart once today and I was out there on the green at the same time as he was….Perhaps Nan has stopped giving him baked beans for his lunch before he turns out to play….Old Billy the Poo….Eh? ... He is suspected of using it as a secret weapon when he is up against any decent Players…Eh?"

Not one of the other persons present expressed any sort of response or reaction to Bernie's unnecessarily barbed remarks. They clearly elected to completely ignore his obviously vindictive ignorance.

There could be little doubt that the members of the victorious team were all very pleased with themselves. Peggy sounded full of enthusiasm as he confidently announced,

"I say….It has to be said Chaps….Those two young Lads….The pups of our litter…Ricky and dare I say it…Joe Summers….They definitely look as if they will be the stars of this Club in the future and no mistake…I know we all have our own justifiable opinions about Joe but he's becoming one smashing player…Natural talent…Getting better every time I see him play."

Ralph responded,

"Today Gentlemen we saw an excellent performance by all concerned….There are many encouraging signs giving us all considerable confidence in the future continuing success of our beloved Club….I feel sure we are all in very good hands….A sight for sore and aging eyes and no mistake…What a pity Joe doesn't grow up enough so he can be sensible at all times….He is still a loose cannon when he takes a skin full on board…And that's still far too often in my book."

There was tacit yet unanimous agreement.

Alf, the Steward, joined them from the other side of the bar. His usual role of serving beer to the Members and their Visitors all afternoon had been adequately and efficiently filled by Denise, the popular Barmaid. This rare and enjoyable situation facilitated the opportunity for Alf to make one of his infrequent appearances on the green playing for the first team. Denise had just taken her leave to take a well earned break before she would be required to return later in the evening at which time they would both be needed in order to deal with the now expected heavy demand for bar service during most of the evening session.

What a satisfactory, pleasant and reassuring, situation the Club had now found itself enjoying. Not too long ago their entire future had been at serious risk. Only the timely injection of much needed cash from the mysterious and still anonymous 'Kenneth Gordon Trust' had saved the Club from expected and even anticipated extinction. Nodding a friendly greeting before speaking Alf politely addressed them,

"I'm thinking about closing down for a couple of hours if no-one objects…I think we could all do with a breather and may I also add…..Perhaps we could all benefit from taking on board something quite substantial to eat before we return later to enjoy our usual not to mention much appreciated Saturday evening drinking session…Every one O.K.? … My bloody stomach thinks my throat has been cut again and I have one of Mavis Greens' rather large individual steak and kidney pie to deal with....By now it should be in prime condition and ready for eating now....So shall we adjourn please until we meet later on? Eh? O.K? I don't want my pie to overheat in that oven up there...And before anyone asks there is definitely only enough for one...Sorry...O.K.?"

Although a slight reluctance could now be detected it was merely simmering under the surface because every one of the Men still remaining obviously realised that Alf's suggestion was not only sound but was also a very sensible proposed course of immediate action bearing in mind the relatively early time of the day and the amount of beer already consumed.

***

In keeping with the now familiar trends enjoyed each and every Saturday night the Clubroom was very close to being packed with members all enjoying themselves without restraint, even if there was a need for it. The company was almost exclusively male with a cross section of men from all age groups, sampling the beer, playing darts and dominoes, with a few others either playing or waiting for their turns to play on the ever popular snooker table. The developing culture of providing regular paid entertainers had not yet been adopted by Lapley Vale Bowling and Social Club although the increasingly popular, modern, 'Disco' evenings were sometimes arranged to provide for the increasing demands emanating from the numerous Younger Members' modern requirements.

Bert and Norman had returned directly to the Club accompanied by the two County bowlers, Woody and Eddie. They arrived shortly before 9.30pm. Bert had been saving himself all day, being mindful of his essential as well as necessary driving duties. He was quickly making up for any lost time as only Bert could.

Woody and Eddie were enthusiastically talking through their afternoon matches to a captive, admiring audience, namely Eric, Sam Best and Damien 'Specky' Harris. The three young men were genuinely thrilled with the astonishing glory their childhood heroes were now able to revel in at the highest levels of their chosen sport. Norman, perched comfortably on the top of his specially adapted stool, was quietly sipping his beer because he and Bert had already listened to a blow by blow account of both matches on their journey back home from Blackpool whilst travelling back home, virtual prisoners, in Bert's car. Specky was genuinely interested in all aspects of the game of crown green bowls although he unfortunately possessed absolutely no personal playing ability. This did not prevent him from finding himself in awe of all the skilled players who were gathered around him. This elite group now included his close friend Eric. Sam was definitely interested in the game but preferred to play darts because he had discovered that he was more than able to distinguish himself whilst standing at the oche. His lack of bowling ability prevented him from making a similar impression whenever he ventured out onto the crown bowling green, but as he immodestly accepted, even he could not expect to be brilliant at everything.

Damien carefully picked his moment before asking a pertinent question.

"Tell me this please….Woody…..And you too please Eddie…. How much actual difference do you experience when you're playing for Lancashire as opposed to turning out for the Lapley Vale Squad? … Travelling up to Blackpool must put an added strain on you……Then you have to consider another fact…You have to play your games on what everyone concerned with the sport readily accepts is not only the finest but the most testing playing surface to be found anywhere in this Country…Or in the North of England to say the very least."

Eddie was pleased to respond because he felt confident that his chosen sport would continue long after he had gone if the younger men continued to demonstrate as well as express such keen levels of genuine interest.

"Personally speaking Damien I find that wide expanse of manicured grass found at the Trafalgar Hotel actually suits my style of play…. Obviously the Opponents we meet on there are all top class players so you need to be on your best form at all times to make any sort of a favourable impression…At the end of the day I am delighted to be

honoured by my selection to play there but to be perfectly honest Boys....
I much prefer our own beloved green out there...That's where I still get
the most pleasure from playing...I've always enjoyed playing with my
friends of many years standing and that's what makes all the difference
to me...Most of the Chaps I come across playing in the Opposing
Teams on our green have been personal friends of mine since my earliest
days of bowling...If they ever played the World Championships on our
green I bet Woody and I would reach the final to end up playing against
each other....I think he knows every blade of grass out there and I'm not
far behind him in that respect...What's that old saying....It's true as far
as I'm concerned....'*There is no place like home*"....Eh?"

Eric responded to Eddie's remarks with a cautionary tone quite evident in his tone.

"Christ Eddie....Don't start quoting sayings or proverbs or the like....You'll only start Woody off....Have you chanced to hear one of his latest wise sayings? Eh? Listen to this....'*A bird in the hand is worth two in the back of a taxi*' ....And that's one of his cleaner ones."

They all chuckled, smiling, as Woody attempted to appear shy and coy. He did not speak but clearly indicated his displeasure with the remarks made by gesturing to Eric using two fingers.

Woody then nodded to indicate his concordance with Eddie's comments but he was unable to curtail his natural urge to allow his wicked wit to instantly rise to surface.

"Eddie is quite correct to give his complimentary assessment of the excellent playing conditions there for all to witness at the Trafalgar.... No dispute with me on that particular account it is magnificent and a credit to all concerned with the preparation and maintenance that obviously has to go into it.... Mind you...They do actually require the much sort after and cherished services of an exceptionally talented Green keeper and that's just what they've got in Ernie Wardale...With years of experience behind him...Oh aye....The Big Boss as they all call him and his...Ahem....And his two...Yes TWO full time and four temporary assistants...Eh? ... Caught that did you....Eh? ... Adding that all together I think you'll find that is a grand total of six staff? ...

Christ…I have to cope with all the demands made upon my horticultural skills out there on our beloved green more or less on my own…Well…. I mean to say….Young Ricky here is about as much use to me as a one legged man would be at an arse kicking contest…And that's when he's working to the best of his ability."

They all chuckled because they were well aware that he was merely speaking in jest.

"What a Tit….Bloody hell…In the pre-season one of the corners of our green needed to have new turf laid on it….I did the hard part by preparing the ground leaving the rest of the job to Ricky whilst I got on with something else but I was unable to concentrate all of my attention on the job in hand because I was obliged to continually keep calling over to him….'No! … Try again Lad…Green side up…Remember Ricky…. Always when laying turf….Green side up'…So you can easily appreciate what I'm actually up against maintaining that…Ahem….Let us not forget that our green out there has been….Highly recommend by the powers that be if you care to recall… Yes….It is a pampered square of hallowed turf out there that we are all very proud to call our crown green and although it is small in size when compared to the Trafalgar square inch for inch it could present a bloody good account of itself…. Eh?"

Eric pretended to attack his mentor, throwing a wide swinging punch which misses by a distance. Woody exaggerated the act of avoidance as he continued to speak,

"Seriously though…I agree with Eddie's comments but I also have to add that this afternoon's contest was a pushover….An absolute synch… The Jock I played against was half pissed when we shook hands before we even started to play and then he kept topping himself up from a hip flash he had cunningly secreted in his sporran….Had me worried the first time I saw him pulling it out from there I can tell you."

They all laughed as Bert and Charlie Walsh walked across the room to join them.

Bert was smiling from ear to ear. He had now established a nice routine with the Treasurer of the Lancashire County Crown Green

Association. He picked up his expenses in respect of their previous trip at the same time as he handed in his claim for the current journey being undertaken. Despite the fact that they all knew he was carrying extra cash in his wallet they were also acutely aware that they had little or no chance of sharing in his good fortune. Bert had his prudent reputation to preserve.

He placed his arm around his son's broad shoulders to speak to him with, obviously, intentional, false sincerity.

"Hello Sonny....Did you miss your Daddy this afternoon then? ... Eh? ... Eh? ... I have been informed by Uncle Charlie here that.... Possibly....Yes....In thirty or forty years time or so you might...Just might....Make the grade...AND....Yes listen now....Become a fairly decent bowler...Eh? ... Eh? ... You were the first person Charlie and I thought of as we were draining our glasses Ricky...We don't want much...Just a pint each....Eh? ... Eh? ... Mustn't be looked upon as being greedy."

Pretending to be offended, Eric wriggled away from his Father's hold at the same time as he was nodding towards Denise who appeared to have already anticipated the imminent need for her services.

"Can you give this scrounging old Bugger a pint of best bitter please Denise....Before we all choke on the intense smell of bullshit suddenly circulating around these parts....Give his little Friend one as well please...So make that five pints all together...I dare say Specky and Sam will be able to force another down under duress."

Instantly and in unison his friends slammed their empty glasses on top of the bar. Sam sounded resigned, complacent,

"Bloody hell fire....You can always tell when it's your round Ricky... We have to stare through the bottom of our empty pots for a while before you even start to take the hint."

Norman joined in the conversation,

"I wonder where he inherits that from then?...I mean to say we are all perfectly aware of the way in which his Daddy has gained such a great reputation for unsolicited generosity often guilty of throwing his money around with gay abandon...Eh?"

Woody chirped up,

"Oh yes….Like a man with no arms….Bert has an unfortunate impediment in his reach….His hands can't reach the money he stashes down in the lowest parts of his trouser pockets….When you get a chance Denise love… My friends and I would like another pint each as well…If you'd be so kind… Thanks awfully much I'm sure…..Drink up Eddie….And you Norman."

They needed no encouragement whatsoever.

The evening had drifted along in a smooth manner affording everyone present the opportunity, and personal comfort, to relax in the friendly, pleasant, highly desirable, ambience which had prevailed throughout. Eric with his Mates Sam and Damien had taken their leave. Despite having eaten enough 'Meat and Tatter Pie' to fill the stomachs of several grown men at Nan Dawes's table earlier in the evening Eric was now beginning to yearn for their usual fish and chip supper on their ways home. They made their way towards the Butcher's Arms, which amongst other things, was close to Billy the Chip's shop on Huddersfield Road where they intended to purchase their suppers. Sam wanted to have a quick word with the Landlord, Steve Crispin, regarding the arrangements for the next home match arranged for the Lapley Vale Villa Football Club. As the Captain, Sam also hoped that Freddie Franklin, the well respected Manager of their team, would happen to be present in there. The Butcher's Arms was the official Headquarters of the local football team. Steve the Landlord was a regular player as well as a life long supporter and benefactor of their Club.

The infamous 'Bitter Enders' were still to be found in their usual positions close to the bar in the Clubroom. The time had now inevitably slipped past the bewitching hour into the early hours of Sunday morning. Ralph and Victor were still seated on their stools across the bar from where the others were sat. These two friends had enjoyed a long day and the after effects were quite apparent in their slightly inebriated state which was clearly emphasised by their general demeanour as they desperately strived to maintain some of the elements of normal dignity. The majority of the Members had consumed their quota of beer before making their various ways home. Denise had arranged for Billy Hancock's Taxi to collect her, she had taken her leave about an hour earlier. Ever dependable Alf had remained at his station, alert, ever ready for action behind his bar.

Charlie Walsh was loosening up after a long enjoyable drinking session, mainly in Bert's company. He had been forced to withdraw after only one drink following his bowls match earlier in the day because he had to take Mrs Walsh out on a shopping trip in their car. As you could well imagine, he had now managed to make up for any lost time accompanied by an added bonus or two. He managed to hold onto their casual attention as he spoke,

"I got a hell of a shock the other day Chaps....I was pottering about in my garden at home after enjoying my evening meal...It was just starting to go dusk when suddenly my Missus let out a very loud scream....She dropped the cup of tea she was carrying out to me...She literally looked as if she had seen a ghost....She pointed down the street and I have to admit I also thought I had caught a glimpse of a ghost."

Woody, Eddie, Alf and Norman's attention was instantly focussed on every word Charlie had to say. Bert seemed to be fairly indifferent. Charlie's voice then took on a more sinister tone,

"The late lamented Jedd Clampett regularly carried out many odd jobs for my Missus and I and she always fed him well for his trouble... Well...I spotted this Tramp approaching me from a short distance away and in the fading light I definitely thought it was Jedd...Honestly.... I don't mind admitting ....I nearly filled my trousers....Really I can tell you...I think he must have heard the Wife's scream because when I called out to him the shady figure literally took to his heels to swiftly disappear out of our sight....I had to sit down with a large brandy to steady my nerves I can tell you...Anyways...I cautiously called in to see our friend...The fearless Sergeant here...First thing the following morning....Unbeknown to many folk in the Town Jedd's place has been taken over by one of his long term mates....What did you say his name is Bert?" Bert responds with calm authority in his tone,

"Spud Murphy....That's what he's known as in these parts...Aye.... That's him Spud Murphy....Probably not anything resembling his God given name but still...Eh? ... Eh? I don't have to remind anyone about the shock we all got when Jedd's true identity was revealed...Eh? ... Eh? ... He does look rather similar to Jedd in build and general scruffy appearance...He's even taken over the vacant possession of the humble concrete pipe down alongside the Municipal Tip where Jedd lived in stinking squalor for many years....He's a fairly harmless type....Doesn't want much out of life....I don't know if he's as keen on doing the odd jobs as Jedd always was....Eh? ... Eh? ... Anyways.... Successfully applied to me for the vacant post of Town Tramp...There were no other applicants...Unless you consider the famous Larry the Lamb as a possibility....Eh? ... Eh? ... Mind you he is the current holder of the office of the Town Idiot mainly due to the fact that he has one more brain cell than Amos Quirk the wandering Holy Man...Eh? ... Eh? ... So bearing all of that in mind I considered that it might be dangerous to place too much pressure on him...Eh? ... Eh? ... I can understand Charlie's shock though... An understandable and genuine mistake to make Charlie...Only time will tell if Spud will make a suitable replacement for Jedd....My Lads and I will be keeping a close watch on him until he has time to settle down properly and he gets into his own routine....I wonder if he has met up with Larry the Lamb yet....That could be an interesting event for any neutral observer to witness....Eh? ... Eh?"

Charlie nodded,

"Thanks Bert....Just to make absolutely certain that my Wife and I would not be subjected to the fear of any suspected mysterious workings of the dark forces of the occult ever again...Just to make sure for myself... I carried on after seeing Bert to make a personal visit to the Tip to see if I could check out the new man...And....Sure enough Spud was there in Jedd's former place of abode and I have to admit he certainly is a dead ringer for Jedd....Uncanny...No wonder we were mistaken there is a genuine similarity and no mistake....He was more than a bit nervous when we met especially after our unfortunate first encounter the previous night…In actual fact I would say on reflection that he had been more frightened by our hysterical reactions towards him than we were when we thought he was the spirit of Jedd returned to haunt us but we have made friends now…I've even arranged for him to take over Jedd's odd job duties as and when the need arises….He's calling round to cut the grass for us tomorrow….I promised him a roast dinner and he seemed to be keen….We'll see….Anyways I want to make sure the Wife meets him in order to convince her that Spud is a new odd job man and not a spooky reincarnation of poor Jedd…The Wife and I are both fully recovered from our shock now but…Honestly…We genuinely thought we had seen a real ghost until things were logically explained and later suitably established beyond a reasonable doubt for us."

The group were suitably impressed by Charlie's fascinating story, enough to cause them all to sit back for a few quiet moments whilst they permitted themselves enough time to fully digest all of the many and varied possible implications the fascinating story had raised. Norman seemed to be more curious than any of the others. He was sincere as he asked Bert,

"I know it's all a load of nonsense Bert…You know….Ghosts and ghouls and all that sort of thing but is there any basis for belief in the supernatural because I believe there are some people who are genuinely convinced it does actually exist? … In your experience Bert have you ever had any ghostly or perhaps mysteriously unexplained encounters or the like?"

Bert took a swig from his glass before smiling, whilst he quickly adopted a strangely ironic look, which appeared to be quickly spreading across his familiar features.

"Norman…..Norman my dear friend let me tell you this….I have been in some bloody weird and wonderful places in my time and have been faced with many very unusual situations to say the least in my long and exciting journey through my adventurous life so far….Eh? … Eh? … But….But let me tell you this … I can honestly say that if there were such things in existence then I would certainly have seen at least one of them….And….Rest assured Norm I'm still waiting to meet my first ghost….Ghoul…Apparition….Or any other such unexplained creature or similar imaginary creation….Eh? … Eh? … Oh and by the way despite the fact that many people are convinced there are fairies at the bottom of our gardens I haven't ever seen any trace of them either…. Eh? … Eh? … "

Woody reacted instantly,

"And knowing you Bert you'd probably have got some of them to pay you rent and to buy your ale for you if your paths had ever managed to cross….Bloody hell Bert….Are we going to catch a fleeting glimpse of the colour of your Blackpool money or are we all going home…. I've run out of readies and I don't intend to chalk up any sort of bar bill even if Alf would allow me to do so….Come on Bert…Before we all expire and pass on to the great bar up in the sky…Get the bloody drinks in please!"

Bert pretended to be mortally offended by Woody's vicious remarks.

"What a way to treat your Chief of Police and incidentally…I might also add for your information….Eh? Eh? That for all you know I might possibly be another of those shy and reserved secret war heroes…Like old Jedd….Keeping all the facts under our hats as is the custom with us strong and silent types….Eh? … Eh? … You're a cheeky Bugger you are Woody….You are…Bloody hell….You'd think I never ever treated my Friends to a bloody drink…."

This comment was met with raucous, ironic, laughter which soon spread across the bar to include the now seriously half puddled Ralph and Victor. Bert realised that there was, inevitably, a time when piper had to be paid. He nodded to Alf, who appeared to be highly amused by this whole turn of events,

"Bloody hell fire Alfred….Just to demonstrate that these scandalous hurtful and downright slanderous comments about my tendencies to be a tightarse are totally and completely unfounded….Eh? Eh? Please…. Set them up….Drinks all round…Eh? Eh? Yes that's correct… I wish you to include yourself as well as Ralph and Victor in this open handed offer to generously treat all of my Friends…Eh? … Eh? … Mind you that's as far as I go…Just in case any sneaky Bastards are hiding in the toilets waiting to take advantage of this new found generous side to my nature…Eh? … Eh? … That's got rid of all my expenses money in one foul sweep… Now I've ended up out of pocket on the day.…Eh? Eh? The cost of petrol isn't cheap these days you know?"

Eddie led the chorus of *'Cheers Bert'*. Norman chirped in

"And that's something you don't get to hear in this place very often…Eh?"

They all laughed as Alf added his observations, whilst pulling the pints,

"In your complicated calculations which tend to leave you of the opinion that you have lost money on the day's transactions I don't suppose for one minute you have included the total cost of all those pints you've forced down in here tonight purchased by almost everyone in this room including myself have you Bert? … I think I'll have this cash of yours stuffed and mounted to be displayed in a glass cabinet prominently positioned next to the coveted Bowling Trophies at the back of the bar.….You may laugh but let me assure you all that catching sight of Bert's money is as rare as discovering the presence of a Virgin inside a brothel."

Again there was laughter as smiling broadly Bert dramatically placed a crisp new five pound note on the bar. This action was accompanied by loud sarcastic cheers.

They all settled down once again to contentedly drink their beer. Alf replenished his own glass after he had attended to all of the others. He took the top of his pint before he began to address his Friends with something resembling a genuine ring of sincerity apparent in his tone.

"You may scoff and find the whole subject of the occult and the after life highly amusing but I can tell you that I have met many people in my travels all around the World and many other places who do genuinely believe in these sort of things.….During my days in the Royal Navy or the Andrew as we called it when my Ship was stationed around the Caribbean Sea under orders to patrol the seas surrounding the hundreds of Islands as goodwill ambassadors for a year or so…This was soon after the War had ended…We actually saw many public demonstrations of voodoo and similar evil and frightening practices… You would definitely need to witness these goings on…And even then you would hardly believe that you'd actually seen some of the things taking place in front of your own eyes.…Some of the resident peoples around those parts.…Especially a lot of those living in Haiti and some of the other many surrounding Islands who actually worship their dead ancestors and as if that isn't scary enough they also believe in the existence of horrible creatures they call *'Zombies'* which is their name for the living dead.…Hard to describe them but they could possibly be mistaken for some regular Oldham Athletic supporters when caught in the right circumstances and in poor light.…Anyways from what I saw and heard.…If they really do exist they must be truly revolting and evil things.…These people genuinely treat the whole subject as a well established and highly respected type of religion…Honestly…I've seen it for myself and I bet Voodoo still holds considerable influence over the vast majority of those Natives to this very day."

Eddie had listened intently to every word spoken by Alf, apparently he was totally spellbound. He spluttered as he asked Alf a burning question,

"Did you ever see one of those Zombies for yourself Alf? … I have to admit I've heard a lot about them although they were never mentioned much in the West Indies as far as I was aware.…I've often seen pictures of Voodoo Priests in their full frightening regalia and believe me they're enough to scarce seven colours of shite out of me just looking at images of them."

Alf, smiling, is pleased that he had been able to influence his friends by generating such a positive level of fascinated interest towards his contribution to the late night conversation.

"Never Eddie.…Not even when I was pissed out of my tree drinking their home brewed rum…And that stuff.…Hell fire.…Talk about strong.…Eh? … It will burn a hole in your clothes if you happen to spill any of it on you…I once saw one of those Priests sacrificing a chicken.… But as far as I can remember I think they then roasted it and served it up for supper with sweet potatoes or yams or the like…All complete bullshit as far as I am concerned."

They all chuckled before Woody consciously composed himself, as he confidently took over the lead in their ongoing, most interesting, discussion.

"I am not claiming anything one way or the other but I can certainly tell you that when I was serving in H.M. Forces I once heard what I believed to be a true story about one of those *'Séances'*…You know that's the name they have for one of those strange spiritualist meetings…I'm sure you must have heard about them it's where they sit around in small groups asking *'Is there anybody there?'* … Knock three times for yes and all that kind of nonsense…Anyways this one I was told all about took place high up in the mountains in the bleakest and wildest inland reaches of darkest Central Wales…Imagine the scene…Well…The visiting Medium.…That's what they call the special Bloke…Or sometimes it can be a Woman…Well…This was a famous bloke from Aberavon who had earned himself a well respected reputation because of his so called special powers and gifts.…He had consented to conduct one of these séances at the request of one of the locals farmers who wanted to find out from his late Wife where she had successfully hidden her handbag before she died rather suddenly…Anyways the Medium had four Local Men seated around a table with him…They were all sitting there holding hands.…A sight rarely never witnessed before in those particular parts.…A Bloke could be strongly suspected of being a *'Willywoofter'* if he was reported to have washed himself more than once a month let alone be found holding hands with another male person…Honestly…So you can work out the significance of the achievement of this Bloke actually persuading these Mountain Men to touch each other's hands… I was going to add that they had the lights dimmed low…But as they didn't have any electricity up there all the bloody lights were inevitably fairly dim.…Anyways.…They were all seated there with a flickering candle burning away in the centre of the table which was throwing eerie shadows all around the room.…They were all conscientiously throwing themselves into the spirit of this special occasion…Each one of them willingly giving his full and undivided attention to the ongoing proceedings…Their concentration was sharply focussed on every word the Medium spoke to them…After they all settled down he asked them in a spooky shaky strange kind of voice….'Has any person here present tonight ever experienced any sort of an encounter or perhaps had a personal relationship with a ghost?'….And one of the men suddenly went rigid…He was a middle aged Shepherd called Idwal Davies who was known to be a little hard of hearing but was far from being deaf…Idwal lived alone in an even more remote and desolate part of the area….Anyways…He suddenly and without any prompting shouted out…With a strangely sincere ring to the tone of his voice….'Yes….Here you are….Yes over here….I have'…. Even the cocky Medium really was quite surprised at this interruption but obviously he was also quietly impressed with the unexpected speed of this most positive kind of response…However he sought further clarification of Idwal's bold and brave statement….'Are you saying you have met or had a relationship with a ghost?.' He asked…Idwal replied, 'Yes that's right…I have….definitely.' The Medium was delighted that things now appeared to be going so well but he again pressed Idwal to elaborate on his statement by asking… 'Yes thank you…Well…Tell me please…Was this a really close and friendly relationship you personally experienced?'….. Idwal responded without a pause…'Oh yes….It was very close….Being perfectly honest with you….It was….Well….Intimate in the full sense of the word if you know what I mean…We made passionate love on more than one occasion actually.' This stunning and revealing statement caused the Medium as well as the other Men present to gasp out aloud with clear astonishment….Finding it hard to believe his own ears the shocked Medium once again sought clarification of the statement being made by Idwal for his own benefit as well as that of all those present…He now earnestly enquired…'Are you telling us here that you not only met but you also had an intimate sexual relationship with a ghost?….A spirit? … A deceased person coming out of another dimension?'…Idwal paused this time….He then stared deeply into the Medium's face….The excited tone in his voice noticeably faded away as he spluttered his reply….'Oh sorry….Did you say a GHOST? … Oh I am sorry Boyo….I was under the impression you said a GOAT.'

Possibly jumping the gun slightly the entire company roared with laughter as Woody's sharp sense of humour managed to steal the show once again. At this point Ralph and Victor, their sides now aching and with tears running down their cheeks caused through uncontrolled laughter, decided to call a halt to their involvement in the evening's proceedings. The others all very sensibly agreed to join them by taking positive steps to vacate the premises.

"Sergeant…Her Ladyship wishes to speak to you in private."

Inspector Bill Kinley and Sergeant Bert McCabe had finally received official notification and conclusive confirmation from the Chief Constable's Office that they would retire from the Lancashire Constabulary on full Police Pensions as and from the 30th of September, 1969. This official disclosure obviously meant that they could no longer keep their imminent, and certainly not by personal choice, departures from Public life a secret. The cat had already been well and truly let out of the bag as a result of the publication of an impressive and informative front page feature, with photographs and brief career histories, which detailed both of their impeding retirements in the latest issue of the Lapley Vale Examiner. In fairness, Lenny Jopson, the Editor, sincerely considered his extravagant article to be complimentary but it was also true to comment that neither Bill nor Bert had any wish to have their regrettable fall from Public stature so well publicised locally.

Bill and his Wife were currently completing their move into a small bungalow which they had recently purchased in a beautiful little Village on the Coast near Fleetwood where Bill would be concentrating on what his dear Wife has managed to convince him was his passion for gardening. Bert, being of lower rank than Bill, could not really afford to live on the reduced income his pension alone would provide. His full, enjoyable and carefree lifestyle throughout his many happy years in the Police Force had never really created any real opportunities for putting aside monies or other forms of savings in preparation for the arrival of that inevitable rainy day.

In all fairness, Bert and Alice did have some modest savings. They were far from being destitute but as they did were not fortunate enough to own their own house all ready for them to move into at the time when they would be required to quit their rent free Police House, Bert needed to find a way to earn some sort of added income to support them in the manner to which they had become comfortably accustomed over the years.

Bert was recently called upon to attend a formal meeting at Lapley Manor chaired by Lady Lapley and attended by Major Sebastian Kinsley-Porter, Horace 'Pinky' Pink, Her Ladyship's Game keeper, and Isaiah Chadderton, one of the famous Chadderton Brothers. The Chadderton Brothers were the acknowledged experts in all of the many required, necessary, regulations legally in place relating to the safe treatment of exotic wild animals in captivity. They were also skilled in every aspect concerned with the setting up and maintaining of the increasingly popular Public attraction now being provided by various Safari Parks up and down the length and breadth of the whole Country. They had now taken full charge of all the arrangements for the painstaking, yet vital, preparations which were required to be put in place prior to the official opening to the General Public of the Manor Estate now renamed the Lapley Vale Safari Park and Visitor Centre. An announcement had already been made and details had been publicised nationally. All the arrangements were in place for the ceremonious opening of the gates to take place on the 1st of October, 1969.

The absent Brother was Ernest Chadderton. He was the Senior Partner. He was also considered to be the more practical member of their family. He had many years of hands on experience dealing with Lions, Giraffes, Rhinos, Primates, Camels and all manner of other wild and potentially dangerous Beasts which were soon to be brought into the Park to live on a permanent basis. One of his utmost priorities would be the safety and comfort of all of the animals within the precincts of their new and strange surroundings where every species would need to be expertly and comfortably accommodated. His other main concern would be application of the highest priority given to all aspects concerned with Public Safety as well as the comprehensive training and management of the Specialised Staff required. This was all in addition to the overall stringent requirements necessary for keeping the Public safe as well as the maintenance of order, as laid down by the letter of the Law. All these statutory requirements had to be enforced in order to comply with all the specific conditions listed in an essential, comprehensive, insurance bond which had to be in force before they could legally open to the General Public.

As stated Ernest was the 'hands on' man in the Partnership. Isaiah, his younger brother, was more of an administrator, a sophisticated wheeler dealer, whose expertise was clearly obvious for all to witness through his handling of all types of legal contracts, money transactions, and many and various other associated fiscal matters.

Incidentally, they were uncannily similar in build and general appearance for Brothers who were not natural twins. However Isaiah could easily be identified on closer examination because, due to an accident of birth, his right eye was set higher up on his face than his left one. As you could probably imagine their Parents were not devoid of a sense of humour even when they were faced with such an unfortunate handicap to cope with at the time of Isaiah's birth.

Just as a matter of interest, this information was not really capable of being verified. Pinky was a staunch Bachelor who prided himself upon the fact that he had always enjoyed a close relationship with his immediate Family. He was especially fond of his Niece whose name was Denise. It was strongly rumoured at the time when Pinky's Sister, Janet Pink, who did not actually have a Husband or even a Male person that she could positively identify as her Children's Father, asked her Brother to register the births on her behalf when her new born identical twins arrived on the scene. Unfortunately Pinky carried out this essential task much too soon after he had been enthusiastically wetting the babies heads in keeping with the fashion of traditional celebration welcoming new births. It was again a, definitely unconfirmed, rumour that he initially managed to register Denise's twin brother, whose was called Dennis, as Denephew, but this event was never positively proved to have really happened. Although the Registrar for Births, Deaths and Marriages at that time, a strange looking and rather odd person, Jonathan Wills-Harper, a local man made good, was a close friend and drinking partner of Pinky. Mr Wills-Harper had been regularly identified as a member of Pinky's group of dedicated drinkers at the relevant time. It was strongly suspected that the Registrar had been as heavily involved as all the others during the head wetting ritual. Needless to say the silly mistake, if it actually happened, would have been swiftly rectified when the effects of the drink had subsided and Jonathan subsequently checked over his records.

The extensive preparations for the opening of the Safari Park, which involved a large proportion of the total of the available land within the boundaries of the Lapley Manor Estate, were now reaching a state of advanced development. As well as being impressed by the professionalism being exhibited by the Chadderton Brothers Company, Bert McCabe was now beginning to realise that he could well be out of his depth taking on a position in any kind in a management capacity working with them. Lady Lapley, being an empathetic person, very soon appreciated Bert's mounting anxiety so as consequence she arranged to see him privately after the official meeting had taken place and then had been formally closed. The Major surreptitiously communicated with Bert as they were all leaving the large withdrawing room inside the Manor House.

"Sergeant....Her Ladyship wishes to speak to you in private.... Please...Before you leave today... It concerns a matter she considers might be in your overall future interests."

Any apprehension felt by Bert soon disappeared as Lady Lapley explained to him that Henry Randall, one of her loyal and faithful retainers, had recently lost his dear wife to illness. Henry was about to move out of the small, yet picturesque as well as comfortable, Cottage he had been occupying alongside the Lake inside the most beautiful and secluded part of the Estate. Henry had accepted an invitation to live with his Daughter and her Family who lived in a little village somewhere in the Cotswolds. Henry was packed up ready to leave the Manor for good that very weekend. Bert listened patiently and with interest to what Her Ladyship was relating to him but remained slightly bemused as to the reason why she was going to all the trouble of telling him about one of her retiring workers in the first place. Suddenly the reason became apparent when she arrived at the point where she offered Henry's Cottage to Bert and Alice at, what could only be described as, a peppercorn rent for as long as they required the use of it. Lady Lapley explained this generous gesture was her way of acknowledging the excellent service and her appreciation for the close personal friendship he had always provided for herself and her many Estate Workers over the years he had been the Officer in Charge of Lapley Vale Police Section. Bert was not only surprised but also moved by the generosity of Lady Lapleys' offer. However, he instantly appreciated that she was genuine and sincere in her expressions of admiration and affection felt by her for him and his Wife. Bert was never lost for words but when he took his leave from Her Ladyship and the Major that day he had a lump in his throat because the gesture would come as a great relief to Alice as well as him. He was sincerely grateful for the unexpected turn in events which would be vital for his and Alice's future welfare and security.

Bert obviously discussed the offer at length with Alice. After making a brief visit to the Cottage Alice actually hugged and kissed Bert in a way which was devoid of the usual signs of her natural reserve. She then confided in her husband that this latest news had been responsible for her wildest dreams being about to come true. She had been worried about their immediate future and genuinely wondered where on earth they were going to live after they would be obliged to leave their ex-officio Police house. This generous and welcome change in luck had been able to put her mind completely at ease in an instant. Apart from many other important considerations she had been most anxious to remain in the local area because of their close attachment to all of their Family and many Friends. She felt content enough to happily reflect upon the fact that Bert was, and always had been, a very loving and caring Husband to her and the family. This was how he had been throughout the many years they had been together. Despite his little personal weaknesses he had always ensured their health and happiness were paramount and this was reflected through his thoughts and deeds. The sheer delight she was now able to feel was clearly apparent in her tone as she confirmed her absolute approval to a much relieved Bert. Her voice was cracking with pent up emotion,

"Bert McCabe....You possess a strange yet wonderful knack of being able to make me happy...I don't know why I was worried or why I was so surprised because despite your annoying tendency to be over fond of beer and your aptitude for mainly socialising in any sort of Licensed Premises I do love you....The Cottage is the answer to a dream...It is gorgeous and it's well within walking distance of Ricky and Jenny's house...As if that's not enough let me assure you for once and for all that as far as that job in the Safari Park is concerned I just hope and pray that no one will be knocking me up in the middle of the night to inform me that you have been eaten by a lion or some other vicious creature...I just wish there was a nice safe job in the offing as well....But anyways...Bert....Well....I don't really know what more I can say....Come here...Give us a kiss."

The couple hugged and kissed each other demonstrating beyond any question of doubt their enduring love and genuine affection for one another which was clear for anyone to witness.

When Bert returned to confirm and gratefully accept the settlement with Lady Lapley his only nagging concern was the possibility of the uptake of the tenancy of the Cottage being in any way conditional to his anticipated future employment in the Safari Park Management Team. When Her Ladyship explained that her gesture was in no way connected with any of the future Safari Park plans or commitments whatsoever, Bert was able to inform her that he had shared some serious misgivings with Alice over the offer of his employment in the Safari Park. This had been further complicated after he had recently received a firm offer of full time employment as a Court Usher at Rochdale Magistrates' Court. This Monday to Friday, nine to five, appointment with every Saturday and Sunday off, known through Police circles as an E.S.S.O. job, had been gifted to him by the Clerk to the Magistrates, Mr William Green, a man with whom Bert had been frequently associated over the past years at various Courts up and down the County. The job of Usher was far from taxing for anyone with any kind of experience in Court procedures and a piece of cake for someone with Bert's background, personality, and familiarity with the protocol involved.

Lady Lapley was genuinely sincere when she advised Bert to accept the Usher's job if that was what he really wanted to do. She hoped that Bert would make himself available for informal consultations with her if and when required. Bert was delighted to commit himself to this reasonable request wholeheartedly and without a moment of hesitation.

As the long summer was drawing to a close and his inevitable retirement from the Police Force continued to rapidly approach, Bert was satisfied that he was doing the right thing by accepting the job at the Courts and humbly taking up the generous offer later made official by written and sealed legal deeds duly exchanged with Lady Lapleys' Lawyers.

The ongoing arrangements were now being made for the joint retirement party planned for Bert and Bill Kinley with added genuine enthusiasm emanating from the wily old Sergeant, who had once again landed happily on his feet.

"Bloody Norah!"

The surprisingly patient group of people lined up in a queue inside the Lapley Vale Sub Post Office on High Street was much smaller during the mid afternoon period when compared with those witnessed during the invariably heavy morning queues, all requiring various essential postal services. However, the 'Terrible Twins' as they were popularly known to the locals, the two fearsome Counter Clerks, formidable elderly spinsters Bella Briggs and Lily Forest, remained no more accommodating or pleasant to any of their unfortunate Customers. The now familiar serene and churchlike ambience continued to prevail inside the Office, which was invariable spotlessly clean. This Office was recognisable at all times by those who visited it by the faint, yet clearly distinguishable, smell of wax furniture polish. It was true to say that many of the people using these facilities were apprehensive; some were even frightened, when faced with the anticipated unpleasant prospects of carrying through any sort of transaction they had to necessarily make with either Bella or Lily.

These two Ladies had ruled over their unfortunate Customers with a rod or iron in these premises for many years. They were, without question or doubt of any kind, accepted as the official representatives of H.M. Post Office. Not too many Local People would ever be tempted to push their luck with either of these formidable yet completely efficient and dedicated Post Office Employees.

Two rows of Clients were neatly lined up behind the two Persons at the front of the queues who were actually being attended to by the

Clerks. Nellie, the Police Station Cleaner, had just tagged on to the end of Bella's queue. She was there to post off a medium sized parcel, which she had carefully addressed, to one of her grandchildren who were living many miles away in New Zealand. She never ever forgot to post off their annual Birthday or Christmas cards always enclosing modest, but thoughtful, gifts. Her parcel was not very large but she had to balance it in her left hand because she was carrying her full and quite heavy shopping basket as well as her handbag in her other hand.

Suddenly, without any sign or warning, the figure of a Youth, wearing a dark duffle coat with the familiar hood pulled up over his head, dashed through the open front door into the Office. He urgently rushed past the waiting people to make his way straight up to the counter. In his haste he accidentally knocked Nellie's parcel out of her hand. It landed on the floor with a loud bang. The desperate looking Youth had his right hand rammed down inside his duffle coat pocket. He was pointing whatever he was concealing in there in Bella's direction. Bella stopped her ongoing transaction with a young Lady at the counter. The Youth shouted out in a loud, threatening, yet oddly, quite noticeably nervous, voice,

"O.K. Missus…..This is a stick up…..Just hand the money over and nobody will get hurt…Come on! Hurry up!"

He anxiously turned momentarily to issue a warning to all the others in the room,

"Stand still! Nobody move….Or else."

Without the slightest sign of alarm or shock, Bella peered at the Youth through the glass window which was there to separate her from the public. She responded sounding much more threatening than the youth had been.

"I beg your pardon Sonny… What the hell do you think we are running in here? Eh? This is not a bloody Charity Shop? If you think you can just barge in here…..Jumping the queue….To demand money you must be a few slices short of the full loaf…And….If you think you're getting anything from me you'd better have another thought coming….I have to work bloody hard in here all week to earn my wages and I won't be parting with any of the Post Office's money to the likes of you....So you can just piss off before I am obliged to come around there to sort you out....Personally!"

The youth was clearly stunned, bemused, by Bella's unanticipated reaction to his earnest and unlawful demand. The top of his right hand accidentally appeared in view for a second or two, as it rose from the cover of his pocket. Terry Bridges, an elderly retired Gentleman, was one of the Customers patiently standing in Lily's queue. He happened to notice that the youth was holding nothing more dangerous than a green, firm, banana in his right hand. He laughed, loudly, if rather nervously, as he called out,

"What are you threatening to do Son? ... Are you going to hit Bella over the head with that banana are you eh? ... Or perhaps you are going to throw it at her eh? ... Hey....Now be honest...Is it loaded? ... Eh? ... Take her advice Sonny...Beat it....You might have a big problem trying to put the skids under those two Ladies behind that counter...You have more than met your match...Eh? ... What?"

The Youth suddenly panicked. He turned with the intention of making a hasty retreat. As he moved towards the door Albert Kitchener Snooks, the elderly, rather eccentric, local Park keeper who was in charge of the Lapley Memorial Park, just happened to be making his entrance. Albert had his head down whilst he concentrated upon the sorting out all the loose change he was holding in his hands. The Youth tripped over Nellie's parcel, which was still lying on the floor, causing his panic stricken face to collide, accidentally, with the top of Albert's bowed head. A perfectly delivered, if completely unintentional, head butt. The Youth, blood streaming from his nose and mouth, dropped to floor like a stone. Although he was obviously shocked Albert had no true inkling of what had just happened because he was practically unhurt. He was quickly attempting to come to terms with what was actually going on when Terry shouted out,

"Nice one Albert....Didn't reckon on an Old Soldier being in his way did he? ... I saw Eddie the Gentle Giant partaking of a brew inside Dick Rigby's Butcher Shop as I was making my way up here....Quick....

Give him a shout someone....Hurry up before Pancho the Bandit here gains consciousness again."

Even before anyone could respond or react in any way, the large frame of Eddie appeared in the doorway. He looked as shocked and surprised as any of the others. A passer-by had managed to see what was happening and he had immediately directed Eddie to the scene. Eddie stood back for a moment before he loudly declared,

"Bloody Norah!"

A few of the customers snapped out of their enforced silence to make it perfectly clear to Eddie that he should immediately arrest the helpless Youth. He effortlessly lifted the still semi- conscious Lad unsteadily up onto his feet. He then spoke calmly to him.

"Bloody Norah Sonny boy....What's going on? Tell Uncle Eddie... Who's been a naughty Boy then? Eh? You're going to be locked up now....O.K.? ... Now try to stand up straight for me please whilst I put these bloody handcuffs on you."

Eddie struggled to pull his cuffs out of his back trouser pocket just using his free hand. The heavy metal manacles dropped to the floor with a very loud clatter. Nellie instantly and effortlessly picked them up to quickly hand them back to the Constable. Nodding and smiling his thanks to Nellie, Eddie soon snapped the cuffs on the Youth's wrists before, now smiling from ear to ear, he smartly frogmarched the young offender out onto the street. There were obvious signs of relief from all of the Customers but Bella and Lily remained unmoved, resolute, and defiant. Bella shouted out as loudly as she possibly could,

"Lock the Bugger up and throw the keys away Constable."

In total agreement with her Friend and Colleague Lily joined in,

"Give him a bloody good pasting first...The cheeky swine...Whatever next? Women will be raped in broad daylight before too long."

Excited by the unexpected ongoing situation and now really chancing his arm, Terry Bridges could not prevent himself from shouting out at the top of his voice,

"I think you and Bella should be safe there Lily...I don't think either of you need to worry too much about that unlikely eventuality."

There were some stifled chuckles which subsided instantly when the Terrible Twins glared out from behind their counter expressing their indignant disapproval of his rather personal derogatory remarks.

Eddie was about to march his prisoner along High Street to the Police Station when Bert McCabe, also alerted by a concerned Member of the Public, arrived on the scene. He had been driving along in his Ford Prefect motor car. The Youth still stunned and now in some urgent need of first aid treatment to stop his nose from bleeding, was transported without further delay to a waiting cell at Lapley Vale Bridewell.

When all the dust eventually settled and the whole story gradually enfolded it turned out that the desperate Youth was in fact an absconder on the run from a nearby Home Office Remand Home for Youths in Rochdale. The C.I.D. Officers from Whiston wasted no time arriving at Lapley Vale Police Station. They were soon able to make their presence felt. Much to Bert and Eddie's delight, also their relief, they took over all the formalities concerned with the arrest. They also accepted the full responsibility for the laborious task which was then required in gathering and collating all of the evidence together absolutely necessary when preparing a prosecution file for Court with quite surprising gusto. By the time their full file of evidence was eventually completed and presented to the Court, Eddie would barely get a mention but Detective Sergeant Bruce Smedley, never known to be a prolific thief taker, would probably be well in line for at least a commendation from the Chief Constable in recognition of the swift, fortuitous, and highly efficient capture of a potentially dangerous and definitely desperate fugitive from justice. At least that was what Bruce would be emphasising in his statement of evidence as the adopted Officer in Charge of the case.

Albert Snooks quite soon appreciated what he had actually done after Eddie had effortlessly removed the offending Youth from the vicinity of the Post Office. His clearly unintentional but nevertheless most effective actions were suddenly being transformed into a heroic and self sacrificing deed of daring do. Albert would now have fresh ammunition for his frequent chats to any of the Visitors who might care to listen to him if they ever entered into his Park. This incident would now provide all the actual evidence he needed to enhance his fearless reputation as the brave and fearless Custodian of the Park for many years to come.

One of the most satisfying aspects of this whole event was the resulting Letter of Commendation which together with a small cash award was presented to Albert. Bella and Lily were also rewarded accordingly. All were paid out of the special funds held by the Head Postmaster in charge of their area. The Youth ended up spending his, now seriously extended stay, at the taxpayer's expense, residing in H.M. Prison Strangeways instead of the rather less depressing as well as undaunting surroundings of the Remand Home from whence he had escaped. Despite the remarkable upheaval which occurred at the time of the attempted robbery Nellie still managed to post her parcel off to her loved one in far away New Zealand.

"I am delighted to see you looking so well."

The British Racing Green Austin Mini proudly owned by the Reverend Jeremy Smith-Eccles, the unfortunate and often found to be hapless, Curate of All Souls Parish Church Lapley Vale, still managed to maintain the stylish, sporty, much admired, appearance it originally possessed when he first appeared driving it around Lapley Vale. Most people were surprised, to say the very least, when he turned up confidently sitting behind the steering wheel, actually driving the car along the roads. In the opinion of those who had witnessed his attempts at driving whilst he was a learner, it was a genuine miracle that Jeremy had somehow managed to pass his driving test. These generally agreed and accepted points of view still prevailed probably due to the unfortunate fact that Jeremy had been involved in more than a few scrapes and minor prangs whilst using the vehicle to transport himself around the Town since that time. The undoubted skill of local Garage Proprietor Barry Hancock as a Panel Beater was evident for all to see. Or should it be fairly said that as a result of Barry's abilities the evidence of these repairs were difficult, if not nye on, impossible to detect. Barry's experience and talent as a first class all round Motor Mechanic had been exhibited to the Locals for many years. Consequently he had earned an excellent, trustworthy and reliable reputation with most of his many Customers, most of whom lived in the immediate Lapley Vale area.

Jeremy's car was currently parked in Hillside Avenue outside a double row of red brick terraced houses. This type of housing was quite typical and prevalent in this particular area. There was a total absence of any defensible space or garden area to the front of any of the buildings. The actual front doors opened out directly onto the pavements on both sides of the road. Great efforts were made to enhance the individual appearance of the frontage on these houses. Women could frequently be seen; down on their hands and knees, applying, mostly a glossy red staining called 'Red Lead', expertly using a specially purchased and designed stone. This practice made finding any particular address even more difficult because, outwardly, they all looked very similar especially to any persons who were not familiar or acquainted with these local surroundings One side of the road appeared to be almost identical with the other..

Amongst the many tasks undertaken by Jeremy as the Curate of the Parish of Lapley Vale he was primarily responsible for the visiting and administering of comfort to the sick and injured living in their Parish. There were modest funds available which usually allowed for the presentation, to those persons considered to be in need, of a basket of fruit, or occasionally a bunch of flowers or even a box of basic groceries. Whenever this type of generous gesture was under consideration liaison meetings would be formally held which necessarily involved himself and Whistling Reggie, the Vicar, with further full and final consultation made with the Church Elders.

The basket of fruit presently being carried by Jeremy had been carefully prepared by Kay Brown in her capacity as the Manageress of 'Bloomers' Flower Shop, on the High Street, which was, as you might recall, owned by Eric and Jenny McCabe. As well as being amongst the McCabe's closest friends, Kay together with her Husband Sam had proved herself to be a real asset to the prosperity of their thriving, fledgling, business. She had been responsible for greatly increasing their turnover from the flowers, plants, wreathes and had introduced other miscellaneous gardening equipment all for sale in their recently modernised and extended Shop. She had also been instrumental in the latest offering of fresh fruit and vegetables now available for sale alongside their standard stock of flowers, shrubs, and the like. Although this profitable branching out involved yet another commitment for Eric, who now had to travel into Manchester three early mornings a week to visit the Wholesale Markets, the whole enterprise was proving to be something approaching a roaring success.

Jeremy wished he had left the basket of fruit on the rear seat of his, rather cramped, Mini when he found himself struggling to pull out his pocket note book from his jacket pocket. He was wearing a modest tweed sports jacket which was worn over his long black cassock. Eventually he needed to get out of the car to place the basket on the pavement before he could freely examine and check his detailed written instructions. He was glancing around anxiously looking at all the numbers on the doors when Freddie Furnace, a retired labourer in his late sixties with a deserved reputation for being a bit of an opportunist, opened his front door at number 28.

"Are you looking for anyone in particular Reverend? Can I be of any assistance to you perhaps?"

Jeremy, as ever, was delighted to accept any help which might be available from any source.

"Oh…Yes….Oh how kind…Thank you….As a matter of fact I'm looking for a Mr and Mrs F Furnace…I am afraid I cannot clearly identify the number of their house from my own rather hastily scrawled notes….Thank you….Can you help?"

Freddie's face broke into a broad smile as he replied without the slightest hint of any hesitation

"Look no further Sir….I happen to be Mr Freddie Furnace….Now isn't that what you might call a coincidence…Eh?"

Jeremy's face lit up instantly. He immediately lifted up the basket from where he had placed it on the pavement, "Well most convenient I must say….Mr Furnace….I don't think I've had the pleasure of meeting you have I? No…..Nevertheless I am here today bearing a gift for you and Mrs Furnace to enjoy….Are you feeling better?"

Freddie appeared to be momentarily bemused by Jeremy's enquiry but still managed to respond positively.

"Oh yes…..Thank you for asking….Er Your Holiness….I still have a lingering cough but I think I'm in reasonable shape for a man of my age and working class background....Thank you for asking....Would you like to come inside the house?....The Wife is at the shops at the present time but I can soon make you a nice cuppa if you so desire."

Jeremy glanced at his wrist watch. He instantly realised that he was, as usual, well behind his schedule for the day. Smiling, sounding polite and most apologetic, he responded,

"How kind Mr Furnace....May I leave that pleasure for another day perhaps....I find there are never enough hours in any day for me.... Thank you all the same....Please accept this offering of fruit with the compliments of the Parish Mr Furnace....I am delighted to see you looking so well....Now if you will be kind enough to excuse me.....I must press on."

Jeremy handed the heavy basket to Freddie who glanced over it expressing unbridled delight and glee. Freddie placed the basket inside the house before he returned to open the car door for Jeremy. Jeremy nodded his appreciation for this gesture as he settled back into the driver's seat. Freddie slammed the door closed. Jeremy wound down the car window before he turned the ignition key to start up the engine.

"Thank you Mr Furnace...God Bless you."

Freddie stepped back to wave as he spoke,

"No thank you Sir....It's so kind and thoughtful of you to bring us such a welcome gift....I mean to say...It was only a bad cold but it kept me in for a couple of days....Perhaps I should tell my brother Frank who lives up the road there at number 58 to expect a similar visit from you....After all he has just come home from the Cottage Hospital after having undergone urgent surgery....I shudder to think what kind of wonderful present he will be getting....Still....Thank you once again most sincerely...Er Vic...Er....I mean...Er Rev...Anyways...Thanks and goodbye....Thank you."

Freddie retreated into his house, swiftly, closing the door after him.

Jeremy paused to stare at the now closed door for a few moments. His face contorted slightly as he again pulled his note book out of his pocket.

Jeremy sat in the stationary vehicle with the engine running for several minutes obviously attempting to come to terms with the current situation he had just created. He soon decided in his own mind that he would be required to face up to his stupid mistake. He closely examined his note book and almost instantly his worst fears were realised. The fruit was in fact intended for Mr F Furnace at 58 Hillside Avenue not number 28. That familiar look of despair slowly began to spread across the Curate's tortured features once again. He quickly decided that discretion had to be much the better part of valour. Asking for the return of the gift from Freddie Furnace would be unthinkably embarrassing so he did not allow himself to linger in the vicinity of Hillside Avenue for very long. He engaged the car's first gear with a slight, yet discernable, crunching noise emanating from the vicinity of the clutch and gear box before he drove off along the road.

Kay Brown was quite surprised to see Jeremy back at 'Bloomers' again so soon on the same day. At his urgent request she quickly prepared an extra special basket of fruit. She was even more surprised to find that Jeremy paid for this extra gift out of his own pocket. Kay was completely at a loss to understand why Jeremy had bothered to go to such great lengths to emphasise to her that, under no circumstances whatsoever, should any mention be made in respect of this extra purchase to anyone at all before he eventually dashed out of the shop to make for Frank Furnace's house at 58 Hillside Avenue without any further ceremony or delay.

"Yes it's a small world isn't it?"

A prolonged spell of dry, sunny, warm, weather throughout the traditionally glorious months of June, July and August had thankfully prevailed at Lapley Vale. This pleasurable experience had ensured that the majority of the local residents experienced a most enjoyable and memorable 'Sixties Summer' in what was the final year of 1969.

The four happily expectant Mothers were all literally bursting at the seams with rude good health, dare it be said? Also bursting with pent up expectation? They all seemed to be growing slightly larger by the day, especially Kay Brown who, as you might recall, was the only one of our small group of Ladies who was actually about to go through her first confinement.

The Lapley Vale Bowling and Social Club had once again proved themselves to be the undisputed, outstanding, not to mention the finest exponents of their chosen art of crown green bowling as a result of their latest appearances in the South East Lancashire Bowling League throughout the long Summer Season. They had comfortably swept all before them both in matches played at home as well as away but especially on their own 'Highly Recommended' Crown Bowling Green. This hallowed square of lovingly manicured grass continued to enjoy and benefit from the masterful maintenance developed through cultured care willingly provided by Woody Green, not forgetting his worthy assistant, his avidly keen to learn understudy, in the person of Eric McCabe. Every home match had been won by an embarrassingly large margin of points despite punitive handicaps being imposed on the Champions and the desperate, fervent, genuine efforts of all their unfortunate opponents to beat them.

The much admired, in some cases worshipped, outstanding stars of the Club, Woody Green and Eddie Brown, had both made excellent starts to their County Bowling Careers. They had enjoyed a number of thrilling trips to various parts of the North of England to play their sport at the highest level currently being made available to them. The Lancashire County Crown Green Bowling Team suffered defeat only once during the entire Season. This loss was painfully inflicted by the old enemy of Yorkshire in what turned out to be a closely fought contest on a beautiful sunny day in front of a huge crowd of Spectators, on an excellent and well presented green situated very close to the sea front at Scarborough. This glorious victory rapturously recorded by the Tykes was later avenged when Lancashire were able to well and truly thrash their old adversaries on their own Trafalgar Hotel Green in Blackpool. The Season's coveted honours were thus shared equally.

Lancashire secured the title of Champions of the North of England League due to their far better winning margins which finally provided them with an excellent average point's difference. Yorkshire reluctantly handed over the trophy for safe keeping at Blackpool until they would start, all over again, in 1970.

Eric and Jenny McCabe, together with their closest friend, Kay Brown, continued to build up their flourishing business empire. Their overall turnover through their flower, fruit, vegetable and now much more shop, 'Bloomers' had increased so much that they now employed a full time shop assistant, a pretty seventeen years old girl called Mary Kelly. Mary was one of the granddaughters of Victor Callow and his Wife. Mary's appointment had allowed Kay more time to concentrate on the ever increasing demands brought about by the administrative side of their business. Jenny still served in the shop occasionally, as and when required, but Eric's mother Alice had now taken full advantage of her well earned retirement. This break from the necessity to engage in daily toil had allowed her to enjoy spending more quality time with her gorgeous little, but growing fast and turning into a delightful little chatterbox, Granddaughter Amy. For Alice looking after Amy was a true labour of love from which she derived enormous personal pleasure. She revelled in the closeness she was now able to freely share with the Child and also with her busy Parents. This close family relationship was fully supported and much desired by Jenny and Eric who were ever mindful of the great support guidance, enduring love as well as the unsolicited generosity, shown to them by all of their Friends and Relations over recent years especially by Bert and Alice.

As ever Eric continued to concentrate his considerable efforts on the practical side of the family business. This had always been his preference probably because of his weakness in the academic field he positively avoided dealings with any of the absolutely necessary administrative demands and legal business requirements. One strong talent in his personal makeup was his exceptional will to work very hard without question or complaint.

Sam Best had now been appointed as a legally established full partner with his long time employer and mentor, Freddie Moore the Builder. Similar to his closest friend Eric, Sam enjoyed carrying out the practical side of the business, leaving all the paperwork for Freddie and his Wife to deal with.

Damien 'Specky' Harris and his fiancée Bernadette Dougan were eagerly looking forward to their impending marriage which was due to take place in the near future. The actual date would undoubtedly be much influenced by Bernie's final qualification as a fully fledged solicitor. They were planning to tie the knot on Christmas Eve following the enormous success of Sam and Kay's wedding the previous year but nothing had been finally set in concrete as yet.

Last of our featured friends to be mentioned, but by no means the least and bringing us all bang up to date, Bert McCabe and Bill Kinley were the centre of everyone's full attention as they entertained all of their Friends and Relatives at their *Joint Retirement'* or *'Leaving Do'* in the familiar surroundings of the Lapley Vale Bowling and Social Club main Clubroom.

Alf and Denise had two young paid Assistants helping them to cope with the urgent, heavy, demands for the supply of drinks. In particularly they were kept busy collecting and washing used glasses. One was a youth of eighteen, Trevor Simons, one of the Grandsons of Peggy Hackett and his Wife. The other was Trevor's close friend, of a similar age as himself, a spotty and miserable, hungry, looking lad called, William 'Billy Boy' Speke. They were almost entirely engaged in, what was always one of the most important and vital tasks on a busy night, the collecting and washing of empty glasses but they were also expected to perform the duties of Waiters engaged in the distribution of food and the disposal of plates and what have you which would inevitably follow the taking of refreshments.

Although there was still little local evidence of the, gradually to become famous, 'Swinging 60's', influencing too many of the good Folk contentedly residing in Lapley Vale and some of the surrounding Districts it was fair to say that certain indicators were clearly evident without them causing too much disturbance to the established *'Status Quo'*. Many young men in particular were now sporting *'Beatles'* hair styles often accompanied by *'Mexican Bandit'* or *'Pancho'* type droopy moustaches. Their clothing was much more extravagant and colourful but this was nothing compared with the bravery now being exhibited by the girls and young women in particular. Many were now wearing, ultra modern, undoubtedly daring, *'Mini Skirts'*, whose introduction had definitely enhanced the sales of new styled tights and flashy knickers, with cheeky *'Twiggy'* or *'Tom Boy'* much shorter close cropped hair styles. By the way, Bert McCabe had amused many of the Guests by stating that most street robbers were now carrying out their crimes in pairs since the inevitable demise of old fashioned nylon stockings had forced them to use pairs of tights over their heads instead of the traditional single stocking.

Another noticeable area of change had been established with exciting new music which was now available to all in abundance. This new music applied in particular to *'Rock and Roll'*, a lot of which seemed to be generally well received and accepted across the ever increasing age gaps. Having said this it also needed to be said that the vast majority of Local People continued to live their lives in the same way as they had always done for many years. They had observed the antics of the many eccentric exhibitionists, mainly in London but also in many other major conurbations, on their television sets, now to be found in most homes, without the slightest appreciation of the fact that they actually lived on the same Planet as the persons they were watching in those flickering images let alone that they were sharing the same Country with them.

To everyone's delight, Mavis Green and Alice McCabe were in overall charge of the catering for the evening. At Bert and Bill's special request, the Ladies had baked an enormous meat and potato pie, which was expected to be more than enough to feed the Gathered Throng of somewhere in the region of one hundred Guests. Nan Dawes had taken full responsibility for the preparation and supply of the compulsory ancillary delicacies of mushy peas together with many bowls of home pickled red cabbage. She would also be ensuring that her Husband Billy did not get a helping of the peas to accompany his serving of the pie attempting to avoid any nastiness occurring later in the evening bearing in mind his famous tendency, or perhaps weakness, to be extremely flatulent. The Ladies were ready and willing to feed the hungry hordes whenever they were given the nod to do so. Young Trevor and Billy Boy would soon be setting up the trestle tables before the made themselves available for their other duties connected with the distribution, and disposal of, all the food as well as all of the necessary eating equipment. After they had carried out their duties the two Youths would be anxiously awaiting their turn to enjoy the, sincerely hoped for and keenly expected considerable remainder of left over pie. With Trevor and Billy Boy on board there was a built in guarantee that there would be little or nothing left over at the end of these particular proceedings.

Chief Superintendent Cyril Wolfenden, the Divisional Commander for the Rochdale Division of the Lancashire Constabulary, was present as the main Guest of Honour. He was about to be called upon to make a speech before he would be expected to carry out the formal presentation of a number of leaving gifts to both Bert and Bill. Bill's Brother-in-law,

Superintendent Arnold Spratt and his Wife, Bill's sister Elsie, were also present sitting at a prominently positioned table with other close Family Members. Arnold would always be keen to assist in the usual formalities if he was given even the slightest opportunity or chance to do so. Eric and Jenny were seated at a table with Nan and Billy Dawes. They had reserved chairs for Alice and Mavis for their use when they had finished in the kitchen and were able to relax themselves by eventually joining them. Sam Best was standing at the bar with Woody, Eddie and Norman because Kay was absent because she was looking after little Amy overnight, yet another definite labour of love.

Ralph, the Club Chairman, standing in the middle of the small, slightly elevated, stage switched on the newly installed microphone; this simple act was accompanied by loud screeching noises which abated as he swiftly and deftly adjusted the volume control.

"Ladies…..Ahem…Ladies and Gentlemen…Ahem if you please….. May I please have your undivided attention for a few precious moments of your time….No don't worry….I'm not going to make a speech."

This comment was greeted with a rather unkind, unanimous ripple of applause and raucous cheering from all around the whole room. Ralph pretended not to notice this obvious slight to his oratory competence as well as his reputation as he continued,

"Ladies and Gentlemen please….The best of order…Thank you… Please….Thank you….All around the room…Please….Please! ... It is my great honour and indeed…Ahem….My privilege to welcome Chief Superintendent Wolfenden from Rochdale Police HQ to say a few words to us all about our two Hosts for this evening….Ladies and Gentlemen….Our dear Friends….Yes….Inspector William Kinley and Sergeant Bert McCabe."

This part of his announcement was met with genuine and sincere cheering and rapturous applause. Ralph was attempting to calm everyone down but Cyril seized his chance to gently push him aside and by doing so it allowed Cyril to firmly grasp hold of the microphone.

"Thank you Ralph….Sorry….Er Brother Jones….Oh no….Mr Chairman….May I first of all thank you for inviting me to this special

'Do'….I don't get out much these days….Not if the Wife's watching anyways…Ha…Ha… Thank you….Well….What can anyone say about the two men present here tonight who are leaving the Force to take up their just rewards for the many years of dedicated and distinguished Public Service they have both provided to a grateful and yes…. Appreciative public….To enjoy their well earned retirements…As many of you will already know….Our very own Sergeant Bell who has been stationed at Whiston Sub-Division for a good few years now has been promoted to take Bill's place as Rural Inspector which covers Lapley Vale Police Section as well as many other surrounding areas…And… And despite rumours that at least three experienced Sergeants were being intensively trained before being drafted into Lapley Vale to fill the massive void being left as a result of the retirement of Bert McCabe I am in a position to break some fresh news….Hot off the press information for you all tonight…This really is stop press news because I was only informed about it myself this afternoon…The replacement selected for this demanding post is none other than Sergeant Norman Blackburn…. Who is….I am given to understand…Locally connected…Oh yes….He is the nephew of your local Vicar…Yes it's a small world isn't it?"

This information was instantly answered by an anonymous voice which emanated from somewhere amongst the crowd,

"Yes it might be a small World but I wouldn't want the job of cleaning all the bloody windows it has in it."

This comical comment was followed by another one,

"No…. Nor would I like to be charged with mowing all of the bloody lawns neither".

Cyril wisely paused to allow a short burst of chuckling to die down before he continued with his obviously well prepared address,

"Thank you…There's always a couple of Smartarses in any crowd of more than twenty people gathered together isn't there? … As I was saying…A much experienced Officer Sergeant Blackburn is about to move from his present post in a very busy Division on the outskirts of Liverpool so that he can set about attempting to fill Bert's boots…I'm given to understand that Sergeant Blackburn is well known to be a devoted Lay Preacher as well as a prominent member of the Ancient Order of Rechabites….You know…Those people who abstain from touching any kind of alcoholic product?"

This news, which was definitely a shock to many systems, was met with gasps of disbelief. He had managed to stun almost everyone present. There were muttered comments of *'Oh my God'*, *'Are they serious?'* and *'A teetotal Sergeant in charge of Lapley Vale Police? I don't believe it.'* Cyril ignored all of these remarks as he continued,

"Anyways it might well turn out to be something like a breath of fresh air for us all to have a man of Sergeant Blackburn's standing in charge of our Local Policing Policies…We shall see….Right….O.K. then…That's enough prattle from me…Now…Over to the presentations…Bill….. Bert…..Come forward please."

Bill nudged Bert, who definitely seemed to have slipped into a state of shock after discovering for the first time the identity of his replacement. They stumbled forward as Cyril quickly checked with Alf that the relevant presents had been placed on the table at the side of the stage. Cyril greeted each man with a warm handshake. Some of those in the audience would have been aware of the significance of the special handshake exchanged by two Brother Freemason's, as far as the one with Bill Kinley was concerned.

"Well Ladies and Gentlemen this table is laden with gifts and tokens of thanks as well as expressions of appreciation and respect for these two worthy men….I am not going to hand all of them all over because it would take all night…They can sort them out afterwards…Remains for me to invite Bill and Bert to say a few well chosen words….Bill would you like to go first?"

Bill genuinely appeared to be rather emotional as, with trembling hand, he took over the microphone. Bert still seemed to be in a state of deep shock or possibly he was fully concentrating.

"Thank you very much indeed Sir….Ladies and Gentlemen….Er…. Thank you all for coming and good luck to you all in the future…Thank you."

There was a sudden brief ripple of applause as those present realised that was the full extent of what Bill was going to say. The elderly Inspector appeared to be choking back real tears as he anxiously pressed the microphone into Bert's limp hand. This action was greeted by loud cheering accompanied by spontaneous and enthusiastic applause. Bert instantly managed to give one of his famous broad grins but all those who knew him well could clearly see through his currently projected demeanour that Bert was certainly not at his usual ebullient and confident best.

Waiting for the noise to abate Bert cleared his throat to speak clearly and loudly into the microphone, there was more than a slight hint of disbelief detectable in his tone,

"Whistling Reggie's tea total Nephew is taking over Lapley Vale Police Section from me? Here? ... My arse....Eh? ... Eh? ... Has the Chief Constable gone raving mad? I think he might find himself somewhat out of place in these cherished and hallowed surroundings....Eh? ... Eh? ... That's to put it mildly....Eh? ... Eh? ... He'll feel just like a Palestinian Arab would feel stranded inside a crowded Jewish Tabernacle on a busy Saturday morning or maybe as nervous as a Virgin straying into an Egyptian brothel... Eh? Eh? Oh dear...Sorry...Sorry Ladies....Eh? Eh? Bloody hell fire....Has the Chief Constable gone daft? Eh? Eh?"

Bert's sincere outburst had stunned everyone into an eerie state of uncomfortable silence. Bert then realised that the focus was still squarely upon him. He rapidly managed to adequately pull himself together,

"Anyways....Thank you all for your many welcomed gifts and all the kind wishes...Eh? ... Eh? ... Believe me I feel I owe it to my flock to have words with Sergeant Blackburn just as soon as I have an opportunity to do so."

There was a coarse comment shouted out by another Heckler from the crowded mass,

"Not over a pint of Best Bitter I'll bet....What do you say to that Bert? ... Eh? ... Eh?"

This remark was generally greeted with ironic laughter in all parts of the room. Bert sadly nodded as an indication of his complete and frustrated agreement,

"O.K....Good point there...Well perhaps not....But....We'll see.... Eh? Eh?"

He touched the side of his nose with his index finger in a sinister yet strangely familiar and endearing manner. He suddenly began to look very much like the real Bert McCabe once again.

Never previously known to be a wilting violet, Arnold Spratt pushed himself to the front to invite Alice McCabe and his sister Winifred Kinley to step forward. Self consciously Alice received a very large bouquet of flowers from Cyril whilst Winifred confidently accepted her offering by landing a big wet kiss on Arnold's cheek just before she bustled back to her chair tugging Alice along behind her.

Taking the opportunity to draw a line under the formalities forthwith Ralph leapt onto the stage intent upon making an announcement,

"Thank you....The bar is still open....Stand clear please.... Ladies first please....I am also informed that the nosh is ready to be served so get yourselves suitably equipped and prepare yourselves for engagement with a rare treat...A well prepared banquet....Thank you....Thank you.... Plenty for all don't worry...Christ go steady!....Victor....Vic!....Watch out for my full pint standing on the bar there will you?...Christ.... Steady....Someone will be having it over....Order!....Now come along Ladies and Gentlemen please...Gentlemen....Can we have some order please....Please do not panic."

Victor managed to switch on the new sound system which emitted soft and sweet background music for the enjoyment of the whole assembled Group as everyone quietly munched away at their delicious food generously lay out before them on their plates. There was now a strange muted hum which had replaced the familiar sounds of the many different voices happily chattering.

Bert appeared to have recovered from the shock and had gained back enough of his composure to greedily tuck into his favourite dish. There was a slight incident when Billy Dawes attempted to take possession of a portion of mushy peas on his plate. Young Trevor Simons refused to be cajoled into submission by the old man, wisely choosing to comply with the strict orders given to him by Nan in the kitchen. Billy protested,

"What's going on here Trevor? Can't a man have a small portion of mushy peas with his cockeyed meat and tatter pie? What's the cockeyed world coming to?"

Eric McCabe shouted across to the cringing Lad,

"Don't listen to him son…Carry on Trevor.…Giving mushy peas to Billy is like giving whisky to an alcoholic…Good Lad.…Your brave action has saved us all from a potential fate worse than death.…Well done."

Eric's comments were applauded, much to Billy's obvious annoyance.

"Stick your cockeyed peas where the cockeyed monkey sticks his cockeyed nuts…See if I care."

This short interlude was greeted with spontaneous ripples of laughter.

In a notable sign of the times there was little or no notice taken when Trevor and Billy Boy cunningly switch over the soft background music being played to rock and roll music from the latest Groups. As there were many younger persons present on the auspicious occasion the small dance floor was soon filled with gyrating girls and boys rapidly wearing off the effects of overdoses of meat and tatter pie and peas, not forgetting pickled red cabbage.

The celebrations continued until the early hours of the morning. Denise was obliged to tend to the needs of the 'Bitter enders' because Alf fell prey to the demon drink soon after the passing of the official closing hour. He was barely capable of standing without having firm support which he managed to achieve by leaning quite heavily on the bar.

As you might expect Bert still appeared to be reasonably fresh. He wondered why everyone around him now seemed to have lost their powers of speech. The end had surely come to what would long be recalled as a monumental night for all those present to remember and no mistake.

"None are quite as beautiful as you."

Although he was quite often seen wandering around the Town carrying out his necessary shopping expeditions and he occasionally enjoyed a few drinks, Douglas Minto, known as 'Minty' by most of the people who were familiar with him, was a quiet solitary man who outwardly appeared to be happy, settled, and quietly contented with his station in life. By preference he liked to engage in the minimum possible personal contact with others although he was always polite and pleasant when approached.

Now in his early fifties, Minty had lived in a small Cottage inside Lapley Manor grounds all of his life. His late Father, Dougie, a Labourer employed on Lady Lapleys Estate, had brought him up to the best of his rather limited ability ever since he was a small child in the unfortunate absence of his late Mother who passed away from natural causes whilst he was still an infant.

As a boy Minty had always shown a great interest in his environment and he enjoyed the company of all types of wildlife in the absence of human friends. His real passion was for Pheasants and over the years he managed to develop this interest so well that he was very soon respected as an accepted and acknowledged specialist in the breeding, rearing and provision of all types of Game Birds. He was soon, justifiably, promoted to Assistant Game Keeper. His immediate Boss was Horace 'Pinky' Pink and following the death of his father Pinky had become his Father figure as well as his closest friend. It would be fair to remark that Minty was not blessed with many of the usual social graces. In particular he had always experienced great difficulty relating to any members of the opposite sex. As a consequence of this he had always endeavoured to avoid them as far as possible. Some of his less sensitive acquaintances had given him a local nick name, *'The Pheasant Plucker'*. Minty was not too fond of this name but he had grown to accepted it without making too much fuss. However, over the years, by way of implementing a natural defence mechanism, he had developed an amusing retort by informing anyone who addressed him as *'The Pheasant Plucker'* must surely be mistaken. It was impossible for this name to refer to him because it could not possibly be him as he was and always had been a nasty Bastard.

Minty's Cottage was situated in one of the most beautiful, yet remotest, areas inside the Park. It was one of two identical buildings owned and managed by the Estate. When the other Cottage became vacant, Major Kinsley-Porter, Her Ladyships Estate Manager, had allowed it to be offered for rent on the open housing market. This was done in the interests of his desperate efforts to bolster the flagging financial standing sadly being experienced by Lady Lapley during recent times. The buildings were small but cosy. Both shared long gardens, adequately fenced off from the open Park at the rear. These gardens abutted together although they were equally divided by a well establish low privet hedge. A fast bubbling brook ran along the bottom of these gardens and there were old fashioned toilets, called *'Privies'*, purposely constructed over the flowing water in order that they could naturally carry away anything deposited in the toilets up above. There were no inside toilet facilities in either home. Mains electricity had recently been connected at considerable cost to the Estate. There was one cold water tap placed over a large stone sink inside each of the compact and rather basic kitchens. Original hand pumps outside the back doors were still operational but were now chiefly utilised for the necessary watering of the flowers and vegetables in the gardens. The main downstairs room was heated by an open fire range which could easily be used for boiling kettles and other cooking purposes when the peat and log fires were lit. Although far from being modern or fashionable these dwellings were comfortable and even after considering their obvious deficiencies they very pleasant places to reside in.

The tenancy of the other Cottage had been taken up by Barbara Flynn, the Lapley Vale Public Library's Senior Assistant. Barbara was a quiet, unassumingly attractive single woman in her mid forties. She enjoyed the facility of a small Morris saloon car which was essential for her getting to and from her place of work. Barbara was a friendly type of person but she had no really close friends in particular although she was popularly known by most of the Townsfolk and could never be described as the typical middle aged spinster type.

Much to Pinky's pleasant surprise Minty had instantly become attracted to Barbara although he only saw her occasionally because of each of their working commitments. Barbara had lived next door to Minty for six weeks and they had never even spoken to each other although Barbara did shyly smile at him one Sunday morning when she was getting into her car on her way to attend Church.

Minty badly needed help. He arranged to meet Pinky in the Flying Horse Public House on a Sunday evening under the pretext of simply enjoying a few drinks together. Pinky was instantly aware that his friend had something of a serious and pressing nature on his troubled mind. After a couple of relaxing pints of best bitter Minty eventually plucked up the necessary courage to appeal to his Boss for help and guidance. He made it perfectly clear that he had been smitten by Barbara and he was desperate to strike up a conversation with her with a hopeful view to the development of some sort of relationship. Pinky could detect from Minty's demeanour that he was serious about making contact with this particular Lady. He was as open and candid as he could possibly be as he appealed to Pinky,

"I haven't the slightest clue when it comes to women Pinky....I go to pieces when I think about speaking to her I need help....Please....Can you tell me what I can do....I've never felt like this before....Ever?"

Pinky, a single man himself but definitely more worldly wise than his friend, having served his King and Country all over the World during World War Two, gave the matter some thought before he spoke,

"You really like her do you Minty?"

He nodded enthusiastically,

"Right then…Do you manage to catch sight of her at any particular time or times? Preferable in the daytime when it's light….Don't want to frighten her off do we?"

Pinky grinned but Minty was far too eager to hear what he had to say to him. After considerable contemplation Minty's face suddenly lit up as he answered,

"Yes….Yes I see her every evening after tea…She walks down to the privy at the bottom of her garden to spend a little time inside before she walks back up her path back to her Cottage."

Pinky was instantly inspired by this reply,

"Great….Right….Now then you need to be quietly pottering about in your garden when she comes out as usual to go to the privy…. Right…..Wait until she's on her way back and then you greet her in a friendly manner….Saying *'Good Evening'* or the like…If she doesn't respond very favourably she may not want to be bothered with you and if that's the case there's not much more can be done…But most people will say hello…Then….Talk about the weather….Most people will comment on the weather….Right….Now you've got her and this is where you zip in with a well chosen complimentary remark…I don't know tell her how pretty she is or something on those lines….Then…. Then my boy….You will have cracked it…Stand back….Dip your bread in."

Absorbing and clearly liking what he had been told Minty grasped Pinky's right hand shaking it over exuberantly,

"Thanks Pinky….Really thanks….I appreciate what you've done for me….I know what to do now…I will start to prepare myself accordingly and as they say when waiting for their photographs at Boots the Chemists after you take your film in…Let's see what develops…Eh? Now then what will you have a double of on me?"

Minty walked home that night as if he was treading on air. He felt as if he now had found a true mission in life and he was now confident that he had the necessary ammunition to give it his very best shot.

Monday turned out to be a blur for Minty as he robotically carried out his routine jobs. Quite understandably he could hardly wait to get himself prepared for the expected and desired encounter with the Lady, in his back garden, straight after tea. He was ready for his first real contact with a woman.

By the time Barbara opened her back door to walk down the path to her privy Minty was already starting to have nagging second thoughts. Because of the self generated tension building up inside of him Minty thought she had remained inside the privy for a much longer time than usual but then, eventually, she was walking back up her path to her back door. Minty almost snapped the handle on his hoe as he pulled together all his reserves of courage to lurch forward. This sudden manoeuvre actually gave Barbara quite a start, he was almost yelling, as he said,

"Good evening then".

Smiling sweetly Barbara replied,

"Oh Hello....Good Evening".

Without a moment's hesitation Minty continued,

"Been a lovely day today then"

Barbara still smiling said,

"Yes....We are enjoying a very pleasant late summer spell of decent weather....Yes."

Minty gulped as he physically forced himself to carry on speaking. He was managing to display an apparent outward self confidence, he took a deep intake of breath before he said,

"There are some beautiful flowers growing in the gardens....But.... None are quite as beautiful as you."

Barbara gasped, she was most impressed, and there was no doubt about that,

"Oh....Thank you....Thank you very much....Do you know I don't think anyone has ever said anything as nice as that to me before.... Ever....Thank you."

There then followed a silent pause which was soon becoming far too long. Cringing as he found himself unable to think of what to say next Minty suddenly blurted out,

"Had a good shit then?"

As soon as those words left his lips he knew that this had not been a well chosen question. He felt himself fainting on the spot so he turned on his heels dashing inside his own Cottage, slamming the door behind him. Once inside he placed his back against the wooden door, before he slowly sunk to the floor. He was feeling desperate as he placed his head in his hands. Because of his perceived stupidity he thought that he was very close to crying out aloud.

Ten minutes later Minty was still sat on the floor with his back to the door when Minty suddenly heard a faint knocking noise on his door. Puzzled he stood up, cautiously opening the door to be greeted by a smiling face. Barbara was standing there holding out to him a sparkling glass of delicious looking beer,

"Here….Have a drink on me…Please don't be shy.…I really enjoy a nice drop of beer myself.…Please.…Let's not allow things to get off on the wrong foot.…My name is Barbara.…Did you know that?"

Minty, now dribbling out of the corner of his mouth slightly, was only capable of nodding, she carried on,

"You're Douglas aren't you?"

Again he could merely nod,

"I'm really pleased to meet you Douglas or do you prefer to be called Minty?"

Once more just a pathetic nod,

"Well cheers Minty.…Here's to us.…I don't know about you but I've been longing to get to know you since I first moved in and I think we should be able to get on with each other very well…Cheers"

They chinked their glasses together before they each took a drink.

What had just happened at the rear of the Cottages inside Lapley Manor Park was shortly about to prove to be the beginning of a long and eventually close loving relationship.

"You're entitled to a little practice"

Jenny McCabe was clearly delighted when she heard the knock on her front door which heralded the presence of Bernadette Dougan. Bernadette was the latest, or perhaps better described as the newest, Member of her close Group of Friends. During the past year or so Bernie and her fiancé Damien 'Specky' Harris had endeared themselves to everyone in Jenny's circle of true friends and relatives.

On the face of it this couple were not very similar to their counterparts because Bernie was a Lawyer and Damien was a Planning Officer at the Town Hall. They both hailed from working class backgrounds and shared elementary and secondary schooling with the others. Bernie and Damien then went on to study at College followed by University because they were well above the average both in their intellect as well as their application to studies. They had remained true to their roots displaying no signs of any airs of superiority at all. Since they became firm friends with the others, Bernie and Damien had proved to be considerable assets to them especially when Eric and Jenny, as well as Sam and Kay, decided to become property owners. The professional advice and guidance provided to them convinced them that the future was in property as opposed to their parents' generation who had been content to live in either tied or rented accommodation without thoughts of home ownership. Bernie owned her own little terraced Cottage where she lived alone except when Damien was in residence.

Kay, still Jenny's undisputed best friend of many years standing, now employed as the Manageress of Eric and Jenny's thriving business, was already present in the house paying a visit. Kay had arrived there straight after she had closed their shop, "Bloomers", after another busy, not to mention profitable, day of business. Kay eagerly took the opportunity to play with little Amy whilst she enjoyed a nice chat and a cup of tea. She settled down for the evening after delivering a large bag of money to her employer for safe keeping. They had a variable system as far as the handling of their shop takings was concerned. Some days Kay left the shop in the care of her latest girl assistant, Bernie Prices' granddaughter Emily, who was working for them during the summer break from her College studies, to pay in the money at the Bank on the High Street. This deliberate alteration to their usual routine was done in the interests of crime prevention as recommended by Sergeant Bert McCabe. This other method of leaving the cash with Jenny for her to pay into the Bank the following day was only occasionally used. Kay would use any excuse to spend a little extra time with her beloved little God Daughter. Again, because of the rising possibility of crime in the area, Eric had installed an old, yet extremely heavy and efficient, metal safe on their private premises.

After the usual polite exchanges of greetings and the delightful little Amy rushing to hug and kiss her new Aunt, Jenny expressed her pleasant surprise at Bernie's visit so early on a Friday evening. The girls frequently enjoyed each others' company much later on a Friday whilst the men were out playing darts and filling themselves up with beer. Bernie, as you will recall was engaged to be married to Damien, better known to all of his male friends and acquaintances as *'Specky Harris'*, who for obvious reasons had been welcomed as the latest recruit to the all male branch of the *'Friends United'*. Both Jenny and Kay were soon conscious of the fact that Bernie definitely appeared to be less than her usual exuberant self for some reason. Kay got the ball rolling,

"I hope this visit is being made so that all those final arrangements can be made for a little celebration to take place Bernie….I hear congratulations are in order…..Damien was telling Sam and Ricky that you are now a fully qualified Solicitor....Well done love....What a marvellous achievement....What do you say Jen? ... Our clever mate eh?"

Nodding and smiling, Jenny enthusiastically agreed as she associated herself with Kay's comments. Bernie smiled but before she could politely respond she broke down, despite her best efforts to desperately hide her distress from them all, in particular from Amy.

Jenny reacted without hesitation to comfort her friend by affectionately placing her arm around her now heaving shoulders.

"There... There Bernie love....Whatever is wrong? Have we upset you in some way? Please sit down and tell us what on earth is causing you to be so very upset."

The distraught woman managed to control herself sufficiently enough to be able to speak.

"Jen....Kay.....You haven't done anything....It's me....And Damien....Oh God....I don't know how to explain this to you.... Well....I've been stupid enough to allow myself to fall pregnant."

The effort involved in relating her news had caused Bernie to commence weeping uncontrollably. Jenny looked completely unfazed as did Kay. They both positively stated, in unison,

"Is that all?"

Jenny continued,

"Thank God that's all....I was getting worried there was something really seriously wrong for a minute or two."

Bernie was sufficiently stunned by their completely unexpected reactions that she ceased her weeping forthwith. Jenny cuddled her friend and smiled as she felt obliged to explain their unexpected reactions and subsequent conduct.

"Bernie love.....You have just well and truly joined our gang in every proper sense of the word....You might not be aware of the fact that Ricky and I also found ourselves in exactly the same state you currently find yourselves in.....Believe me Bernie...This is nothing to be so upset about....You are properly engaged to be married....You're entitled to a little practice in the long run up to your wedding day....Good grief love….I thought…Well I don't want to even think about what I thought when I saw you bursting into tears."

Kay was anxious to emphasise with Bernie but as usual her natural aptitude to be humorous came rushing to the fore.

"Christ Bernie….I know you planned another Christmas Eve wedding like Sam and I did last year but this development just means that the date will need to be brought forward a bit….And it might well end up saving you a hell of a lot of dosh because you can take my word for it Church weddings with all the expensive afters and what have you will cost the happy couple a small fortune….We actually thought it was going to be another of those very rare posh wedding where the blushing bride is not a couple of months up the spout….Sam and I did everything bar the actual dirty deed before we eventually tied the knot….We were so bloody keen and anxious to do it properly at long last…You know what I mean? … We couldn't wait to get on with it and I can tell you that without any doubt whatsoever I definitely fell pregnant on my wedding night…..Or possibly on more than a couple of occasions during the day after….Talk about having a Merry Christmas…..Best present I ever got by far…Damien says he wants the same pressy again this Christmas and he's already told me not to bother wrapping it up for him….Mind you I'm not shouting too loud about anything like that until after the baby is born because I've had a very smooth ride up to now and I have been told many horror stories and eye watering accounts of what I'm in for there….Bloody hell girl….This is not the end of the World….Not a bit of it….Your life is now beginning….Anyways….I don't think the NHS can afford the funds for another mass conception all occurring on the same night….Look at the state of us two now….And Linda and don't forget Susan."

To underline her point Kay and Jenny both pushed their formidable lumps forward in an exaggerated way.

"Come here….Give us a nice huggle….Come on Bernie."

Kay and Jenny dropped to their knees at the side of the chair where Bernie was seated. All the three women ended up joyfully entwined around each other enjoying, if that's the word, a combination of laughter and tears. This is a physical attribute available only to the female of the species. The combination of both laughter and tears was now being liberally gushed out all round them.

It took a few minutes for the friends to settle down after enduring such a traumatic interlude but it was amazing what soothing sips of tea combined to feelings of sheer relief can do to promote an aura of well being and inner contentment.

Bernie, now almost completely at ease, was able to get to the nitty gritty of the plan of action she had already discussed at length, albeit also tinged with much panic and some signs of despair at times, with Damien.

"I only have my much older married Sister to concern me as far as family goes both Mum and Dad are up in Heaven I'm afraid….Damien has broken the news to his Mum and Dad and they seem to be taking the news quite well….Mrs Harris wasn't too impressed initially but she soon started talking about the hidden benefits of Registry Offices and how much money it would probably save us sneaking off to get wed instead of making a bid for the title of *'Wedding of the Year'*…. So what we hope to do is wait until all of you Ladies have completed your jobs in the Maternity Hospital….Then allow a couple of weeks for everything to settle down and then we hope to be booked in with the Registrar before the end of next month….The 30th of October looks like the favourite at the moment but Damien is waiting to hear from me because we decided not to make definite or final plans until I had concluded these deliberations with you today….So we now need to be cancelling all of the former arrangements before making the amended formal bookings….I'm sorry I was such a cry baby but I can't really talk to my Sister and you two….Not forgetting Susan and Linda of course are the only close friends I felt confident that I could confide in….I'll only be just over a couple of months gone and hopefully none of us will be showing on the wedding photos….Thank you girls….No really…. Thank you very much….I feel as if a heavy weight has just been lifted off my shoulders….I realise that there are a few more hurdles to jump before we can settle this whole sorry situation but I am now confident enough to just grit my teeth together and to get stuck right into it."

This heartfelt expression of gratitude and true friendship subsequently resulted in another mass flood of tears, hugging and kissing taking place. There was absolutely no doubt on this occasion that all the tears were being caused by genuine feelings of sheer, unadulterated, happiness. Even little Amy was somehow aware that something momentous and traumatic had taken place. She had quietly contented herself with her necessary duties as her dolly's mummy when the tension was at its peak. A loving child she was only too pleased to join in mass hugging and kissing anytime, especially if this involved her Grandpapa Bert. For such a young child she was able to display a remarkable strength of character. She had proved that she was able to keep her head down and leave the big girls to get on with whatever they needed to get on with when the circumstances called for her to do so.

Although Bernie was now feeling much relieved and comforted by the unexpected reaction her devastating news had evoked from her friends she suddenly remembered that she still had more problems to discuss.

"You are all most kind congratulating me on becoming a fully qualified Solicitor but I'm afraid there is a down side to this wonderful news as well. I have to find somewhere else to work because the firm where I have been a poorly paid Articled Clerk….Damien thinks he's very funny calling them *Art Bart and Fargo'*…Anyways they are a fairly small family firm and they won't be able to pay me the proper rate for the job now….I had almost forgotten about this little problem when the famous tick failing to appear on my calendar for the second month running immediately out ranked any other pressing considerations… There are very few decent prospects available to me locally and you need a lot more money than we are ever likely to have to even think about starting up on my own…I have heard from one of my University friends recently she has arranged for me to be interviewed for a vacancy to fill a full time Solicitor position with a Local Authority….Very well paid and excellent prospects and she tells me that the job will be as good as mine if I want it…But….And this is a very big but….The job is in one of those New Towns we keep hearing about nowadays…In Milton Keynes…I had to look on my *'Girls Own'* map of England just to remind myself where it is situated….I don't know much about Buckinghamshire…Sounds posh doesn't it? … It's not that far away but I'm afraid that given any sort of choice I don't want to leave Lapley Vale and all my dearest Friends."

Bernie was upset again. She was close to tears. Jenny put her arm around her shoulder to demonstrate her enduring support for her.

"Bernie love….If you can land a job like the one you've just described you have got to give it very serious thought….Thanks in no small way to yourself and Damien we have all managed to set ourselves up nicely for our futures and the likelihood of any of us ever getting the chance to move to one of these new up and coming places is remote to say the least….It's not on the other side of the World is it?"

Kay indicated her agreement,

"I would rather be well off in Milton Keynes with a decent job…A new Husband…And a new baby to share the rest of my life with than end up hanging around this smoke ridden dirty old dump of a Town not knowing, or worrying, where your next mortgage payment was coming from…What does Damien think?"

Once again Bernie felt a heavy weight was being lifted off her shoulders as she recovered her poise considerably.

"Well Jenny its funny you should mention that…He's the same as me in his desire to remain in this area but with his qualifications and experience he would have no problem getting a job with any Local Authority Planning Office anywhere in the Country and it so happens that there are suitable vacancies at the same Town Hall as I might be ending up at…He was on the phone to someone down there the other day and it seems that they are prepared to go out of their way to fill all of the vacancies they have currently by offering all sorts of incentives to the right applicants…Like moving allowances and help with the purchase of brand new homes…It's not as if we can't see that we are on the brink of a life time opportunity but it's still tearing us away from our roots…That's the major downside."

Jenny responded with surprisingly well considered logic,

"Bernie love…You are starting out in life and I know you and Damien will be able to settle into any new surroundings with consummate ease…Don't get me wrong…We don't want you to go but…"

Kay cheekily interrupts,

"When you've got to go…You've got to go."

They all sat back and took a few moments to fully absorb the possible future prospects of all concerned.

Now that all of the worrying news had finally been aired and fully understood they were feeling much happier and relaxed. Kay was still at her jovial best as she followed up with her frank and honest observations.

"I know that you and that randy Damien are now getting hitched sooner rather than later but for Christ's sake be very careful when you tell Susan Summers about the arrangements whatever you do."

Jenny was ahead of the conversation because she started to roar with laughter well before Kay completed her pertinent deliberations.

"She has four kids already and I think she might murder Joe if she thought for one moment there was the slightest possibility that she could be in line for having yet another one.…I say that bearing in mind what happened on Christmas Eve last year.…Know what I mean?"

They all smiled with clearly, far from genuine, rueful expressions across their pretty faces.

Bernie ended up her visit by dashing away from Jenny's house when she suddenly realised that time had managed to pass very quickly in the company of her true friends. Her abrupt departure was caused because she managed to remember that she had arranged to meet Damien outside the Town hall at 5pm. She actually arrived a few minutes late but Damien was pleasantly surprised by the intensity of her greeting kiss, especially on the Street and in full view of anyone who happened to be passing by. He obviously deduced that she was feeling much better for some reason but was wisely waiting for her to take the lead.

Bernie was in high spirits,

"Come on Darling....Let's have a coffee in the Café I have a lot to tell you before we meet Jeremy whatshisname that so-called Curate up at 'All Souls'."

Bernie clutched onto his arm as she purposefully steered him along the Street.

"When we've done with this matter I think we will need to give our working futures some careful thought...Leave that for now...Don't mention Milton Keynes until I indicate that I am receptive to that subject please."

A now much more confident couple met, as arranged, with Jeremy Smith-Eccles in the Church Vestry shortly afterwards. He graciously shook hands with them both bidding them to sit facing him on chairs he had placed on the other side of a large wooden desk. As ever Jeremy was polite and friendly.

"Well I have been told you wanted to discuss an urgent matter with either myself or the Vicar...Is it concerning the forthcoming arrangements for your marriage on Christmas Eve? I always think that is a wonderful choice of day....If I ever meet Miss Right I shall endeavour to bear it in mind for my own convenience and delight. Now what is it? What can I do for you?"

Bernie was much more competent as an orator so she automatically spoke up for them both,

"Well first of all thank you Sir for being so kind as to see us at such short notice....I only wish we were here for a much better reason but unfortunately we are not....I'll come straight to the point Reverend... We need to cancel our arrangements with the Church...We find that we will be using the alternative legal services provided by the Registrar and that will be happening sooner rather than later and much in advance of what we had initially planned for the tying of our knots."

Jeremy was strangely puzzled by the content of Bernie's address. He failed to understand what she was talking about.

"Sorry Bernadette my dear....Let me assure you...It is not a problem for me to make a cancellation....In fact some other couple may well be delighted to hear about it....But...Why? ... Do you require me to set another date for the service to take place? ... I must confess I do love conducting Marriage Ceremonies...I have found by experience that very little can go wrong with them....Well....Usually...."

Jeremy giggled nervously as the confused vision, of his sometimes getting the names mixed up and also of one occasion when he attempted to marry the Best Man to a Bridesmaid by mistake in his early day's swiftly, flashed before him. Bernie nudged Damien who suddenly shot forward to offer an explanation.

"Oh no....Sorry Vic....Rev....Er Sir....We won't be in need of the services of the Church at all now I'm afraid."

There followed a short period of silence whilst Jeremy attempted to put together the exact meaning of what he was being told. Not wishing to expose the fact that he was totally bewildered he managed to respond coherently,

"What are you saying? Have you cancelled your engagement? Oh dear....How sad."

Bernie shook her head. She was getting a little stressed by the slowness being exhibited by the Curate. She sounded rather sharp,

"No...Not at all....If anything we've actually cemented our commitment to each other and we now consider a Church service would be totally inappropriate in view of the entirely relevant not to mention prevailing circumstances."

There was another short period of silence before, inevitably, Jeremy had to come clean,

"Sorry Bernadette....Damien....Sorry....I do not comprehend what your intentions happen to be at all I am afraid....I am unsure concerning what in exactitude you might be requiring from me."

Damien attempted to take the bull by the horns,

"Yes well...We have decided that a Church service will now be inappropriate because.....Well."

He paused to glance at Bernie, hoping for assistance. She nudged him even harder as she impatiently gesticulated to him to get on with it. Damien gulped down a deep intake of breath before he spoke,

"Does the Church or more pertinently…Do you…Believe in sex before marriage Sir?"

Another silent pause prevailed before, obviously after due consideration, Jeremy gave them his considered response,

"Wouldn't that make the Ceremony rather long Damien?"

The couple were so frustrated at this remark that they both actually felt like screaming out aloud. Bernie rose up onto her feet; her patience had now ebbed away completely,

"Make the Ceremony rather long? What on earth are you rabbiting on about? … Listen….Carefully…..I am up the duff…With child…. Pregnant….Do you understand now? … We are getting married as soon as possible and without any fuss to alleviate some of the embarrassment we are feeling and we do not consider ourselves worthy of a Church wedding with all the usual pomp and circumstance involved….No white dress? … No pretending to be the blushing bride…Understand? … We are not hypocrites…We are with child…We just want you to cancel our appointment…That's all."

Damien tugged on Bernie's arm attempting to calm her down as he steered her back onto the chair.

This time there was no expected silent pause, Jeremy, realising that he had been somewhat inadequate, responded, he was smiling from ear to ear,

"Oh I see….Oh yes….Well in that case would you like me to book in the Christening for you whilst you are here?"

The couple rose up, both glaring at the hapless Clergyman, speechless, before they stamped out of the Vestry shaking their heads both experiencing feelings of sheer disbelief with regard to the content of the conversation they had just endured. They were back standing on the High Street before one word was exchanged between them. Suddenly they both stopped in their tracks. They gazed deeply into each others eyes for a few seconds before they, still without any exchange of words, uncontrollably, burst out laughing. They laughed until tears ran down their cheeks. Damien could hardly speak but he eventually exclaimed,

"Wait till we tell the Gang about this."

They chuckled again as Bernie responded,

"Damien….I don't think for one minute they will believe a word of it."

Damien corrected her,

"Bernie my little dumpling….Oh yes they will….Just watch their faces when you tell them… They have experience of Jeremy whatshisname before and they know exactly what a steaming twit he really can be."

Again they hugged and kissed in public as Bernie headed off to re-join Jenny and Kay again as Damien headed for the Bowling Club to catch up with Eric and Sam confidently expecting a thoroughly enjoyable evening that had appeared to be highly unlikely earlier in the day.

"Gentlemen……Call me Blackie."

Susan Summers was experiencing a feeling of acute discomfort as she sat on a rather solid, uncomfortable, seat on the lower deck of a Rochdale Corporation Transport Omnibus travelling back to her home in Lapley Vale. She hoped that the uncomfortable pains she was feeling were not what she thought they might be because of her delicate stage of pregnancy. Joe, working the night shift at the Factory, where to many persons astonishment he remained a model Employee, considered to be an asset by his Employers as well as his Colleagues, had been left in charge of the kids. He not only collected some from their school but he was also responsible for looking after their baby. This situation was not unusual; as far as his beloved children were concerned his sacrifice of precious drinking time was acceptable. He had been left in charge in order to facilitate Susan attending to some last minute shopping, which she considered to be essential in connection with her now due confinement from the well stocked shops in Rochdale Town Centre. Susan felt as if the bus was deliberately travelling over every little bump and pothole present on the road surface. She was rapidly and relentlessly becoming more and more anxious and distressed.

After she had boarded the Bus at the Terminus near the Town Hall in Rochdale there had been quite an incident when Amos Quirk, local drunken religious fanatic, insisted upon carrying his cumbersome placard onto the platform of the Bus on his way to impart the *Holy Messages'* that he often felt prone to preach to the General Public on any streets and highways where he was not moved along by the Police. His current placard carried the message "GOD SAVES" on one side and "REPENT YOUR SINS BEFORE IT IS TOO LATE" on the other. He had managed to win the argument with their rather timid Bus Conductor. Then much to the annoyance of the other passengers travelling at that time he struggled to place it in the luggage compartment, which was found under the flight of stairs leading up onto the upper deck. He had then precariously seated himself on one of the long bench seats at the rear of the Bus so that he could hold onto his precious placard, which in his humble opinion was bearing urgently required information for the saving of all potential sinners. As an indication of how important and vital Amos considered his equipment to be to his cause he was prepared to suffer some considerable discomfort in his efforts to prevent it moving or falling over during the journey.

After reading a copy of the Lapley Vale Examiner, the one which highlighted the retirements of Sergeant Bert McCabe, he had decided to return to his flock in Lapley Vale after considering that his life ban from stepping foot and visiting that area had now become null and void because of Bert's departure from the Force.

Amos had been drinking; in fact he was very close to be formally classified as clinically drunk. However, this condition would never stop him from preaching his particular version of the holy word to anyone unfortunate enough to come into contact with him in any street or other public area. Amos was a strange, even quite complicated, character because when he was sober he was quite justifiably considered by many of his Clients to be the finest repairer of leather boots and shoes in the area. He conducted a roaring trade in a small wooden shop premises just off Yorkshire Street in Rochdale Town Centre. Amos had started work in this same, now rather old fashioned, shop for many years before as an apprentice clogger. At that time much of the considerable available trade was directed at anyone who could mend or put new irons on wooden clogs. Most Mill workers wore clogs as their everyday foot wear up until the end of the 1950's. He had eventually inherited the business after his late Father had passed away. This happened many years after he had been trained as a fully fledged Cobbler. Unfortunately

Amos transformed himself into a religious fanatic whenever he imbibed alcohol. This usually happened at weekends during the winter months and at anytime when the weather was clement. His outrageous conduct, whilst he sincerely considered himself to be acting as an agent of God, had in no short measure caused him to remain a bachelor. Over the years he had earned a well deserved reputation for being a total *Pain in the arse'* with a Police record of arrests for minor public order offences which would require several pages of inscription. Strangely, for a person with such a colourful background, he had never been sentenced to a term of imprisonment. This was probably because the Magistrates who had dealt with his cases were all well known to him and they consequently accepted and dealt with him as an stupid eccentric rather than a nasty villain.

Another couple of Passengers were sitting between Amos and where Susan was seated, which was very near to the front because the Bus had been quite full when it set off from Rochdale. The Bus frequently and monotonously stopped to allow Passengers to get on and off every few miles or so. As each and every Passenger did so they found themselves being serenaded by Amos singing, very loudly, *'Onward Christian Soldiers'* at the top of his raucous voice. This was clearly to the annoyance of most but also to the amusement of many others. If they offered any money to him he had been known to turn very nasty. He had actually done so on numerous occasions over the many years. As another couple boarded the Bus they were suitably greeted in the *'Lord's name'* as they passed Amos to take their places on seats on the lower deck.

The ancient Bus re-started with a noisy jerking movement which eventually proved to be too much for Susan. Suddenly her waters broke and she found that she was about to give birth where she was sitting on the Bus. The Conductor instantly panicked, pressing the emergency stop bell. The Driver slammed on his brakes but bearing in mind the prevailing circumstances this proved to be less than helpful. Susan had now found herself in serious difficulties.

As if by some miracle the Conductor just happened to spot the local District Nurse, Fanny (Sorry Frances) Costain, riding her bicycle along the street towards them. He leapt into the roadway and by frantically waving and shouting he managed to attract the elderly Nurses' full undivided attention. She reacted in a swift and impressively formidable fashion. She swept along the narrow deck of the Bus ready to assist the desperate, as well as helpless, Susan. Astonishingly soon the sound of a new born baby crying was heard. Amos, momentarily half asleep, woke up wondering why the Bus was stopped. He was at a loss to realise what had happened. He clumsily staggered along the length of the deck towards the front of the Bus where he was genuinely shocked at the sight of Fanny carefully holding the tiny newborn infant whilst, at the same time, she was also doing her best to administer care and attention upon Susan. She bellowed to the Conductor,

"Get someone to ring for an Ambulance immediately this Lady and her child need to go to the Hospital right away."

The Conductor almost tripped over his own feet in his haste to dash into a nearby shop where he intended to use their telephone. The formidable and vastly experienced Nurse Costain had made full use of the fairly limited equipment she inevitably carried around with her in her black bag. Despite his drunkenness, Amos was also in a state of real shock. He dropped down to sit, mouth open, silently, on a seat just behind Susan.

The Conductor, still clearly in a state of panic, informed Fanny that his Driver had already instructed a passer-by to ring 999 and that as a consequence the Ambulance was already on its way to them. Susan was quite understandably distressed which caused Fanny to desperately need to give Susan her full attention so that she could tend to her in a proper manner. She glanced around and without giving too much thought to what she was actually doing, she passed the Baby wrapped in her once spotless white apron to the hapless Amos. She placed the child firmly on his lap. He instinctively held onto the little bundle, staring down at the baby with an expression of sheer disbelief on his face.

Within a few minutes the Ambulance, bells loudly clanking, arrived at the scene. Both of the Attendants were soon carrying Susan, securely fastened down on their stretcher, along the deck carefully removing her from the interior of the bus so they could place her in the back of their Ambulance. Fanny cautiously supervised Susan's safe departure from the Bus into the Ambulance. She made sure she was as comfortable as could be reasonably expected before she returned to retrieve the baby from Amos. Amos now appeared to be, at least, partially aware of what was happening around him. Fanny gestured for him to carefully pass over the screaming child to her. With great tenderness he did so. Smiling down at the child he tenderly said,

"Off you go then little one….Go to the nice Nursey….And don't you ever… ever…EVER! Go up there ever again."

Fanny was concentrating so hard on the whole situation as it stood that, perhaps rather fortunately for Amos, she failed to hear his stupid remarks.

With the new born child lying in her Mother's arms the Ambulance soon roared off in the direction of the Cottage Hospital with those bells clanking, apparently sounding ever louder. Fanny then, without a word to anyone, retrieved her bicycle and literally tore off down the road, riding so frantically, she gave the appearance that might not just follow behind the Ambulance but she could actually overtake it.

Astonishing as this may seem another similar emergency was taking place inside "Bloomers" Shop on the High Street at almost the same time. Kay suddenly realised that she had started to go into labour and she panicked. She had desperately telephoned Jenny at home. Eric happened to be at home when her call was made. As Amy was presently being taken around the shops in her pram, being pushed by her devoted Grandmother Alice, he was able to transport Jenny straight around to the Shop without any undue delay. Within moments of them arriving at their shop Jenny, at first thinking she was merely experiencing sympathy pains, soon realised that she was starting her labour as well. They left the shop without delay with Mary Kelly, their new full time shop assistant, left in charge with strict instructions to telephone or somehow get in touch with Alice McCabe and Sam as soon as she possibly could. Eric then unceremoniously took both of the groaning women to the Cottage Hospital in the back of his rather old and less than prestigious delivery van. He padded the vehicle as well as he could with pillows and cushions supplied from upstairs by Mary.

The Ambulance carrying Susan and her baby had recently arrived at the Maternity Unit at Lapley Vale Cottage Hospital. A Sister and a Nurse had taken them into the Ward. Within minutes and before the Ambulance had been able to clear from the entrance, Eric came screeching into the car park looking and also sounding as if he was driving on two wheels in his desperation to deliver up his two damsels in distress.

Talk about panic. The absolutely dedicated Staff immediately dashed out to the vehicle ready willing and able to admit Kay and Jenny into the waiting Ward. Eric was formally given what is known as the *'Bum's rush'* out from under their feet. Inside the Ward all those, who were necessarily present, soon settled down to get to grips with the urgent matters in hand. Eric headed off intent upon taking whatever steps he could to locate and inform Sam of the exciting developments. At this time Eric was totally unaware that Susan and her new baby Daughter were already Patients in the Hospital.

Despite the desperate urgency of their arrival both Jenny and Kay had to face several hours of dreadful pain and suffering in the Labour Ward before they each delivered delightful, healthy, bouncing, baby sons. As if to add to the miracles already taking place Linda Chumley was then brought in later in the day. She managed to beat both Jenny and Kay in the delivery of her healthy new baby daughter, albeit as a result of her responding to a pre-arranged appointment to have another caesarean section.

Now if proof was ever needed in order to establish that all four of these women actually conceived at almost the same time on the night of Christmas Eve into Christmas Day these two little girls and two boys born within 24 hours of each other would certainly tend to provide more than sufficient support for such primary evidence. Many things astonish us from time to time but these happy circumstances would undoubtedly live within the memories of numerous happy Families concerned for many years to come.

***

A magical ambiance prevailed in the Crump Ward of Lapley Vale Cottage Hospital as all four of the proud Fathers and some other, perhaps less essential but nevertheless welcome, Visitors admired their new born babies and their equally proud, if a little bit exhausted and sore, Mothers. The atmosphere seemed to be electric through a mixture of relief, excitement and downright unadulterated happiness. The four close Friends were the only Patients occupying the Ward which probably explained the surprising extent of the latitude that was shown by the infamous Sister Murphy, the vastly experienced person who had been in charge of the Maternity Ward for many years. She was actively turning a blind eye to one of the Hospitals strict rules of not allowing more than two Visitors to each bed. Sister Murphy had earned her reputation for being a strict disciplinarian who suffered all Fathers equally badly. She was, somewhat cruelly perhaps, sometimes referred to as *'Hitler with tits'* and also as *'Attila the Hen'*, especially by those persons who fell foul of her by even threatening to disobey any of the carefully laid down Rules and Regulations without her leave to do so.

In a fascinating continuation of, what can only be referred to as astonishing happenings or even miracles, Joe Summers was present in the Ward visiting his long suffering Wife Susan in a state of cold soberness. As a consequence of his unexpected condition he was behaving himself accordingly which was a great relief to Susan. Perhaps it should be said that by the time Joe had managed to deal with all the immediate needs of their four hungry and demanding Children at home, and then followed that by arranging the urgent requirement for a baby sitter to cover for his absence, he had not found time, as yet, to take any celebratory drink. As he was lucky enough to secure the services of his trusted Mother to sit for him there was nothing surer than the assurance that he would be taking a drink or two or even more just as soon as he could decently leave his Wife and his Child in the Hospital.

Joe was at that time nursing his new Daughter, who was to be named Elizabeth after Her Majesty the Queen, also chosen because they had already used up their favourite girls names of Shirley and Rosemary on their other two daughters. Joe was openly exhibiting for all to see the obvious love and pride he has always genuinely felt for Susan and his Children despite his frequently displayed unfortunate shortcomings.

Sam Best could hardly speak he was so proud. He was also amazed with the suddenness of the events. He was lovingly gazing down upon his baby Son, being named Edward after Kay's Grandfather Eddie Brown, as he lay sleeping in one of those skimpy looking Hospital cots that were not particularly enhanced by the big labels stuck on them bearing the Mother and Child's names. Kay was bravely attempting to mask the agony she was feeling after suffering prolapsed haemorrhoids as a result of her necessary exertions during her tortured stay in the dreaded Labour Ward.

Linda Chumley was still groggy from the effects of anaesthetic necessarily administered to permit the Doctors and their staff to perform her caesarean section operation but she was gamely attempting to convince her pale, fragile appearing, husband Malcolm, that all was well. She was delighted and very contented with the arrival of her new Daughter, who would be named Sonja, a little sister for Jane their other Child.

As far as the McCabe's were concerned they were absolutely delighted with their Son who would be called William after his Great Grandfather Billy 'Cockeye' Harris. His Grandfather Bert was also present. He had been unable to wipe the broad smile off his face ever since he received the news of the birth. He had expressed his approval of the Child's name but sincerely hoped that he had not inherited one or two of Billy's less attractive characteristics. When Bert added this caveat to his consent for the name he had them all roaring with raucous laughter when he stuck out his tongue to make a rasping 'Farting' noise accompanied by the waving of his hand under his nose in a most jocular way.

A loud clanking bell, why they should have such a thing anywhere near a Ward housing tiny sleeping infants was difficult for the men to understand, rang out denoting the necessity for all of the Visitors to leave forthwith. This was much to the disappointment of majority of those persons present. The volume of hugs and kisses given and received all around the Ward made an audible humming and smooching noise. Susan and Jenny were reduced to tears; these were the female ones of happiness this time of course.

The excitement of the visiting hour had now given way to an opportunity for the Patients to enjoy quiet relaxation and contented reflection on all the exciting events that had happened over the past 24 hours. No matter how she tried Kay was unable to make herself comfortable. This was where the exceptional qualities of someone with great Nursing skills came to the fore. Sister Murphy caringly attended to her equipped with a rubber surgical glove which had been filled with frozen ice and had then been carefully wrapped in a towel before it was placed on top of a rubber sheet on the mattress of the bed. She tenderly, carefully, positioned this soothing device under Kay's most tender parts instantly bringing her enormous heartfelt relief. She was soon in a much better frame of mind to join the others in their quest for a well earned sleep. Her humour still managed to survive despite her many recent ordeals as she whispered to Jenny, who was not quite asleep as she lay on the next bed,

"Are you awake? … Bloody hell Jen….I never thought I would possibly entertain the thought of having a frozen hand placed under my arse….But….I'll tell you what love….At this present moment in time I would be prepared to highly recommend it to anyone in the future."

They both quietly chuckled as they drifted off into a contented and well earned sleep.

***

As far as most of the clearly thrilled men leaving Crump Ward behind them after visiting time were concerned the perfect end to this wonderful day could not be spent anywhere other than in the Clubroom at the Lapley Vale Bowling and Social Club. Exceptions, at least initially, included Joe Summers who wanted to spread the news of his new arrival around all of his usual watering holes and Malcolm Chumley who wanted to get back to his Mother and the baby Daughter waiting for him at home. Malcolm was a rarity amongst the Blokes living around these parts. He did not really enjoy drinking alcohol of any sort and consequently never really mixed on a casual basis with the other men in the group although he never exhibited dissent or disapproval and always friendly as well as approachable.

Great Grandfather Billy Dawes was almost carried home shortly after, what was laughingly called, closing time by Eric and Sam. Eddie also left early but had managed to retain sufficient dignity to make the journey under his own steam albeit under watchful supervision. Eric and Sam were ably assisted by Damien 'Specky' Harris, who eventually managed to join in the celebrations with them inside the Clubhouse. After they had attended to Billy, Damien decided that he would carry on to Bernadette's cosy and comfortable little House. In view of all of the prevailing circumstances, taken together with their present condition, Damien had now moved in with his Fiancé instead of just living there for the majority of the time whilst pretending he did not. He was unable to fully enjoy the wetting of the babies heads celebrations because he had been forced to leave Bernie still suffering from *'Morning sickness'*. She had been cruelly struck down soon after arriving home from work early in the day. Much to her disappointment her sorry disposition had unfortunately meant that she was then unable to visit the Hospital to see her three Friends in their moments of glory. As it happened Damien had been quite anxious to ask his more experienced Friends why this sickness caused by pregnancy, mostly in the early stages, was prefaced by the word *'Morning'* because Bernie seemed to be suffering from it most of the time recently but obviously this was not the right time make such an enquiry. Billy had managed to live up to his well established reputation by breaking wind loudly soon after he inevitably started to sink slowly in the west. He brought joyous laughter to his all of his closest Friends and Relatives as he was clearly heard to be mumbling,

"A miracle….A cockeyed miracle…."

As he had to be substantially assisted out through the door of the premises. The way things appeared to be going there was a very strong possibility that the remaining pair of Good Samaritans could well be requiring the same personal service for them later.

Having discharged their Good Samaritan duties with distinction Eric and Sam were now able to quietly enjoy the special occasion. Grandfather Bert was now really revelling in the company of Woody, Eddie Brown the other Great Grandfather and little Norman Smith. Alf was in sole charge behind the bar after Denise had taken her leave to catch the last Bus home. Denise, a Single Lady, who had no children of her own always doted on all and any small infants. She was as delighted as anyone over the arrival of the four new souls. Chairman Ralph and Secretary/Treasurer Victor were also there to represent the *'Bitter enders'* who never knowingly missed a celebration of any shape or form.

Bert was describing his recent arrival as a tenant on Lady Lapleys Estate after his much heralded retirement from the Force and his removal from the Police House where he had lived happily for many years.

"I managed to do a deal with the bloke from Oldham who runs those Auction Rooms….You know who I mean don't you?….Eh? … Eh? … Does House clearances and flogs the stuff by auction….Eh? … Eh? … Well…As our new place of abode is considerably smaller than the Police House we needed to part with quiet a large quantity of excess furniture…O.K.….Eh? … Eh? … Mother managed to give some of the better stuff away locally.….And when I say give.….I do mean GIVE IT AWAY! So I did a deal with him to keep the surplus gear free and gratis just as soon as he had dropped all the stuff we were taking with us at the Cottage using his big van.…..Worked like clockwork.….I heard about someone being quoted an arm and a leg from a specialised furniture removal firm recently when they were moving out of the District so I think I've saved myself a small fortune and at the same time I've also got rid of the rubbish I didn't want to keep….Eh? … Eh?"

They nodded their approval for Bert's cunning strategy but Woody was sharp to respond,

"Great news Bert….Does that mean you might buy us another round? I know the normally rare opening of your wallet ceremony has been abused a bit of late but now that you are a humble Court Usher and you no longer wield all the powers bestowed upon the Officer in Charge of the Police you might find that you may have to pay for your own beer more often…Stands to reason that does."

Eddie and Norman agreed with Woody's sentiments but, as expected, Bert was quick to respond.

"Aye….Maybe so….Maybe not….Have I told you Boys about the fistful of genuine complimentary tickets I have been given for free entrance into the new Safari Park?....Eh? … Eh? … Save anyone a good few bob they will…People getting those from me so they can sample what the Park has to offer free and without paying the entrance fee will obviously want to express their gratitude won't they? … Eh? … Eh?"

They readily appreciated that Bert was far from dead and buried which resulted in ironic, wry, smiles all around. Norman, who had, up to now, been reasonable quiet perked up to add his comments,

"I would be surprised that after all the years you have managed to drink heavily mostly with other folk's dosh buying the beer has not given you some special powers in this respect Bert…I have heard it said that you could convince a monkey of his need to give you his peanuts… Hey you will be able to test that particular theory won't you? Unless I'm mistaken Bert you've got monkeys living in your back garden now haven't you?"

Bert agreed and through laughter he replied,

"It's not the bloody monkeys I'm worried about boys….Eh? … Eh? … It's all those ferocious lions and other wild things that are wandering around the Estate behind those electric fences…..Horace Pink….You know Old Pinkie don't you?....Well he accidentally strayed into one of the enclosures the other day and had a very narrow escape…He was chased by a big male lion…He managed to execute a hasty departure but only because the lion kept slipping on the shit."

Norman was on the brink of asking *'What shit'* when he quickly realised that Bert was being his amusing self once again.

The bewitching hour passed as the two weary, newly established Fathers, filled to capacity with celebration drinks, had forced themselves to go home. Both had to attend to their work early the next morning.

Both were happy to be in full employment. Sam together with, as he was now his employee, the joiner Isaac Wells, were fully booked with enough jobs to keep them ticking over in the building trade for the next two months. Freddie Moore, Sam's original Boss who was now his Partner had retired from the practical side of the work but was invaluable to Sam carrying out an administrative role.

Only the real hard core were left enjoying what would probably not be their nightcaps. Suddenly the door leading onto the car park flew open to reveal Bert's successor the new Officer in charge of Police, Sergeant Norman Blackburn. He was in full uniform accompanied by a frightened, possibly desperate, looking Constable 'Sooty' Sutcliffe. Their dramatic entrance was enough to give them all a nasty shock. Norman, a tall, well built, imposing man in his early fifties with quite handsome features really put the wind up everyone as he announced, using a noticeably officious tone,

"Everyone stay where they are this is a Police raid."

All those at the bar were stunned as Norman aggressively glared in their direction. Sooty appeared to be very embarrassed by the whole situation he had unfortunately found himself facing. Norman picked out Bert as his initial target,

"Right…..Now then…I assume you are the famous Mr Bert McCabe….Note that Mister McCabe…I thought you might have shown more regard for the law after enforcing it for so many years…. What have you to say?"

Bert swallowed nervously sounding oddly strange as he replied,

"Well….Sergeant….As I am confident that you are already aware…. There are many different and varied ways of achieving satisfactory enforcement….Er Sergeant…..Eh? … Eh? … I think you'll find that the lid has been kept firmly placed upon this Town during my long reign as Police Chief even if my methods were sometimes…And I must stress this point….By some of those less practically minded than yours truly…Eh? … Eh? … Considered to be in breach of the Book or the Queensbury Rules or let's face it…Any other written Rules and Regulations whatsoever you might care to quote to me…Eh? … Eh?"

There was a moment or two of silence before Norman went around each person at the bar as he sternly asked them for their names. All answered without hesitations as the atmosphere by now had quickly turned from one of delight to one of despair verging upon horror. There was another short silence before Norman's face suddenly broke into a broad smile. There was a trace of a chuckle in his voice as he said,

"Right! ... Case proved beyond a shadow of a doubt....You have been fined at least two pints of best bitter to be handed over for destruction by the Constable and myself forthwith....No...No let's make that fifthwith....It's quicker...Come on Chaps let me introduce myself properly."

An enormous sense of relief could now be sensed from every one of the *Bitter Enders* still present. Norman gave a funny (Masonic) handshake to Ralph, Victor and Alf. This clandestine signal was probably not noticed by those not, in any way, connected to the famous Secret Society, namely Bert, Woody and not forgetting little Norman. The whole company were soon enjoying fresh pints of frothing bitter. The new Sergeant smiled, he had now changed his tack completely as he displayed a genuine desire to be friendly. He spoke directly to little Norman,

"Norman I must compliment those responsible for giving you such a worthy and respectable name....As I share this honour you might be pleased to hear that I am far better known by my nickname.... Blackie....No points for anybody guessing that was there eh? ... I much prefer to addressed as Blackie and this fact will therefore resolve any future problems when we enjoy the pleasure of meeting together..... Please....Gentlemen call me Blackie."

They all raised their glasses in unison to mutter "Blackie".

After another pint was eagerly supplied to the Sergeant, Bert was somewhat curious as he eventually realised that they had now reached the conclusion to the particularly, initially trying, interlude. Having introduced themselves to each other as well as quickly supplying them with a brief account of his life to date from a career point of view, Bert had to ask him,

"Just a minute....Tell me something Norman....Sorry....Blackie.... I don't wish to be too personal but we were given to understand from a reliable source that you were known to be a non drinking Lay Preacher..... Eh? ... Eh? ... A Member of the Ancient Order of Rechabites....Who's been kidding who?....Eh? ... Eh?"

Norman sat back roaring with laughter,

"Bill Kinley Bert....Your old Boss and pal Bill Kinley told his Brother-in-law Arnold Pratt....In confidence of course and Arnold actually made the announcement using all his skills as a Superintendent to give everyone the impression that he was being totally sincere...Let me inform you once and for all Gents....I left the Rechabites when I reached the age of sixteen or seventeen and this happened immediately after I discovered just how nice beer tasted....I am a Religious Man and have been known to Lay Preach but that was many years ago.... Take my word for it Bert you have just met for the first time a drinking man who might even be your match...We shall see....I look forward to many happy hours of briefing without missing any of the ins and outs of your experience looking after your old Patch over countless pints of this delicious bitter....Bill Kinley must be laughing his bloody socks off up their in Knot End or whatever it's called where he lives now....It was all his idea.....No permanent harm intended Bert....He even told me exactly how you used to make your entrance in here when you were being playful....How was it?.....Was I O.K.? Convincing I trust? O.K.? ... Shall we be all be friends from now on?"

Bert's cup was now full and running over. He almost cried with tears of joy as they all warmly shook hands with each other once again. They actually ended up hugging each other in a less than masculine but extremely agreeable manner. Bert still needed to know more about their new friend,

"Is the connection with our esteemed Vicar just another of Bill's funny pretences Blackie? We were informed that you were his nephew.... This probably gave credence to the other bullshit."

Blackie laughed,

"That piece of information is absolutely correct Bert....Whistling Reggie is my late Mother's little Brother....I have to confess that I have rarely had the pleasure of meeting him and I have not done so for many years but it is a fact I am the Nephew of the Vicar of All Souls."

They all made a toast to Whistling Reggie the Vicar of 'All Souls' the Parish Church of Lapley Vale.

Ralph, who had been extremely subdued, now fully recovered from Blackie's shock entrance, possibly due to the amount of beer he had consumed, enquired politely,

"You also know him as Whistling Reggie then do you Blackie? ... We all affectionately call him that for obvious reasons but let me assure you he is held in high esteem by the majority of our fellow Townsfolk."

Taking possession of another pint Blackie responded keenly,

"Oh Yes....He has always whistled through his teeth...As a young man I recall the amusement in our family when he got married to Sybil....Eh? ... Bloody hell fire....What was wrong with marrying a woman called Nellie or Jane?....She must be so used to his whistling by now that she probably manages to ignore it completely....They had no children of their own and as we lived up near Lancaster I only ever came into contact with them on rare Family gathering occasions....I'll tell you what though....I wouldn't mind being in his Will as a beneficiary....Has a few bob stashed away over the years...He was a Padre in the Army during the War....The first one that is....There's a lot people will not know about the famous Whistling Reggie....He is a most interesting character to say the very least."

The company was rapt by their new friend's line of conversation. He glanced out through the windows to catch sight of Sooty smoothly arriving on the car park driving Blackie's own new Triumph Herald saloon car. This would not have happened in Bert's day because he would never allow anyone to drive his precious Ford Prefect under any sorts of circumstances.

Sooty quietly sloped in still looking a little apprehensive. Blackie gestured to him to join them at the bar.

"Thank you Sooty....I am time expired and I fear that my dear Lady Wife will be waiting for the sound of my arrival home before she can enjoy a really deep sleep....Bert....Thank your Bride and compliment her for the way we found the house Bert....Ursula would love to meet her probably because she guesses they are definitely of a very similar ilk...Right... I'll bid you all a very good night Gents or should that be good morning....I look forward to occasions when I will be able to enjoy your sparkling company again in the future."

Victor, now almost in a coma again jolted into action having what proved to be the final word,

"Sergeant Blackburn....Blackie....Your name will be inscribed in the register as a Full Member of our beloved Club."

Formal handshakes preceded the disappearance of Blackie and Sooty and the now much happier Bitter Enders finished off their drinks before they retired to their homes in an orderly fashion. Alf locked up before he also retired to his comfortable and convenient quarters upstairs.

"You nasty old Bastard"

The true facts surrounding what really happened, not just inside but then also on the pavement outside, at the 'Light of Bengal' Indian Restaurant in the early hours of a Sunday morning (In this particular case it just happened to be the continuation of a Saturday night out) would probably never be known. Suffice to say that what had been an extended, most enjoyable evening; visiting selected night spots in the Town Centre of Rochdale had eventually come to an abrupt and disastrous end.

Bridget Nolan, semi retired Prostitute, known locally, in what is her home Town, as *'Charlotte the Harlot'* and her two friends, Mary Picard, Lapley Vale's own amateur *'Lady of Pleasure'*, notoriously called *'Worthington Mary'* because of her addiction to bottled Worthington Pale Ale, especially their product called *'White Worthies'* or *'Looney Juice'*, together with Dan Smith, a Scrap Metal Dealer, Mary's part time Boyfriend come Customer, although cash never ever changes hands payment in kind was expected and generously given. (For those not familiar with Mr Smith, Dan is a wealthy self made Lapley Vale character who was often referred to as *'Dan Dan the Scrap Yard Man'*. Although he was a married man with a respectable Wife and Family he had been intimately and overtly associated with Worthington Mary for many years), had all spent the later part of the remainder of their night out locked up in the Cells at Rochdale Police Station.

Charlotte and Mary had been close friends ever since their school days. They had made arrangements to meet Dan and his friend Tommy

Cox, a well to do Business Associate, by appointment earlier in the evening. The foursome had purchased and managed to consume many drinks in a number of the Licensed Premises; these were liberally distributed around the Town Centre, before deciding to finish the evening off by taking a meal as a prelude to their adjournment to Charlotte's flat with a view to the participation in pleasures of the flesh (Locally referred to as *'Percy Filth'*). After they had been refused entry into their chosen place for eating their chosen food, a respectable place called the *'China Star'* Chinese Restaurant, Tommy, foolishly, took exception to the attitude of the large non-English speaking Chinese Bouncer, who was rumoured to have easy access to a huge cleaver, which resulted in him being on the wrong end of a sharp smack in the nose that unfortunately would not instantly stop bleeding. Feeling that he had had enough for one night Tommy decided to forego the meal and other treats on offer by calling an abrupt end to his night out. After flagging down a taxi Tommy, swiftly, retired to his home where he had earlier left his Wife and Family watching television. The remaining three Revellers had carried on to the, less desirable, *'Light of Bengal'* Indian Restaurant where they were initially made welcome. They were able to enjoy an excellent meal, perhaps unwisely accompanied by a fine bottle of wine or two. Mary invariably insisted upon substantial sustenance after a long drinking session. Dan was aware that she might not be as receptive to his disgusting desires, planned for later that evening, if she did not get a square meal inside her first.

What then occurred was not clearly established and was likely to remain a mystery for evermore. Dan paid in cash for the meal and wine giving the Chinese Waiter, who Dan had annoyingly insisted upon addressing as *'One Hung Low'* much to the amusement of his Companions, a generous tip. They wanted to remain for another couple of drinks and that was definitely the point when the trouble started. After harsh words had been exchanged all three in the party were unceremoniously thrown out onto the pavement outside. Instead of going quietly to Charlotte's flat they foolishly chose to remain remonstrating with the Staff. The Police were called and after a considerable amount of pushing, shoving and swearing, two burley Constables had finally decided to arrest all three of them for being drunk and disorderly. As if he had not managed to get himself into enough trouble, Dan then petulantly put his foot through a glass panel on the entrance door leading to the inside the Restaurant. Obviously this clearly stupid act was carried out in full view of the Officers.

As the three Accused Persons climbed up the concrete steps into the Dock from the Holding Cells on the floor below they made a pathetic, shocking, sight for any of those Persons who were present in the public gallery of the Courtroom to witness. Dan looked particularly rough because he had a shocking hangover, needed a shave and had been obliged to sleep on a hard wooden bench with all of his clothes on but he was in quite a reasonable state in comparison with his two Female Co-defendants. They had both been crying on a number of occasions, initially at the time of their arrests and then later when they eventually realised that they were definitely going to be incarcerated, without bail, to appear before the Court the following morning. This weeping had causing black coloured mascara to run down their faces, their hair was dishevelled to say the least, resembling half destroyed bird's nests and their make up was smudged and some of it had almost worn off. They could have confidently applied for and easily landed the staring roles of the *'Two Ugly Sisters'* in any top Christmas Pantomime.

All three were blinking due to their exposure to the sudden brightness of the open room. Mary instantly spotted Bert McCabe, the Court Usher as he was now gainfully employed, standing near the double doors alongside the dock. Bert looked extremely smart wearing a school master type cloak over his best suit, worn with smart collar and tie. The three Accused Persons were firmly pushed onto a wooden seat which faced towards the bench where the three Magistrates were seated. Mary immediately and desperately called out,

"Sergeant McCabe….Bert….Darling….It's me your friend Mary…. Oh please….Can you do something about this terrible state of affairs please? Please Sergeant."

Bert grinned, as only Bert could. A female Constable and her large Male counterpart standing in the Dock with them insisted upon their silence in no uncertain terms. Mary quickly realised that Bert was not going to come to her aid. She resigned herself as she quickly stared up at the Bench. The Chairman of the Bench of Magistrates was Major Reginald Duckworth a local war hero who was famous for his keen attention to discipline and good order at all times. There were two Female Magistrates, one on either side of him, present to assist him in any necessary deliberations. These Colleagues were obviously quite classy Ladies; both were very well dressed and were wearing fancy looking hats.

The Magistrates' Clerk, Horace Mayo, who was actually in overall charge of the proceedings, read out the charge of being drunk and disorderly to all three Prisoners at the Bar. He asked them to enter their pleas. Charlotte bowed her head as she muttered, sounding sorry for herself,

"Guilty…And I would like to say sorry as well."

Mary was next but she felt the urge to ask a question,

"Sorry….But….What exactly do you mean Darling? Do you want me to tell what little I can actually remember of what happened last night? Or what?"

The stern looking Clerk glared at her as he almost shouted,

"I want you to plead guilty or not guilty Madam….That is all…. Please refrain from calling me or anyone else here present 'Darling'….If you must speak to the Bench kindly address them as 'Your Worships'….. Now what is your plea?"

Mary clearly did not care for his tone but she did realise that he was not about to stand for any messing about.

"Sorry Darl…..Oops…..Sorry….Your worshipfulness…I am as guilty of these charges as my Companions….I would like to ask for mercy please."

These remarks brought laughter from all corners of the public Courtroom. Bert was obliged to keep them quiet. Hence the descriptive title of his new job *'Usher'*, he was there to make people hush.

The Clerk demanded order before he nodded in Dan's direction. Dan replied, sounding and looking rather meek and forlorn,

"Guilty Your Honour".

The Clerk then read out the additional charge of willingly committing criminal damage accusing Dan alone. Again he was humble and submissive,

"Guilty My Lord and I am quite prepared to pay the cost of any damage forthwith."

The Clerk then nodded to the Prosecuting Police Inspector, Leonard Smithe, who stood up to clearly and distinctly read out a summary of the brief circumstances surrounding all of their arrests. Each defendant was asked if they had anything they wished to say to the Bench by way of explanation or mitigation. All three declined the offer without speaking. Inspector Smithe then mentioned that Charlotte had some previous minor convictions, Mary had a clean record but Dan had some convictions for assault and also for receiving stolen goods but these were from a few years back in the distant past.

The Major got into a huddle with his two Lady Companions. They chatted in low voices for a few minutes. He then leant forward to consult Horace, the Clerk, who was sat in front of the bench. There followed a further little muffled conversation between them before the Major sat back to have a final discussion with the two Ladies. Bert remained in the Court grinning; he had been seen to be shaking his head and was even tutting as the Inspector outlined the sorry story of their disgraceful behaviour which had resulted in their arrests for the charges they were now facing.

The Major politely coughed to trigger the Clerk into action again. Horace called out loudly.

"All three Defendants will please rise."

They shuffled to their feet looking even more bewildered. The Major commenced passing sentence on them,

"Bridget Nolan and Mary Picard you are both mature women and should be able to conduct yourselves in an orderly fashion at all times. Your conduct was nothing short of disgraceful....You will be fined ten pounds each. The said fines are to be paid forthwith and you will be remanded in custody until payment has been duly received."

Possibly with some sort of relief Charlotte turned to Mary to cheekily say,

"I'll have to take my knickers off first to earn the money because I've a horrible feeling that my purse is empty."

The Women both laughed but the Major was far from amused. Perhaps unwisely he chose to react to the humorous remark,

"One moment please….I may be getting older but I am glad to say my hearing is still extremely acute…I gather from those comments you are far from remorseful for your outrageous conduct….You will pay a fine of twenty pounds instead of the ten in your case Nolan…I strongly advise you to keep your trap shut unless you wish to find out just how severe the penalty could be….Oh and incidentally Nolan I think it has to be said that I estimate that there must be a considerable number of those amongst us who would gladly pay you at least that sum on condition that you keep your knickers on."

This comment was greeted with loud laughter. Although he was enjoying the proceedings just as much as everyone present in the Courtroom, Bert was still obliged to carry out his basic duties of cajoling them all to be quiet and also demanded that they settled down. The two Women were steered back down the concrete steps to the Custody Suite from whence they would only be able to regain their freedom after payment of their fines had been duly made.

The Chairman of the Bench then turned his attention to Dan.

"You Smith have a record of dishonesty and violence in the past… You have very clearly not learned your lesson….You will pay the full sum claimed by the owners of the 'Light of Bengal' and as an example to others who misbehave so atrociously you will go to Prison for 28 days….Take him down Officer."

Dan could hardly believe his ears. Rather than being stunned he became aggressively argumentative.

"Prison? Prison? What the bloody hell are you going on about? You impose fines for the two Women who caused most of the bloody trouble in the first place but it's got to be Prison for me….No way….You nasty old Bastard."

With that he charged into the Constable, using his broad shoulder to do so, causing the Officer to stumble as he lost his footing. He was sent sprawling until he was flat on his back on the floor. He almost fell down the concrete steps positioned behind him inside the Dock. Dan burst out of the hinged door at the side of the Dock. Bert instantly removed his false teeth and glasses in his familiar precursor, which always formed part of his ritual preparation for the anticipated need for his involvement in physical violence. Bert hurriedly passed these very personal items, wrapped in his handkerchief, to a trembling Lady Usher who was standing nearby. Bert was ready for action. He met Dan at the front of the Dock, in the well of the Courtroom. He dropped him with a single adeptly placed sharp punch to his stomach region. Dan doubled up, groaning. Bert was suddenly aware of the presence of Major Duckworth roughly pushing past him to dive in on top of the temporarily incapacitated Dan. On witnessing Dan's behaviour the elderly, but still very fit, Chairman of the Magistrates had athletically vaulted over the bench into the well of the open Courtroom in a flash. A scrum developed until the angry Constable, who had been knocked off his feet by Dan, managed to place his handcuffs on Dan's wrists. He then bodily carried the prisoner back into the Dock and down the steps to the Cells below ably assisted, all the way, by both the Major and Bert.

The few remaining cases being heard by the Court were an anticlimax for most of those present but the Bench were able to proceed as soon as the Major returned to his rightful place as their Chairman. What was amazing about the whole interlude was the fact that, apart from the two Lady Magistrates. Horace Mayo the Court Clerk and possible the Female Usher, no-one appeared to have been greatly shocked by the actions taken by the Prisoner Dan, the Usher Bert or the even the Magistrate Major Duckworth.

Bert dashed back to retrieve his teeth and spectacles from his still trembling and ashen faced Colleague. He swiftly placed the teeth back into his mouth, again in compliance with his tried and tested routine, he cautiously applied a couple of test bites to ensure they were soundly bedded in, before he also replaced his glasses back where they belonged. He then turned to glance all around the room, immediately breaking out in his broad identifiable toothy smile for all to see.

"Paddy is Larry's horse Serg."

Dawn had already broken about an hour or so before Lawrence Walter O'Brien, better known to most of the Inhabitants of Lapley Vale as 'Larry the Lamb', woke up suffering from a horrible, throbbing and pounding, headache. As if this was not enough these symptoms were accompanied by a very dry mouth which felt, to him, as if he had somehow left his tongue lying on the bottom of a parrot's cage. These were the classic symptoms of a severe hangover which Larry had found himself having to cope with once again. The dawn chorus provided by the wide variety of wild twittering birds was very loud and piercing. Probably the various little creatures were innocently celebrating the fact that the sun was shinning brightly and the skies above them were blue without a cloud in sight.

You will probably recall this Character. Irish born Lawrence was commonly called *'Larry the Lamb'* in Lapley Vale where he spent most of his time. He did, however also share some of his time in a nearby Town called Stretton. Just to confuse things he was commonly known over there as *'Wandering Wally'*. As if that was not enough confusion he had recently gained another nickname from his friends and acquaintances in Lapley after being involved in an unfortunate incident with Peggy Hackett. He was now also called *'The Wild Linoleum Boy'* by certain, naturally humorous, Local Citizens. He had lived all of his life since he was first born in a genuine wooden *'Gypsy type'* Caravan. This quite valuable dwelling place had eventually been inherited by Larry after the death of his late Father. He was the current owner of a black and white cob called Paddy who, as well as being his constant and faithful companion, provided him with his sole means of locomotion. Paddy was regularly utilised for Larry's journeys between his two Towns. Paddy would be secured between the shafts at the front of the Caravan in order that he could convey Larry in a sedate and stylish, certainly not fast, fashion to and from his destinations. The trustworthy and strong Paddy was quite capable of towing the heavy Caravan for many miles if he was required to do so. The Local Children in both Towns taunted him. Some thought he was a Gypsy many others considered him to be an Irish Tinker, although he was neither, they had somehow resolved to call him *Stinker the Tinker'*. Larry did not really care too much what People called him as long as he could make his meagre living carrying out any odd jobs or other types of various menial tasks requiring his attention in both Towns.

He had enjoyed the benefit the of long standing, convenient, parking and pasturing agreements with Whistling Reggie at 'All Souls' Parish Church Lapley Vale and also with Emmanuel Snoddy, the Vicar of St Peters Parish Church in Stretton for as long as he could remember. In lieu of the payment of any rent at either venue Larry conscientiously tended to the gardens, graves and other grassed areas which were the property of either Parish. Larry (or Wally) had built up the trust of both of these generous Vicars. Both valued him as a considerable asset to them over a period of many years. Paddy not only managed to keep both of the large paddocks closely cropped but he was also used to graze upon the grass on the Lapley Villa Football Pitch as well.

Now in his fifties Larry had always enjoyed excellent health. He was generally accepted. He had become quite popular with his many of his Regular Customers in both of the Towns. As you may have already guessed Larry did have a slight drink problem. Fortunately this *'Achilles Heel'* was only ever noticed on the rare occasions when he had enough money to spend on buying large quantities of *'Guinness'*, his favourite tipple. Larry's late Mother had almost reared her son on Irish Stout from a tender age. She was remembered in some quarters for her forthright opinions on the value of natural breast feeding. She would draw attention to Larry's fine healthy physique as a prelude to often stating sarcastically,

"Just look at the fine figure of this Man I am proud to call my Son....Reared mainly on Guinness...I can assure you that he never had a Woman's Tit in his mouth until he was sixteen years old and he started courting...So that well known saying, *'Breast is best'* is a load of codswallop."

Alas she died at a relatively young age from a serious liver disease caused in no small part by her frequent consumption of the black stuff as well as any other alcoholic beverages she could manage to get her hands on.

The sole reason behind Larry's temporary woeful state was an unexpected, surprisingly peaceful, meeting which took place between him and the latest, unofficially appointed, Town Tramp, a new face around Town called Spud Murphy. They happened to meet up by chance outside the Slip Inn Public House, situated next door to Lapley Vale Police Station, at a time when both had been paid for their various services and were unusually carrying cash in their pockets. At that particular time of the year Larry was known to specialise in the provision of freshly picked fruit, mostly apples and plums. His Customers were mainly found amongst the Elderly or Infirmed People in the area. He was easily able to undercut the Green Grocer by considerable amounts due to the fact that Larry *'Found'* his supplies hanging from trees which were liberally distributed all over the Town and the surrounding countryside. He had never ever been brought to Justice for this activity, which strictly speaking was Larceny in legal terms, because he used all of his *'Living off the Land'* skills, which he had developed through practice since he was a small child. In some ways it could be said that he provided a Social Service to the less fortunate Members of Society who would not normally have been able to enjoy fresh, healthy, British grown fruit.

Probably because both Men were cautiously unsure of what their relationship with each other was likely to be they rather apprehensively, not to say wisely, decided to shake hands with each other in an unmistakable gesture of good faith before they thought about even beginning to establish themselves as potential friends. They had already realised that they were not really in any kind of serious competition with regard to their existing customers because there always appeared to be much more than enough casual work available for each of them to make a reasonable living. So, there and then in bar at the Slip Inn, they bonded, not only as friends but also as sworn *'Ale Brothers'*. The two new Comrades had then spent the remainder of the evening drinking themselves into the sorts of serious states of drunkenness not too often witnessed. When they eventually did run out of money their conditions would have easily qualified them in medical terms as being in advanced stupors.

Through many years of past experience Larry had become to realise immediately upon awakening that he had been in a sad alcoholic state at the time he had fallen asleep the previous night. One definite indicator was the fact that he was still wearing his boots. Although he usually wore most of his outer garments when sleeping in his tiny bunk bed he did normally removed his boots. In a, possibly, forlorn gesture towards personal hygiene he usually left his footwear outside in the open air to rest overnight. In fairness it also needed to be stated that Larry was also in the habit of keeping his galvanised *'Toilet'* bucket, used for solids only, under the Caravan at all times when it was not in use. He claimed two pertinent reasons for this action. Firstly he thought the contents of his bucket would keep the flies out of the inside his Caravan. Secondly, now this would not be received as good news for those of his many Clients who consider him to have *'Green fingers'* and an astonishing aptitude for growing strong and healthy shrubs and plants, he never wasted anything he considered to be of even the slightest practical use.

His next task after he had discretely emptied his over filled bladder at the side of his Caravan was to attend to the provision of Paddy's oats. He had pulled the sack out from under the Caravan before he casually walked to where he expected to see Paddy securely tethered on a long rope. He was not unduly alarmed initially when he could not see his horse. After first glancing, then feverishly gazing all around the

Paddock, he very soon started to panic because, for some inexplicable reason, there was no sign of Paddy. Larry was instinctively aware of the seriousness of this situation because Paddy was normally impatiently awaiting his feed of oats every morning as soon as he realised that Larry had woken up. The long standing routine, considered to be of vital importance, for the setting up of the animal's general health, strength and constitution for the day ahead, had always been rigorously adhered to in the past.

In an effort to revive his addled brains, Larry plunged his head under the surface of his water butt, spitting and spluttering loudly after he did so. He then noticed that the Paddock gate was ajar. He realised that in the state he had returned home from the Slip Inn the previous night it was undoubtedly his own fault. He dashed out stopping briefly at the gate to anxiously peer all around the Church and Vicarage grounds. Then he carefully scanned up and down the road. He was then conscious of the low rumbling noise which emanated from inside the newly opened Safari Park, now abutting onto the Church properties. He had been reliably told by Horace 'Pinky' Pink, Lady Lapleys' Game Keeper, this frequently audible noise was being caused by the hungry Lions in particular as they wandered around inside their extensive compound. Although Pinky had a reputation for being ever vigilant in his duties and he quite understandably considered Larry to be a potential poacher, Larry was satisfied that this information had been true because the unusual noise could sometimes be heard accompanied by proper bloody curdling roars.

The first person he happened to meet was the Curate Jeremy Smith-Eccles. Even someone as humble and low down in the pecking order as Larry, actually considered Jeremy to be a bit of a twit. Jeremy greeted Larry in a most cordial fashion.

"Well good day to you Lawrence…What a glorious autumnal day the Good Lord up above has blessed us with today.…Makes one happy to be alive.…What?"

Larry nodded, tried to smile but failing to do so. Before he could respond Jeremy added, in a concerned yet friendly and inviting manner,

"If I may be as bold as to say so you look a mite out of sorts.... Perhaps somewhat upset or even disturbed Lawrence....Does something ail you?"

Larry gulped hard before he managed to splutter,

"Morning Sir....You haven't seen my Paddy this morning have you?"

Jeremy paused, thinking momentarily,

"I trust we are referring to that fine Animal you keep tethered in the Paddock are we?"

Larry was becoming most impatient, anxious to find his horse.

"That's just it Sir....He should be in the Paddock but I can't find him....He's missing."

Not for a single second did Jeremy even consider the possible impact of his words as he replied in a rather jocular fashion,

"Let us hope he has not strayed into the Safari Park to become breakfast for a Lion or some other ferocious Beast...Eh?"

Jeremy allowed himself a chuckle as poor Larry instantly experienced a feeling that he was about to faint. He turned to dash down the road without uttering another word to Jeremy. Jeremy observed Larry's frantic reaction to his comments with a modicum of curiosity but even then he failed utterly to realise the shuddering effects they had had upon the obviously seriously distressed and genuinely concerned Larry.

Two hours soon passed by from the time when Larry had commenced his search for Paddy. He was growing more and more desperate with his abject and total lack of success in finding any trace of his faithful, cherished, animal. He had even been prepared to take a chance by visiting Pinky at his Cottage, inside the original part of the Park to no avail. He was still far from convinced that Paddy was safe despite Pinky genuine assurance that the Lion enclosure was seriously fenced off and almost impossible for a Horse to get through without assistance. In a moment of sheer desperation Larry noticed the door leading into the

Police Station was open. Without another thought Larry dashed inside. Constable Sooty Sutcliffe was on the telephone so he was obliged to anxiously wait until he could speak to him. Sooty finished his call by which time Larry was so upset he was on the brink of bursting into tears,

"Constable Sutcliffe I can't find Paddy....I think he might have strayed into the Safari Park by mistake and ended up as Lion meat.... Please....Please help me....Please sir."

Sooty was about to speak when Sergeant Blackburn, the new Officer in Charge, suddenly emerged from his Office to enquire,

"Lion meat? What do you mean? Who is Paddy? Is it your mate? Not your child I trust....Please do tell me more."

Sooty intervened before the panic stricken Larry could respond,

"Oh sorry Sergeant....You may not have had the pleasure of meeting Larry the Lamb....He lives in a wooden Caravan in the open air Paddock alongside the Parish Church....Paddy is Larry's horse Serg...It's a big black and white animal....A Cob I think is the correct description of the type of horse he is Serg."

After he had verified that there had not been any information remotely associated with horses or any other animals being observed on the loose reported to the local Police, Larry quickly departed after thanking them for their assistance. He then ran off down the High Street pathetically calling out Paddy's name. Larry soon found himself approaching the Municipal Tip where he happened to come across his new friend Spud Murphy. Spud, who was still in a shocking state of health after their sojourn the previous evening, was most sympathetic to Larry's situation. He instantly agreed to thoroughly search every inch of his locality in an effort to find the missing animal. By mid morning there were few People in the Town who were not aware of Larry's unfortunate circumstances and many were actively out and about looking for the missing horse.

Larry's attention was suddenly drawn to the loud tooting of a car horn. He turned to see Jeremy driving his little Mini car towards him. The Curate was flashing his headlights as he gesticulated to Larry enthusiastically indicating that he had some vital information. The car stopped and Jeremy, perhaps rather foolishly, invited Larry to sit alongside him on the front passenger seat. After he apologised for the tactless comments he had uttered earlier on in the day he went on to explain that the Vicar, Whistling Reggie in person, who had also joined in the search for Paddy, had driven outside the Town into the semi rural parts with the intention of conducting an extended search there. He had subsequently telephoned Jeremy in the Vestry with instructions for him to find Larry forthwith and then transport him up to Pringle's Farm on the Lancashire/Yorkshire Borders.

With all the windows open Jeremy drove with a purpose for more reasons than the sole desire to reach his destination as soon as possible. Larry was ecstatic as they drove into the ramshackle Farmyard because the first thing he saw was Paddy, in what might be described as an excited sexual state, securely tethered to a long heavy concrete water through. Basil Pringle and Reggie were standing alongside Reggie's car which had been carefully parked nearby. The sincere joy and pure relief pouring out of Larry was a joyful pleasure for anyone to witness.

Hugging and kissing Paddy continuously Larry eventually managed to express his heartfelt gratitude to everyone present for their help. Basil explained that his Mare, called Matilda, had come into season and despite the fact that his Farm was several miles away from the Paddock at the Vicarage Paddy had somehow followed the scent to find her. He had forced his way into the Stable where Matilda was being kept indoors. The Animals had no doubt got straight to work on what they had both been desperate to get on with. Larry was more than happy to walk Paddy back home. Paddy was not too keen to leave but Larry was able to force his Animal to accompany him out of the Yard as Reggie called out to him,

"It would appear that Paddy had his mind set on a different variety of oats this morning Lawrence….What?"

Jeremy actually laughed saying,

"By Jove Reginald that was a good one….How amusing another variety of oats….Yes I see….Oh yes you are a wit."

Basil, who was not noted for his natural sense of humour, actually managed to break out with a twisted smile on his gnarled face and he was obliged to choke a definite chuckle as it emerged.

One Man and his Horse happily made their way out of the Farmyard, at least one out of the two extremely relieved at the outcome of what had proved to be a most trying day. They were heading purposefully in the direction of their home base where the aforementioned other type of oats would be ready and waiting.

"I'm Goff…..Has he mentioned me?"

A mysterious crisis meeting, arranged to take place at Jenny and Eric's home, had been called by a rather flustered, agitated sounding, Bernadette Dougan. Kay, who had only recently returned to her duties as Manageress of Eric and Jenny's Shop on the High Street after giving birth to her child, was confidently able to leave her now fully trained Assistant, Mary Kelly, in complete charge of 'Bloomers' in her absence. She had swiftly wheeled baby Edward in his pram the short distance arriving at Jenny's home before any of the others. Linda arrived soon afterwards driving her, almost new, Ford Cortina car, a gift from Malcolm for being such a clever girl in the *'Giving birth'* stakes. She was accompanied by both of her small Children, Jane and new baby Sonja. Susan Summers was unable to attend because she had to collect her Children from school due to the fact that Joe was at work on the Afternoon Shift. Eric quickly managed to locate Sam who, fortunately, was working on a local building site. The men arrived together just as soon as Eric had been able to collect Sam before driving him around to their house.

After going through the delightful procedure which involved all present admiring all the new additions as well as paying due attention to little Amy and Jane Chumley, who were soon playing together in perfect harmony and with obvious glee, the grown ups all settled down over cups of tea and biscuits. Everyone keenly waited for Bernie to reveal the reason for all the intrigue and urgency.

Bernie, quite accustomed to addressing Groups of People through her job as a Solicitor, thanked them all for responding to her urgently sent contact message so quickly. After she thanked Jenny for providing her usual hospitality, she got down to explaining the reason for the crucial meeting.

"Well Boys and Girls I already thought Damien and I were being rushed at an indecent speed into a state of Holy Matrimony before this latest bombshell exploded….As some of you may already be aware Damien has an Elder Brother who emigrated to Vancouver in Canada many years ago….Well out of the blue he has sent two plane tickets and a generous cheque to his Parents inviting them to visit him and his Canadian Wife and their three rapidly growing Grandchildren…Whom they have never actually seen in the flesh."

Jenny, cautiously relieved with the input so far, was smiling when she said,

"Oh how lovely…What a smashing treat for the Couple…That's really nice."

There were mixtures of various sounds which all indicated total association with those remarks. Bernie continued,

"Yes…As anyone can well imagine they can hardly wait to go…. And that is where the problem area has arisen….They are flying out next Tuesday morning from Manchester Airport and they will be staying in Canada for just over a month….Now as you might well appreciate Damien and I have no wish to delay our Wedding for too long because of….Well you know….So…To get down to the crux of the matter Ladies and Gentlemen…We are booked in at the Registry Office at 4pm this Saturday for the deed to be done."

There were gasps accompanied by excited hand clapping from Kay and Linda.

"We appreciate that this is very short notice but Damien who was able to arrange this vital appointment this Saturday mainly through his connections at the Town Hall and as you have probably noticed he unfortunately cannot be with us until later because he has been run off his feet sorting out his Parents Passports and what have you because they have never been out the Country before…Damien and I would not dream of getting hitched without our closest Friends being there to witness the actual deed being done and of course be present to share our happy day together…And Mr and Mrs Harris would be extremely unhappy if they were to miss seeing their youngest Son safely married….So Saturday at four of the o'clock at the Town Hall it is…. Please make sure you are all there for us…And believe me…I really have got everything crossed here… Honestly….Please…Please don't tell me that these sudden but necessary arrangements will be likely to cause anyone any serious problems….Please."

Silence prevailed for several moments whilst all present took time to absorb and digest the exciting news. Suddenly everyone wanted to speak at once. Eventually they all agreed that the arrangements were fine which made Bernadette a very happy and relieved Lady. Eric volunteered to call at Susan and Joe's home to deliver the vital information, hot off the press, just as soon as he had dropped Sam off back at the building site where he had left Isaac working alone.

By the time Damien actually arrived at the house all the others had left. He hugged and kissed Bernie in front of Eric and Jenny after she indicated to him with a subtle nod that their hastily arranged plans would be going ahead without a hitch. Jenny and Bernie enjoyed playing with the Children whilst Eric and Damien were partaking of a much needed face to face chat. Damien appeared to be very relieved,

"Bloody hell Buddy…If it's not one thing it's another….I have managed to sort out all of the Folks travel documents…Still…The show must go or that's what they say….Now listen Ricky…Some of my many Colleagues want to have a few drinks with me on Friday evening and obviously I want you and Sam to be there as well."

Eric, pretended to be seriously shocked, as he glared at his friend,

"Did you think you could have a 'Piss up' without us being there to keep an eye on you then?"

They both laughed and then Damien continued,

"I know you're playing an away match in the Dart's League on Friday evening but as good luck would have it you will be over at the

'Dog and Duck' by the Canal which is not that far away from the 'Wellington' Pub where the Gang from work regularly meet together because my Boss Geoffrey Holmes….We all call him Goff….Well he lives close by…We are all planning to meet in there straight after work…. About a dozen of us at the most…Anyways the Landlord's Missus will be making a few butties and there will be some pies and sausage rolls and what have you …So I hope you and Sam won't mind….Play your matches and then make your way around to the Welly to join up with us….We can eventually end the evening's proceedings in the bar of the Club later…That's provided we are still able to walk by then."

Again they laugh as their devoted Ladies both gazed across at them expressing genuine relief that the clear evidence of a state of concordance was pleasantly being reached between the two Friends.

On the night Eric and Sam had been unavoidably delayed in the 'Dog and Duck' as a consequence of the very close outcome of their Dart's Match. The other Members of the away team had left immediately to enjoy their hard earned victory in the familiar surroundings of their own Clubhouse. Eric and Sam soon found themselves standing in a big comfortable room, called the 'Snug', inside the well appointed and roomy Wellington Hotel.

Although they could see that there were quite a few persons seated and standing around inside they were unable to see any sign of Damien or his Friends. A middle aged, quite frail looking, man dressed in a smart suit with collar and tie was seated at round table close to a serving hatch. They soon noticed that he was gesturing to them,

"Ricky….Sam…Are you here for Damien's Bachelor Night?"
Both nodded eagerly,
"I'm Goff…Has he mentioned me?…This is my local pub I only live around the corner…Not far away…Get yourselves a couple of pints before I fill you in with the sorry details."

He pressed Sam to take a pound note out of his hand,
"I'll have a Scotch…No make that a double Scotch and here"
He passed a small jug to Eric,
"Get some fresh water for me please….No ice."

The Barmaid was already attending to the order as Sam turned to face her. Goff smiled as he remarked to Eric,

"I love beer but unfortunately I can't drink it these days I have to stick to the shorts….Not got the capacity nowadays…Still it's better than being without a drink at all…..Eh?"

Goff patted the top of a stool placed alongside where he was sitting,

"Sit here Ricky…How do you do by the way."

Goff extended his right hand to Eric which caused Sam to deftly duck back from the bar to do the same. With drinks on the table Goff got on with the explanation,

"Sorry but I'm afraid it was all too much for Damien and the rest of those other Youngsters…The Youth of today cannot take their drink….Still….As you can probably deduce I am the sole survivor of the drinking session…About a dozen of us started on the booze straight from work this evening….When things started sinking slowly in the west Johnny the Landlord was kind enough to telephone Bernadette and she collected her drunken Fiancé and took him home in her car…. About half an hour ago that was…He was starting to talk broken biscuits and the rest of them were either in the bog puking up or they had stopped drinking all together…Still no permanent harm done eh? … I enjoy partaking of a Whiskey or two most evenings…I find it helps me to relax and get a good night's sleep…Makes the wife look better and more agreeable as well…Anyways….I'm very pleased to meet you both because Damien has told me a lot about your exploits together …He's been a new man since he joined up with you two…Unfortunately on the downside he appears to have suddenly discovered what his knob is really for…But anyways… I think all young men need to have good Mates around them when they are going through the long process of maturing that's what I always say…So let's get down to seeing off a few nice drinkies together eh? … Oh give Nellie behind the bar a shout…We put a couple of nice plates of food aside for you….Damien said you were always ready for a feed….In fact I think he intimated that you could both eat for Lancashire…Or was that England Eh? …

I really am pleased to have the chance to meet and get to know you both a little before the dreaded formalities start tomorrow…I always feel much more comfortable at these sort of formal Ceremonies when I find myself able to recognise at least some familiar faces….Drink up boys….Cheers…I'm really in the mood for a good session….Cheers Ricky…Cheers Sam."

They had then chinked their glasses together in a relaxed and convivial fashion.

After about an hour or so had passed by Eric and Sam were rapidly becoming more and more anxious about the obviously drunken state Goff was steadily getting himself into. His speech had now become slurred and he had started to chuckle to himself quite a lot. Eric and Sam were quite keen to move on, hoping finish the night off in the Club, so they politely asked Goff if he would care for a nightcap before they had to take their leave of him. Goff lurched forward on his seat, instantly causing Eric and Sam to appreciate that this suggestion might not be such a good idea bearing in mind the prevailing circumstances. Goff had now started to dribble slightly as he chirpily replied,

"Certainly….Absolutely…Is it my shout?"

Eric and Sam, whilst casually drinking a few pints of beer, had both made visits to the toilet in order to relieve themselves but Goff had not moved from his seat since their arrival. They soon dispatched their nightcaps. Eric and Sam both rose to their feet in preparation for their imminent departure. Goff seemed to be struggling to stand so they both stepped forward to assist him up onto his feet. Although he did seem a little unsteady they cautiously released their hold on him. Goff dropped like a stone knocking the table and the two stools flying on his journey to the carpeted floor. He narrowly avoided taking a nasty smack on his chin from the edge of the table on the way down. They quickly assisted him to his feet again and in an effort to avoid any further embarrassment, Eric and Sam, between them, bodily carried Goff outside the premises onto the pavement. Although Goff seemed to be in a rather limp state, once again, they carefully released their grip on him. Instantly they were required to react again because, Goff, then grinning and dribbling from the sides of his mouth, again dropped like a stone.

Eric and Sam were then getting most concerned about the drunken condition their new Friend had clearly got himself into. As good luck would have it, Goff had written down his home address and telephone number on the back of a beer mat well before he started to lose his senses completely. Eric had placed this information in his wallet so they were aware of his desired destination.

In the circumstances they decided to carry him the short distance to his home. Goff was draped between them with his shoes dragging along the pavement. They firmly grasped one arm each to enable them to hold Goff securely over their broad shoulders. Outside number 28 Lord Street, Goff's home, the three stopped. They decided to chance another attempt to get him to stand by himself, hopefully before his Wife or any of his Neighbours managed to catch sight of him. Again their new Friend immediately plummeted on his way to the ground. Fortunately they were able to anticipate this was about to happen even before they completely released him from their grasp. Fearing an unpleasant face to face confrontation with Mrs Holmes, Eric and Sam carefully placed Goff, seated in an upright position, propped up against the front door on his doorstep. Anxiously gazing into each others eyes they both nodded a signal before Eric nervously pressed the door bell and they ran down the street like Whippets. They were out of sight in a matter of seconds.

After this trying experience Eric and Sam decided that they would forgo any more of the demon drink. They headed straight for Billy the Chip's Shop on Huddersfield Road where they bought delicious fish suppers for their beloved Wives who had, presumably, been waiting patiently for them both to return to their homes as usual after their Dart's Match.

Eric had some necessary work to carry out the following morning before he even thought about getting ready for the important gathering at the local Registry Office. He was putting stock out in the shop when Jenny shouted down to him from Kay and Sam's flat above him,

"Ricky….Phone….It's Damien….Says it's urgent."

Eric quickly spoke to his friend,

"What's up with you Buddy not got cold feet have you?"

Without the slightest sign of a snigger or titter, Damien adopted a most serious tone,

"No….Don't be daft….Listen Ricky what happened to Goff last night? I hope you can help because his Missus has just been on the phone to me with a terrible attitude….She says he's in a shocking state…May not be able to make the Wedding unless he bucks up quite considerably she reckons."

Eric felt a blush rapidly working its way through as he hastily attempted to explain what had happened,

"Look….He was really pissed and we decided the best thing we could do was make sure he got home safely…It wasn't far away as you probably know….We carried him all the way and then we just left him outside his house on the door step….I have to admit we didn't hang about for a number of very good reasons."

There followed a fairly long silence which Eric found was quite unnerving, not to mention, frightening. Eric now found himself shouting down the phone,

"Hello….HELLO! Specky! Are you still there?"

Damien's voice then took on an even more sinister tone,

"Eric….Listen carefully to what I have to say now Buddy…What is puzzling Mrs Holmes as well as myself at this moment in time I might add…Is how the hell Goff managed to get himself home without his bloody Wheelchair."

Eric instantly felt that he was about to pass out, he actually felt his knees buckling, he almost lost his composure as well as his balance,

"WHEELCHAIR! What wheelchair? What are you talking about I don't know anything about any bloody Wheelchair."

Damien could then be heard sighing very loudly and deeply,

"Ricky…. Goff has been confined to a Wheelchair for many years…. He is paralysed from the waist down….He pisses straight into a little bag fastened to his leg….He has his own personal little Nook inside the snug at the Welly adapted so that his Wheelchair slots in without any problems Oh no….Don't tell me you….Oh no! … Bloody hell fire!…. Ricky I'm sorry Buddy but I think you had better keep quiet about this whole incident….I'll phone Johnny at the pub I'll ask him to make the necessary arrangements to drop Goff's chair off at his home….Bloody hell fire Ricky…. This really is hard to believe. I suppose we will laugh about this at some stage in the distant future but let's get the rest of today behind us without any further shocks before then…..Bloody hell fire Ricky!"

Without further comment Damien put the phone down. He had already started to splutter with laughter as he tried very hard to actually visualise the astonishing scene as it had been acted out the previous night outside the Wellington and on the way back to Lord Street.

Eric needed to call in at Mitchell's Nursery, which he and Jenny now part owned ever since Dickie's semi-retirement. He needed to collect fresh supplies of flowers and vegetables for their shop. He just happened to spot Sam and Isaac as they were doing a *Foreigner'* working on the roof of a house on his route. After carefully attracting Sam attention the two men walked a short distance away from any prying ears whilst Sam updated his friend on what Damien, the current man of the moment, had just told him about Goff. Sam was understandably shocked and immediately concerned.

"Bloody hell fire Ricky….Is he O.K.? … No-one mentioned a Wheelchair…Not even Goff….Or anyone else in that bloody Pub…No wonder we had to carry the poor Bastard….I realised he was quite pissed but you might have expected a mention of something as important as that by someone….Eh? … I have to admit I thought he must have had a bloody big bladder capacity because I had two slashes without him visiting the bog at all….I know he was on shorts but even so…."

Eric interrupted him in mid sentence,

"He has a bag fastened on his leg Sam….Pisses straight into it without the need to undo any buttons or pull any zips down….Specky reckons we should keep quiet about it because he doesn't think Goff will be able to remember anything himself…So…Mum's the word….

I just hope he doesn't end up missing the Wedding…Oh and another thing….Bernie has booked the Private Room at the Vaughan Arms for a meal and drinkies after we clear from the Registry Office….Thank Christ the Happy Couple are not short of a bob or two….We should get a good feed there….Bloody hell fire…Sounds like another thick head tomorrow…Right….Well I'm off or I won't be going to the Wedding myself….Tarra for now."

Eric drove off in his van leaving Sam to stand quietly on the pavement alone. He had found himself having great difficulties as he tried his best to take in all the incredible information he had just been given. After a few minutes he slowly started to shake his head, he then smiled to himself, and eventually began to laugh out aloud. Suddenly he, rather self consciously, glanced up and down the Street to check if his strange behaviour in Public was being observed by anyone, before he hastily returned to his roof job.

"Oh no…..The mind boggles."

What fantastic, exciting, alas also sad, nevertheless extremely memorable events have been taking place in the small Mill Town of Lapley Vale over the twelve months which had elapsed since those, Christmas Eve of 1968, celebrations got off to a fabulous start with the Church Wedding and Reception brought about by the marriage of Sam Best to Kay Brown.

Possibly considered to be the most outstanding occurrence above all of the other things happening over the period was the welcome arrival of the four healthy, Bouncing Babies, all coming into the World within a 24 hour period. Evidence, if proof was ever needed, that one small Group of close Friends had all shared their individual conceptions at more or less the same time. This astonishing outcome probably occurred as a result of them all being able to feel completely relaxed so that they could extract the maximum enjoyment from those extra Christmas Festivities. This happy co-incidence would now be forever etched into all of their memory banks for ever and a day. Each Member of the Group of true Friends would from now on be able to revel in masses of enjoyable, happy, reminiscences as a consequence of the inevitable arrival of their annual four joint Birthday Celebrations.

There was the tragic and sudden death of the familiar Town Tramp Jedd Clampett which was then followed by all of those astonishing revelations about his undisputed heroic past. Not one person in Lapley Vale would have credited the subsequently established fact that Jedd had been a highly decorated Army Officer during the Second World War before he drifted into the life of a humble Vagrant. On the plus side there had been a most satisfactory, rewarding and morally acceptable, result to the impudent and unjustified claim made against the Dead Man's considerable estate from his estranged Widow of long standing. Bearing in mind the multitude of obvious difficulties faced this was an excellent achievement with merit being shared equally as a result of the high level of co-operation and determined dedication to search for fairness which had been exhibited by the Army, Bert McCabe and some of the members of the Lapley Vale Section of the Lancashire Constabulary not to mention Whistling Reggie, the Vicar of All Souls Parish Church, his dear Wife Sybil and finally, but by no means in the least, Jeremy Smith-Eccles the Curate.

Then there was the much heralded opening of the Safari Park in the magnificent grounds of Lapley Manor. This monumental modern type of advancement in, the increasingly common provision of new and exciting places of Leisure, Interest and Amusement, opening up for the convenience and pleasure of the General Public had been welcomed with open arms by all of those involved in such a gargantuan task. This event was in a large part responsible for the most welcome restoration to an acceptable comfort zone of Lady Lapleys once embattled and sadly declining Family finances. As might well have been anticipated, the ever popular local aristocrat, Her Ladyship had boldly displayed considerable courage and formidable foresight when she elected to embark on such a potentially precarious project. There were clear signs to indicate that she would very soon be guaranteed a sound financial footing in the future as the interest in the attraction had been so great the Visitor figures were rapidly exceeding even their most optimistic expectations. Lady Lapleys personal security also ensured a happy future for the entire Group of Employees and other Dependants who unashamedly rely upon her to make a considerable contribution towards their comfortable existing standards of living. This thrilling and attractive Leisure Feature had also been responsible for helping to put the small Town of Lapley Vale on the Tourist Map, so to speak.

Following on from these events there was the enforced retirements, by reason of age, of Inspector Bill Kinley and Sergeant Bert McCabe after their long and mostly distinguish careers in the Police Service. Bert was extremely reluctant to go. Fortunately, through Bert's enduring mutual admiration and genuine friendship with Her Ladyship, both he and Alice had now been able to settle into a beautiful Cottage inside the remaining Private Portion of the Lapley Manor grounds. Bert was able to avoid taking any unnecessary risks with his and Alice's' future by being able to decline the offer to be an Employee of the Ultra Commercial Chadderton Brothers at the Safari Park. He was able to take advantage of a much less taxing role as a Court Usher at the local Magistrates' Courts. Obviously familiar with his new working surroundings and vastly experienced in Court procedures this job had now afforded him, the not previously available, guarantee of taking every Saturday and Sunday off. This desirable and much sort after state of affairs had always been fondly referred to in Police circles as an E.S.S.O. turn. These turns were cherished by many of those engaged in the Fight against Crime because most necessarily worked shifts over each and every 24 hour period. Many other Office Workers throughout the entire Country also enjoyed a familiar mnemonic relating to Fridays. This was known as P.O.E.T.S day (Piss off Early Tomorrow is Saturday). Popularly practiced in most of the various Businesses you may wish to contact as a matter of urgency after 4pm on any Friday afternoon.

To top off all of these magnificent milestones there was the marriage of Damien and Bernie Harris, albeit unscheduled due to Bernie's unexpected but nevertheless welcomed pregnancy. Joe Summers actually behaved impeccably at all the formal stages of the rather muted celebrations despite the ready availability of endless supplies of free drinks. This less than predicable outcome in the sobriety stakes had been achieved, in no small part, as a result of the very close supervision he had been subjected to by his long suffering Wife Susan. Damien's immediate Boss at the Town Hall, Goff Holmes, accompanied by his Wife, attended without a hitch. As correctly anticipated by Damien when he conversed with Eric earlier in the day, Goff had no recollection whatsoever of the actual happenings during the later portion of the Bachelor Night's booze up. This state of affairs had been greeted with great deal of personal relief by Eric and Sam. This had been because they had rather unjustifiably considered themselves in someway responsible for the dreadful drunken condition Goff had fallen into. The Newlyweds set off on their Honeymoon in Bernie's car. The Group of Friends were all aware of the prospect that the Young Couple would be moving to Milton Keynes very soon. They were setting off on a touring Honeymoon around the Cotswold and Home Counties including a trip to Milton Keynes to enable each of them to be available to attend Pre-arranged Interviews built into their tight schedule. If, as anticipated, everything went according to plan they would be taking up their new jobs and moving to a Brand New Detached House at the beginning of the New Year.

This Small Group of close Friends in Lapley Vale were currently wondering what the coming year would bring as the, soon to be infamous, 1960's would inevitably become the 1970's on New Year's Day.

The obvious changes in British Society were now beginning to filter through to some of the less Cosmopolitan parts of our Country. Giant strides in Technology were now being enjoyed, directly or indirectly, by most of the wide spread Populace. There was little doubt that the quality and availability of daily television newscasts together with many new exciting films, programmes, and productions, mostly emanating from the U.S.A., had been one of the most noticeable factors which heralded massive social changes, not just to people's life styles, but also to the much less submissive attitudes now frequently being demonstrated towards all forms of accepted Authority and even affecting Law and Order. Very few homes were now without a television set although quite a significant few people had deliberately not purchased one through their own personal choice. This sort of deliberate isolation soon convinced the vast majority of the People that the folly of the *'Ostrich Syndrome'*, hiding of heads in the sand, would eventually be seen as an insular, unhelpful and poorly thought out, disastrous course of action.

The spread of much less subservient, bolder, attitudes directly effecting many ordinary People, who had previously been prepared to suffer in silence, were being heavily promoted and encouraged by the ever increasing completely new, and in soon cases quite over powering, varieties of popular music. This had been made readily available to anyone wishing to listen to these new innovations on their much improved wide choice of affordable, now available in portable form, transistor radio sets. The old fashioned BBC Home Service, Light and Third Programme, had suddenly become outdated and had rapidly become a thing of the past. They had been replaced by more relaxed BBC Radio One, Two, Three and Four. Numerous Independent Radio Stations, some illegal, were also broadcasting, some of them for 24 hours a day, available to Listeners in many parts of the Country. One popular Station was actually broadcasting from a Ship moored three miles off the British Coast. A bold Commercial Enterprise created to avoid breaking existing Laws proved to be very popular and surprisingly heavily subscribed to. These new approaches to the provision of all aspects of news forecasting and frequent reporting together with the introduction of the more and more daring and outrageous music mainly recorded on *'LP's and Singles'* by *'Groups'* or *'Bands'* rather than solo Tenors, Sopranos and other Individual Performers were slowly but surely being accepted by the vast majority of People as the modern norm. The on and off stage conduct exhibited by some of the Members of these Pop Groups, as they were being called, left a lot to be desired. There was a genuine fear that their bad influence on the Younger Generation had definitely become a major cause for concern in many quarters. Possibly emanating from across the Atlantic Ocean the pushing and taking of so called *'Performance enhancing'* or *'stimulating'* illegal, not to mention dangerous, Drugs was soon becoming quite common place. An enormous future problem was rapidly building up with certain tragedy on the horizon for many trusting Families and their Friends alike. Inexplicably there now seemed to be a complete lack of any positive action being taken by *'The Powers that be'* (That Ostrich Syndrome again?). Many tried and tested traditionally held values were being surely and steadily eroded without any signs of redress. Perhaps this was inevitable as People were now starting to believe the *'You have never had it so good'* speech, famously quoted by former Prime Minister Harold McMillan some years previously. There was also a growing fear that the clearly increasing power and influence of the Trade Unions was becoming far too great and the looming probability of serious future conflict was now starting to seem very likely.

Apart from the stunning new hair styles and the wearing of more daring, colourful, clothing, now regularly being worn and accepted as normal, little had really changed as far as the vast majority of the average Citizens of the Town of Lapley Vale were concerned. The strong bonds formed by close Family contacts as well as an inbred devotion to considerate caring within their Community would need a considerably long period of time to die out. They would definitely not simply fade away overnight.

In keeping with their updated and recently adopted fresh approach to their provision of entertainment in the Clubroom the Committee of the Lapley Vale Sports and Social Club had laid on a modern Disco complete with ridiculous looking Disc Jockey (Sammy Baxter an operative in a horrible foul smelling tanning factory in Oldham) as well as two houses of 'Bingo' (Unfortunately for those pioneers of modern trends and practices the numbers were being called by Charlie Walsh). This now enormously popular game was formally known as the children's pastime of 'Lotto'. These special features were still enhanced the by the usual, ever in demand, Christmas Eve supper of meat and tatter pie, mushy peas and pickled cabbage. The Committee had been able to authorise the distribution of most welcome vouchers, redeemable at the bar, to all the Old Age Pensioners amongst their Membership. These generous gifts were given with sincere wishes for them to treat themselves to a Seasonal round of free drinks paid for out of the ever growing Club's profits. Every Pensioner also received a free raffle ticket on entry into the Clubroom which guaranteed every one of them a nice prize ranging from bottles of Sherry, Sacks of potatoes and other Vegetables to several Oven Ready Turkeys. All the prizes had been generously and willingly donated by many of the Local Business and Trade Folks.

The whole evening turned out to be a massive success, made even more enjoyable and memorable by the unexpected arrival of Dick Rigby, local Butcher and Fishmonger, in his other popular role as the Band Master and talented Conductor of the Lapley Vale Brass Band. He arrived in the company of a few of his best Musicians all carefully carrying their own precious instruments. They made sure that every Person present in the Clubroom was treated to a thoroughly enjoyable Christmas Carol interlude. This initially appeared to be resented by the modern Disco fanatics but before the Musicians had completed their recital everyone, including Sammy Baxter, joyfully joined in singing the familiar, traditional, and much loved Carols. Ralph, Victor and Alf later reflected and then appreciated just how fortunate they had been to catch Dick and his Troupe of Musicians during the earlier part of the evening because their annual Christmas performances inevitably tended to deteriorate as the provision of free drinks at every venue visited all became too much for them to maintain their ability to play as well as talk and in some cases to actually walk.

In what might be considered a sign of the times even most of the more Elderly Members now no longer expected a Disc Jockey to be on horseback or even remotely associated in any way with Racing.

At the Club's Annual General Meeting, held earlier in the year, Bert McCabe had been voted onto the Committee as a replacement for the antagonistic and mostly abrasive and unhelpful Bernie Price. A development much welcomed by his life long arch enemy, the quite harmless and unfortunately often hapless, Billy 'Cockeye' Dawes. Ralph Bates the much respected Chairman, Victor Callow the dedicated, trustworthy, Secretary/Treasure along with all the other long serving Committee Members were re-elected without any further challenges being made. Alf, not an elected Member of the Committee but ever present at Meetings as an Advisor, remained as the trusted and valued Bar Steward. Finally The Lapley Vale Bowling and Social Club could never be the same without Woody Green as their cherished Green keeper.

Fortunately Woody had been ably assisted for some considerable time by his enthusiastic understudy, none other than, Eric McCabe. Although Eric's heavy work load had been increased again since Woody and Eddie Brown had been honoured with their selection to the Lancashire County Crown Green Bowling Team, the Young Apprentice had never been found wanting. Neither had he ever been heard to utter one word of disapproval or complaint. Eric exhibited a healthy attitude and a commendable aptitude, as well as a vast capacity, for taking on seriously hard work.

The Clubroom emptied surprisingly early as Christmas Eve was surely giving way to Christmas Day. The most likely reason for this happening had to have been the inherent desire of the majority of the Members to be at home in the bosom of their Families, in particular with their Children, at this emotional and extra special time of the year. This exodus had allowed the 'Bitter enders' to enjoy one of their usual quiet nightcap sessions seated around the bar with Alf tending to their every need.

Reflecting upon the evening, Eddie Brown raised the conduct of the infamous Joe Summers once again. During the course of the evening Joe had called in with his equally stupid drinking partner Fred Bates. They had been much the worse for drink when they arrived. They had soon managed to draw attention to themselves when Joe, possibly in his own twisted way, attempted to join in the Happy Festivities when he stood up to yell out, "Never mind the bloody mistletoe….Where's the sage and onion?" This remark was much to Fred's amusement but swift and positive action had been called for and duly taken. Eddie was delighted to point out that the two Annoying Presences had been thrown out by a few unimpressed Ordinary Members who were intent upon enjoying the evening, without unwelcome interference from Idiots, in the company of their Wives, Families and Friends. Norman perked up to merrily chip in,

"No need for you to take your choppers out tonight then Bert."

Grinning broadly Bert retorted,

"I would have happily left Joe to you Norm….One word from you and both of those Brainless Efforts would have crapped themselves… Eh? … Eh? … As I clearly overheard someone remarking it would be rather nice if Father Christmas put a new fully operational brain in Joe's stocking this year…Mind you….He would be in for a bloody good hiding from Susan when he got home in the state he was in…Eh? … Eh?"

Ralph remarked upon the great pleasure everyone had derived from witnessing their older Members enjoying such a memorable night. Victor was quick to recollect their, not so far in the distant past, brush with near Financial Disaster,

"What a treat for us to find ourselves in a position where we are able to give money away without any worries….That Kenneth Gordon Trust….Remember that? This Club will be for ever grateful for the timely financial intervention provided….Even though we still have no idea who was behind it you may take my word for this it my Friends the Trust was definitely responsible for putting us squarely back on the road to a safe and secure future and I consider that things might well have been very different without the unselfish generosity shown by that Wonderful Benefactor."

Bert allowed a crafty wink to pass between him and Woody. Woody exhibited no noticeable reactions at all as they all grunted their agreement with Victor's comments. Of all those present only Bert was aware that Kenneth Gordon Green, exclusively known locally as Woody, had been the anonymous Benefactor. His secret would continue to remain safe so as long as Woody wished for such a State of Affairs to continue. Due to his unbridled generosity which, taken together with Woody's affection and loyalty to the Club, a man with no real desire to be rich, ensured that the Kenneth Gordon Trust had long since been exhausted and then wound up but not before a great deal of genuine happiness had been liberally shared amongst Woody's many chosen Friends.

The elite Group of Friends exchanged sincere Seasonal Good Wishes whilst they were all enjoying their nightcaps. Alf then drew their attention to the fact that a heavy fall of snow was quickly covering over the surface of their Car Park. Although this offering from the Heavens was especially desirable at Christmas, Bert was the first to remark,

"Well that certainly makes for the end of a perfect night Gents….Eh? Eh?….Can you imagine the sheer thrill it will provide for those Children of all ages waking up to eagerly see what Santa Claus has left for them in their stockings left under their decorated trees….Eh?….Eh?… Looking out through their frosted windows on a Christmas Card scene in their own Streets and Gardens…Having said that I don't think we should tarry much longer if we want to be safely in our own beds tonight….By the looks of things there could be a strong possibility of us getting snowed in….That's a good enough warning for me….Can I offer a lift to anyone on as I make my way home to my new exclusive place of dwelling? … Eh? … Eh?"

Ralph was first to respond,

"Bloody Hell Fire Bert…What a tragedy that would be….Stranded inside here with a cellar still half full of delicious beer….Hardly a fate worse than death to my way of thinking….Oh no….The mind boggles… Seriously though I agree that the most sensible course of action for us all is the one already suggested…That is if we want to enjoy the rest of the Christmas still talking to all of our loved ones."

They all laughed as Eddie said,

"If I don't get myself home to my own bed very soon I will be finding out what they serve for Christmas Dinner at the Cottage Hospital…I'm very much afraid that my Missus would not be able to see the funny side of any accidental occurrence like that…Anyways….Bert…I am given to understand that we will be sharing the Special Day with our new Grandchild….Or should I say in my case….Great….Grandchild… I have been told that you have got them visiting you for Dinner and then we will be having them round at ours for their Tea….I wouldn't miss that for a million quid…Little Edward Brown the Third….Sorry my mistake Edward Best's first Christmas….Beautiful name that Edward…Eh? … …Just imagine that….Starting up all over again….Having your very first Christmas."

All those present sighed. They were able to appreciate that Eddie had spoken those words straight from his big heart. They all knew exactly what he meant, even the two single men in their company. The warm glow being felt by the Friends was not entirely being enjoyed as a result of the consumption of a large quantity of quality beer they had all merrily consumed during the course of a most memorable night.

Christmas Day was duly celebrated by all of those concerned, without any untoward incidents or disasters occurring. The 'Bitter-enders' had been well advised to leave the Clubhouse when they did because the snow fall had been very prolonged and because of the prevailing freezing temperatures was not thought likely to thawing for some considerable time. The carpet of thick snow caused the Industrial, grimy and dirty, Mill Town to take on the false appearance resembling some picturesque Alpine Town, at least for as long as the weather remained constant, because everywhere was entirely covered by a perfectly white, clean, and crisp covering blanket.

The celebration for New Year's Eve provided a stark contrast to those of Christmas Eve inside the Lapley Vale Bowling and Social Club. Sandwiches and shop bought meat pies, not to mention seasonal mince pies, were plated up and served by way of refreshments. These had been prepared earlier in the day by the ever capable and accommodating Mavis Green together with her little band of eager helpers. The vast majority of their Older Members who enjoyed Christmas Eve in the Clubroom were noticeably absent. Many were carrying out overnight babysitting duties which had enabled the Younger Members of their Families to enjoy what would invariably end up as nothing short of a monumental piss up.

Sammy Baxter had been in his elements playing all the latest and most popular music records to a mainly receptive and very appreciative and interactive Audience. Every inch of the small dance floor had been in use causing many of the Revellers to be forced to cautiously gyrate, sorry dance, around their tables which were all covered with their drinks and food on paper plates.

Alf and Denise had been ably assisted by their new apprentice Barman, Trevor Simmons. Trevor had been selected for promotion from Waiter and Glass gatherer to be broken in as back up to the regular Bar Staff. His mate Billy Boy Speke and one of their other Mates had been carrying out all of the most menial, yet essential, tasks. In fairness they had also been making a very good job of it until they eventually lost the use of their wits swiftly followed by their powers of speech and then their legs. Billy Boy and his Assistant, another spotty youth called Stevie, greedily ensured that the glasses they were charged with collecting were well and truly empty before they were offered up for washing. A not too brilliant idea as events turned out.

There had been an expected heavy demand for draught Lager because of the very impressive presence of large numbers of the Younger Generation but the 'Bitter Enders', ensconced in their usual positions, probably managed to down a greater volume of Best Bitter by far, despite their comparative lack of presence in actual numbers.

There had been mass chaotic frivolity when the New Decade invariably arrived on the stroke of midnight. The sound system was able to transmit the actual gongs from Big Ben after Sammy had managed to tune into Radio One. Mass shaking of hands, kissing, hugging and crafty feeling of arses and the like were accompanied by a prolonged deafening volume of sound. Although probably not appreciated by the Older Generation this momentous occasion was definitely considered to have been suitably greeted as far as most of the Younger Generation were concerned. Alf had taken the precaution of instructing his Staff to stop serving to most people when drunkenness could well have been responsible for the distinct possibility of unwanted unpleasantness rearing its ugly head had inevitably threatened. Most of those present had had enough anyways. A very joyous and mostly contented Crowd swiftly cleared after the first tentative moves had been made. As might have been expected as usual the 'Bitter Enders' were left to continue the welcome joyfully being extended to the arrival of the 1970's.

"What did you charge him with Bert?"

The New Decade was not very old at all when the first notable incident occurred in the small, now fairly well known, due to the amazing success of the new Safari Park, Town of Lapley Vale.

The clock on the Town Hall was striking 10pm as Constable Eddie Littlejohn; the 'Gentle Giant', was inside the front Office fully engaged in the recording of telephone messages which were being received at Rochdale Divisional Headquarters as a result of the *'Hour end'* Policing System adopted for practical reasons at Lapley Vale Police Station. All telephone calls made to the Station were automatically transferred in the event of the absence of Officers from their Station because it was never continuously manned. There was a familiar blue *Police Box'* imbedded in the wall at the front of the Building prominently situated alongside the stout metal studded wooden Front Door. This Box was there for any immediate use by any member of the General Public wishing to make immediate contact with their Police. The telephone kept inside the Box connected the Caller with an Officer at Rochdale DHQ at all times throughout the 24 hours. If the call was not deemed urgent it would be passed on later to any Officer from Lapley Vale Section as and when they happened to call into their Station. In normal circumstances this would be at the end of each hour. Hence the term *'Hour end Police Station'* used quite extensively in many of the more Rural Areas of mostly County Police Forces.

Eddie was carefully writing on a message pad as he leant over the elevated desk situated alongside the, tried and trusted yet possibly old fashioned, telephone switchboard. His new Sergeant, Blackie Blackburn, was relieving himself in the toilet inside number one cell when an urgent '999' call was relayed through to Eddie from DHQ. Blackie and Eddie had just been out and about paying routine visits to Licensed Premises throughout the evening. They would have been considered either rude or possibly strongly suspected of acting in a devious or strange manner if they ever chanced to decline any offers of a drink in each and every one of the many Licensed Premises on their long visiting list.

Eddie was able to instantly recognise the panic stricken voice of Dick Turpin, who was the Landlord of the 'Tim Bobbin' Public House on the High Street,

"Oh thank Christ it's you Eddie can you get yourself down here tout bloody suite please….We've had to barricade a Group of those weird Hippie Flower Power People or whatever they're called in our Snug for their own safety…I was forced to protect them before my Regulars set about them and really flattened them….Please come Eddie….Ben…You know Ben my First Man don't you? … Ben is holding the Mob back but I don't know for how long…"

Eddie responded with enthusiasm,

"Bloody Norah…Keep them there Dick….We'll be with you in a flash."

Slamming the phone down the young, now highly excited Constable, yelled out,

"Serg….Give it a final shake will you….We're needed at the Tim Bobbin without further delay and as soon as possible….If not even sooner….Bloody Norah….Stand by for action."

On their arrival at the popular and very well patronised 'Tim Bobbin', generally considered locally to be a rather rough Pub, the mere presence of the two Burly Policemen was sufficient to cause most of the angry Regulars, who had been doing their best to attack a small Group of four outrageously dressed people, to back off immediately. One or two of the Hippies were merrily singing as they enjoyed the benefit of the security being provided by a small annexed room, known as the Snug, just off the much larger Main Bar. Dick was in a highly excited and flustered state which seemed to ease slightly when he saw Blackie and Eddie had arrived. All of the Aggressors were now back in the Main Bar sitting quietly and peacefully at their tables sipping their drinks. Dick glared at them before, clearly influenced by the presence of Blackie and Eddie, he felt brave enough to mock them.

"Oh….Butter wouldn't melt in their mouths now….A few minutes ago they were all very keen on carrying out Mass Murder by Lynching.…"

The floor of the Bar was strewn with crushed and damaged flower blooms and many long stems. Ben the Barman, under considerable pressure, shouted to Blackie,

"They've sneaked a bloody old wreck of a Charabanc onto the car park round the back….You can't miss it has been daubed with every bloody colour of the rainbow and then some more….The Soft Bastards wandered in here singing and throwing flowers at all the Chaps in the bar….They were chanting something like *'Make peace not war'*… That was it wasn't it Dick?"

Dick nervously nodded without speaking as Ben continued,

"They wouldn't be told when they were strongly advised to… Ahem….Clear off….They kept throwing the bloody flowers around all over the place….As you can well imagine they were soon under attack…Most of the Attackers were going to shove their flowers up their arses….And they meant it as well…I managed to push them into the temporary safety provided by the Snug.….Thank Christ you got here quickly I was starting to lose the Battle…Can you get them out of here Serg?…Please…They're definitely getting on everybody's nerves…. Mine included."

As usual Eddie was smiling as he adopted his familiar amenable approach. He carefully scanned all of the guilty looking faces belong to the Men who were now sitting quietly in the bar. Eddie was big enough to deter even the most desperate person from even contemplating any sort of attack on him so; inevitably, he rarely needed to be aggressive. Blackie quickly weighed up the four scruffy looking People who were dressed in long loose fitting fleece trimmed sheep skin coats which were draped over their ragged yet colourful casual clothing. They were all wearing really delicate threaded daisy chains around their necks and they were showing lots of colourful strips of embroidered braid and silk ribbons especially entwined in their long, unkempt and dirty looking hair. They were still holding onto lots of freshly picked flowers available for use as peace offerings, or ammunition depending on your personal point of view, cradled in their arms. These flowers definitely looked very similar to those known to be growing in a number of the private gardens in the Street running alongside the rear car park of the Pub.

The Sergeant addressed them firmly,

"Right….Outside! NOW! Out!"

The smiling, apparently unconcerned, Hippies shuffled past Blackie making their ways towards the front door without a sign of haste, but suddenly one of them decided to shout out,

"Make peace not war".

This seemed to trigger them all off because they immediately started to throw their flowers around inside the Bar again. The Regulars in the Bar roared their disapproval which caused Blackie and Eddie to unceremoniously force the Hippies through the door to the forecourt outside. They whisked them around the side of the Pub straight to the place where their vehicle was parked. Blackie then insisted upon them climbing on board without further delay. Blackie was clearly annoyed because he was noisily growling,

"Right Eddie get yourself behind the wheel of this load of shite and drive it up to the Police Station…NOW! We can sort this out up there. I'll go ahead of you…I'll open up ready for your arrival…Don't stand any messing from them Eddie…Christ what a Shower….Whatever next?"

After swiftly making himself familiar with the controls on the vehicle, Eddie tentatively started the engine which suddenly erupted with a very loud backfire bang and rattling noises accompanied by clouds of black smoke. Very slowly and gently the Constable drove off heading in the direction of the Police Station which was situated further up the High Street with all four Hippies, still singing, showing little adverse reaction to what had definitely been a very close encounter with violence. They were obviously content at being driven along in their own vehicle by the friendly Constable completely unperturbed by their current state of close arrest.

The scene to be witnessed inside the Bridewell was one of chaos. The persistently annoying behaviour of the Hippies had very soon convinced Blackie that they would need to be locked up in the Cells for the night. They would be officially charged with using conduct which was likely to cause a breach of the peace contrary to Common Law before being arraigned before the Court. There was no provision for bail under Common Law so the four Guests were assured of staying in custody until they appeared before a Magistrate in Rochdale Magistrates' Court the following morning.

Blackie was soon astonished to find that one of the four Scruffy Prisoners sharing the two available Cells was a Female. Eddie had been able to remember the Hippies from a previous visit they had made to the Town. They eventually ended up fist fighting in the Precinct with a very strange Band of *Hare Krishna Followers'* which had been, sort of, refereed by none other than the drunken religious zealot, Amos Quirke. Eddie was not sure if they were in fact the same Group of People but he considered them to be very similar because of their outlandish appearances. He was soon able to dig out the *'Occurrence Register'* kept at the Station as a permanent record of the entire previous incident.

"I've just checked out our records Serg….I think she…The one with Tits….May be called Myfanwy Owens…I think I recognise her…She originally comes from Abergavenny in Wales of all places and I bet the Others were all Locals at one time or at least not far from it before they took to their nomadic life style….Bloody Norah….No wonder they stink….That old Bus they use reeks like a Ancient Skunk's Shithouse…. Oh by the way Sergeant Bert just kicked their asses out of it after he had administered one of his World famous Double Barrelled Bollockings…. Didn't bother to officially charge them just made a record for future reference in the Books at the time….They never learn do they?"

The identity of the Woman was soon established. She freely admitted that she was the very same Myfanwy as had been strongly suspected by Eddie. The three Men had all originally been natives of the Oldham and surrounding areas up to the time when they decided to take to the road as Ambassadors for Peace. As they had now been legally classified as *'Of No fixed abode'* their fate for enforced incarceration was doubly sealed. They all quickly fell asleep chanting to themselves as if they did not have a worry in the World. The three Men were separated from Myfanwy for the usual reasons of decency. The Men were highly amused by this action as they were all very familiar with every nook and cranny of the Woman who they apparently considered to be the joint property of the whole Group. She was glad to have a Cell to herself; the Men were rather cramped but never raised even the slightest hint of any complaint.

Early the next morning, much to Sergeant Blackburn's initial annoyance, Kitty the Station Cleaner made the Prisoners mugs of tea accompanied by unlimited rounds of thick buttered toast, all provided at her own expense, without her even thinking about making any charge to anyone. Kitty would have provided the exact same treatment for the Devil himself if she thought he had been in need of her tender care and attention. The Divisional van had been called in to take the four Hapless Clowns to Rochdale. Blackie caused the Charabanc to be moved to the Scrap Yard at the rear of Barry Hancock's Garage for safe keeping with a view to it eventually being disposed of or more likely destroyed. The question of valid road tax, driving licenses and third party insurance cover, had been put to one side for the time being. Blackie considered that charging them with traffic offences would probably end up delaying their desired departure from the locality because there would be little or no chance of them being able to find any money to pay fines. In his opinion the best outcome was for the Court to issue *'Common Law Binding Over Orders'* for each one of them. If necessary they could always take further appropriate action at a later time.

The vile stench of mainly body odour was wafting up into the Courtroom well before the four bedraggled Defendants actually made their appearance in the Open Dock. Bert McCabe, wearing his official

Court Usher's gown, was standing with his back to the door, happily grinning from ear to ear. There were a few cries of disapproval and sounds indicative of disgust emanating from some of the Members of the General Public who were present in the room. Even some of the Court Officials were annoyed and distressed as the Hippies actually emerged from the Cell Block to appear at the top of the concrete steps as they shuffled into the Dock. The unfortunate Constable, who was obliged to stand in the Dock with the prisoners, looked distinctly unhappy and appeared to be visibly gagging. Alas, luck was far from being with the Hippies because Major Reginald Duckworth JP just happened to be the much feared and strict Chairman of their Bench.

Horace Mayo, the Magistrates' Clerk, called for order before all four of the Prisoners at the Bar duly entered admissions of 'Guilty as charged'. Then Inspector Leonard Smithe, the Prosecutor, adeptly got on with his task of outlining the circumstances of their arrests to the extremely attentive Bench. The Major was flanked on the Bench by a Male and Female Colleague. The Inspector concluded his formal narration of the fairly short statement of facts by purposely stressing the final points. He coughed politely before he purposefully stressed,

"The four Defendants were all singing *'We are all going to San Francisco'* as they were being ejected from the Licensed Premises known as the Tim Bobbin Public House….However…Sergeant Blackburn and Constable Littlejohn diverted them from their intended journey to take them directly to the Cells at Lapley Vale Police Station where they were detained overnight."

Lenny Smithe's intentional injection of humour caused a ripple of laughter to circulate all around the Courtroom.

The Female Magistrate, who was sat next to the Major, was carefully holding her small and ornately perfumed handkerchief under her nose as the stench coming from the Hippies was already reaching every corner of the Courtroom. The Major, unable to disguise his disgust with the four pathetic Creatures lined up before him, asked if they wished to say anything before he pronounced sentence upon them. Perhaps to everyone's surprise, Myfanwy confidently stood up to say,

"We don't know what all this fuss is about Man....The last time we were in Lapley Vale...Sergeant Bert."

She turned to smile sweetly at the nodding, still grinning, Bert,

"Oh…Hello Sergeant do you remember us? Yeah Man…Well he just gave us a damn good talking to and sent us on our way Man….. We find all this formality quite unnecessary…Man….Make Peace not War!"

The Major was having great difficulty controlling his temper but after displaying his disapproval of the Young Woman addressing him as 'Man' he did manage to rather aggressively ask each of the Men in turn if they wished to say anything. They all declined the kind offer. Glancing to see if they were in unison they then started to quietly chant *Make peace not war Man*. Horace lost his self control lurching forward to shout,

"Shut it! Just shut it or you will be unceremoniously slung back into the Cells until you can learn some respect and exhibit some Common Courtesy to this Court….Now…Shut it!"

Even the bold Hippies realised that they were now pushing their luck too far so they complied instantly.

The Major had been on the brink of screaming his disapproval yet he struggled to remain in control of himself as the Horace the Court Clerk competently dealt with the situation. He pulled himself together to address them firmly but politely

"Thank you….You have been very wise to obey the instruction bidding you all to shut up…..Well done…Now I want you to remain silent for a little bit longer….Constable….They have received their final warning for today….They must now keep the mouths shut….Or else… Ahem…I have been informed by Mr Mayo the Clerk that by Law we can only impose a Binding Over Sentence upon you this morning….If I was empowered to do so I would order you all to be given a damn good wash before you are permitted to mix with decent respectable People again….Nevertheless….You will each be bound over in the sum of Fifty Pounds to be of good behaviour for a period of twelve months….You will be asked to sign a declaration to this effect and should you happen to transgress sufficiently enough for you to be brought before any Court within the next year you will forfeit the said sum of Fifty Pounds each in addition to any other Penalty you may face."

He paused, appearing to be momentarily hopeful, he added,

"Unless of course you refuse to be bound over and in that case we can send you all straight to Prison….Where you will definitely be given a hygienic carbolic soap scrub down and a disinfected bath…Ask them please Mr Mayo."

Horace quickly established that they were all quite amenable to a *'Binding over Order'*, much to the obvious chagrin of the Major. His disappointment was apparent as he finally snapped out his closing remarks to them,

"So be it….Get them out of our sight please Constable."

The Hippies shuffled down the concrete steps leading to the Cells waiting until they considered that were well out of the earshot of anyone inside the Courtroom before they cheekily started chanting again,

"We love you Man….Make peace man."

Because of his extraordinary powers of hearing the Major then needed to be restrained by one of his Colleagues. He had to be persuaded to remain on the Bench before he was once again allowed to exhibit his surprisingly adept athletic ability by vaulting over the bench into the well of the Courtroom, undoubtedly with the implicit intent of physically setting about them.

Bert McCabe had thoroughly enjoyed the whole of the proceedings from start to finish. He was chuckling to himself as he purposefully made a point of meeting up with Blackie and Eddie just outside the Courtroom in the ornately panelled corridor.

"His arsehole was chewing the gusset right out of his underpants in there the old Major…Eh? Eh? He would willingly have given them all a bloody good scrubbing down himself just as long as he would then be entitled to give them all a bloody good hiding….He badly wanted to send them down…He's a one off is the Galloping Major…Eh? Eh?"

Blackie and Eddie grinned as they quietly nodded their agreement. Blackie took the opportunity to explain,

"Bert….I'm not entirely in keeping with your more Liberal Methods of dealing with these sort of incidents but as I was of the opinion that it would probably be a total waste of time fining them or sending them down and I also to use the old Common Law Statutes because sometimes a binding over works….Not sure why perhaps they feel they have something to prove to themselves as well as everyone else…They won't be moving that Mobile Shithouse they have been driving round in unless they manage to establish that it's completely roadworthy and then they have to show me some driving licences road tax and insurance so with any luck they may just fade away.….They might piss off home…. That'll teach their Parents to bring them up properly.…I'd love to see their Mums and Dads if they all returned to the roost in the state they're now in…Eh?"

Laughing, Eddie chipped in,

"Did you remember them Serg? Er sorry Bert."

Bert smiled,

"Eddie…..Eddie my Bonny Boy how on Earth could anybody ever forget any encounter they may have had at any time with that smelly lot…Remember that day do you Eddie? … Eh? Eh? The Hare Krishna Mob and there right in the middle of it all was Amos Quirk…. Rochdale's very own answer to John the Baptist…Eh? Eh? You couldn't make up incidents like that even if you were making a Film or a Play for showing on the telly.…Eh? Eh? Mind you scruffy and smelly as they undoubtedly are I have seen worse in my many years of dedicated Public Service.…Eh? Eh? "

Eddie appeared to find Bert's comment highly improbable but Blackie nodded his head, displaying the look of a Man who was not easily surprised. Bert was clearly keen to embellish his statement,

"I once saw a youth who was standing in the centre of a busy Town Shopping Precinct in full view of everyone and this Bloke was sporting a haircut which I had only ever seen previously on the head of one of the Last of the Mohicans…That Indian Tribe on the telly… Eh? Eh? … But this Bugger had the pathetic remaining tuft of hair running up the middle of his head heavily lacquered so it stood on end like the plumes often seen on an ancient Roman helmet…Eh? Eh? And as if that wasn't enough he had sprayed this ridiculous monstrosity with different very bright coloured dyes…Eh….Eh? … He didn't seem to mind People staring at him….Most People were pointing at him and let's face it…. Laughing at the soft Bugger….Eh? Eh? … So I took him on one side to have a little heart to heart chat…Eh? Eh? … Eventually I got round to asking him how long it took him to set it all up before he turned out in the morning….He said it took him at least two hours so then I asked him what would he do if a bird shit on it….Eh? Eh? What do you think he said? Eh? Eh?"

Blackie and Eddie both shook their heads allowing Bert the opportunity to declare with gusto,

"I'd pack HER in straight away….Eh? Eh? Honestly that's exactly what he told me."

They all ended up laughing so loudly that they were obliged to quickly move away from the vicinity of the Courtrooms before they were the one's being told to hush.

Bert happily accompanied the two Officers as they walked to the front of the Building. Blackie and Eddie were about to take their leave when Bert had to pass on to them another of his interesting facts. He was clearly keen to relate another story to them. Blackie did not know Bert well enough to know when he was being serious and when he was taking the Mickey. Bert then pretended to be offended,

"Anyways…. Hold on a minute Blackie don't you think for one minute that I never had occasion to use any of those useful old Laws during my long and distinguished Career…Eh? … Eh? Those one's that have been in existence since time immemorial or even longer set in stone to enforce authority on miscreants….Eh? Eh? Do you remember when that Liverpool Tramp called Scouse visited our area Eddie?….He was so smelly that even Jedd Clampett gave him the cold shoulder…. Anyways….He tried his luck out by bumming a hand out at the St Mary's Roman Catholic Presbytery but Father Murphy….You know who I mean Eddie….Better known locally as Father Bunloaf? … Eh? Eh? Well he very soon gave him the full bum's rush and rather foolishly

Scouse chose to turn very nasty…Father Murphy was a match for anyone in his day and he was all set to throw him out by the scruff of his neck…The sight of Father Murphy advancing towards him made Scouse panic…..He definitely frightened poor old Bridget….The Priest's Housekeeper…Because she was mopping the front steps with a bucket of hot water laced with Domestos…You know what I mean? … Eh? Eh? Well Scouse tried to defend himself by picking up Bridget's bucket and throwing the contents over Father Murphy…I got there handy and took the Tramp straight down to the Bridewell…Eh? Eh? Saved him from a bloody good hiding the Priest was going to justifiably give him….."

Blackie was now fascinated,

"What did you charge him with Bert?"

Just as soon as Blackie had asked the question he instantly realised that he was, once again, falling into another of Bert's traps. Bert could hardly disguise his delight as he delivered his well practised punch line,

"I charged him with causing a Bleach of the Priest Blackie…. Obviously…What else? Eh? Eh? Get it? Bleach? Domestos? Bleach of the Priest … The sharpness of my enormous brain is even a surprise to me at times."

All three Men were soon almost helpless, laughing until tears ran down their faces and their sides started to ache.

Before undertaking any further actions that day they were all obliged to seek immediate relief as they swiftly headed towards the toilets.

"Alright then.....I got the name wrong."

There was nothing in particular out of the ordinary about Victoria Street, Lapley Vale. The entire hundred yards or so of straight Urban Roadway had impressive, if slightly dated, looking two storey double bed-roomed Terraced Houses, without front gardens, along either side of the entire length of the thoroughfare. As the street name might readily suggest all the existing properties were built around the turn of the Twentieth Century during the long reign of the late Queen Victoria. No expense had been spared in the choice of the materials used by the Builders which had resulted in all of the Properties being of solid reliable quality as they were definitely made to last for many years. The unique red coloured Accrington brick facades exhibited an impressive appearance that made the Houses seem as if they had been polished. In certain lights, usually when the sun was shining brightly or perhaps when it was raining heavily, they really did look as if they had been finished off with a coat of varnish because they really did glisten.

Most of the many Families with their Homes in this Street had been able to enjoy their pleasant surroundings, close to the Town Centre and other desirable amenities, for many years without much change either to the overall general appearance or to the Inhabitants. The vast majority of the People who resided there were quite familiar and quite well known to each other. The Resident Families also shared many valued relationships with some of their various Friends and Relations with their Neighbours. Many had been able to share similar upbringings and life styles by reason of the fact that they attended the same Schools together before many moved on to take up employment in Local Factories or Mills. In all relevant respects Victoria Street was deserving of the good reputation it had always strived to maintain and it was currently enjoying because this Street comfortably typified a respectable and desirable working class environment.

Since the recent dramatic birth of baby Elizabeth Summers, which took place on the lower deck of the Rochdale to Huddersfield bus, Nurse Francis Costain had been able to modestly reflect in the glory of being, quite justifiably, considered a genuine Heroine in the eyes of most of the Local Inhabitants. Francis, only ever called Fanny behind her back, invariably addressed as Nurse Costain at all times, was not the easiest person to interact with at a person to person level. Although there was no doubting the fact that she was very caring and a most competent person she was also impatient, abrupt and positively rude at times in her determination to tackle all of her complex and revealing dealings with the numerous Patients she had been called upon to treat in her esteemed position of District Nurse. Someone once said of Francis Costain *'She loves and cares for people until they hurt'*. A phrase commonly referred to as being *'Back handed compliment'* but this comment was, alas, very close to being the case.

A Single Woman by choice Fanny was now in her late fifties. She was a private and self sufficient type who could be described as a Pillar of Society in all ways. She had never seriously attempted to become the driver of a motor vehicle. This was due to her unfortunate experiences during a very brief and ill-tempered first driving lesson under the tutelage of Harry 'Bleeding' Longfellow, the Local Driving Instructor, many years before. You will have already guessed why Harry had earned the nicknamed *'Bleeding'* because of his frequent use of this half swearing word inevitably included in his familiar vocabulary whenever he opened his mouth or if he was being quoted elsewhere for any reason. Alas Fanny had never been able to permit herself to be instructed or told how to do anything by anyone other than a fully qualified Doctor ever since the earlier days when she had started off her long and illustrious career as a Young Student Nurse. Obviously this happened a long time ago in far and distant past and her self sufficiency had been developed through her constant Professional Relationships with her Patients. As Harry was reported as quoting at that time, whilst sitting in the Bar of the Slip Inn shortly after the conclusion of the encounter with Fanny, nursing a throbbing, freshly slapped, right ear,

"She's a bleeding maniac….Take my bleeding word for it….She should never be allowed behind the wheel of a bleeding car as long as there's a hole in her arse."

A few of the highly amused Onlookers, who just happened to be present in the Bar at the time, humorously, responded, almost in unison,

"And that's forty years after you die".

The ill-fated lesson had lasted all of ten minutes. It came to rather a swift end when Harry confidently asked Fanny to start the engine on the car they were sharing. This only happened after he had competently given a brief introduction to the basic purpose and workings of the clutch, the brakes and other familiar equipment to be found inside any motor vehicle. On turning the ignition key to start the engine the car stalled, abruptly, viciously lurching forward, causing Fanny to bang the top of her head on the inside of the windscreen. As a direct result of this unfortunate occurrence Fanny instantly abandoned the car together with any thoughts she ever had ever held of becoming a Competent Driver. Consequently she invariably travelled around to visit all of her Patients on her trusty bicycle, complete with basket pannier on the handlebars which she mainly used for the conveyance of her precious black medical bag. This enduring practice had caused Fanny to achieve a personal level of physical fitness which was the envy of many Persons much younger than she was.

Nurse Costain was standing on the pavement hammering on the front door of number 30 Victoria Street, where Bertie Brough and his daughter Nellie resided. Bertie was now an Elderly Retired Man who had worked as a Labourer at one of the local Cotton Mills for fifty-five years before he took his well earned retirement. He had been lovingly cared for by his rather shy, borderline introverted and naturally nervous, youngest Daughter Nellie since his Dear Wife passed away several years before when Bertie was still a relatively Young Man. Bertie was in the process of slowly recovering from a very nasty bout of Quinsy; this was a distressingly painful version of Tonsillitis. This illness, the treatment of which was being supervised by Doctor Berry, required the daily attendance of Fanny. Her duties were to administer an antiseptic spray internally to his throat and also to give her Patient a course of injections.

Nurse Costain was angry; she rattled the brass letter box as she continued to thump her fists upon the solid wooden door. All her efforts were apparently to no avail. She had been able to see that Nellie was cowering inside the front room. For some reason the timid woman was defiantly refusing to open the door to admit her. Fanny kept stepping back towards the edge of the pavement to enable her to glare up at the front bedroom window, as she was shouting,

"Bertie Brough….Get your Nellie to open this door forthwith… Come on now…Or there's going to be big trouble….Come on….Open up….You need this injection if you want to get better….COME ON! … Open the door."

She then returned to continue her relentless onslaught upon the solid wooden door, now she was not only using both of her fists but this was now accompanied by a couple of hefty kicks as well.

Suddenly the bottom section of the transom type bedroom window above her head, slowly, noisily, slid up to open. This caused Fanny to step back again so that she could get a better view of what was going on up above her. A bucket full of, what initially appeared to be water was swiftly thrown out through the open window. This water hit the target by falling directly into Fanny's face just as, open mouthed, she was staring skywards. Fanny was drenched. She spluttered and reeled about on her feet until she eventually fell over her carefully parked bicycle ending up sprawled on the road in a most undignified manner showing her next weeks washing as she did so to anyone who happened to be passing by at that moment in time.

Circumstances then revealed that during these poignant moments Sam Best, accompanied by his joiner Isaac, just happened to be driving along the Street in their flat backed builders' truck. Not immediately knowing what was going on Sam slammed his brakes on rather suddenly. As soon as their vehicle came to a stop Isaac leapt out of the passenger seat at the front of the truck to dash across the road to Fanny's aid. Fortunately Fanny was relatively unhurt but her temper had now reached a dangerous and extremely volatile level. Isaac just managed to briefly catch a glimpse of the terrified face of Nellie as she peered out from behind the thick net curtains inside the front room of the house. On seeing Isaac she instantly darted straight back out of sight. Bertie, thick woollen scarf around his neck, wearing his cloth cap, dressed in his pyjamas, then suddenly appeared in the frame of the bedroom window. He seemed to be almost as annoyed as Fanny had been as he yelled out to her,

"I warned you Nurse…I warned you….Didn't I? I told you this would end in tears….Incidentally I have to protest that this is no way to be treating a Sick Man."

He then disappeared again inside the bedroom. The window came down so fast there was a grave danger that the glass would shatter which called for Isaac and Sam to instinctively jump out of the way just in case.

Sam lifted Fanny's bicycle onto the rear of the flat truck before he helped Isaac to climb up to sit alongside it. Fanny was then gently steered into the passenger seat at the front of the vehicle before they drove off heading towards Fanny's own home, which Sam happened to know was situated close by. She was so frustrated and enraged that she defiantly refused to respond to any of Sam's persistent questions to her. He was attempting to discover exactly what had been going on just prior to them arriving on the scene. Sam soon noticed that there was a rather unpleasant smell coming from, the soaking wet, Nurse making him suspect that the bucket they had witnessed Bertie emptying over her had not contained something much less acceptable than ordinary tap water.

Fanny remained in no mood to speak even when they eventually arrived outside her home. Isaac carefully unloaded her bicycle placing it over her garden wall into the safety of her enclosed, concreted, front garden. Fanny sprung out of the truck before she furiously stamped up her front path. She then entered her house slamming the door behind her with such force that both of the Men involuntarily blinked. Not a word of explanation or thanks or anything for that matter was offered to either Sam or Isaac by the obviously distressed Nurse.

Sam and Isaac were somewhat at a loss. They were wondering what their next step should be. They decided that they would go to the Surgery where they ardently hoped they would be able to speak to Doctor Berry. Fortunately for them the Doctor was just about to leave on his daily rounds and was at home. He made himself available to speak to them immediately. Sam, ably assisted by Isaac, related what they had seen and then what action they had subsequently taken. Malcolm Berry, a distinguished, elderly and most respected, Medical Practitioner who had served the people of Lapley Vale for many years was instantly annoyed. Malcolm had never been known for his forbearance although he very quickly realised and soon appreciated that Sam and Isaac were merely doing the right thing by reporting the matter directly to him.

They all retreated into his Consulting Room where Malcolm decided to fill in, what he thought could possibly be, the probable background to this incident.

"Nellie called in here yesterday asking me if I would instruct Nurse Costain to visit her Dad before she went to make her call at Ernie Carr's at number 17 and Mary Picard at 10 in Victoria Street on her daily rounds....She wouldn't explain the reason why Bertie wanted this change to the Nurses routine but as we are all too aware he can be a funny old Bugger when it suits him to be so....She said her Dad had begged the Nurse to do this on two separate occasions but she had blatantly chosen to ignore what Bertie considered to be his reasonable request....Anyways....She is so timid and frightened by nature Nellie.... I told her that my Authority did give me either the right nor the powers to instruct the Nurse on what specific route she should take when out on her rounds and I also told her to tell her Dad to stop moaning and get on with his prescribed course of treatment without causing any unnecessary fuss…Mind you I have to admit Sam… Nellie was really looking shocked and horrified when she scurried out of here but I didn't think any more about it…Really…Perhaps I should have taken a bit more notice of her…Hindsight is a wondrous gift eh? I'll nip round to the Nurses house first to check on her and then I'll be paying a visit to the bold Bertie….Thanks Chaps.…Leave it to me now I'll sort it out… Thank you.…You've done the right thing by telling me…Thanks."

When Malcolm arrived at Fanny's house she had just finished bathing. She was dressed in a long, fluffy, buttoned right up the neck, pink coloured dressing gown. Being Fanny she would never even consider permitting any Man, not even the Doctor, to enter her house whilst she was not fully dressed in her complete outside attire. Fortunately she was soon able to convince him that she had calmed down and she had now managed to regain full control over her emotions. Malcolm was able to assure himself that she was physically uninjured without actually examining her. When he mentioned Bertie's name Fanny almost instantly lost her composure as the mere mention of his name had started her up all over again. Realising the delicacy of the situation Malcolm decided to back off immediately. He made a hasty retreat,

"I am going round to Bertie's house now Nurse please take your time to recover…You have suffered a nasty shock.…Take the day off.… Leave it to me.…Don't you worry now.…I'll sort him out."

Malcolm drove away already in a state of steadily mounting trepidation. He was anxiously wondering what could possibly be waiting for him when he got to 30 Victoria Street.

As soon as Malcolm stopped his car outside of the Brough house Nellie threw open their front door. She frantically gestured for him to enter urging him to do so without delay. Once inside the door was quickly locked behind him by the highly excited and emotional Woman.

"What's been going on Nellie…I've just seen Nurse Costain and she has had a terrible shock…I cannot understand how an incident like this can occur when a District Nurse is merely and I must say conscientiously carrying out her duties to her Patients.... What on earth caused this nasty incident to happen?"

Nellie was so upset and excited that she was experiencing great difficulty trying to speak, however she did manage to splutter,

"Upstairs please Doctor Berry....See Dad...He's upstairs in his bedroom."

Then, in complete, inexplicable, contrast to her outwardly apparent state of high excitement, she politely enquired,

"Can I make you a nice cuppa Doctor Berry or would you like a drink of Dad's Brandy?"

Malcolm brushed aside her kind offer choosing to head straight up the steep wooden stairs without making any further comments.

Bertie was obviously still in an acute state of pent up frustration. He was sitting up in his bed in his thick cotton pyjamas. He was still wearing his cap with the woollen scarf wrapped snugly around his neck. It was then that Malcolm needed to call upon all of his vast experience and training to manage to keep him calm,

"Now Bertie....What has been going on Nurse Costain is in a right state...I've spoken to young Sam and his Mate but...What on earth's been going on....I'm still struggling to understand any of it...What the Hell was it that caused this fracas?....Now....Tell me the whole story...What is wrong with you why have you attacked Nurse Costain? Please tell me Bertie because this matter needs to be nipped in the bud before anyone else suffers."

Bertie was extremely eager to explain his actions,

"Listen Doctor Berry I sent our Nellie around to see Fanny Costain at her house yesterday to press home a reasonable request to her.... I asked her on two occasions to make her visit me before she did her other visits in Victoria Street...No difference to her I would estimate.... Reasonable request....She just ignored me."

Malcolm was unable to think of any reason why Bertie would need to make such a request in the first place.

"Sorry...Why did you want her to do that Bertie?"

Bertie responded with even more vigour and genuine conviction,

"Because Doctor Berry….Because she called at Ernie Carr's house first at number 7 and then she called at Worthington Mary's house at number 10 and this was before she came to me three mornings on the trot this was…I wanted her to come down the Street from the opposite direction so that she could see me first…Before Mary and Ernie…. Nothing unreasonable about that Doctor Berry."

Malcolm still had no idea what on Earth Bertie thought the problem was,

"Why is that so important to you Bertie? I'm sorry I'm doing my best to understand…Why did the timing of her visits to Ernie and Mary matter to you?"

Bertie reacted very angrily

"Matter to me?! Matter to bloody me? I'll tell you why Doctor Berry…And incidentally you should know what I am about to tell you for a fact yourself.….Ernie has got painful boils all around his arsehole and other parts of his unmentionable nether regions…I know that is the case because his Missus in person told our Nellie in detail about the dreadful state he was in…Right.…So she calls there to treat him first.…Getting my drift are you Doctor? Then she goes into Mary's and our Nellie says she has something called.…Er Robins…What is it called our Nellie?"

Nellie, nervously standing in the background, boldly corrected her father, "Thrush Dad.…It's a Lady type complaint…I heard from one of the Neighbours that she was suffering from Thrush."

This requested interjection seemed to antagonise Bertie even more,

"O.K. alright then.…I got the name wrong.…It's something nasty concerning her Fanny Region isn't it?"

Malcolm, tutting, shook his head; his voice was cracking with emotion as he spoke,

"Bertie…. Mary has got a very nasty chest infection.…CHEST! Inside her chest.…She's bronchial…Has been since she was a little girl…She has to have injections similar to those you been receiving to fight off the serious infection in her....CHEST! It has nothing whatsoever to do with her Fanny...Good grief man I wish you would stop listening to gossip and nasty rumours...I should not be discussing other Patients complaints with you or anyone else...Bloody Hell Fire Bertie you appear to have gone off half cocked on this occasion and poor old Nurse Costain has ended up getting soaked insulted and then publicly humiliated...This will not do Bertie."

There followed a short, yet poignant, pause. Bertie suddenly sounded a little more conciliatory,

"Well I wouldn't be surprised if it had been her Fanny the way she offers it around to all and sundry....And anyways....All I did was ask to be seen before she treated them two dirty Bastards...I didn't like the thoughts of her touching me after she had been handling them.... I don't think I was being unreasonable...Why didn't you order her to visit me first....That's why I told our Nellie not to let her in and she got my bucket over her because I thought she was about to smash our front door down....I still say she should have been told to visit me first so there...Would have saved all this trouble and strife"

Exasperated, Malcolm passively turned to Nellie,

"What was that you mentioned to me about Brandy Nellie? Fetch two glasses up will you please? I need a drink and so does your Dad."

Nellie was gone in a flash. Malcolm returned to address Bertie,

"Look Bertie....Nurse Costain is a very experienced not to mention highly trained District Nurse...She is specially trained in matters concerning cross contamination and she of all people knows exactly how to avoid spreading any disease or infections....She would sterilise herself after treating any of her Patients...What sort of a Nurse do you take her for Bertie...I'm not saying she might...Only might mind you....Have been a little more flexible but....Did you mention to her the reason why you wanted her to visit you first?"

Bertie, sipping his brandy, was by now beginning to look rather sheepish,

"Well....Not in so many words Doctor Berry....I didn't want her to think I was sounding too personal....Cheers....I still say it was a reasonable request but will you ask her to call round again please and I will definitely apologise to her for everything that happened…Cheers Doctor Berry….Fanny Costain likes a drop of this Brandy as well you know and I've got a spare bottle kept in reserve for these sort of occasions…By the way…This whole incident is hardly in keeping with the needs and caring treatment needed to ensure the comfort and recovery of a very sick Elderly Man you know…Cheers….Drink up…By Christ Doctor I'll tell you what…This Brandy is making me feel a lot better already….Cheers"

Doctor Berry shook his head before he cautiously allowed himself a happy, possibly more of a relived, smile. He then drained his glass.

"Right you can take that bloody scarf off for me now Bertie I might as well check you over whilst I'm here….Bloody Hell Fire Bertie….Is nothing at all straight forward these days?"

Bertie, carefully removing his scarf did not respond.

"What a marvellous man he was and no mistake."

Woody and Mavis Green had just finished enjoying their evening meal. Woody had been so happy and contented since the elderly couple had taken the shock, not to mention bold, step when they decided to get married. The idea of the two apparently settled Single Persons throwing their lot in together was probably, at least in the first instance, created when Eric and Jenny McCabe announced that they were rather hastily tying the knot. Although the prevailing circumstances were vastly different for these two couples they did successfully manage to arrange a double celebration by marrying on the same day and the same place by courtesy of the Registrar at Lapley Vale Town Hall. Apart from any other favourable considerations, Mavis was, as was confidently anticipated, a really marvellous Wife. Although Woody had always lived in his cosy Terraced House ever since he had been born there he had spent many years alone after his Mother had passed away, he had never ever experienced the sort of personal happiness he had revelled in during the past couple of years since he became a Married Man for the very first time. Woody and Mavis had proved to be a perfect match for each other and both had derived enormous comfort and pleasure from their Matrimonial State.

As a pleasant and most welcome side effect their surprise Marriage had been a terrific boost for Eric and Jenny because at that particular time the young pair's future was under threat because of severe financial pressures being brought to bear upon them. Apart from the small outlay involved with the Celebration of their Marriage they were also awaiting the imminent arrival of their first born child with the obvious cost incurred proving to be a great strain. Mavis, who had been widowed for many years, agreed to sell her desirable house to them at a more than reasonable selling price. Apart from their sincerely felt joint wish to willing assist the young couple in their time of need they found that they were able to be very generous because Mavis, who had no close Family, no longer needed to own her own home after she became Mrs Green because she had chosen to move in with Woody. Bert and Alice had been able to prop up their meagre savings to enable the young couple to obtain an affordable Mortgage. The manner in which Friends and Relatives had rallied to the assistance of Eric and Jenny was far from unusual in their sort of close Working Class Communities.

Mavis had treated Woody to one of his favourite dinners, liver and onions with mashed potatoes accompanied by fresh, home produced, mixed garden vegetables. As usual he had devoured his meal with gusto. She had then pressed him, if that was a real possibility bearing in mind Woody's enormous appetite, to finish off their repast with jam roly poly pudding covered with thick and creamy custard.

Woody was soon contentedly loading his trusty pipe with tobacco preparing to enjoy a nice smoke after having filled his belly to maximum capacity. He rubbed one of his hands across his now slightly extended stomach region before he spoke,

"Have we any of those tablets Mavis? I think I might be suffering from a slight attack of Indigestion."

Smiling sweetly, Mavis stood up to walk through into the kitchen, collecting some of the dirty dishes off the table as she was doing so.

"Perhaps you wouldn't need the tablets if you slowed down a bit when you are eating Woody…I've seen ravenous starving dogs demolishing their food slower than you at times….I've got some of those tablets you like to take in the kitchen cupboard…I'll make a nice pot of tea for us both whilst I am at it."

Mavis was aware of Woody making a slight grunting noise as she was preparing the pot of tea. She dismissed any concern because she thought it was Woody naturally relieving the pressure built up whilst he had been eating and consequently she carried on regardless. On returning to the living room she instinctively knew something was very wrong. Woody had slumped forward on his chair and although his eyes were open their usual sparkle had suddenly disappeared from them. She almost screamed at him,

"Woody….Woody.…Are you alright dear? Oh no Woody….What has happened?"

She desperately attempted to check for his pulse but she very soon began to realise that, in what had only been a matter of minutes, she had lost her beloved Husband. In sheer panic she dashed next door to ask their Neighbour if he would contact Doctor Berry or an Ambulance as soon as possible. Their Neighbour was one of the few Residents in the Street who had a telephone. He was able to contact Doctor Berry at his home without any delay. Malcolm Berry instructed him to ring for an Emergency Ambulance telling him to inform Ambulance Control that he had asked him to do so. The Doctor arrived within minutes skidding his car to a halt outside their house. The Doctor was just dashing through the front door when a speeding Ambulance with screeching tyres turned into the Street with the bells clanking noisily.

Doctor Berry was visibly upset, as he was soon forced to turn to face the clearly distressed Mavis, following his quick examination of Woody,

"Mavis love…There is nothing I or anyone else can do for Woody now….I'm awfully sorry…He's gone."

They then ended up weeping in each others arms. Obviously in a state of shock Malcolm sat down at the table. He then attempted to do his best explaining to Mavis why the Ambulance would still have to take Woody to the Hospital and that by Law he would be obliged to contact the Coroner because he would be unable to issue the Death Certificate because he had not seen Woody as his Patient for many years. Malcolm was keen to stress that although a Post Mortem Examination would have to be carried out there was no doubt in his mind that Woody had died from natural causes, almost certainly, a sudden fatal heart attack.

Alf was the first person to be informed. He quickly contacted Ralph by telephone to pass on the dreadful news. The two stunned Men made an instant decision that they would be keeping the Club open so that all of Woody and Mavis's many Friends could be properly informed first hand of the tragic circumstances and of any subsequent developments as they unfolded. His voice was cracking with heartfelt emotion as Ralph was speaking to Alf,

"I can't see you selling much beer tonight Alf but as Woody spent almost every evening of his adult life in our Clubroom I think he would approve of the action we are going to take by not closing for the night.… We can all show our respects and express our feelings at the appropriate time."

Both men were seriously stunned. They were struggling to cope with what had happened so suddenly. It was very hard to accept and believe.

Alf and Denise would never be able to forget that dreadful evening serving behind that bar. They were in the front line as the bad news gradually percolated through the various avenues available to people in a small Town. The distress and devastation genuinely felt by many of the people, who were mostly suffering from shock, was prominently displayed throughout the whole of the evening's proceedings. Denise, who had always been very fond of Woody, found that she had been unable to maintain her brave front for too long; consequently Alf sent her home early. Alf might well have been able to close the Premises well within the prescribed closing times laid down by the Licensing Justices as their permitted legal opening and closing hours. Alf was close to tears as he finally closed the door behind 'The Bitter Enders' saying,

"This would never have happened if Woody had been here."

His unintentionally poignant comment re-kindled the grief and sadness which was being acutely felt by all of them.

The next day Mavis was pleased, not to mention relieved, to receive a visit at her home from Bert, whom she had always considered to be one of her Dearest Friends. She was aware that Bert could be trusted and relied upon at all times. He was accompanied by Alf. Both men were clearly trying to display a practical, matter of fact, approach but they were both, quite clearly, still in distressing states of severe shock. Bert, knowing that the need for all of his strength of character would be essential in the prevailing circumstances, set about attempting to sort out all the many urgent and pressing matters which had to be faced by Mavis. Bert coped with this ordeal despite having to bravely put aside his own deeply felt feelings of sorrow and loss which he was experiencing as much, if not more, than many of the others.

Alf was soon on the receiving end of a further stunning shock when he realised that Woody had been the mysterious person behind the famous *'Kenneth Gordon Trust'*. Only Mavis and Bert had been aware of the real facts but now Bert suggested that the ongoing tragic events had created a suitable time for them to come clean so that Woody could receive the credit he had always shunned but so rightly deserved.

As the men were about to take their leave, they assured Mavis that they would deal with all of the necessary Legal Requirements on her behalf. As they were talking through the provisional arrangements for the funeral, Mavis, who in the circumstances was coping extremely well, informed them that although Woody had rarely ever suffered from any life threatening illnesses he had made it clear to her that when he did pass away his dying wish would be for his body to be cremated so that his ashes could be scattered over his beloved crown bowling green. She had broken down at this point. She was caringly comforted by Bert because Alf was in need of succour himself because he was almost distraught. All three of them allowed a little time to recover their composure once again. Mavis had soon recovered sufficiently enough to say,

"He was 79 years old you know…He didn't want anyone to make a fuss but he had reluctantly agreed to allow me to put a on a 'Do' in the Clubhouse for his 80th Birthday Celebration….Sadly that won't be happening now…However I do definitely think he would wish his many Friends to have a final drink with him in the Club after the funeral and I'm sure Alf will be able to make all the necessary arrangements for that to be done…Fortunately I find that I am in a comfortable financial position so please do not spare any expense."

Tears were then streaming down Alf's face; he nodded his head as he desperately attempted to smile but without any success.

H.M. Coroner was able to very quickly dispense with the need for an Inquest because, as Malcolm had correctly suspected, Woody had died from natural causes. As it had been Leonard Skillet and his son David, the Local Undertakers, had finally removed Woody's body from the house on the instructions of the Coroner Mavis was content to allow them to handle all the detailed funeral arrangements on her behalf.

The Funeral was duly arranged to take place at the Crematorium at 3pm on Monday afternoon. The Ceremony would be followed by drinks and refreshments provided for all Mourners at the Club, a place where Woody had spent a considerable number of happy hours of his life over many years.

Saturday night in the Clubhouse was difficult for most of those Persons who were brave enough to be present but, as always seems to be the case when tragedy strikes, people soon began to get on with their lives again although the sad atmosphere was still very evident especially in the vicinity of the bar. No-one dared to use Woody's stool. Eddie, Norman, Charlie and Bert were all present with Ralph and Victor in their usual places across the bar from them. The death of Woody had hit young Eric more than most because he genuinely loved and admired the Old Man. He had greatly benefited from his association with Woody in so many different ways. He had learned most of what he knew about gardening and how to produce and maintain the finest bowling green to be seen in the entire vicinity from him. He had been so confident of their enduring friendship that he would never hesitate to seek his advice on any and all of the subjects under the sun. Unbeknown to Eric and Jenny, Woody and Mavis had also been their loyal and genuine Mentor in many other ways mostly through their own close friendship with Bert and Alice. As Eric and Sam slowly approached the saddest corner in the whole room they were obviously feeling uncomfortable.

Both Young Men were clearly consumed with grief. Norman tried to ease the tension,

"Ricky…We have been talking and we think that as his natural successor you should have the use of Woody's stool from now on whenever you want it."

They all nodded and grunted with expressions of their complete agreement. Unable to make a response, Eric was carefully steered onto the stool by Sam and Damien. Not one of them could manage to speak for several minutes. A quiet night ensued with all of Woody's friends unashamedly expressing that they were already missing him badly. They all dreaded the thought of the forthcoming funeral yet every one of them would be present at the unwelcome ritual to a man.

The short Non-religious Service which had been held at the Crematorium was a heart breaking experience for Mavis as well as for many more of those attending. She was closely comforted throughout the entire torturous day by Alice McCabe at her side. The turnout was exactly what had been expected. The room was filled to capacity. Ralph Jones was sufficiently composed to deliver an excellent Eulogy. He summarised Woody's life without giving away too many delicate details. For once one of Ralph's speeches was well received by all present.

Many people had taken the trouble to attend as a genuine demonstration of their sincere desire to exhibit their respects as well as to bid farewell to an Exceptional Man who had never ever maliciously upset or hurt anyone throughout his long lifetime.

Lenny Jopson, the Editor of the Lapley Vale Examiner, had made certain that the tragic death of one of the Town's most colourful, popular and well respected Citizens had been prominently featured in the popular and well circulated Local Weekend Newspaper. Somehow the Editorial Team had managed to show a photograph of Woody in full Army uniform which had been taken just before his final demobilisation from the Forces after World War Two in 1946. Even Woody himself might have experienced some difficulty recognising him. If Woody had been fortunate enough to have borne a son this photograph would have been very close to what he could have looked like. This did not detract from the full and empathetic Obituary written with genuine feelings of admiration and respect by Lenny himself in person. There was no mention of his, no longer being kept as a secret, and fortunate win on the Football Pools which had subsequently allowed his generous disposal of a large amount of money through *The Kenneth Gordon Trust'* although his death had been reported using his full name with *'Better known as Woody'* added for ready recognition. If Readers were not surprised by his actual name they might well have gasped at his age. Woody's appearance had never seemed to change very much from when he was about 50 years old. He certainly did not look the 79 years of age that he actually was.

Back at the Clubhouse Leonard Skillet and his son David, who had carried out their undertaking duties with sensitivity and calm efficiency, joined all the other Mourners for drinks and sandwiches. These light refreshments had been prepared by Alice with willing assistance from Nan Dawes, Denise and Mrs Callow, Victor's wife. Nan later kept a close eye on her Billy because she knew how much he had always admired and worshipped Woody. She was afraid he might eventually spoil the dignity of the occasion by allowing himself to get well and truly pissed. As things turned out Billy was too upset to drink very much at all. He could barely manage to continuously mutter,

"I can't believe he's really gone….It's a tragedy….A cockeyed tragedy."

Most of the Ladies withdrew from the mainly Male gathering quite soon after they had affectionately raised their glasses to the fond memory of a well loved and respected Member of their close Community.

The 'Bitter Enders' soon began to settle down to their normal routine with Eric now feeling bold enough to take his new personal place by proudly sitting on Woody's stool. Tearfully, Mavis had thanked and kissed all of Woody's true Friends. She had an extra hug for Eric. This gesture was readily accepted by all those present as a demonstration of her approval for his rightful succession to the coveted post of *'Head Green Keeper'*. Bert had now decided to try his best to snap everyone out of their lingering feelings of sadness and grief. He shouted across the crowded room to attract Leonard's attention. Leonard had been quietly circulating around the room. Bernie Price, true to form, whispered to Peggy Hackett that he was probably sizing up his potential future Customers. When he uttered,

"It's a wonder he hasn't got his bloody measuring tape in his hand."

Peggy purposefully glared at him before he walked away in disgust. Bert asked Leonard, most respectfully,

"When will Mavis have the Urn containing the Ashes Leonard? Sorry to ask you about such a delicate matter but we need to make arrangements so we can carry out Woody's final wish to be scattered on his beloved square of grass out the back…Eh? Eh?"

He nodded discreetly in the direction of the bowling green at the rear of the premises. Leonard cautiously glanced all around before he responded, lowering the volume of his normal tone,

"I'll be making a point of collecting them on Wednesday Bert….I'm going to make a special trip up to the Crematorium to do so….Without giving you too much of the finer detail….The….Er…..Ashes you are referring to will need a short time to cool down…If you understand what I mean."

To a man, they all instantly realised exactly what Leonard meant. Leonard asked if he would to be allowed to perform the task of scattering the Ashes personally because there was a definite knack in doing so. Bert was happy to assure him that Mavis would be pleased if he would be kind enough to do so. Content that the proceedings had passed without a single hitch and that all other delicate matters were being dealt with Leonard and David took their leave soon after Bert had agreed to make them aware of the exact arrangements for this ritual to happen as soon as they had been made. As only a few chosen close Friends would be present to witness this final gesture they hoped to carry out Woody's wishes as soon possible and considered that Wednesday afternoon would probably be most suitable.

Bert, having established all they needed to know about the Ashes, then elected to make a special effort with a view to the easing of any possible embarrassment being felt by any one of them,

"Remember when old Freddie Swift passed on? You must remember old Freddie? Eh? Eh?...As far as anyone could tell he never did an honest day's work in his entire life...Gave his Missus a terrible time by leaving her to rear a house full of hungry children Eh? Eh? She just about managed to scrape enough food together to keep them clear from pending starvation...Freddie would be straight down to the Pub if he managed to get his hands on any money...She would then get him out of the Pub using any means she could muster always hoping she would be able to salvage any cash still remaining in his pockets....Eh....Eh? ... I bet Leonard would remember him for many good reasons"

Bert, quickly looking around before he recalled that Leonard and David had just left continued,

"Well when Mrs Swift got his Ashes back she went out of her way to get hold of an old fashioned and very large Egg Timer....Eh? Eh? Poured the sand out so that she could replace it with Freddie's Ashes instead...She and the rest of her Family turned that timer over every bloody chance they got...Night and day....She said that she couldn't get the Bastard to work when he was alive but she was making bloody sure he was kept active by putting in some work in after his death. Eh? Eh?"

Everyone soon realised that Bert was relating one of his humorous tales well before he got to his punch line. They all managed to raise a laugh. The gloomy atmosphere was, at long last, starting to lift slightly.

As the evening passed along and the beer flowed the friends gradually began to feel sufficiently recovered from the ordeal of the whole sorry day to enjoy one of their usual chats.

Eddie, a Major Beneficiary at the time, genuinely sounded as if he still found it very difficult to believe that Woody had been his and many other People's Benefactor. He had been genuinely astonished when the stunning truth behind the famous Trust had been disclosed after having remained such a mystery for a very long time,

"When I was told about Woody's real name….You know Kenneth Gordon?….The penny eventually dropped…Then I remembered the wonderful trip that Mary and I had back to the West Indies with all expenses paid but it still took me a little while before I finally twigged that it was none other than Woody who had footed the bill…He never ever hinted that he was responsible and if I am to be honest he was one of the last Persons I would have suspected as being the Benefactor responsible for one of the greatest demonstrations of anonymous generosity I have ever been fortunate enough to witness and also benefit from…I still find it hard to believe but I'll tell you this Woody made Mary and I extremely happy and we would never have been able to afford that Trip without the gift….What a marvellous man he was and no mistake."

Norman, who was deftly putting two and two together, as more and more formerly unknown facts were being revealed, turned to question Bert,

"I bet one of us here present knew all about it….Am I correct Bert?"

Bert smiling coyly nodded, positively indicating that he had appreciated that Norman's powers of perception were almost as sharp as his own. Every one of them was now agog with the keenest of interest as Bert was delighted to reveal the long protected secrets,

"I actually found out by accident Norm…Eh? Eh? I just happened to be searching a copy of the Electoral Roll up at the Police Station looking for a Bloke's address when I noticed that someone calling themselves Kenneth Gordon Green was listed as the person living at Woody's address….When I really thought hard about it…Well it was bloody obvious…Eh? Eh? First of all there was that horrible Woman….We all called her Doris Karlof…Remember? Eh? Eh? The short tempered Woman who used to do all the cleaning for Alf and also took it upon herself to help him behind the bar when the mood took her…Remember her? Eh? Eh? She suddenly inherited just enough money to provide her with sufficient funds to pay for her Immigration to Wales where she longed to impose herself on her daughter...Eh? Eh? Well Woody hated her serving him with his beer...Never enough to actually put him off it but she definitely tended to spoil his enjoyment through her nasty personality...Then of course there was the miraculous provision of a state of the art brand new artificial leg for Peggy...Now then who used to really annoy Woody by sinking his wooden peg into his beloved green especially on those occasions when the weather happened to turn inclement....Eh? Eh? Then....Sorry about this Alf if I'm telling stories out of school but then Alf was provided with a brand new superdooper Car with all expenses paid...Eh? Eh? I think it is fair to say that this came about at the same time as his old Jalopy was Scrap Yard bound even Alf had to admit that only the wing mirrors and ashtrays on it were still serviceable...Now Woody...Not a Driver himself had regularly been a grateful Passenger in your old Car am I right Alf? He was wasn't he? Eh? Eh? But....All of these wonderful gifts were beginning to mount up but the clincher as far as I was concerned was the mysterious deposit of all those substantial funds in the Coffers of this Club...Eh? Eh? Saved us from certain extinction they did...Victor can certainly bear witness to that fact...So...When I put all these separate yet somehow connected facts together I found that I was able to tackle him about these acts of unselfish but possibly self indulgent distribution of gifts...Eh? Eh? Woody was not surprised at my amazing powers of deduction but he did make me promise to keep the whole matter secret and I have done just that ever since...Eh? Eh?"

All of those present were eventually beginning to appreciate that there were, without any doubts whatsoever, many things they had not known about Woody. There was one thing they would be certain to unanimously agree upon. They were all confident that they would never see the likes of Kenneth Gordon 'Woody' Green ever again and that he would be missed tremendously by each and every one of them.

"My face went bright red."

The bitter disappointment and heartfelt grief and sadness evoked by Woody's sudden death was gradually becoming a fading memory to many of the Younger Members of our close Group of *Friends* living in Lapley Vale because, as the familiar saying goes, *'Life moves on'*. Steady progression to this much more bearable State of Affairs had been helped along, in no small way, by the gathering of all concerned to witness and celebrate the 'Mass' Christenings of the four new additions to the Gang. The New Babies had been able to enjoy their most welcome initiation Ceremonies whilst experiencing their very first Easter holidays.

Baby Edward Best was the first to be baptised at St Mary's Catholic Church in the presence of the other Families. Sam was not a Roman Catholic neither had he ever been associated with any other Religious Sect. Kay and her Family had always been staunch in their Faith so Sam had not offered any objection whatsoever to his Son being brought up in the Catholic Faith.

There were quite a number of People gathered together for this Special Day, well over sixty Guests. This large coming together included all the invited close Friends and Relatives of the four main Families, with the additional most welcome attendance of Damien and Bernie Harris proudly accompanied by their tiny new Daughter Rachel. They had willingly undertaken the long journey north, all the way from their new home in Milton Keynes, to join their Friends for the day. Most of the Group were taking the opportunity to see Rachel in the flesh for the first time although they had all enjoyed viewing the photographs taken with loving attention to detail by Damien, the proud new Father.

This considerable Group of Happy Souls had then moved swiftly along, en masse, to All Soul's, the Lapley Vale Parish Church, where William McCabe, Sonja Chumley and Elizabeth Chumley were all baptised at a joint service conducted by the Vicar, Reginald Blackburn, who, on this extra Special Occasion was being ably assisted by, his often rather accident prone and generally considered hapless Curate, Jeremy Smith-Eccles. Pronouncing the names of Sonja and Elizabeth together in the same sentence brought Reggie's slight speech impediment to the fore. Any of those present who had not previously met him immediately realised why he was affectionately known as *'Whistling Reggie'*. This time it was the Best family's turn to be the witnesses. To everyone's joy and amazement not one of the Babies cried or did anything to make things embarrassing or difficult for all of the Grown ups. After the formalities had been finalised in a proper and satisfactory manner for all concerned almost everyone had taken their eagerly sort after photographs which took some time in the prevailing circumstances. Then they had all descended upon The Lapley Vale Bowling and Social Clubhouse to participate in a most joyous Joint Celebratory Party.

At the forefront of the essential Backroom Girls, who were responsible for the provision of all the delicious party food, was Mavis Green. Mavis had clearly been in her elements as she was always at her best when she was able to generate joy and happiness for so many others. She had been very proud, as well as delighted, to have been given the honour of being a God Mother to all four of the Little Children. This was a cherished duty which Mavis could be depended upon to take seriously and conscientiously with each one of the Children equally.

Susan Summers was greatly relieved when Joe had to make his excuses before leaving the Party early to take up his work on the Night Shift at the Factory where he was still considered by all concerned to be a much valued Employee. Even Easter holiday breaks were excluded from their full work schedules in the mainly manufacturing and Light Industrial Companies, many of whom had been long established in this hardworking, productive, area. Joe Summers, despite his well known serious weaknesses personality wise rarely shunned his work duties. As all of their other Children had been present throughout the long day Joe, definitely not by choice, had managed to keep well away from the demon drink. Irrespective of many other less than complimentary opinions frequently expressed about Joe all of the Children in their loving and close Family Group obviously adored their Daddy without even a hint or the slightest signs of any reservations.

Some of the Smaller Children, including little Amy McCabe, Jane Chumley together with Joe and Susan's older kids were having the time of their lives. Denise, a mature Single Woman, was being treated to a break from her Barmaiding duties so that she could thoroughly enjoy the rare experience for her of having lots of Little Children for company. They were all quite easy to amuse with the well tried and tested provision of simple balloons, ensuring there were more than enough to go around, as ever proving to be a great success with Children of all ages. The proud Mothers, including Bernie, were all quietly feeding their Tiny Babies in a secluded corner of the Clubroom. This somewhat infrequent gathering of the whole Original Gang provided an excellent opportunity for them to indulge themselves with a really nice girly type chat. Bernie was anxiously watching that Damien did not overdo his reunion with his old Friends at the bar in view of the fact that she was being mindful of his need to remain reasonably sober to face up to their long journey back later in the evening.

After they had all adequately expressed and exchanged their individual joy and delight with their new arrivals, special attention obviously paid to baby Rachel Harris, it was Kay who was soon able to bring out their smiles,

"I hope this wonderful gathering of all of us together in one place doesn't result in producing a similar effect on us girls as what happened after Sam and I tied the knot....I wouldn't mind a fruitful outcome too much but I bet you Jenny…And you Linda have enough on your plates to cope with for the time being…And you Susan…Well if you have any more kids you'll have to move out of your House to take up residence in a Shoe…Eh?"

The smiles turned into laughter but, as might be expected, Susan humorously retorted,

"Well Kay love….When you and Sam tied the knot…As you called it…It wasn't the only bloody knot to be tied if you know what I mean…If we have anymore Kids we won't have any trouble choosing a name for it…No…Boy or girl it will be christened Houdini Summers…"

They all continued to enjoy the experience of their own close company as once again Susan deftly managed to demonstrate that she had not lost any of her natural sense of humour.

Linda was the next of them to regale her friends,

"Malcolm and I haven't decided on anything too drastic yet in keeping with the interests of contraception but the way I am struggling to cope with two children…Well….I think enough may well be enough as they say…I have to tell you what happened the other day when I was in Littlewood's Café in Oldham Town Centre…My Mother was at home minding Baby Sonja for the day which allowed Jane and I the chance to go out on our own little shopping spree together….After visiting all our favourite shops I was carrying three full shopping bags and I was also trying to hold onto Sonja's little hand all at the same time so I decided we would take a break in the Café….I bought some juice and a iced bun for Sonja and I also treated myself to a nice cup of frothy coffee and a large chocolate KitKat wafer biscuit….I treated myself to the biggest one…The one with four delicious fingers all for myself…The place was packed but we were lucky enough to find a vacant seat on a small table for two positioned quite close to the way out…Sonja was sitting on my knee but I was having a Hell of a job putting my shopping bags in a safe place as I was also struggling to put our refreshments down on the table…As son as we had settled down I noticed this weird looking Youth…Who was already seated at our table…He was a frightful sight…Long straggly dirty looking hair…Definite unwashed appearance with a big dangly brass ear ring hanging from one of his ears….He appeared to have been dressed by a Rag and Bone Merchant by the scruffy look of him…Anyways….The thought crossed my mind that it was little wonder no-one had wanted to sit at the table with him but I was desperate so I didn't care…I managed to get Sonja sorted out and was about to enjoy my coffee and KitKat biscuit when I saw that this horrible Youth was snapping off one the fingers from my KitKat bar…As bold as brass he started to munch on it so I really glared at him before I snatched the remainder of the biscuit off the table…He didn't say a word but I could tell that he was a bit shocked because he suddenly didn't seem to be enjoying the biscuit as much as he had been doing…. Well…He soon wilted under my best disgusted gaze…Then…..Looking as if he was terrified he shuffled up onto his feet before he disappeared through the door still without uttering a word of apology or anything… Little Jane was not aware that anything untoward was happening as she happily tucked into her bun so I sat her on the chair the Youth had just vacated and then sat back myself to cockily snap off another of the remaining three fingers of chocolate biscuit to enjoy…It was then that I was gently tapped on the shoulder by one of the Young Ladies from behind the Counter who had served me with our refreshments…She smiled politely as she passed me a small plate with a whole KitKat bar on it…All four fingers still intact inside it's sealed wrapper….She placed it on the table in front of to me as she said *'You left this on the Counter love…You paid for it so you might as well eat it'*….I didn't know what to say…My face went bright red…I quickly looked out onto the Street but there was no sign of the Youth….I had stolen his chocolate biscuit from him and the poor Lad never even uttered one single word of protest…Now bearing that incident in mind can you imagine what sort of tricks I might get up to if I had taken both of our Children into Town with me."

Her Friends were happily chucking as each of them tried to visualise the scene inside Littlewood's Café and the shocked expression that must have been exhibited on the Youth's face that day. Perhaps it was an illustration of the sayings, *'Looks can often be very deceptive…Never judge a book by its cover alone'*

Jenny was the first to react,

"I bet he thought he was being filmed for that Candid Camera… You know that really funny show on the television…Poor Lad…Just shows you should not go by appearances alone."

They nodded their tentative agreement as Jenny continued,

"Funnily enough Grandpapa Bert was telling us about them secretly filming in a Café somewhere near Bury Town Centre some time ago and the Actor who does all the daft tricks….You never actually see his face…Er…Jonathan somebody…Anyways…He was in there sneakily pinching chips of this Blokes plate…Just an ordinary Chap sitting across the table from him reading his newspaper as he ate his dinner…It was suppose to be amusing but when the Bloke caught sight of what the Actor was doing and without a word he just smacked him so hard that he sent the poor Chip Thief flying across the room upsetting several tables and also making a right mess of 'What's his name's' ugly face…The Police were called but after they settled everybody down there were no actual charges made…Apparently the aggressive Bloke didn't lose out and the whole filmed incident has not and never will make any appearance on anyone's telly."

Everyone was extra keen to hear how Damien and Bernie were settling down in their new unfamiliar surroundings of Milton Keynes. Her demeanour and excitement, as she updated them with all the new developments, was a clear indication that the Young Couple had definitely made the correct and sensible decision when they reluctantly moved away. They obviously missed all of their Friends but as they were both very happy with their new very well paid Jobs and they were delighted with their splendid New Home they were confident that they would soon be reaping the many benefits their bold move would undoubtedly be producing for them. Bernie fondly remarked on how her memories of the comments made by the new Mothers after the mass births in Lapley Vale Cottage Hospital had actually proved to be a comfort to her and some others she shared her experiences with.

"I don't have to remind you girls what actually giving birth was like because we all know from experience now don't we? … I was happy despite being very tender and sore and I soon rallied round when I recalled some of the remarks made about eyes still watering for a few weeks after the birth and the selling of bicycles…Cheered me up no end…One of the other Mothers in my Ward also benefited from Sister Murphy's remedy for painful bottoms…At first they were sceptical but when she discovered the unexpected comfort to be found from a frozen hand on her arse she was most grateful and I think some of the Nursing Staff learned something new as well."

As might have been predicted on such a Family occasions the Parents and Children soon gathered themselves together to make their ways home from the Clubroom after they had all spent the type of splendid day which they would remember for a long time. One of the main beneficiaries of the day's proceedings was Mavis Green. She was not the sort of person who would be likely to allow herself to suffer for too long, particularly as a result of self pity. Although she would never completely recover from her loss she was now looking forward to being able to enjoy a fruitful, useful and enjoyable, life as a Widow once again.

Bernie made sure Damien was not amongst the last of the Friends to leave the vicinity of the bar. She expertly managed to get him safely into their car and off down the road well before he was in danger of losing the use of his legs or talking in the style of broken biscuits.

"Alfred please pull another pint of bitter for our honoured guest."

The Sun was shining brightly on a delightful mid-summer afternoon as a battered, dilapidated, old fashioned Bedford pick up truck was seen to be very slowly edging its way along Westminster Road. This particular Road was proudly situated in one of the most prestigious and desirable Residential Areas in the whole of the Lapley Vale area. Bert McCabe was often heard to comment that wild birds flying over the area automatically flipped over onto their backs in full flight so they would not drop any crap on the roofs of any of the very expensive houses. He was also known to humorously allege that most of the Residents had padlocks fitted to their dustbins as a deterrent to any common, ordinary, People who might be tempted to pinch anything from them.

The driver of the truck was purposefully crawling along the Thoroughfare carefully checking the progress of a second scruffy looking Youth who was marching up and down the neat pathways and paved driveways knocking on the front doors of all the Houses in turn. The Residents behind the majority of these doors, which were actually opened instantly, slammed them closed again in the Youth's face. He eventually managed to encourage a Well-to-do Elderly Lady from one of the Houses, displaying a large and impressive sign denoting that the House had been named 'Shangri-La', to accompany him to take a look into the rear of the truck which was loaded with a collection of all sorts of colourful concrete Garden Gnomes. They were of various shapes and sizes and were neatly displayed on the floor of the truck. The Lady, called Mrs Alice Withington, made a considered selection before the Youth happily carried two of the chosen Gnomes down her pathway to deposit them on her front doorstep. She then disappeared inside her home soon returning in possession of her bulky looking purse before some cash changed hands. The Youth tugged on his forelock after he had deliberately spit on the money in his hand. Smiling broadly and in the view of the Driver he then placed the money in his pocket. He then continued along the Road to the next House.

As the two Men and their vehicle reached a secluded, quite shaded, stretch of the road where large Copper Birch trees blocked out most of the daylight two other Men were seen to suddenly leap out from cover. After the Driver of the truck had been dragged out of his cab a fully fledged Street Fight ensued involving all four of the Men. More than one of the Residents, who had probably been carefully watching the entire proceedings from behind nets and curtains, immediately telephoned '999' asking for the Police to attend to sort out the uncalled for disturbance in their Road as a matter of urgency.

The Shifts were changing over at Lapley Vale Police Station at the time when the Emergency Calls were being received. Constable Sooty Sutcliffe was handing over the reigns at the end of his Shift to Constable Eddie Littlejohn, better known as 'The Gentle Giant'. Sergeant Blackburn was also present in his Office attending to some of his necessary paperwork. The 999 calls received from various Residents in Westminster Road at Rochdale DHQ had been immediately relayed by internal telephone to Sooty who instantly relayed the breaking news on to Eddie. His response was typical of his usual engaging eagerness,

"Bloody Norah Sooty....Sergeant!...There a mass punch up taking place on Westminster Road at this very minute...Headquarters have dispatched a Crime Patrol Vehicle 'Z Mike Two'...They are making their way from the other side of the Division...Bloody Norah...Serg... Can we get there before they do? ... "

Without further comment all three Men dashed out of the Station, locking the front door behind them as they did so. They then jumped into Blackie's Triumph Herald which was parked outside the front door and they were off down the High Street travelling as fast as the vehicle could go.

On their arrival at the scene they saw that the Crime Patrol Car 'Z Mike Two' had already arrived. Two burley Constables were struggling in the roadway fully engaged with the four Men who were still fighting with each other. Eddie and Blackie immediately weighed in and all four Offenders were soon handcuffed and rendered harmless. To the shock and amazement of the local Officers Larry the Lamb and Spud Murphy were quickly identified as the two Assailants. The Driver of the truck and the other Youth were obviously Irish Tinkers. The Tinkers had definitely come off worse in the fracas. Blackie and Eddie, supported by a worried looking Sooty and the two Crime Patrol Constables lifted all four Prisoners into the rear of their own truck carefully arranging them amongst the remaining Garden Gnomes. Blackie had a quick word with the 'Z Mike Two' crew. They were quite happy and grateful to leave the Local Men to get on with whatever was now required which allowed them to be available to respond to any other Emergency Calls anywhere else in their Division.

With consummate ease Eddie drove the truck back to the Police Station. Sooty took his place riding in the rear *Riding Shotgun'* over the four manacled Men. On arrival at the Bridewell Eddie halted the truck directly outside the front door. Blackie, who had arrived before them, had already opened the front door and had also cleared the way through to the waiting Cells. On returning outside the Sergeant signalled to Eddie and Sooty that they could unload the four stunned Prisoners, who had made no attempt whatsoever to escape, to fetch them inside. Eddie, beaming with a broad smile, responded but he still managed to find time to inject a little humour,

"Can you please move around a little bit Chaps…We need to make a head count of the number of Garden Gnomes we've got here…Eh? It's bloody hard to tell much difference between them and you scruffy Buggers… What do you say Sooty?"

Sooty was far from feeling at ease but he did manage to raise a weak smile as he carefully assisted the Men out of the rear of the truck before they were guided into the Police Station.

Larry and Spud were placed in Number One Cell and the two Tinkers were locked up next door to them in Number Two Cell. After allowing things to calm down over freshly brewed mugs of tea in the kitchen at the rear of the Building Sooty was given permission to go home leaving Blackie and Eddie to do all of the sorting out which was now required. Eddie waited until he had gone before he remarked to his Sergeant,

"Probably needs to change his underpants as a priority Serg…Sooty isn't a physical type of Copper…He was sent here years ago from Bury Division because he had thrown a wobbler….He's fine now but he still avoids any nastiness whenever possible…I thought he did very well today…What a start to the Afternoon Shift….Bloody Norah."

Chosen for interrogation first Larry and Spud were anxious to be co-operative. Larry wasted no time at all informing them that he had recently been over in the nearby Town of Stretton on one of his regular jaunts spending some time attending to the needs of the Reverend Emmanuel Snoddy at St Peters Church as well as some of his Regular Customers who resided in that particular neck of the woods. According to Larry he had been, without warning or justification, hauled in to the Police Station over there because as Sergeant Baxter, the Officer in charge of Stretton Police Section, informed him they had been receiving a disturbing large number of calls from the Public reporting miscellaneous items mysteriously going missing from their Yards and Gardens. Lawn mowers and other gardening equipment had disappeared but above all there had been a considerable number of Garden Gnomes of all shapes and sizes that could no longer be accounted for. Because of his tendency to operate in the Area as a casual Gardener, taken together with his somewhat scruffy outward appearance, Larry had been nabbed and taken in as their Number One Suspect. After a long, frustrating, and at times very uncomfortable, interrogation Sergeant Baxter had released him for the time being but the Sergeant had made it crystal clear to him that he had definitely not been let off the hook and that he would be very carefully watched in the future.

Larry had been most distressed by this nasty experience so he decided to make his own enquiries into the mysteries surrounding the missing Gnomes and Miscellaneous Gardening Equipment and other Items of Garden Furniture. It did not take him too long before he discovered a small Colony of very shifty and untrustworthy Irish Tinkers who had made a Temporary Camp in a secluded lay-by on the outskirts of the Town. Putting two and two together he sneaked into their Encampment under the cover of darkness where he soon found lots of stolen garden items and a stash of dozens of Garden Gnomes. Although they were not exactly out in the open they were barely hidden from sight casually stuffed under and behind their ornate, and very valuable, Caravans and alongside some of their usual piles of miscellaneous debris.

Rather than placing his trust in the Stretton Police Larry hastily made his way back to Lapley Vale. He was intent upon making contact with his new friend Spud Murphy, who had fairly recently replaced Jedd Clampett as Town Tramp. They both agreed that due to the prevailing circumstances Spud would also be in line for selection as another Prime Suspect in the eyes of the Stretton Police. Spud readily agreed that he had no wish to share a similar experience to that suffered by Larry. He had no intentions of sitting back waiting be dragged in by the Police so there and then the two Men decided to join forces determined to deal with this whole distasteful matter without any official assistance.

Fortunately for Larry and Spud the Tinkers were stupid enough to opt for offering the stolen Items for sale, door to door, just a couple of miles away from where they had been stolen, namely in the leafy suburbs of Lapley Vale. The two Companions had skilfully, not to mention furtively, followed the clapped out Pick-up truck when it turned into Westminster Road. As soon as they witnessed the actual sale of some of the Stolen Property taking place to Mrs Withington, who just happened to be one of Larry's Regular Customers, at 'Shangri-la', they honestly considered that they were entitled to make a Citizen's Arrest. As Blackie and Eddie were satisfied that this was the sole reason why the Street Fight had broken out they were prepared to accept their version of events. Blackie explained to them that they had been arrested and locked up because the Police had been called to a Fight taking place in a Public Place which was at the very least a Breach of the Peace and therefore warranted the action subsequently taken which had caused them to be incarcerated along with the Thieves. As Larry had been given a nasty smack around his ear from Blackie and Spud was sporting a Black Eye after he had chosen to struggle with 'The Gentle Giant' Blackie informed them that he would be calling it quits and they would not be facing any Formal Charges. He warned them that they would be liable to be called as Witnesses for the Prosecution if required in any future Proceedings taken against the Tinkers. Arrangements were then made for both Men to make and sign Police Statements.

Blackie then triumphantly telephoned his opposite number at Stretton Police Station. Sergeant Baxter confirmed with him that all the salient facts, now exposed and accepted, after being anxiously and carefully related by Larry to Blackie were absolutely correct in all the relevant respects.

After expressions of gratitude together with gestures of admiration had been coyly accepted by Blackie, Sergeant Baxter informed him that he together with one of his Men would soon be on their way to collect the Tinkers from Lapley Vale Bridewell. Blackie was highly delighted with the whole outcome because apart from the fact that he had been able to release Larry and Spud without Charge, although they were severely cautioned about taking the Law into their own hands, because, in truth, Blackie did honestly accept that their actions had been quite reasonable in the prevailing circumstances, he also realised that he would have little or no paperwork to deal with because the Prisoners were going to be Charged with numerous individual Thefts from Gardens around the Stretton area and consequently they would be detained and then arraigned from there. He later expressed his genuine admiration for the determined action taken by the two wrongly suspected Offenders, Larry and Spud.

Detective Constable Jimmy Cross from Stretton CID together with another of Sergeant Baxter's Men raided the Tinkers Temporary Camp later the same day when further arrests were subsequently made and a considerable amount of outstanding Stolen Property was successfully recovered. This Property would need to be retained by the Police as evidence but after convictions were eventually secured they would all be returned to their rightful, grateful, legal Owners. Everyone concerned, with the possible exception of the Irish Tinkers, who were not deserving of any sympathy whatsoever, was happy with the way everything had turned out. Mrs Withington was only too willing to make a full Witness Statement after the Criminal Offence of 'Handling Stolen Property' had been poignantly pointed out to her. The two Gnomes she had paid good money for were also seized as evidence. Her chances of receiving them back or being paid a refund were virtually none.

Because of the anticipated Kudos, justifiably warranted by the numerous successful arrests being made, would be bringing to Sergeant Baxter and his men at Stretton Police Station, Larry and Spud were generously rewarded with a couple of quid each out of the Official Funds to enable them to enjoy a drink or two at the expense of the Police.

Later that Evening when all the dust had finally settled Blackie joined Bert McCabe and the 'Bitter Enders' for a welcome drink or two in the Clubroom at the Bowling and Social Club. They were all enthralled when Blackie rapturously related all the exciting events, blow by blow. Ralph, ever the Creep, was the first to offer Congratulations to him,

"I must say you are already having a remarkably impact on Crime and Criminals at Lapley Vale Blackie...And also sorting out the Felonious Swine who have infested Stretton as a side line....Well done...Alfred please pull another pint of bitter for our honoured Guest."

There were grunts indicating approval and agreement. Norman added,

"Whenever those thieving Bastards descend upon an area the Crime Rate rockets we've been lucky here over the years...Not merely by chance I'd be prepared to wager....Down to your Trusted Predecessor I think...What about it Bert."

Coyly accepting the obvious compliment generously being paid to him, Bert responded,

"Thank you Norm....Nice to receive deserved recognition from the adoring Public even if they made me hang my boots up well before I was ready to go...Eh? Eh? ... Seriously though that was a nice capture Blackie and I'm glad Larry and Spud were able to clear their names...I don't know Spud very well but I have known Larry for many years and basically he's not a serious threat to anyone...Eh? Eh? It's all too easy for Folk to blame the innocent in these sort of annoying cases...I hope you've made a full report of all these goings on to the...Er...Gnome Secretary at the Gnome Office Blackie....Eh? Eh?"

Everyone roared with laughter but it was Blackie, who managed to have the last word,

"Of course Bert...But we also made sure that the Er...National Elf Service was suitably informed as a matter of protocol also."

This happy Group of 'Brothers in Ale' were soon settling down to what would eventually turn out to be an enjoyable and seriously extended evening of informed social intercourse accompanied by unrestrained boozing.

Early the following morning, around 7am, Albert Kitchener Snooks, the current Locally Hero Worshipped Park Keeper at Lapley Vale Memorial Park and Gardens, was resplendent in his uniform as he proudly carried out his daily duties by raised the Union Flag on the pole alongside his hut (Sorry his Office). Albert, an Elderly Man by any standards, looked and conducted himself in a manner likely to be envied by a Guardsman a third of his age. He was still basking in the glory of his recent accidental arrest of a Desperate Criminal inside the Post Office. He was ever keen to relate the whole story to anyone unfortunate enough to ask him to elucidate upon what had actually happened on that now fateful day.

Frank Gelder, a Council employee who also had the Part Time Seasonal Job of running a small sweets and ice cream Shop in a purpose built Building, next to the Public Toilets inside the Park, from where he also looked after the daily care and hiring out to the Public of the small fleet of colourful Motor and Rowing Boats for popular use on the Ornamental Lake, called Albert's attention to one of their Rowing Boats drifting aimlessly in the middle of the Lake. On straining their eyes they could just make out the unusual sight of a pair of redundant oars, resting motionless in their rowlocks hanging from either side of the boat. Strangely, they could also see part of a right leg dangling over the right side of the boat with a human arm and hand, pointed towards the sky, showing on the left side.

They soon reached the Rowing Boat by using one of their little Motor Boats. To their astonishment they then saw Larry the Lamb and Spud Murphy both fast asleep lying in the well of the Boat where they had obviously fallen over and slipped into slumber whilst attempting to row the Boat. Albert cupped his large hands together to throw cold water, scooped from the Lake, over the two Men's faces. They were both awakened rather abruptly almost causing the Small Vessel to capsize.

"What the bloody hell are you two doing in the middle of the Lake at this hour in the morning? Frankie doesn't even start to hire out the Boats until 1pm sharp...Eh? I want the truth now or I'll be taking you both into custody for Theft and calling for the Police."

It very soon became blatantly apparent to both Albert and Frank that the two Characters in the Boat were suffering from very bad hangovers.

They quickly attached a towing rope to the stricken Boat before they towed it back to the Moorings. This necessary exercise allowed Larry and Spud a little time to utilise in their desperate attempts to regain some of their befuddled senses. Once they were all back on dry land Larry suddenly turned on Spud,

"It was you Spud...Last night after we spent our reward money and all the other cash we had between us...I remember now...We somehow ended up in here after a long thrash on the Ale and you suddenly got all upset saying you wanted to visit your old Mother in Ireland...You reckoned we had somehow managed to find ourselves by the Irish

Sea…Remember? Bloody hell I said it was too far to start rowing all that way at that time of night but you wouldn't listen."

Spud instantly looked suitably ashamed of himself as he spluttered,

"Sorry Lawrence my old Pal I'm afraid the memory is rather fuzzy this morning but I must admit I sometimes get very nostalgic especially when I've had a skin full…Christ how much did we drink last night…. My lips and finger ends have gone numb…That's never a good sign you know."

Albert took his first opportunity to telephone the Police Station. After he had been given the full facts relevant to all of the events which had taken place the previous day from Sooty Sutcliffe his whole attitude changed completely. In view of all the circumstances Albert then made them all a nice strong mug of tea. He informed them that after due consideration he would not be pressing any Charges with regard to the unofficial use of one of the Park's Boats. Their penance for this act of mercy, mingled with generosity, was to be made to listen to a blow by blow account of that day in the Post Office when single handily Albert had captured a dangerous and possibly armed Felon without any regard whatsoever for his own personal safety. He had a Framed Certificate of Thanks signed by the Post Master General himself proudly displayed on the wall of his hut positioned next to a Lapley Vale Examiner black and white photograph of Albert, in full uniform with two rows of medals prominently displayed on his tunic, receiving the actual Certificate from the Mayor of Lapley Vale, none other than Councillor 'Oily' Crump in person.

Had Larry and Spud realised what they had let themselves in for before Albert started talking they might, quite happily, have preferred to serve a six months Jail Sentence on Bread and Water Rations with Hard Labour as a punishment for the taking the Rowing Boat without permission.

"Right……Now it is my turn."

If anyone wanted proof that the 1970's Decade was already bringing forth rapid and remarkable changes to the everyday life and times in our Country they were merely required to make a visit to any of our mainly industrial and Manufacturing Areas. The best examples of these could be found situated in the North West of England as well as many parts of Yorkshire and other principally manufacturing centres operating in and around the whole of the Northern Areas of England through the Borders into larger Cities in Scotland.

It would have been nigh on impossible for anyone to miss the ever increasing presence of Asian People amongst our Communities, especially in the predominantly Cotton Mill Towns. Thousands of Indian and Pakistani, who were mainly manual and Semi-skilled Workers, had been targeted and then actively encouraged to move to Great Britain primarily to carry out the kind of tasks they had been trained to perform back in their Native Environments.

As so many new and varied opportunities were being offered to the Indigenous Population, particularly in the fields of Technology, Communication, and many other less labour intensive and manual types of well paid employment, the Cotton Mills Owners were finding themselves having to face up to a struggle as they attempting to find sufficient suitable Operatives to maintain their desired output in order that they could continue with their profitable and efficient Production of Goods. Not only were many of the Asians able to carry out the majority of tasks required for the production of cloth and other textiles, there was a growing suspicion that the greedy Directors and Shareholders had suddenly discovered that an apparently unlimited source of a much cheaper, competent, labour was available to them in great numbers. These Socially Naive Immigrants were prepared to work for much lower wages. They also made fewer demands on their Employers through their immediate Managers for any kind of improved Working Conditions or even, normally expected everyday, Welfare matters. A very liberal Immigration Policy along with an ever increasing influx of Illegal Immigrants had very quickly created this profitable opportunity those prepared to exploit it.

Many of the old, back to back, Terraced Properties in Towns like Rochdale and Oldham had been bought up, mainly by enterprising Property Developers, at ridiculously low cost. These very basic dwellings were soon being utilised as homes to an extraordinary number, at least by British standards, of Male Asian Manual Workers. Every one of these uncomplaining Lodgers was required to pay rent for very poor and over crowded sub-standard accommodation. Some Local People were reportedly commenting that the countless number of beds, stacked inside these houses, never actually got cold. As one Man got up to go to his work another Man took his place in the same bed having completed his work stint. All of these Immigrants also had an obligation to find sufficient money to enable them to repay their debts, greatly increased by the adding of exorbitant rates of interest, to various Intermediaries, mainly in their home Countries. These were the People who had provided the initial finance for their long journeys from their homes to our Country. Without getting too political there was clear evidence that a considerable level of cruel exploitation was being allowed to take place. Not all these ill-gotten gains were down to British sponsored manipulation because most of the monies being repaid were lining the pockets of more affluent, educated and intelligent, Asians in all of the Mother Countries involved. However the vast majority of these Workers seemed to be willingly accepting the conditions they were obliged to live and work under probably because at the end of the day they were earning the sort of wages they could only dream of getting at home.

After meagre living expenses and instalments on loans were paid out most of them were still able to send money home to the Poverty Stricken Families they had left behind them, many of them still living in very poor conditions.

The British style of life was gradually becoming more attractive to many of these people who had been brought up in totally diverse Environments and Ethnic Cultures. As they gradually adjusted to, what to them was a brand new, much improved, way of life, many became intent on settling down in the United Kingdom on a permanent basis just as soon as they could earn enough money to have the finance available to move their Families over to our Country to join up with them.

The previously experienced influx of Afro-Caribbean people to our County which first started in the 1950's, probably reaching its peak in the early 1960's, had not really been, what anyone could honestly call, a great success. After some initial harmony was enjoyed during a short period of time when the Immigrants keenly carried out hard work legitimately employed in low paid unrewarding, and sometimes downright dirty, jobs that most of the locals were not prepared to do, many social problems soon started to arise. Instances of Racial Prejudice increased as the next generation of British born West Indians were found to be naturally mixing with white men and women and somehow the resulting *'Half Castes"* they often created were openly being shunned by both the Black and White Communities. The result was that this growing number of misfits became more and more isolated and found them unwanted by almost everyone. They were considered to be practically impossible to employ which obviously caused them to become an increasing burden on Society in general. Some turned to Crime which caused even worse critical attention to be levelled against them. The more they were subsequently caught and punished was the more they tended to rebel.

The initially submissive nature and attitude exhibited by the vast majority of Immigrant Asians was in stark contrast to the more laid back, *'Happy go lucky'* approach seen with Afro/Caribbean Persons.

They could not really be fairly compared with their Counterparts. The many Asian's Ethnic Backgrounds taken together with their totally different basic Cultures were as diverse to the West Indian way of life as they were to the indigenous British people. Great Britain was well on the way to becoming a Multi-cultural Nation whether this had been the actual intention of the Government or not. At that time many ordinary Citizens, both Black and White, were becoming concerned that future problems were steadily building up. These warning signs were not being dealt with in a positive manner so they were inevitably being allowed to evolve as the eventual cause of much undesirable Social Unrest. This was generally considered to be more of a certainty than a dread. Many feared violence and there was the now infamous *'Rivers of Blood'* speech delivered by a prominent Politician whose words were not only ignored but were even ridiculed in some parts of the Country. These clearly precarious courses of action appeared to have been irresponsibly condoned by *The Powers that be*[*] as well as some of those Persons who could justifiably have been accused of having vested interests in the developing situation being allowed to steadily make progress without having the slightest care for any probable, undesirable as well as disastrous, consequences.

Not all of the Asian or the many other Resident Ethnic Minorities residing in our Country were engaged in carrying out menial tasks or manual labour. Hospitals were recruiting fully qualified Doctors and Nurses from all over the World in last ditch efforts to ensure their essential facilities were adequately staffed. In the Birchfield Infirmary near Rochdale the Staff had been drawn together from a far ranging mixture of differing Nationalities in such proportions that they could fairly be described as *'Staggering'*. The now established and generally well accepted familiar Irish Doctors and Nurses were being replaced, in no small way, by mainly Asian and Afro/Caribbean Contemporaries.

Although the Medical Profession continued to be dominated in their Top Echelons by typically British people the undoubted skill and dedication readily exhibited by the majority of Overseas Personnel was not only deemed competently acceptable but was also becoming vital in order to preserve the longer term smooth running of a Service which was having to face up to the ever increasing demands continually being made upon it.

Many of these extra pressures were being caused directly as a result of some of the many marvellous advances in the availability of new Drugs and Medicines as well as radical, revolutionary, Treatments now there for every Patient to take advantage when necessary.

Our Universities still continued to churn out huge numbers of Medical Graduates, many of them originating from Overseas, mainly Commonwealth Countries. Many of the newly qualified British Doctors and experienced National Health Service Trained Nurses were all too often being tempted to emigrate to all corners the World especially to the United States of America, Canada and Australia where they could expect to be given the opportunity to enjoy a much higher Social Status at the same time as they were comfortably making their personal fortunes. It was a fact that British trained Doctors and Nurses were in great demand all over the civilised World.

Doctor Deepak Shantha had already successfully qualified as a Doctor at the University of Bombay in India some years before he moved, with his wife Amma, to take up a Junior Post at a well known London Teaching Hospital. He had then continued to diligently study gaining further qualifications in more than one specialised area of Medical Excellence. After another couple of years of purposeful self advancement at a number of other London Hospitals he moved with Amma and his young Family, children Vicram and Indira, to take up a highly regarded and prestigious post as a Resident Consultant at the Birchfield Infirmary.

The Shantha family had moved into a large detached house situated on Westminster Road, Lapley Vale, which readers may recall was considered to be the most desirable and upmarket part of the Town. They encountered a few minor problems whilst they adjusted to the new slower pace of life in their unfamiliar locale. Living in London during the 1960's had prepared the Family very well for life in any part of the British Isles. They were generally well received by most of their Neighbours, with one notable exception.

There was little contact between the Shantha Family and the elderly Mr and Mrs Elgin, who owned and lived in the house on one side of them although they were committed to being polite and friendly to each other. The McAvoy Family on the other side were a very different story. The McAvoy Family had two Children almost identical in their ages to Vicram and Indira. James and Hannah McAvoy soon became close friends with their new Neighbours. As was often witnessed with Young Children not even a slight problem over language seemed to deter their sincere friendship from developing. Amma Shantha and Grace McAvoy were slightly more distant but, as most Mothers appear to be compatible, they were both delighted that their Children were able to get on so well with each other. The language and cultural differences were a definite handicap to their everyday interaction between the Wives but they were committed to being quite tolerant as well as cautiously comfortable together. The McAvoy Children had developed a taste for new foods like curries, rotis and naan bread whilst the Shantha children enjoyed fish and chips with liberal amounts of tomato ketchup added amongst many other typical British dishes.

However, Gordon McAvoy, a successful Chartered Accountant with his own quite small but nevertheless thriving Company in Oldham, unfortunately was neither impressed nor enamoured with Deepak. Thankfully this was not for any reasons which could have been even remotely classed as being of a racial or ethnic nature. Gordon disliked his new Neighbour for one reason alone. He considered Deepak to be a penny pinching frugal miser. In his opinion, a view not shared by anyone else of any note, Deepak's considerable income was sufficient to avoid the necessity for him to literally live off the land in what Gordon considered was a respectable Residential Area.

Deepak had utilised every inch of the large area available at the rear of his home filling it with an assortment of fruit trees and bushes. Where there was spare space he had cultivated several vegetable patches which were packed with many varieties of home grown produce. He had also erected a small greenhouse in which he lovingly nurtured and grew oriental herbs and chilli pepper plants as well as the usual tomatoes and cucumbers.

Gordon was not too upset by this initial development but when Deepak set up a small wooden Henhouse complete with a Cockerel and several laying Hens he considered that his Neighbour had gone a step too far. The Hens were kept in close confinement behind a Chicken Wire Fence but Poultry being what they are by nature, on occasions, had managed to successfully escape allowing them the freedom to wander aimlessly around pecking at everything in sight. Thankfully they merely roamed within the immediate vicinity of the Henhouse but they also considered their Neighbours gardens to be within their extended range. In addition to this inconvenience, Gordon strongly objected to the *'Bastard'* of a Cockerel waking him and everyone else up at the crack of dawn every morning with his ridiculous, loud and annoying, crowing.

Due to a total lack of any solid support from other People living nearby Gordon had been reluctantly forced to tolerate *'The Chicken Ranch'* next door, as he called it. He commented to one Neighbour that they would live to regret not making a stand when Deepak inevitably increased the inhabitants of his Menagerie by moving in sheep, goats, and possibly some sacred cows.

One Saturday morning Gordon just happened to be present in his rear garden when a startled Hen leapt up in the air directly in front of him as he was quietly approaching his wooden garden shed which was situated close to the impregnable perimeter fencing. The surprised Hen was clucking ten to the dozen, making, what could fairly be described as, a dreadful racket. Gordon immediately noticed that the Hen had laid an egg in a small indentation scrapped out on the surface of the ground in a sheltered portion of one of his cultivated flowering borders. Deepak had been fully occupied busily toiling in his vegetable patches until his attention had been drawn to the loud noises being made by the frightened Hen. The terrified Creature did manage to fly over their dividing fence, landing straight back inside the confines of the Chicken

Coup. This action was accompanied by even more noise and left clouds of dust as well as loose feathers flying all around.

Deepak first checked to ensure that his Hen was secure before he peered over the fence. He was just in time to witness Gordon as he picked up the newly laid egg off the ground. Deepak coughed politely before he spoke,

"Sorry about that Gordon…I will strengthen that bloody fencing around the Coup at my very first opportunity."

Gordon merely stared at him as he stiffed a growl. Deepak then politely and quietly asked his Neighbour,

"Can you please hand my egg over to me now? I have been missing quite a number of them recently…Thank you."

Gordon appeared to have been unimpressed with this request,

"I beg your pardon Friend….Your egg? Sorry but you seem to be slightly mistaken there…This is my egg now."

Deepak was defensive and clearly curt in his reply,

"Your egg? What do you mean? It's your egg? Sorry but that is definitely my egg….Hand it over please…There is a good chap."

Gordon defiantly shrugged his shoulders,

"Sorry this is my Garden where the egg was laid and this is a natural product it is therefore my property…Thank you."

Gordon was about to walk away carefully holding the egg in his hand. Deepak was now getting most annoyed,

"What! You are mistaken there Old Boy…It is my Hen and therefore my egg…Hand it over to me please."

Gordon stood his ground, unmoved,

"Look…Let us both carefully examine all of the known facts here… I found this egg within the legal confines of my personal Garden area…Right? Now I don't dispute for one moment that the said egg was laid by one of your Hens but….Under British Common Law as it stands….My Garden…..My egg….I will do the decent neighbourly thing by refraining from suing you for allowing your Hen to wilfully trespass upon my Land…I am mindful of your status as the *'Ears nose throat dandruff and bellybutton Specialist'* up there at the Hospital and as such you would obviously not welcome that sort of adverse publicity being directed towards you."

Deepak was then almost speechless,

"What are you talking about Old Boy? What nonsense are you speaking? It is obviously my egg…Hand it over right away."

Gordon then very calmly walked over to confront Deepak, face to face, over their dividing fence,

"Look….Old Boy….There is a traditional civilised British way to decide the rightful outcome to this dispute which has been passed down from Generation to Generation since time immemorial.….Are you interesting in hearing about this?"

Deepak thought for a second or two before he vigorously nodded his head positively. Gordon confidently continued,

"Join me over here on my lawn.….If you please…The lawn…That is this green bit here…Cannot be eaten by Humans…I mention that just in case you don't recognise what the Area is called by name.…Right?"

Deepak adeptly vaulted over the reasonably low fence showing natural athletic prowess. Gordon nodded his approval for Deepak's impressive response by nodding his head before firmly saying,

"Right"

He then paused for a few moments. He was looking into Deepak's face as he went on to say,

"You have questioned the rightful Ownership of this egg…Now.… As it was you who had the bare faced audacity to impugn my veracity in this matter it falls to me under the prescribed Rules governing the conduct of these Contests to inform you……That this therefore entitles me to have the first go."

Deepak appeared to be puzzled as well as strangely fascinated; he demanded some basic clarification,

"First go? What do you mean? First go.…I fear I do not understand."

Gordon was only too keen to explain,

"We….That's you and I…We.…Stand facing each other on this neatly manicured square of grass…Right?"

Deepak nodded adjusting the position of his body slightly in order to directly face Gordon.

"Right….You will be the first to stand with your legs in an open position or stance as it is called in order to facilitate me as I aim one kick at your Balls….Sorry Doctor…The official Medical Term is as you probably know….Your…Er… Testimonials….Just one kick each at a time…. Right?"

Deepak appeared to be a little reluctant to comply but he intimated that he did understand. Gordon was concentrating upon getting himself ready, as he added,

"This Contest will be decided when one of us reacts to the kick by falling down onto the surface of the grass…After I have taken my go it will be your turn….So…The First Man who allows any part of his anatomy…Other than his feet…To touch the grass…Do you comprehend?....That is any part with the stated exception of feet of course… Will then be deemed to have been the Loser of the Contest and will thenceforth forfeit any rights or any claims whatsoever to the Legal Ownership of the egg in question…Do you clearly understand these tried and tested Rules?"

Deepak anxiously nodded as he was determinedly gritting his teeth together, preparing himself. Gordon then took a short run up before kicking Deepak squarely in his Testicle area. The Doctor immediately let out a piercing squeal. He then reeled around the lawn almost falling over at least twice but managing, with great difficulty, to maintain his vertical position on his feet, still within the confines of the lawn. Slowly re-gaining his normal stance he painfully teetered and tottered almost falling to the ground once again, yet after a couple of minutes of sheer agony, he skilfully avoided losing his balance and therefore prevented himself from illegally touching any part of the grass. Grimacing as he gently rubbed his groin area, groaning as he still desperately gasped for breath, he glared aggressively at Gordon as he returned to take up his original position. He looked absolutely committed, as well as angry, determined, and very keen and anxious, to move on to the next stage of the ongoing proceedings,

"Right…Now it is my turn…Please would you be kind enough to prepare yourself for my turn to have a kick at your Balls."

Gordon stared directly into Deepak bloodshot eyes before he casually said,

"No….Bugger it….You can keep the egg…"

He then handed the egg over to the stunned and still aching Doctor.

"Shut that gate behind you as you leave my Garden please…Good Morning."

Gordon swiftly walked away in the direction of his back door leaving the still gasping and frustrated Deepak staring down at the egg now snugly held in his trembling hand.

Long Evening shadows were just beginning to appear when Deepak, sweat pouring from his forehead, groaning with aching muscles, finally completed the added errection of a second even more permanent Chicken Wire Fence. This one completely surrounded the whole of the Chicken Coup making the chances of any Hen ever escaping that way again impossible. The Doctor had just experienced one day that he would have cause to remember for the rest of his life.

"Thanks Ricky….I am honoured."

The wooden Pavilion conveniently situated alongside the hallowed square of grass belonging to the Lapley Vale Bowling and Social Club had not noticeably changed at all since the sad demise of Woody Green. The small, lovingly painted in white gloss, Pavilion was mainly use as the store for all the essential equipment required for the upkeep and maintenance of the crown green and also the well stocked surrounding flower beds and all of the neatly trimmed ornamental shrubs. Eric McCabe, unofficially appointed as Head Green Keeper, was still suffering with pangs of sadness whenever he found himself inside there where the two Men had shared so many happy hours of company and friendly conversation whilst skilfully engaged in the course of their duties.

Eric had done a remarkable job of keeping the high standards set by his late Friend and Mentor, who had proved to be a very hard act to follow as his Eric as his successor had discovered to his cost. This achievement, which had frequently been commented upon by many independent observers, was a matter of extreme personal pride to Eric. The proudly displayed 'Highly Recommended' plaque presented to the Club by the *'Powers that be'* was not in jeopardy because even after a long Season of constant use the grass was still in perfect, top quality, condition after being painstakingly prepared for the long dormant winter break.

Vic Callow the Secretary/Treasurer of the Club had authorised Eric to seek out a replacement for himself as the understudy to the Head

Green Keeper. This had not proved to be too difficult a task because Eric had recently taken on an Apprentice at Mitchell's Nurseries, where he and Jenny were now Part Owners, and this appointment had been a great success. The Apprentice had turned out to be just as keen and enthusiastic as he had been many years before at the time when he left school to work under the tutelage of Dickie Mitchell. Eric was conscious of the distinct possibility that his prospective appointment could present him with a slight problem. The Novice Gardener in question was a girl. It was difficult for the casual observer to determine at a glance when she was wearing suitable gardening attire because Myrtle Billington genuinely did look more Male than Female at first glance. She had always been known to her friends as 'Billy' and this had not really helped her to enhance her feminine origins. She was a rather plain, deceptively strong, very quiet, always most respectful and obedience girl. She lived with her Mother in a small Cottage situated in the beautiful surroundings of Lapley Manor. Fenella Billington had been employed by Lady Lapley since she was a Young Woman. The Cottage she now shared with Billy had been her Parent's home until they passed away. No-one, especially Billy herself, was aware of the true identity of her Father. This had remained a secret since the shocking time when Fenella fell pregnant in her teens at a time when she was employed as a Chambermaid at the Manor House.

Eric had been fully informed of Billy's antecedents before he took her on at the Nursery and as far as he had been concerned Billy had already been able to show that she had a promising future in front of her as a skilled and dedicated Gardener. He had invited her to visit him at the Club so that he could put her through one crucial final test before she was given the Understudy's Post.

He had already collected a package of specially prepared chemicals from Harry Jeeps the Chemist on the High Street. Every year after he had been sent by Woody to collect these secret items he was pleasantly reminded of the first time he ever encountered his beloved Jenny. Jenny had been working as an Assistant in the Shop and due to what can now be called an unfortunate misunderstanding she had thought Eric was visiting her Shop to purchase a packet of contraceptives. Her suspicions had been further aroused when Eric had initially insisted upon seeing Mr Jeeps in person. After Eric then went on to purchase a packet of assorted plasters Jenny had taken the bold step of placing a packet of 'Durex' in front of him on the counter with the genuine intention of avoiding any embarrassment or further expense for the naturally shy Eric. However, this potentially disastrous first encounter soon developed into a delightful love affair which resulted in their happy marriage taking place. There was also the, possibly a little too soon than might have been planned, arrival of their daughter Amy which subsequently enhanced their lives for ever more..

Billy arrived on her bicycle, skidding to a halt on the car park at the front of the Club. She had then dashed through to the bowling green at the rear of the Clubhouse clearly anxious not to be late for her prearranged appointment with Eric. Eric had already taken the opportunity to give Billy a full tour of the main facilities when the two of them had called in to deliver some bedding out plants in Eric's van. Eric got straight to the crux of the matter by curtly instructing Billy to follow him as he made his way to the rear of the Pavilion carrying the parcel of chemicals as well as a spade. Billy was fascinated to see a very large wooden barrel complete with a lid which was held down by a large stone placed on top of it which was where the Special Fertiliser for the grass was stored. Eric, smiling in an encouraging fashion turned to address Billy,

"Right Billy….Shift that stone off the top of the barrel will you please."

Billy, a big strong girl, had no problem completing this task. Eric was then bracing himself because he was aware of the nature of the contents inside the barrel. There was a solution of rain water with several punctured plastic bags suspended in the water. These were filled with ripe chicken shit, which was being allowed to slowly dissolve to make a foul smelling liquid which would be carefully applied to the grass on the bowling surfaces in order to keep the square in the outstanding, healthy looking, condition it was invariable found to be in.

Billy did not even flinch when Eric nodded to her to remove the lid. The acrid stench was immediately present as evil looking fumes escaped. Eric carefully opened up the parcel to expose the carefully measured chemicals. He instructed Billy before he covered his mouth and nose by pulling up the collar on his thick woollen sweater.

"When I pour this into the barrel I want you to give it a bloody good stir using the shovel please Billy...Ready?"

As might have been expected the stench increased fifty fold as Billy conscientiously stirred the disgusting mixture. Eric almost collapsed as he desperately gasped for air. Billy's eyes were watering but she was still managing to bear up to her ordeal very bravely. She was doing so much better than Eric was as it so happened. Eric soon signalled to Billy to replace the lid back on top of the barrel. She dropped the spade to the ground so she could do so with a sign of relief then becoming apparent by her twisted facial expressions. Eric quickly ushered her away to the front of the Pavilion. They both filled their lungs with as much fresh air as they could possibly inhale. Eric was still rubbing his eyes as Billy remarked in quite a cool, casual, manner,

"Christ Ricky what the Hell have you got in there?....It smells worse than what I would expect Skunk shite to smell like....And I do have some idea what that smells like because I've cleaned out their cages on the Safari Park a few times when I did temporary work there during the summer holidays...Just before I left school."

Ricky laughed as he was happy to indicate that Billy had passed her test with flying colours.

"It's a secret recipe invented by Woody Green and Harry Jeeps....I won't go into all of the gory details but let's say rotten chicken shite is the base ingredient...If you can stand that pong Billy you are fit for purpose here and I want to offer you the Part Time Job as my Assistant....You can start right away if you like...You might be please to hear that the sink gradually fades after a couple of weeks of fermenting....Woody used to tell me that I would get used to it after a while but I never have done and neither did he if it comes to that."

Billy nodded her head with sheer delight having been able to pass the dreaded test without suffering too much discomfort.

"Thanks Ricky....I am honoured...I must say it took all my inner strength to stop myself from screaming out loud when I started giving it a stir...Thanks Ricky I know you have been influential in getting me this Job and I promise that I won't ever let you down."

Eric smiled as he issued a warning note to his new understudy.

"Just keep your head down for a while Billy there might be one or two of our Chauvinist Tithead Members who might disapprove of a girl working here but I'm sure that won't worry you too much...Just do as I tell you and carry out your tasks in the same way that you do all your jobs up at the Nursery and one day....One fine day Billy...You will succeed me as the finest living Green Keeper in the whole of Lancashire....Nay....Make that England....NO....The World."

They made their way across to the veranda heading towards the kitchen. Eric nudged Billy as he spoke to her in a low whisper.

"Just listen to this now Billy...Don't let on will you? Just listen."

Mavis met them at the door. She was holding a lace handkerchief under her nose as she waved her other hand in front of her face.

"Poo! What a rotten pong....I bet it's that smelly Tanning Factory down the Town at it again Ricky?...They should be prosecuted as a danger to Public Health if you ask my opinion....Come on inside I brewed up and I've made a fresh batch of scones...I take it you are a scone fan are you Billy?"

Billy did not begin to understand the comment about the Tannery but she was aware of how delicious Mavis's scones were so she keenly responded.

"Oh yes please Mrs Green...Thank you very much....I'm always hungry my Mother thinks I've got worms or something...She says I eat like a horse but they eat oats don't they? I don't like oats."

Mavis was dashing into the kitchen as she added,

"Well thank you for that information Billy love...You'd better put a move on though...Because I know a certain Club Steward who could represent England at scone eating and he's already on his way to join us."

Eric and Billy were giving their hands a really good scrub as Mavis left the room for a moment to give Alf a final call. Eric nudged Billy again as he attempted to mouth his words silently to her,

"Bloody Tanning Factory….Eh? We've never told Mavis about our special mix…She blames that Factory every year….Woody and I always enjoyed a laugh over that."

The two Gardeners were giggling as Mavis returned to feed and water them all.

"I think we might have entered into the 'Staggering Seventies'"

The Members of the Committee had been called to attend a Meeting primarily arranged to come to a decision on how they would best be able to preserve the fond memory of Woody Green, their departed Friend and Mentor. As is quite normal for these occasions Alf had attended to his, now familiar, routine by the placing of a large plywood board over the top of the snooker table to provide a desk for the use of the Chairman and the others. They were to be seated around the 'Desk' using tall bar stools because of the unusual height of the adapted facility. Ralph Jones, the Chairman, invariably took his rightful place at the head of the table with Victor Callow, the Treasurer/Secretary, seated alongside in keeping with his position as his right hand man.

Ralph had opened the meeting by welcoming Bert McCabe, the newly elected Member of the Committee, replacing Bernie Price who had lost his place to Bert in a recently held election. This particular announcement was especially well received by Billy 'Cockeye' Dawes who had invariably been the butt of Bernie's nastiness at any given opportunity. This often included undisguised personal attacks upon him during Committee Meetings. Ralph almost broke down when he had to mention the sudden and lamented death of Woody Green. He expressed the unanimous desire of all of the Membership to establish some permanent reminder of such a long serving and totally committed Servant of the Club, not only as the Head Green Keeper but also as the Captain of the all conquering Crown Green Bowling Team. The mere mention of Woody's name brought instant indications of still raw feelings from all of those who were present, who also included Eddie Brown and Alf the Steward. Ralph whilst attempting to save the dignity of the Meeting then called upon Victor, in his role as the Treasurer/Secretary, to outline the current Financial Standing of the Club.

As ever Victor presented all the facts in a most professional manner. All were delighted to hear that the Club was continuing to thrive and prosper. The ever increasing popularity was being reflected in their highest ever numbers of fully Registered and Signed up Members. This fact had certainly been responsible for maintaining their desirable as well as healthy financial situation. Before handing back to Ralph, Victor seized the opportunity to make mention that the decimalisation of currency was definitely going to be introduced throughout the United Kingdom in February, 1971. He pointed out that there would be a need for new Tills to be purchased and that some necessary alterations would be required to their profitable Slot Machines. Victor assured them that all of these matters would be dealt with in plenty of time before the historic date arrived.

The most welcome content, delivered by the smooth presentation of his report, had been responsible for the return of a pleasant ambience to the Meeting. Ralph thanked Victor,

"Thank you Mr Treasurer…And also Mr Secretary of course for your expected efficiency and the excellent news about our financial standing….Seems a long time since we were wondering how we were going to be able to simply survive…I want to mention Woody again in a moment but before I do are there any questions for Victor please?"

Eddie Brown was smiling as he shook his head, Billy Dawes also indicated that he had nothing to say but Alf mouthed words by way of compliments to Victor who, always, relished any sort of praise from any quarter. Bert raised his right hand causing Ralph to respond instantly,

"The Chair recognises you Bert…Welcome to the Inner Circle… What is your question for Victor pray tell?"

Bert, beaming with one of his famous smiles, returned nods of welcome before he cleared his throat in order to speak,

"Thank you Mr Chairman…Thank you all Gentlemen for your warm welcome and kind good wishes….I hope to serve the Club at all times to the best of my enormous abilities…Eh? Eh? You mentioned the decimalisation issue Victor I wonder if everyone present is as ignorant as I am as to the actual details of this massive change to our everyday familiar money Eh. Eh? I know we will get more information before the actual time but I hope that this rumour about the School leaving age in Liverpool being raised to 45 years to allow them sufficient time for most of the Students to be able to understand this new dosh before they set out in the big wide World Eh. Eh?"

They all chuckled, realising that Bert was deliberately being humorous. Billy was first to react,

"Well Bert I was hoping someone would explain this cockeyed change over to me…I don't suppose for one moment that I will get anymore cash in my cockeyed Pension but I have been told the new money will be easier for Old People like me to cope with….I cockeyed hope so."

Alf was stirred to make a comment,

"I bet one thing Billy….It will probably be easier to run out of it if I'm any guess of Government Policies….I'm bracing myself for possible problems and I'm expecting some trouble but we must all try our best not to make matters any worse than they need to be."

Eddie joined in the discussion,

"As I understand things the pound will be made up from 100 pence and when you think about it I suppose it's probably more sensible than having 240 pence and 20 shillings 8 half crowns and the like that we have always had…A quid is a quid in my books and for most of us this change will make little or no difference because we'll still struggle make ends meet…We've had to cope with money problems all of our lives so far…I bet we find things will not as bad as they seem likely to be at the moment as and when this change over inevitably happens…They must be planning to make some allowances for the introduction of such a radical change surely."

Ralph waited until everyone was quiet before he returned to the subject which they were all aware was the main reason for the Meeting taking place.

"Well as they say at Boot's the Chemists when you leave your films…Let's see what develops….Thank goodness we have Victor's vast Banking Experience to fall back on….Vic will make sure we cope won't you? I obviously realise that we all suffer some degree of difficulty talking about Woody but talk about him we must….First of all can we take a vote on the Appointment of young Ricky McCabe to replace him as our Head Green Keeper? Can we have a show of hands please…All those in favour? Thank you Gentlemen unanimous as expected….Victor will you please write to Ricky with the details of his now Official Appointment."

Billy raised his hand whilst he was actually speaking,

"Mr Chairman….I understand that Ricky has already found a replacement for himself as the cockeyed Apprentice…It's a cockeyed girl….Called Billy."

Bert was happy to be in a position to explain,

"As a matter of fact her name is Myrtle Billington Billy….She much prefers to be called Billy… Can you blame her Eh? Eh? Christ who would want to be called Myrtle…What a bloody handle to be stuck with….And…Her Mother…. Fenella! Eh? Eh? Got a bloody good sense of humour that Family if you're asking for my opinion…. Anyways she's a good Lass and Ricky tells me that he's very pleased to have her helping him…That's all that matters isn't it? Eh? Eh?"

Alf suddenly shot forward, almost losing his balance on the stool, anxious to add his observations,

"Does this mean I'll have to order bottles of Babycham to cater for the staff refreshments?"

They all laugh as Eddie said,

"If she's anything like her Mother she will be able to drink us all under the table…Fenella has been downing pints of bitter on the odd occasions when she spends a night on the Town for as long as I have been acquainted with her....And that's a few years I can tell you....If she does the Job half as well as Ricky has always done it she'll do for me.... I bet she'll turn a few heads at first but she has the complete support of Ricky and the backing of all of us as well so she'll be fine."

Ralph regrettably found he was once again obliged to return to the subject which was the crux of the Meeting,

"Right fine....Well Mavis has informed me that she would like to present the Club with a fine Silver Plated Trophy to be called the Woody Green Memorial Cup....To be presented to the Club's best all round player each year...She has set her mind on doing this so I wonder if there could possibly be anyone who wishes to raise any kind of objection to this most generous offer?"

As anticipated there was no response. Victor spoke,

"I think we are unanimous again Mr Chair...Perhaps we could consider the purchase a quality wooden bench to be placed outside the Pavilion at the side of his beloved green."

Billy was very keen to exhibit his total agreement,

"The cockeyed Woody Green Memorial Bench....I'd go for that... What a great idea Victor....We afford a decent bench can't we? I've seen some cockeyed rubbish ones around some of the other greens we play at during the season."

Victor was delighted to respond in a positive manner,

"No problem at all Billy....But I think we should call it the Kenneth Gordon 'Woody' Green Memorial Bench....There may be one or two people who still don't know who was really behind that brilliant Fund which amongst other things was responsible for saving this Club from certain doom...Anyone disagree?"

There were clear and definite signs of total agreement. Ralph took over once again.

"Well that's it Gentlemen....Alf get that beer tap turned on....I'm as dry as a Witch's tit....The Chairman is buying...Any other business? Can I call a close to this most fruitful meeting?"

Ralph allows seconds for any possible response before he rapidly closed the Meeting officially,

"Thank you Gentlemen….All agreed matters will be attended to forthwith…I wonder what the 1970's will have in store for us all…If this Decade turns out to be half as fantastic as the 1960's appear to have been I for one will not be making too many complaints."

It was Alf, who had the final words as he made his way across the room heading towards the bar,

"The Newspapers and those excitable people popping up on the telly seem to be forming the habit of referring to the past Decade as the "Swinging Sixties" whatever that means… I think we might possibly agree that we were swept along to a stage where we could perhaps be described as "Swaying" but having witnessed the general state of drunkenness shown by most of our Members as they were happily leaving these Premises in the early hours of the morning following our 1970 New Year's Day Celebrations I think we may well be entered into what will probably be known when we reach the 1980's as the *Staggering Seventies*'….Speaking for myself personally I am braced ready and prepared to take on whatever is thrown our way….Even the good Folk of our beloved Lapley Vale will be forced to move with the Times or they might find themselves left behind the Rest of the Country"

Ralph responded on behalf of them all,

"Well said Alfred….Don't imagine for one moment that you are only speaking for yourself…We all look forward to *'Staggering'* along whilst we thoroughly enjoy each and every one of the ever increasing new and exciting changes as they present themselves."

These remarks were greeted enthusiastically with shouts of "Here Here!"

All of the friends were laughing as they happily took their places at the bar, ever ready to enjoy their drinks.

The End (Or is it?)

Thank you for reading this book. The Author hopes that you gained as much pleasure from your experience as Readers as he did as the Writer.

If you have not already done so you can easily find other stress free zones by reading the associated stories, "The Swaying Sixties", "Still Swaying" and "Boydie" all written by R.T.Cain. Most of his familiar, lovable and memorable, Characters are to be found in all of the four novels and the now famous Town of 'Lapley Vale' is never found to be too far away from any of the action.

This will not be the end of these adventures.

About the Author

If you have not already been acquainted with *'R.T. Cain'* and his ficticious Town called *'Lapley Vale'* prepare yourself for a heart-warming treat. The enduring affection he holds for his fellow man is reflected in the contents of all of his books. Born on the Isle of Man in 1940 he was in his prime during both of the relevant decades. Natural unspoilt humour continues to be underlined in all of his *'Stress Busting'* stories. The production of his creative writing provides him with enormous personal pleasure and satisfaction a fact which soon becomes clear fo all to see through the enjoyable, uncomplicated, material he offers to all of his Readers.